"MORE THAN A ROMANCE. BLAIR PROVES SHE HAS A HEAD AS WELL AS A HEART. . . . HER CHARACTERS BECOME REAL PEOPLE WE CAN BELIEVE IN AS WELL AS ADMIRE."

—*Publishers Weekly*

FROM THE BEST-SELLING AUTHOR OF *PRIVILEGE*

LEONA BLAIR

A WOMAN'S PLACE

"MARVELOUS! MS. BLAIR IS BOTH KEEN-EYED AND TENDER IN HER OBSERVANCE OF THE HUMAN CONDITION."

—Celeste de Blasis, author of *The Wild Swan*, *Swan's Choice*, and *The Tiger's Woman*

"BLAIR CREATES CHARACTERS WHO ARE BOTH STERLING AND HUMAN. . . . WHILE *A WOMAN'S PLACE* IS ESSENTIALLY FOR WOMEN, IT WILL APPEAL TO MEN AS WELL WITH ITS EXCITING STORY OF MODERN ISRAEL AND MODERN JEWS IN AMERICA."

—*Fort Wayne News Sentinel*

"ENJOYABLE . . . THE ATTITUDES AND FEELINGS OF AMERICAN BIG BUSINESS TOWARD HELPING ESTABLISH THE STATE OF ISRAEL . . . IS EXPRESSED EXTREMELY WELL."

—*The American Israelite*

"RICHLY CAPTURES THE SWEEPING EMOTIONS AROUSED BY HERITAGE, PATRIOTISM, AND LOVE."

—*Booklist*

BOOKS BY LEONA BLAIR

A Woman's Place
With This Ring
Privilege

QUANTITY SALES

Most Dell Books are available at special quantity discounts when purchased in bulk by corporations, organizations, and special-interest groups. Custom imprinting or excerpting can also be done to fit special needs. For details write: Dell Publishing Co., Inc., 666 Fifth Avenue, New York, NY 10103. Attn.: Special Sales Dept.

INDIVIDUAL SALES

Are there any Dell Books you want but cannot find in your local stores? If so, you can order them directly from us. You can get any Dell book in print. Simply include the book's title, author, and ISBN number, if you have it, along with a check or money order (no cash can be accepted) for the full retail price plus $1.50 to cover shipping and handling. Mail to: Dell Readers Service, P.O. Box 5057, Des Plaines, IL 60017.

A Woman's Place

Leona Blair

A DELL BOOK

Published by
Dell Publishing Co., Inc.
1 Dag Hammarskjold Plaza
New York, New York 10017

Dell ® TM 681510, Dell Publishing Co., Inc.

ISBN: 0-440-19629-9

Reprinted by arrangement with Delacorte Press

Printed in the United States of America

One Previous Edition

January 1988

10 9 8 7 6 5 4 3 2 1

KR

For Seena and Stan,
who showed me the way to come home

ACKNOWLEDGMENTS

I would like to thank Yuval Gat of the Israeli Consulate for helping me to make the events which take place in his country as authentic as possible within the framework of fiction.

The research sources I used are too numerous to list, but I am indebted to many authors who so painstakingly gather and record history.

Book
One

1

NEW YORK
MAY 1928

When the doors opened, there was no going back, but Naomi hesitated between her bulky mother and the frail lady who would be her mother-in-law.

"Are you all right?" her mother whispered.

"She's fine," the maid of honor's voice answered from behind them. "It's that carpet—it looks like the Red Sea opening."

Naomi was grateful for Sarah's high spirits, but she was not "fine." Her small laugh stopped abruptly at the pressure of her mother's hand.

At the end of the long aisle she could see the white marriage canopy and the black-suited men figures grouped around it like stone idols. For a breathless moment they seemed ominous, all-powerful, and she wanted more time to think, to be sure of why she was doing this.

For once she didn't want to be the center of attention, no matter how beautiful she looked. She didn't want to be paraded to the altar, like a virgin sacrifice, for people who had no idea what she was really like. No one knew what she was really like.

But Arnold was waiting there. He was solid, secure, the kind of man Naomi ought to marry. The feeling of safety was a comfort. He must be twice as nervous as she was without his sister Sarah to make him laugh.

Then they urged her forward down the aisle, a veiled bride between two women: her own mother, Leah Held, a large battleship in shimmering gray, and Arnold's mother, a small craft lost in the sea of a similar gown. Leah had agreed to a strictly Orthodox ceremony out of respect for Arnold's parents, but everything else was according to her own taste. Leah's one daughter was going to have the most lavish wedding they could afford.

The guests murmured. Seated on small gilt chairs, they were anonymous spots of color to Naomi in the lofty room. This hotel offered every luxury to brides who could afford its services. The same deep red of the carpet paneled the walls in velvet and draped the high windows, shutting out New York's May dusk, making a sanctuary of the hall. Candles flickered in wall sconces. White flowers banked the dais in the distance.

The satin wedding dress was Naomi's enchanted armor, a new self she would wear from this day forward. It was made like a knight's tabard over a slim underskirt that rippled into a train. A satin cap almost covered her bobbed red-gold hair. A short veil hid her face—another custom they followed because of Arnold's parents, even though no one else in either family believed that nonsense. They were doing this because of all her family owed to Arnold's, a debt of loyalty they could never repay, Naomi's father always said.

Through her veil Naomi saw her father turning toward her. Martin Held was the tallest of the men who waited at the long aisle's end, taller than her two brothers. Her father was big and square, like her mother. But Leah was formidable to all three of her children; Martin was strict with his sons and indulgent to a fault with Naomi.

Arnold's father, Leonard Fursten, was a much older man. Leonard's eyes were as gentle as his smile when he looked at her. This quiet, slender man, not much taller than his wife, had hovered on the fringe of Naomi's girlhood, lost in his religion, benign but remote.

The last to turn was Arnold, compact and fair, always seeming taller than his actual height. His eyes were the same changeable green as his father's but with that look he had reserved for Naomi since they were children. She smiled behind her veil. She really did love him, serious as he was for a boy of nineteen, so ambitious and reliable.

Then some trick of light through the white tulle made her see the resemblance for the first time.

He was so much like Joshua!

She had never noticed how the brothers resembled each other from the inside out, even though Arnold was slight and fair and Joshua tall and dark, even though they were so different in every other way.

Joshua. The only member of the family who wasn't here, except by the glaring fact of his absence.

Naomi closed her eyes and went on, borne forward by the two proud women down the long, long aisle to marriage. Inside her white satin armor, behind the refuge of her veil, the only voice she listened to was Joshua's.

"I can't help myself," Joshua said. "God forgive me, I mustn't do this, but I can't help myself." His hands framed her face, and he looked at her in the dimly lit living room with the same love and longing she was feeling, before he kissed her again.

"We didn't plan it," she whispered against his mouth, comforting herself as much as him. "It just happened."

"Naomi, he's my brother. He loves you so much—and I love him, even if we argue about most things."

"I know," she said, touching the face she wanted to watch forever. "I love him too. But not like this, not like us. Would you want me to marry him, feeling this way about you?"

His eyes closed. "That's what makes him only another man for me, not my brother—the idea of you as his wife. Then I have to have you for myself, no matter who gets hurt."

"Don't think about it now." Her arms coaxed him closer to her on the big pillowed couch. She could feel his warmth through the cotton of his shirt. Whatever love was between a man and a woman, she wanted it, all of it, with him. Once, the idea had embarrassed her, even frightened her a little. But she was not frightened now, not with him.

He moved away. "No," he said. "Not until we're married. I'll steal you from my own brother, but I won't seduce you to add to my sins."

She knew he would be shocked if she asked him not to stop. She was shocked herself; she had never felt this need before. Instead she said, "You're still thinking like a rabbi."

He had renounced the rabbinate only a few months ago. Naomi's father said it had broken Leonard Fursten's heart.

"No, that's over, no matter how disappointed my father is." He sighed. "I'm making my own rules now, as well as I can."

It seemed to Naomi that Joshua had always made his own rules.

He cradled her in silence. Her parents had left them alone, Naomi knew, to confront their feelings for each other. It was embarrassing to Leah and Martin Held that their daughter was engaged to one brother and in love with the other, but her father would arrange things for her. Her father always did.

"What will your parents say?" Joshua asked.

"They already know."

Naomi had never been able to hide things from her mother—not her feelings for Arnold when they changed from childhood preference to love, and not her electric response to Joshua when she saw him for the first time without the beard and somber clothing of a rabbi.

She had never really looked at him before that night, the night of her engagement party, never noticed that his strong face was as wonderful as his dark eyes, that his tall body was as beautiful to watch as his hands. She had never realized that although he had worn the trappings of a rabbi, he was a man as well, an exciting man. People had always responded to his passionate beliefs with newly discovered passions of their own. They might disagree with Joshua—as Arnold did—but they were always aroused by him.

"I think my mother knew I loved you even before I did," Naomi went on. "And they both like you just as much as Arnold."

The name made a reproachful silence between them. After a moment Joshua said, "I don't mean that. I mean what will they say about Palestine?"

She knew exactly what they would say if he even went on working for the Zionists. She could hear her father's voice: "Dangerous fanatics, radicals, Communists." *Zionism* was a dirty word in many Jewish households all over the world, a doomed cause that robbed families of their sons and drew attention to Jews who desired only to blend into the fabric of their countries, to become one assimilated thread among many.

As for Naomi's mother, Leah thought going to Palestine was the wild dream of a man without responsibility—a dream no man would pursue if he loved a woman enough to take her from his own brother. Palestine was a wasteland, full of rioting, raping Arabs, and dangers as ugly as those Leah had escaped when she left Russia with the Furstens as a little girl. It was not to send their child back to such a place that she and Martin had worked so hard, moving up step by step from poverty to security and comfort.

Naomi answered Joshua carefully. "It might be better not to talk about it so much in front of them."

He laughed softly. "That'll be easy—we'll be living in Palestine." He saw her face change, and his own clouded. "Naomi, you *are* coming with me?"

She was too surprised to answer him, but a cold feeling enveloped her.

"Naomi, you know I could never give up Palestine," he said steadily, watching her.

"But that was before we . . ." She stopped. She had already learned that there was no point in arguing when Joshua looked like that. He simply closed himself away from those he could not win over. Her hands hid her face, and suddenly she was crying, torn between his will and her own.

He took her hands gently. "Don't cry, my love. There's nothing to be afraid of, you'll see. I won't join a labor brigade. I'll teach or do something else. We can live in Jerusalem or Tel Aviv, and you won't be alone until you get used to the place."

She shook her head. "I can't go there, Joshua. I've thought about it, and I can't." Her blue eyes were filled with fear. "It's another world, a language I can't even speak, a way of life I don't understand. Why can't you stay here and teach—or do fund raising like Mama said? My father will help until you earn enough for us to live on. Joshua, please." She implored him to listen. "I don't really care about all the things they tell me I should have. I only want you. Can't we be just as happy here, in our own country, near our own family?"

He answered from a great distance. "No, we can't. *I* can't." His eyes were very, very dark. "This is a thing I must do, the thing I've wanted to do since I could think." His eyes begged her. "Naomi, I love you. I'm ready to betray my own brother for you, for God's sweet sake! But don't ask me to give up any more of what I'm made of."

"A miserable wilderness . . ."

"Making a Jewish homeland out of that wilderness is what I have to do. Naomi, I had brothers and sisters who were killed because they had no country of their own! And I've still had to

fight my parents, my friends, everyone. But it's part of my life."
He held her hands to his face. "So are you, now. I always
believed there was only one woman in the world I could really
love. I waited until I found you." His hands shook her shoulders
gently. "Naomi, you have it in you to live so much more than a
narrow, conventional little existence. Live with me, come with
me. I need you."

She looked up at him, held by his hands and his voice. She
was ready to defy her parents by working for the Zionists in
America with him. For a split second she was ready to go with
him to Palestine, to be part of his dream. But there was too much
to hold her. Fear held her—fear of the unknown, of violence and
danger such as her parents and his had escaped. The room held
her—the furniture, strong and solid, impregnated with the odors
of her father's cigars and her mother's cooking. Even the carpet
she had crawled on, built blocks on, wheeled her doll carriage on
held her. Home held her.

Her head went down, and he let her hands fall. He turned
away. "We can't see each other again before I go. I couldn't say
good-bye to you a second time." His voice was flat, hollow.

She said nothing, shrouded in sorrow. She held her breath
when he left the living room so she couldn't call him back, so he
would have to come back on his own because he loved her more than
some nonexistent nation.

She heard his footsteps going down the corridor to the front
door of the apartment. The door opened and clicked shut, and he
was gone. In the space of an hour she had been supremely happy,
passionately aroused, honestly in love. Now she was alone, her
body aching with frustrated desire, her pride battered. How could
he leave her? He asked the impossible of her and abandoned her
for failing him. It was cruel to demand more of a woman than
she had to give.

Naomi stood next to Arnold under the canopy and let him
stroke her with his eyes, easing the hurt. He loved her enough to
do that for the rest of her life, if that was how long the hurt
lasted—and even though he would never know it was there.

Her pride wanted this marriage as much as Arnold wanted her.

She began to walk around him. It was another age-old custom
she had agreed to follow to please his parents. His irrepressible

sister, Sarah, had told them it was meant to give the groom a chance to decide if he wanted the bride chosen for him. But Arnold had chosen for himself. That he would marry Naomi was something Arnold had decided when they were both thirteen.

She knew he resented the fuss people were making over Joshua's absence—just as he resented the fuss over Joshua when he was present. It wasn't Joshua's fault, Arnold had confided in her, that he drew people to him like a magnet; but it wasn't easy being younger brother to a crusader. Arnold didn't have such heroic ambitions: he wanted to be rich, successful. It was what most people wanted—Naomi's parents, Naomi herself.

Walking slowly, Naomi watched the faces that were dear to her drift into sight. Arnold's father, Leonard, looked like a contented angel, as he always did during religious observance. Was he really so angry at Joshua for going away to Palestine? It was almost impossible to be angry at Joshua for long.

Manya, Arnold's tiny, indomitable mother, kept her eyes closed while she murmured some kind of prayer—a prayer for Arnold's happiness, Naomi supposed. Or was she praying for Joshua to come back? Or for her children who died in Russia so many years ago?

Naomi saw her mother's face, happy but strained. Leah's hands twisted her handkerchief nervously. Leah had always been nervous around rabbis and synagogues. She had refused to have the ceremony anywhere but here. A hotel was more fashionable, she said; but that was not the reason, and the whole family knew it.

Leah still woke often in the night from dreams of smoke and fire and the village of Savurov burning, burning, after a Cossack raid. In her dream she was back once more in a field outside Savurov, a small, helpless girl watching the flames consume the synagogue and everyone the raiders had locked inside it: her parents, the rabbi, all the village Jews. She had tried then to scream for her mother, but a woman's hand covered her mouth.

It was Manya Fursten's hand—and Leah, struggling, remembered Manya's eyes while her own children perished and the hysterical new-orphan in her arms became the only daughter she had left. Leonard Fursten held a small boy they had managed to rescue when the Cossacks came to make sport of the Jews in another pogrom. Leah still cried for her real mother during those dreams; in her waking hours she turned to her foster mother for comfort, to Manya, who rarely smiled and never laughed but who had always sustained all of them.

It had frightened Naomi and her brothers when they were little to hear Leah scream like that. As soon as they were old enough, Martin and Leah told them why, passing quickly over the horror, talking about how Manya and Leonard had brought them, two small orphans, to America, where it was safe for children to grow up.

They told their children how they had all worshiped Joshua from the day he was born, how they called him an "old soul" and swore they saw all those who had died at Savurov in his eyes. He would be a rabbi, Leonard decreed, in the tradition of the eldest son. They remembered what a miracle it was to have Arnold come along, six years later, when Manya was too old to have children. And then Sarah—they called her Shai, the gift— the next year.

Then they were a large family, and it was planned that Leah and Martin would marry as soon as they were old enough. The flat on Rivington Street was small, and it was indecent for an unmarried girl to live in close quarters with a young man; they had been raised together, but Martin was not Leah's natural brother.

Naomi smiled tenderly when she passed her father, his face glistening with tears. His wife and children and his foster family were everything to him. She knew he was glad she was marrying Arnold . . . and not Joshua, the dreamer. Martin Held was a practical man; he had great admiration for Joshua's learning, but the boy was not a businessman, and Martin Held's major interest in life, after his family, was his men's ready-to-wear business. When Arnold went to work for him right out of high school three years ago, Martin had declared with great satisfaction that Arnold had a head for business.

Naomi wondered what her father would say when Arnold announced he was leaving to go into another business, one he would have to learn for at least a year before he could risk it on his own. Naomi and Arnold had agreed to break the news in the flurry of the wedding. Martin couldn't be angry on his daughter's wedding day.

And Naomi knew Arnold would be successful. He always did what he set out to do, just like her father.

Naomi finished circling and came to a stop beside Arnold again. She watched the rabbi's white beard bobbing, repeating words she didn't understand, his small mouth like two crushed berries in a snowdrift. The rest of the ceremony was a blur; she was thinking about the new little apartment in the Bronx that was waiting for them after a long weekend honeymoon in Atlantic City.

She blushed momentarily at the idea of the honeymoon, wondering how it really felt. Her mother would have told her anything really important, and Leah had said nothing. Sarah said no one had ever died of it, so it couldn't be that awful, and it might even be nice! Naomi deliberately thought of something else.

She was glad Arnold was leaving Rivington Street at last. Martin and Leah had put Rivington Street behind them years ago, but they were loyal to their foster parents, who still felt at home there. One Sunday of each month and all the important holidays they spent with the Fursten family. Naomi knew her parents had secretly hoped she would marry a man from a different background, but they could not object when she fell in love with Arnold.

In love . . .

It was too late to think of Joshua now.

They had placed a glass wrapped in a white napkin near Arnold's foot. He broke it easily, reminding the joyful of those who were not so blessed. The sound of it breaking and the happy cheers from the guests roused Naomi, and she turned to let Arnold lift her veil and fold it back. It was a symbolic uncovering that foretold the real one to come that night.

His mouth touched hers briefly. Then he took her hand in his, and they went back up the aisle together to a small room at the back of the hall. This, the *yihud,* was Orthodox custom too: a few moments of privacy for the newly joined couple even before they embraced their parents and their friends.

"This is the one part of the Orthodox ceremony I like," Arnold said, closing the door. "Just let me look at you for a minute." He took her hands and held them to his chest. "I never saw you look so beautiful. You must be happy if you look so beautiful."

She kept the smile on her face. "Of course I'm happy, Arnold. It's my wedding day." She put her arms around him, hiding her face against his cheek.

"I love you so much," he whispered. "I don't know how to tell you—I'm not good at that—but I love you."

"I know, Arnold," she said softly. "I know."

He waited for more—but he didn't really expect it. He had never been able to say what he felt. Joshua was the one for that, and Arnold had known what was happening between Joshua and Naomi once his brother took off his black rabbinical clothes and let people see that he looked as commanding as he sounded. But giving Joshua enough money to go away had not been enough. Arnold had to get his brother out of Naomi's mind too.

He held her tightly, pushing Joshua out from between them with his body. "I don't think you know how I feel. Nobody in the world loves you as much as I do. You have to believe that."

"I do believe it," Naomi said, her eyes closed. As long as she had Arnold to hold on to, she could forget that she wanted someone who didn't want her. With Arnold life would be what her parents had planned for her; it would be safe; it would be enough.

He had to hear something. "Naomi," he whispered again. "Say you love me, for God's sake, say it!"

She felt like crying. "Of course I do." She held him closer. "I always have. Since we were little. You know that."

Maybe later, he thought, maybe later when she was really his, she could say she loved him. He kissed her. Her mouth was warm, receptive—but there was no answering passion. Still, she was as young as he and totally innocent. What could she know of passion? He would show her. Only he had the right. He held her body closer to his.

She drew away. "I think it's time we went out for the reception."

"Yes, all right." He let her go, disappointed.

"Here, let me fix your hair," she said tenderly. "I can't have a rumpled husband."

She sounded like Sarah, like a sister, not a bride. He felt cheated, robbed of his rights, of his love—and he would never be able to accuse the thief. He walked to the door, his slight frame rigid with resolve, his eyes stormy.

"I'm going to give you everything you ever dreamed of—and more," he said. "I'll make you love me more."

"Arnold," she said, coming to put her arm through his, "I could never love you more than I do right now."

He kept his face as calm as hers, and they left the room together.

2

PALESTINE
APRIL 1929

Joshua grunted, half-blinded by dust and sweat, his muscles still protesting after months of constant labor.

He could smell himself as he strained at the boulder with three other men, all of them breathing hard. He could smell Lazar Kramer next to him, sandy, sunburned, and muscle-taut like the rest of them. But nothing mattered except to dislodge that granite giant, eight feet high, blocking their road.

Joshua's brigade worked midway between the Mediterranean coast to the west and the Jordan River to the east, a shore-to-shore distance of some thirty-five miles. But the untimbered soil was so parched and the sun so intense they might have been thousands of miles from any large body of water.

"*Push!*" Lazar shouted. "It's coming away!"

Suddenly the rock rose, as if by levitation, propelled by their cheers. Seconds later there was a wild scream as the boulder streaked like a comet down the incline forming the shoulder of their road and into one of the men working at the bottom.

"God Almighty," someone shouted, and the four of them grabbed pickaxes and crowbars and plunged down the incline. The man was lying on his back, hidden from the waist down by the massive rock. Inhuman shrieks ripped from his face. Blood oozed from under the rock to sink into the thirsty soil.

"God Almighty," Lazar repeated. "Do something!" He grabbed a crowbar from Joshua and began thrusting at the boulder, as if

he could move it himself. Joshua glanced at Isaac Levy, who
shook his head. Joshua knew Levy had abandoned the practice of
medicine when he left Vienna, but surely Isaac could not refuse
to ease the man's agony.

"A little morphine till he dies?" Joshua whispered to the
doctor. Levy was still breathing heavily from their struggle with
the giant rock.

"He'll be dead from the shock and pain before I can get back
from the tent with it," the doctor said. "Lazar, stop with that
crowbar, it's no good." Then he spoke to the fourth man who
had moved the boulder with them, a powerful man, short and
stocky, with the neck and shoulders of a Minotaur. "Hit him,
Natan, knock him out."

Natan Markevitsch nodded, knelt, and silenced the screams
with a quick blow to the man's head. He remained on his knees
next to the victim, patting the head he had just struck. The other
three stood together, looking. A few men who had been working
nearby joined them in silence.

"How long will he stay unconscious?" Joshua asked the doctor.

"Not long enough to die, I don't think. The pain will wake
him." Isaac Levy's lips were white. His skillful surgeon's hands
moved, knowing what to do, unable to do it.

"Then we have to kill him before he wakes," Lazar said.

"We can't . . ." Joshua began. But the man was virtually
dead. They were miles from a hospital, even if any hospital could
have saved what was left of him. He looked at his companions.
"Which of us?" he asked.

The man who had been working near the victim shook his
head, crying.

"That's his brother," Lazar said. "I'm in charge. I'll do it."
He stepped forward, his hands and body shaking.

Natan Markevitsch, still crouched by the body he had just
mercifully silenced, looked up at Lazar. Then he gave the inert
figure another blow to the head. Before any of them could move,
he had quickly and deftly broken the neck.

Joshua gasped, feeling sick. A few of the others turned their
heads away.

Natan put his ear to the chest and listened for what seemed
like hours. Then he stroked the dead face again and repeated the
shema, the prayer every Jew utters as he dies if he can. Joshua

joined him with some of the others. Lazar Kramer and the doctor were silent.

There was a shout from the top of the rise, and the men turned, almost gratefully.

A thin man in a bush hat sat in a ramshackle cart behind a horse. The cart had wide, heavy wheels to get it through the sand. "What happened?" he called.

Lazar began walking up to the cart.

"Don't waste your strength in this heat," the man called. "Unless it's a major catastrophe."

"A death," Lazar shouted back, still walking. "That major enough for you?" Anger was permissible; open sorrow was not.

The man—he was in charge of another branch of the labor brigade, as Lazar Kramer was of this one—stopped chewing on the cigar in his mouth and nodded. He waited, silhouetted against a bright blue sky, while Lazar plodded up to him. As he'd said, except for labor and catastrophes, the less energy expended in the sun the better.

The men watched without speaking until Lazar came back with the newcomer. At close range he looked a lot younger. His skin was leathery brown. With a bare nod of greeting to the others he looked down at the half-hidden body and the man still kneeling beside it.

"Lucky I came by early," he said softly. "Put him in the cart. We can bury him down there." His head moved in the direction of the small Jewish settlement about half a mile away.

They managed to roll the boulder farther down the incline, exposing the pitifully squashed body, caked with blood-soaked dirt. They brought a length of canvas and rolled the body into it. Then they carried it to the cart and walked silently behind it until they reached the little colony, and some of the settlers came to help them dig a hole near two other graves, one large, one small.

"There isn't any goddamn wood to make a goddamn coffin," Lazar said, punctuating every shovelful of sandy soil with a curse. "The goddamn Turks cut down all the trees for their goddamn trains." The sun glinted on his blond hair. His tall, heavily muscled body was anger in motion.

There was usually small talk and news of progress—or lack of it—along the line when this driver and his cart came through for

a daily inspection. Today there was no talk until the hole in the
sliding, drifting earth was deep enough.

"Orthodox?" the driver asked the man's brother. He took a
carefully wrapped package from his rucksack and handed the
grieving man a prayer shawl, shocking in its gleaming whiteness.
He glanced at Joshua in a silent request to lead the ceremony.

Joshua took a deep breath and began. He knew the words, he
was a rabbi; but he had left the rabbinate behind him. This was
the first funeral he had ever conducted. Yet here in northern
Samaria, for the comfort of the dead man's brother and his
comrades—and for himself?—he said the ancient words.

Then the driver retrieved the shawl and left them to trundle
down the dusty road.

"The horse looks better than he does," Isaac Levy said irrele-
vantly while they walked back to their tents near the worksite.
There would be no more work that day. The only sound as they
walked was the sobbing of the dead man's brother. It had happened before. They all knew it would happen again. Men died in
this country from many things. It was better not to give way to
grief.

"Listen," Lazar said to the sobbing man as they neared the
cluster of tents. "It's better than being killed in a pogrom by a
bunch of Cossacks. And he's buried near his own kind. You
think about that for a while. Doctor, give him the bottle of
brandy, will you?"

They left the man in his tent with Natan Markevitsch. "I
killed his brother," Natan said. "I can sit *shivah* with him."

Lazar put an arm around Natan's massive shoulders. "The
boulder killed him, not you."

Natan nodded as he left them, and the three men walked on to
the next tent. They cleaned up with the small bucket of water
each was allowed for bathing once a day, then sat smoking while
the sun set over the Samarian hills in a burst of color. When the
chill night closed down, they built a fire, letting the flames
consume the shock of the afternoon.

Through the silence Joshua felt with them, so well did he know
these men by now after nearly a year of working with them and
sleeping side by side. Isaac Levy was resigning himself once
again to the limitations of human surgical skill. His marvelous
hands had been as helpless to save his young wife in Vienna as

they had been today. He had come to Palestine to use them on stone—"because rocks can't die," he said, "because my hands can build something here that nothing can kill." His medical practice was limited to first aid—it was safer.

Natan, the Minotaur, sitting just outside the next tent with the dead man's brother, was puzzling over the problem of his great strength. It was one thing to avenge his parents by strangling the two Russian soldiers who had murdered them for sport; it was another to escape to Palestine to build with his powerful body, only to kill again, even to spare a fellow creature an agonizing death. Natan was a gentle soul; he only looked like an angry bull.

And Lazar Kramer, Joshua's first and closest friend out here, was cursing the senseless accident and vowing to avoid another. For Lazar, orphaned at seven, the entire Jewish community of Palestine was his family, and the state-to-be his mother. Any death was his personal bereavement, just as every new settler was a long-lost relative come home. Joshua was the brother he had never had, so instant and complete was the accord between them.

For Joshua, Lazar was the family he had left. Lazar had rescued him from teaching Hebrew to new immigrants several months after Joshua arrived in Palestine. Soon after they met, Joshua joined Lazar's brigade, doing what he'd come to do at last. He could not be homesick, because he had come home. The brutal realities of life out here had not disillusioned him. He had no such demon memories as haunted his companions, and if his heart was sometimes hollow, it was because Naomi's face vanished from his mind when he worked relentlessly on the rocky land of Palestine.

Work had even wiped away the last traces of remorse he felt for the shock and disappointment to his parents when he left the rabbinate. Knowing they were too immersed in tradition to understand him, he had made his decision out of his own convictions. No matter how it affected anyone at home, he knew it was right. If his father could see what they were doing, he would know it was just as important to the perpetuation of Judaism as a religious life.

This road would link the northern Samarian settlements with those at the southern tip of the Sea of Galilee; the more accessible the Jewish settlers—the Yishuv—were to each other, the

safer they would be from marauding Arabs who took advantage
of the Yishuv's poverty and isolation to harass them, rob them,
occasionally kill them.

In this midsection of the Holy Land were tiny settlements that
had tried and failed and tried again to survive. Another string
of kibbutzim—collective farms—and moshavim—cooperatives—
fringed the Mediterranean coast. And the rest of the Yishuv,
apart from those in Jerusalem itself, ranged from the northern
Galilee south along the western bank of that lake of many names:
Galilee-Tiberias-Kinneret. The road would make it possible for
new settlers to succeed where others had failed.

The men watched the fire fingers play. The sky was black
plush before anyone spoke.

"They couldn't build the road around that boulder?" Dr. Levy
asked that night.

"In this terrain you build a road on a rise when you're lucky
enough to have one," Lazar told him.

The doctor shrugged. "I'll take your word—I'm no engineer.
I'm not much of a doctor, either. There was nothing I could do
for the poor bastard."

"There was nothing anyone could do," Joshua said.

"A doctor is supposed to save lives, not assist at murders."

"Stop it, Isaac," Lazar said. "That was no murder."

"Lazar, my dear friend," Levy said. "Don't tell me he died
doing what he wanted to do. I know that. He is still dead. For a
boulder. It's better than a pogrom, but not much."

"He died in his own country," Lazar said. "For me that's very
much."

The doctor looked at Joshua sadly. "This one makes a noble
sacrifice out of everything."

Joshua nodded. "Things are easier to accept that way. Anyhow, the man's a poet."

They were quiet again, watching the blackened skies over the
desert flash with stars in the distance.

"God, it's beautiful," Lazar said. "So beautiful!" He turned
to the other two. "You haven't been here long enough to appreciate the beauty of this land. After a while you will. You'll want
to hold it in your arms, protect it with your body, keep it safe no
matter what the cost."

"You sound like you're talking about a woman," Joshua said.

He thought of Naomi's lovely face, her warm body. He wanted to touch her again.

"No woman could ever make me feel like this," Lazar said, shaking his head. "This is 'passing the love of women.' " He got to his feet. "I'll get us something to eat." He stepped into the tent.

"He means it too," Isaac Levy said. "If only the women who fall in love with him knew that, maybe he wouldn't be so successful, even with his looks." He sighed. "Still, it's probably safer for a man to love what is eternal."

"Of course it is," Lazar said, coming back with pita bread and goat's cheese in a cloth he spread on the ground near the fire. He took a drink from a bottle of red wine mixed with water and passed it to Joshua. "Look," he said, taking something out of his pocket. "Oranges."

"Where did you find those?" Fruit and vegetables were like water out here, as precious and as scarce.

"Someday there'll be citrus groves in this country as far as you can see. But I got these from one of the girls in that settlement last night," Lazar said.

"So that's where you were," the doctor said. "Not surprising—that's where you usually are." He smiled affectionately at the younger man. Better to talk of love than to dwell on death. "Tell me, Lazar, do you remember their names at least?"

Lazar peeled his orange. "Some of them," he said. "I'm sure some of them don't remember mine. Look, there's no reason to make a cosmic event out of it. I don't believe there's only one woman on earth meant for me, the *bashert*."

Joshua shook his head. "What'll happen if you ever fall in love?"

"But he *is* in love," the doctor said, "with this." He waved a hand at the blackness beyond the fire.

"It isn't the same," Joshua insisted.

"No," Lazar agreed. "It's bigger. It's better. It has some of the same qualities: I can see it, feel it, hold it in my hands." He let sand trickle through his fingers. "I can give it love and watch it bloom and blossom under my eyes—watch it be fruitful, if you like. And its beauty not only endures, it's enhanced, not destroyed, by time." He stretched out on his belly, watching the fire, his blue eyes intense, his hands supporting his face under its

mop of blond hair. "Wait until the fields are green and gold.
Wait until Kinneret has more settlements around it with purple
bougainvillaea on white walls in that soft, blue air you can't find
anywhere else. Wait until there are more roads from Haifa to the
Jordan, till you can go easily from anywhere to rest in the light of
Jerusalem."

The men were caught in his vision, bound by his voice,
captured by his spell. In that moment they both would have
agreed that no man, no woman on earth possessed the enchant-
ment or promised the fulfillment of this land.

"Bed for me," Lazar said, getting to his feet in one easy
motion. "Ben will be back early in the morning with the truck,
and we can move on to Giora."

They smothered the fire with sand and went into the tent they
shared with Natan and Ben Horowitz, the fifth member of this
special group of friends, a fraternity of men from five countries,
bound together by loneliness and a single purpose.

The five were always together, with code names they had been
given by the other men: Joshua, the Rabbi; Lazar, the Poet;
Isaac, the Doctor; Natan, the Minotaur; and Ben, the Dandy.

Ben Horowitz had left a luxurious, upper-class home in England as soon as he turned twenty-one two years ago. His fair,
well-scrubbed looks made him invaluable to the Yishuv's growing clandestine army. Furnished with British army papers and
looking every inch the correct junior officer in his stolen uniform, Ben slipped easily into the governing power's administrative offices, picked up information about its plans to restrict
the Yishuv's defenses to a worker-police force—and slipped out
again to rejoin the brigade. Like all of them, he preferred to be
with the elite labor force; like all of them, he was prepared to go
where he was most needed.

Joshua stretched out on the straw mat that was his bed. After
so many months he was used to it, and his bones no longer ached
every morning. Nothing hurt while he worked.

It was when he was alone with his thoughts before sleep came
that he ached for Naomi. His eyes wanted to see her, his hands to
touch her, his body to possess hers. He was not sexually ignorant, only inexperienced—and that was by choice. What he did
not desire with a passion of the mind and heart as well as of the

body, he had not wanted, no matter how many women looked at him with taking eyes.

He was really far more of a romantic than his friend Lazar. He had always believed that there was one perfect mate for every man and that he had been lucky enough to find his. He wanted Naomi. The wanting exposed all the sensuality of his nature, diverted, calmed until now by music, poetry, and his absolute devotion to a new Zion. His joys had been aesthetic joys, and his frustrations had focused on his desire to get to Palestine.

He felt another kind of desire now. The hard physical work he did made him want a physical release. Was it possible that in the life he had chosen for himself, healthy, jubilant amours like Lazar's were better than lonely longing for the woman his brother loved? A woman who wanted security and comfort more than she wanted him?

Then why did he think of her, yearn for her, want her? Miss the sight of her face, the sound of her voice, her eager, quick curiosity, her sweetness, her laughter? Because he loved her. He would always love her.

Love to Lazar was a revel, not a solemnity. In a different land Joshua was beginning to think differently. He admired Lazar so much it seemed only natural that he live like him.

Certainly Joshua had never before made a lifelong friend in a matter of seconds after meeting him. But then, he had never before known men like these.

"A country is like a woman," Natan said to the other men in the truck. "You have to be inside to appreciate."

The truck hit a deep hole in the road, knocking them all off balance.

"That'll teach you to be lewd in the Holy Land, where God is listening," Isaac Levy remarked. He replaced his cap after slapping it against the truck's wooden sides to shake off bits of straw and manure.

The other men laughed.

"What's so terrible?" Natan protested. "Love is beautiful, not lewd. That blue sky is beautiful. This sun is beautiful." He flung his arms wide at the passing landscape. "This whole damn country is beautiful."

Their eyes followed his to the bare countryside with its rocky outcrops, its tattered vegetation. It was softening as they passed from Samaria toward the Jezreel Valley—Emek Yizre'el—but it was desolate still. These men saw the neat villages and streets they would build here, the ripe green fields where now there was only bracken. This part of the country was crisscrossed by narrow dirt tracks where only horsedrawn wagons, a lot like stagecoaches, could pass. They would build highways. Some of the land near the Sea of Galilee was still swampland, breeding malaria and typhoid among the settlers. They would drain it.

This was to be a Jewish homeland. The Balfour Declaration had promised it twelve years ago, and the British were honorable men who kept their word.

Isaac Levy was not so sure. "In 1917 the Brits needed a more stable presence than the wogs' in a strategic area—so they issued the Balfour Declaration to get Jewish support; if they want Arab support, they'll issue another declaration."

But a homeland was not enough for these men. They wanted no less than a Jewish state, and they were ready to fight for it when the time came. They were Zionists in that sense, but they preferred not to label themselves. To the world, Zionism meant communism, socialism, free love—all the vices, political and social. These men cared for none of those things.

They ranged in age from sixteen to fifty because sheer physical endurance was the main requirement of the elite labor brigades, along with discipline and devotion. Their backgrounds were as varied as their original nationalities: they had been shopkeepers' sons, tailors, rabbis, doctors or plumbers, chemists or carpenters, engineers or moneylenders, depending on what trades were open to Jews in their native countries. Right now they were laborers. As time went on, they would become whatever was needed.

The truck rumbled along. An occasional cluster of clay huts was the only sign of life. Ragged bedclothes and white kaffiyehs flapped on lines in the Arab villages; goats nibbled on whatever scrub they could find, and once in a while a small shepherd waved and smiled at the jolting truck.

The man on Joshua's right, in safari clothes and a pith helmet, murmured in upper-class British accents, " 'Unhounded by sordid cares, at ease in Zion.' "

Joshua smiled at Ben Horowitz. "You never had a sordid care in your life."

"No," Ben said. "As it happens, I haven't had any cares, sordid or otherwise, except for telling my family I was coming out here."

"Both of you had that problem," Isaac reflected. "I hope one day they'll understand it."

Joshua nodded at the Doctor. Ben's face remained impassive; he had very little hope of a reconciliation with his family unless he went back to inherit his father's fortune and run the family business for him.

Lazar laughed. "They all think we're heathen out here."

"We look like a bunch of heathen, sure enough," one of the men said.

"Except for the Dandy, here," Natan said. "How do you keep so neat in this place?" He looked down at his own dusty, patched work clothes. "No wonder you pass for a Britisher."

"The Brits can keep Jews out of Palestine—officially," Lazar said, "but they can't keep little Benjy Horowitz out of their own headquarters, because he looks like one of them. Let's hope he continues to fool them."

It was important that he did—and everyone knew that Ben was spying on the British whenever he was absent. Britain wanted undisturbed strategic dominance in the area; she was listening to Arab demands that Jewish immigration be curbed. At the same time, the Jewish presence in Palestine was considered desirable because it was more reliable. What Britain wanted was territorial influence through the Yishuv, but with as few Jews in the territory as possible.

To achieve that goal, the settlers had to be kept firmly under control, restricted to an unarmed police force as a token defense against increasing Arab attacks.

That was not acceptable to the Yishuv. An underground army, the Haganah, had sprung up. The military arm of the Jewish Agency, it was an offshoot of the old Watchman organization of pioneer days. There was not a settlement in Palestine that wasn't beginning to accumulate illegal arms. Each one, small or large, was a link in the chain of common protection. Their destination this day was one of the strongest links in the network—Giora.

It was at the southern tip of the Sea of Galilee, a well-protected, self-supporting enclave that was a perfect meeting place for the worker-police and the secret underground army. At Giora, Ben would feed whatever information he had gathered to the Haganah coordinator; they would be informed of any strategic meetings they might have to attend before they got back to the business of building roads.

Joshua had never been to Giora. He was looking forward to it. Everything out here was not simply another place; it was a discovery. He bounced along in the rickety truck, utterly content to be with these men. Each of them had made a personal crusade to reach this parched scrap of earth.

Lazar Kramer's had not been easy. What must it have been like, Joshua wondered, to come to Palestine from Poland as a frightened seven-year-old orphan? But Lazar had been adopted here by many fathers—some rugged farmers and workers, some rarefied scholars, some violent political agitators—and only one mother: the dream of a Jewish state. The country itself was all to him that a mother could be to a loving son.

Looking at Lazar's tall, powerful body, his deep-set blue eyes under heavy, sun-bleached, peaked brows, his sharply defined upper lip and full, sensual lower one, Joshua thought that Lazar had been well nurtured physically in this rough, demanding land.

As for his character, it had no equal Joshua had ever encountered before. The man was a combination of intensity and indolence. His mind was well honed; he remembered everything he saw or heard without appearing to trouble his handsome, lazy head. And that head was full of the knowledge, literature, lore, and languages of all the men who had reared him. He could write a poem or an article as well as he could build a dam or repair a motor. He could argue politics and philosophy or the best techniques for sewage disposal. He commanded men without a gesture of command. He was fearless and tender.

Joshua had been surprised and proud to hear Isaac compare him to Lazar. "You're like a reverse negative of him. One's blond, the other's dark. One's lighthearted, the other's serious. But you're cut from the same cloth. It's good to have a friend who knows what you're thinking."

"Look!" Lazar's voice interrupted Joshua's thoughts. "There's Giora."

The white stone houses—dormitories, barns, a communal hall, Joshua supposed—had a weathered look, like a person past first youth. Yet Giora had been founded less than twenty years ago.

The fields looked more carefully tended than the buildings, and there were rows of orange trees in the orchards. Joshua knew Giora was neither a collective nor a cooperative but a colony somewhere between the two. The fruits of the settlers' labor were combined and the proceeds shared; children lived in a separate house as soon as they were nine months old. For now, each married couple had a room—small, rough, and meagerly furnished, but their own; unmarried men and women slept in dormitories.

Someday, the settlers hoped, each family would have a two-room bungalow to itself. But life was still hard, even since the founders had cleared and filled the swamps near the lake; if they were to survive, it had to be through a shared endeavor. They had come a long way; they had a longer way to go.

The morning mist had long since burned off the lake. Under the hot sun the blue water sparkled, the sky was clear, the fields were green.

Joshua glanced at Lazar. "It's beautiful," he said to Lazar's smile. And the truck bumped on toward Giora and the banks of the lake they called by the name that described its shape: the harp—Kinneret.

The communal dining hall at Giora buzzed with talk. Grouped around scrubbed wooden tables with the settlers, the laborers exchanged news and gossip with their hosts, or argued politics.

"They can't keep away from politics," Natan grumbled to Isaac Levy as they entered the hall with Lazar and Joshua. "Even the girls talk politics." Natan's eyes swept the crowd, looking for someone in particular.

The women at Giora were a mixture of physical types, although most of the colony's founders came from Russia. Some were as round of figure and as dark of hair as Joshua's own sister, Sarah. Some were as tall as Sarah, but much slimmer, with olive-tinted skin that bronzed so quickly in the sun. And a few, like the delicate girl Natan's eyes finally found, were as blond as Ben and Lazar.

"There's Aviva," Natan said to his friends. "Come this way."

Joshua smiled at Natan's eagerness. "She's lovely," he said to Lazar. "Pale as a Botticelli Venus."

"Probably the result of a Cossack rape," Lazar suggested.

"You never let us forget, do you?" Isaac said.

"Neither do they."

They followed Natan to a table where Ben was already seated, waiting for Giora wine. Joshua and the Doctor were newcomers. This was their first visit to Giora.

Two young women, one dark, the other Natan's blond Aviva, joined them at the table. They both wore rough work shorts and shirts and carried jugs of wine and glasses. A third woman, in her forties and dressed in men's work pants and a wool jersey, carried a plate of figs and cheese. They sat down with the five friends.

"More food!" Natan said. "You gave us a banquet for dinner." He took the glasses from the fair girl very carefully, as if his unguarded strength might injure her.

The dark-haired young woman smiled. "That's to make up for the bread of adversity and the water of affliction you get in the desert."

"If they don't talk politics, they quote the Bible!" Natan complained. "What a country!"

The dark girl poured wine for Joshua and the Doctor. "I'm Rachel, and this is Aviva." She nodded toward the fragile blond girl now sitting near Natan. "And this is Shula."

They all raised glasses. *"Bruchim ha-ba'im,"* Shula said in Hebrew. "Welcome." She turned as a heavyset gray-haired man joined them. "Ah, Reuven, sit with us. You wanted a word with Lazar."

Reuven took the wine she gave him. "It can wait. Meanwhile, enjoy. You've had enough trouble this trip."

They always knew, Joshua marveled to himself. The Jewish community was like a village, and any triumph or tragedy was known to the whole Yishuv within days. They drank silently to the man who had been killed.

"You've done a good job," Reuven went on. "How many men do you have now?"

"Twenty-five," Lazar said. "But they work like fifty. From what I saw, Reuven, you haven't been sitting around either."

Shula nodded. "The entire fence has been rebuilt and two new houses. We're getting in the crop, and it looks like almost double last year's."

"We've cleared more swamp," Rachel added. "Maybe Dr. Levy will have time to see a few of our malaria patients?"

Isaac assured her he would, smiling at the anxious young girl.

Aviva passed a plate of cheese to Natan. "We have a new dairy. Try this—you'll see what a difference those machines can make in taste as well as quantity." She smiled at the Minotaur, who gazed at her in adoration.

"We'll have enough revenue from dairy sales to triple our poultry stock too," Rachel added.

"Any trouble lately?" Ben asked quietly, his anxious eyes on Rachel. The New Grand Mufti of Jerusalem was a religious fanatic, stirring the Arab peasants with stories of Jewish plans to rebuild their Temple over the Arabs' sacred Dome of the Rock. There had been isolated cases of Arab raids on Jews in cities and on farms, strife between once peaceful neighbors of both faiths.

"Nothing we can't handle," Rachel said, "and no shooting since the last time Lazar came through, months ago." She was answering Ben, but she kept looking at Joshua with eyes as black as his own. They were all curious about the American. Who would come from the Golden Land to work on a road gang?

The sound of a violin and a flute broke into their talk. "Oh, good," Shula said. "Somebody got Herzl and Avram to play." She took Joshua's hand. "Come and dance, it'll do you good."

He glanced back at Rachel while he followed Shula to where other couples were dancing. "Our Victrola's broken," Shula said, settling into his arms. "We've been waiting for a replacement part for months, so we have to make the best of a fiddle and a flute. But they play all the latest hits from America."

"I don't even know the latest hits from America," Joshua told her. "And I have to warn you, I'm not much of a dancer."

"I didn't think you would be." Shula looked up at him with laughing brown eyes. "You're the Rabbi. Never mind, with popular songs all you have to do is stand there and sway."

Her body, strong and solid except for the softness of her breasts, moved against his. She smelled like new-mown hay. Over her shoulder he saw Rachel dancing with Ben, and Natan holding the delicate Aviva as if she would break. She was as small-boned as Naomi, but much slighter.

Lazar and Isaac were still talking with other men and women

at the table. The thin warble of the violin sounded good to Joshua. Being in this hall, in this place founded by men and women with the same vision as his own, within sight of friends he loved and trusted, was a joy to his spirit. And the woman in his arms, suntanned and bursting with vitality, was a joy to his senses. But his eyes followed the dark-haired Rachel throughout the dance.

She was exactly what he had thought a woman born in Palestine should be. That long, glossy black hair, the slanted dark eyes under brows like black wings against sun-gold skin, a rounded but compact body that seemed more at home in shorts and work shirt than it would ever be in a dress.

How beautiful Naomi would be in Palestine!

"You're miles away," Shula said. "Thinking about a woman, I'll bet."

He nodded.

"Tell me about her. Maybe it'll help."

For some reason the words came even more easily with this woman than they had with Lazar. She looked as if she knew what total love between a man and woman meant, while Lazar had no idea of love beyond the merry making of it. "Her name is Naomi. She's small and very beautiful, like a perfect porcelain. I've known her all her life, but I never knew I loved her until a year ago."

"And all you ever thought about anyway was coming here," Shula added for him. "Why didn't she come with you if she loves you?"

"She was afraid of living out here."

Shula nodded. "It's no picnic for a city girl, especially one from America. Is she a Zionist?"

"No."

"Well, that's that, then," Shula said. "It takes a very special kind of woman to live like this."

"She *is* special—she doesn't know it, but she is. If she stays back there, living that kind of life, she may never know it."

"What do you mean, 'if'? Is there a chance she'll change her mind?" Shula's voice was sympathetic but doubtful.

"I don't know," Joshua said. "I haven't heard from her, and I've had only a few words about my family from my sister. Mail takes a long time catching up out here." He looked down at Shula. "You don't think she will, do you?"

Shula shrugged. "She'd have to give up so much." She studied his face. "For you she's the *bashert*, isn't she—the one meant for you?" She looked at him steadily. "I know how that can be. But you're here now, for this moment. Why not live for that?"

Her eyes were giving him a frank invitation. There was no innuendo about it, not even the mildest flirtation. It merely conveyed that he was a lonely man and she a woman alone and that they might find comfort in each other. When he nodded briefly, it had nothing to do with his feelings for Naomi, except for the empty place his longing left inside him; it was more the sense of hard work, accomplishment, the realization of a dream, and the feeling of well-being that made him want this, not only as a comfort but as a commitment to this new way of life and a separation from the old.

"Come," she said, taking his hand. They went through one of the doors. The night was unusually mild. A vagrant breeze swept over the fields outside the stockade, bearing the fragrance of orange blossom. The scent of night-blooming jasmine became stronger as they came to a small house tacked on to the long dormitory building where unmarried adults slept.

"This is mine," Shula said. "They let me keep it after my husband died because I do the books for the dairy farm and need a quiet place to work. But it gets lonely sometimes."

Inside the small room were only a rough wooden table and chair, an unpainted chest of drawers, and a bed. Books and papers were piled everywhere.

Joshua barely noticed the room. The sheets on the bed were rough against his naked body, but the feel of her was soft. He had never held a naked woman before, but some subtle sensitivity to what would delight a woman's body, some deep-rooted sensuality guided his hands and his mouth, and she responded with a quiet abandon that matched his own.

He was not prepared for the wonderful warmth of being inside a woman, for the wonderful welcome her body gave to his, a taking-in that excited and comforted at once. And he had no idea that the climax of all this wonder would be so soaring, so liberating, and so utterly fulfilling.

They spoke no more. They slept and loved and slept again, and if a random thought of Naomi threatened to cast a shadow of pain on such peace and soul-stroking as he felt, it was the body of this unknown, generous woman that he reached for in the night.

He rejoined the sleeping men well before dawn, feeling he had made another dear friend in this friendly land. By first light the brigade was preparing to move out and Giora to start work after seeing them off with waves and cheers and bundles of tomatoes and cucumbers and hard-boiled eggs.

Joshua looked at Shula in wordless gratitude, and she waved her straw hat back at him, smiling. His eyes stopped again on Rachel's face, and he shouted good-bye to her. Then the truck's engine labored, started, and pulled them away from Giora, northward to Safed. Lazar had received instructions from Reuven to proceed first to a Haganah meeting for briefing before sending the brigade back to its project in Samaria.

Lazar Kramer was more than a brigade chief: he was a key liaison between the Yishuv and its defense force and between the Yishuv and the outside world. The Jewish National Fund, the Palestine Foundation Fund, and an enlarged Jewish Agency in Europe would work to stimulate and finance Jewish immigration to Palestine. But first it had been necessary to reconcile Zionists, who wanted a Jewish national home, and non-Zionists, who would help needy Jews anywhere but drew the line at inflammatory talk about a new state. The aid of both factions was vital to the survival of the Yishuv, and Lazar Kramer was the kind of man who appealed to everyone. Charming and eloquent, a handsome, nonpolitical product of Palestine's Jewish community, he traveled all over Europe, raising money to finance new settlers. Inside Palestine he helped the Haganah to smuggle them in, defying British attempts to keep them out.

"Why is everyone so quiet?" Lazar asked now.

"They're all in love," Isaac Levy said. "Except you—you're immune."

Lazar laughed. "Happens every time we spend a night in a place with houses. They think it's love, but it's only civilization."

Natan sighed. "You call it what you want. I call it love."

"Aviva?" Lazar guessed, and Natan nodded mournfully.

"Well, cheer up; she seems to like you just as much. And you'll see her again in a few weeks." Lazar looked at the other men. "The Dandy looks bereft too. It has to be the dark-eyed Rachel."

Ben nodded. "But the dark-eyed Rachel kept looking for the dark-eyed Rabbi, I'm afraid." He spoke lightly, but his blue eyes watched Joshua carefully.

"Don't worry, Ben," Lazar said, amused by Joshua's confusion. "She'll have to look so far for the Rabbi that she'll turn to you for comfort."

"What do you mean by that?" Joshua demanded.

Lazar leaned back against the side of the bumping truck, his hands clasped behind his head. "I mean that you and I are going to America."

"Lazar, no! What for?"

Lazar opened his eyes. "For money." His lazy attitude stayed the same, but his voice took on energy. "Look, we've had a recession, more Jews leaving than arriving—and we need every soul we can get. Weizmann needs financial support from nonpolitical Jews, non-Zionists, and America's where we can find them. We need money—for new land purchases and new settlers to farm the land, for supplies, machinery. But mostly for arms. You and I have to go over there and get it."

Ben nodded agreement, but Natan protested. "Arms to fight against what? The Arabs? Sure, there's trouble once in a while, but we can take care of a few knives."

The Doctor disagreed. "The settlers must stand guard themselves and work the land too," he said. "That crazy man in Jerusalem won't stop with a few murders; the Mufti's out for an uprising. The Haganah needs guns, ammunition. Lazar's right."

"But why me?" Joshua insisted. "After all the years it took me to get here. Why me? I don't know anyone with money, Lazar."

"We have the financial contacts. What I really need is a combination guide and apprentice. You have to learn what I've been doing in Europe for years to raise money and buy munitions. The Jewish Agency thinks you're the right man to help me do this job." He was sympathetic but firm. "It has to be done, Josh. Each of us has to do what he's best at. We can't leave ourselves undefended when trouble comes, and we haven't got a kopek in the defense fund the British finally allowed us to have. Do you think they'll defend us in an Arab uprising? They're doing all they can to curry favor with the Arabs now.''

Joshua's new sense of well-being was replaced by a mixture of regret and anticipation. He would see her again. After a year he would see Naomi again and maybe, maybe persuade her to come back with him this time. Yet he had never felt a place was "home" before, and he wasn't looking forward to leaving Palestine.

"When did you hear about this?" he asked Lazar.

"Reuven told me last night. Our people want to send me to America with another man who can learn. You're the man.''

"Thanks, friend," Joshua said, mildly acid. "Your flattery is exceeded only by your *chutzpah* in assuming I'd want to go with you."

"But you will?" Lazar's question had more doubt in it than was usual for him. It was impossible to deny him anything when he asked like that—or to sour their friendship by childish resentment. The job had to be done to protect what the Yishuv had built here stone by stone.

"Yes, of course," Joshua said, smiling. He looked at Isaac, Ben, and Natan. "Where will they be while we're gone?"

"Don't worry about us, old man," Ben said. "We'll get on with our engineering." He seemed completely relaxed now.

"A fancy name for backbreaking labor," Isaac commented.

The lovesick Natan only grunted.

The truck plodded up to Safed, built on a slope, each of its white houses sparkling in the midmorning sun, trimmed with blue against the Evil Eye. Flavius Josephus, a Jewish historian and soldier, had built its fortifications. Crusaders built a castle on their ruins in the twelfth century. Scholarly Jews expelled from Spain in 1492 had made the dreamy little town a center of rabbinical and mystical learning, living peaceably with their Arab neighbors.

Here, for Joshua, were his beginnings. Since earliest childhood he had drenched himself in the history of Palestine—to be here, to walk on streets that had been only dream names to him, was unutterably moving.

But all was not religious devotion in Safed, as a casual visitor— or a British patrol—might think, watching the pious Jews and the devoutly religious Arabs who inhabited the place. There were four "holy cities" for the Jews: Hebron, Tiberias, Jerusalem, and Safed. Of them all, Safed, in the northern Galilee, was a little jewel of antiquity for tourists . . . and a safer place than the frequently patrolled settlements for the meeting Joshua was about to attend.

While the brigade had lunch, he and Lazar, along with Isaac, Ben, Natan, and three others, met with members of the Yishuv's underground army, the Haganah.

The introductions were brief, the comments terse. As a boy Ari, the man in charge, had joined Josef Trumpeldor's Jewish Legion of the British army in the Great War. But there was no love lost between Ari and the British. "Are we supposed to be honored that they put us in charge of the mules?" he blustered.

He was short, with a military bearing. It was difficult to tell his age. But it was obvious that his sole interest in life was defense of the Yishuv. He spoke in short bursts, like a gun firing.

"There's going to be trouble," Ari said, sitting near a table with a map of Palestine spread out on it. Spring sun streamed through the window of the small white house, hitting the map.

"Here." Ari pointed. "And here—and almost certainly at Hebron. We can't stop it. The Grand Mufti is fomenting more hate than we can fight with words. We'll have to fight with guns." He looked at Lazar. "You're arranging to leave?"

"As soon as they replace us in the brigade and get us on a ship." His eyes included Joshua.

"The hell of it is," Ari said, "we need every man we have to fight—so we send you two to give lectures and hold tea parties to get money from American Jews! What have they got against Zionists, for Christ's sake?"

"They don't want to seem disloyal to America," Joshua suggested.

"But if they give to the Red Cross to house earthquake victims at the North Pole, that's not disloyal?"

"Ha!" one of the men snorted. "They're afraid that if they draw any attention to themselves, people will start killing them."

Ari threw the pointer on the table. "Well, all I want for now is enough guns to keep us from getting killed." He rolled the pointer up in a map. "I have to get moving—and so do you. Good luck and good hunting. Bring back all you can, Lazar—and the rest of you be ready for anything."

He shook hands with each of them while his own men gathered canteens and rucksacks. They looked relieved to be moving outside the confines of a house. They had all been Hashomer men—members of the Watchman civilian patrol—before the British permitted formation of the Haganah, the first official recognition of tension between Arabs and Jews over Jewish immigration. "You can always tell a Haganah man," Natan had once said, "by the way he keeps looking behind him."

The Haganah was still not supposed to be an army, merely a loosely organized labor group with no arms to speak of and no military hierarchy.

"So we'll hide the arms," Ari had directed, "and forget to call me General. The English judge everything on appearances. We'll look like farmers, so to them we'll be farmers—with mules, if that's what the bastards want!"

Now, he spoke with Ben for a moment. "Find out all you can about what beaches they're planning to patrol. We have a lot of people to get in—and a lot of guns." He looked back at Lazar and Joshua. "Shalom," he said with a sardonic smile as he left. "Peace." It was hardly the parting wish to men who were going out to find guns.

Lazar and his group made their way back to the truck. "You get the idea," Lazar said to Joshua. "It isn't all milk and honey."

"I get the idea," Joshua told him.

"Come on, then, start telling a savage like me how to behave in rich American living rooms. Do you realize I've never lived in a house with a carpet and steam heat?"

Joshua laughed, but it was a surface laugh. Under it there was a flood of feeling—was it hope or hopelessness?—at the thought of seeing Naomi again. *This* was his land now, in fact as well as spirit. Even the act of love with another woman had punctuated his separation from Naomi, no matter how free of obligation Shula had made it. He and Naomi were worlds apart literally; now they were figuratively so as well, each of them living by different precepts.

And yet he loved her, in a way he could love no other, not a generous woman like Shula, not a black-eyed girl like Rachel. He had the feeling that Rachel was as virginal as Naomi, that she might also be waiting for marriage, but out of choice, not social restriction. Marriage for a girl like Rachel would mean other things than for Naomi. The Shulas and Rachels of this world—his world now—were rooted in the rocky soil of reality.

He wondered if his own idealism had its roots in hard reality now, far more than in the dreams of Zion that had swaddled him all his life. It was time to stop dreaming.

Lazar interrupted his thoughts. "There was mail for us in Safed. Some of it pretty old."

"Who gets mail?" Isaac said. "We're a disgrace to our families."

"Well, I got another poem published in Warsaw." Lazar paused to acknowledge cheers from the men. "Here, Isaac, the medical faculty in Vienna must be asking you to come back. And there's a fat one for the Rabbi." He eyed Joshua with friendly concern as he handed the letter over. He knew the whole story, as Joshua knew his.

Joshua started to open the letter, but its unusual bulk made him stop. Sarah usually hadn't the patience to write such long letters. There might be news in all those pages he had better read alone.

3

NEW YORK
APRIL 1929

Arnold looked around the loft near Union Square with pride and satisfaction. Everything was ready, and he would be in real production by next week. He had earned this: he had defied Naomi's father last year at the wedding, insisting that he would support his own wife in his own way. And then he had gone to work as a salesman for Elizabeth Arden, watching everything, listening intently, and learning even more than he had expected in the ten months he was there.

All the while, he and Sarah, with Naomi's help, ran a small operation on the side. The nights they'd spent together, pasting labels on jars, making up cartons for shipment, writing lists of shops for Sarah to contact—wonderful nights when the three of them shared laughter, hopes, and plans. It had helped him make some of the money he needed to set up on his own. He had never expected to do it this soon.

He frowned. The balance of the money had come from his father-in-law. Arnold had sworn not to ask for a penny, but he had finally yielded to Martin's offer, mainly because it gave Naomi something else to think about when she lost her first baby. Martin Held was so intent on distracting Naomi that he had virtually insisted on making the loan. It was Arnold who insisted on paying interest on it. But Martin wasn't risking his money; Arnold would prove that to him soon enough.

Now Naomi was pregnant again, and that was a good omen, even though Arnold didn't really believe in omens. He looked around the loft and smiled again. Now he could make his own product in his own plant without paying someone else a king's ransom to let him use equipment whenever it was convenient. He stood in the center of the large loft, dominating by his intensity the massive vats, the enormous mixing blades, the huge drums of oil, wax, scents, emulsifiers.

There were shelves stacked with jars and bottles, ready to be filled, labeled, and shipped. And there were orders for them too, enough to keep them working for six months, and more coming in every day, thanks to Sarah. He hadn't wasted his time, selling for Arden. He'd learned the business from an astute woman. He also knew who the clients were, and now they knew him—well enough to be sure Arnold Fursten would provide an equivalent product at a much lower price. It wouldn't be a salon product at first, but that phase wouldn't last long.

The telephone rang, and he left the center of the big loft to answer it.

"Hello, tycoon," Sarah's voice said, and he smiled at her excitement. It equaled his own. "How does it feel?"

"It feels great! Wait till you see the rest of the equipment." He sat down behind a neat desk inside a glass-partitioned cubicle.

"I can't wait to see it. I called to wish you luck."

"The workmen just finished—who else but my partner would know exactly when to call? How's business in Philadelphia?"

"You wouldn't believe," Sarah said. "I think we ought to

rent warehouse space here, Arnold. That way we'll be able to stock and ship quicker than from New York.''

"Who'd run it?" Arnold objected.

"Maresh Skowalski." Sarah was always ready with a name from the old neighborhood whenever they needed help. When she'd first begun traveling outside the city, she had taken one of the neighborhood girls with her. Arnold and their parents insisted on that. Manya and Leonard might even have refused to let her go at all, but they had just lost Joshua because he had other plans for his life; they couldn't risk alienating another child in this modern country—still a mystery to them after a quarter century—where young women wore short skirts, danced the Charleston, and, they had heard, even smoked cigarettes.

Lately, though, Sarah was traveling on her own. She had always seemed much older than she was, and she insisted that she was capable of taking care of herself. Arnold relied on her advice, always considering her suggestions carefully.

"Maresh? He's one of Joshua's, isn't he?" Joshua had organized a class to teach the Rivington Street immigrants how to read and write English. Most of them were devoted to their former teacher and followed his adventures in Palestine as closely as they had followed *The Perils of Pauline* at the movies. "You think that big Polack is smart enough?"

Sarah bristled. "I sure do! And he won't steal us blind—we all started out poor together. Also he won't faint if I say 'shit,' and with me that's a consideration."

Arnold ignored that. "Let's see if the volume we do is enough to cover both lines first."

That was why there were two kinds of jars and bottles—one in white and one in gold—and two kinds of labels: *Aurora* for the cheap line, *Duchess* for the golden one. They would both contain exactly the same product, but Duchess would sell at triple the price. The Federal Food and Drug Act of 1906 didn't regulate cosmetics, and there were no requirements about labeling contents. No one would know that two prices bought the same product, and if that bothered Arnold at first, he had to accept it as established practice in this industry or lose a lot of money.

"You're getting conservative," Sarah commented. "We're going to need a gang of salesmen soon."

"I know," Arnold agreed, "but first there's Naomi's father to pay back and the perfume thing to launch."

"I keep telling you to give Martin a piece of the company," Sarah said, sighing. "Lord, you're stubborn!"

"No." Arnold's voice was as set as his face. He still remembered Martin calling him irresponsible for leaving an established business to work for a stranger, saying Arnold had married Naomi under false pretenses. And he remembered being respectful to executives at Arden who didn't know half what Arnold knew because *they* hadn't started out making cream on a kitchen stove and selling it door-to-door. "Nobody's getting a piece of this company but you and me," he said. "I'll never work my behind off for anyone else again."

"Okay, okay," Sarah soothed. She knew it hadn't been easy for Arnold to work at Arden. Sarah kept talking. "I'm concentrating on Aurora for now, since it's our bread and butter. I've been to every drugstore and corner grocery in Philadelphia, and I'll see the boys who buy for Penney, Woolworth, and some of the Midwest chains before I come back to New York. You still want me to leave the Duchess outlets for another trip?"

"Yes. Keep the two lines separate, even in the selling. If there's one thing I learned from Arden, it was to keep the carriage trade and the *schlock* stores as far apart as possible."

Sarah laughed. "You learned a lot more than that from Lizzie Arden," she said. "But I still need Maresh. I'm only one woman, not a department."

Sarah was a colossal woman in Arnold's opinion. She had a crackling vitality that was contagious, as compelling as her tall, strong figure, her lovely face, her glossy dark hair and laughing eyes. A woman with a complexion and a personality like Sarah's could sell beauty products to anyone.

"So hire Maresh if that's what you want—but you're the best sales force I ever saw. When are you coming back?"

"Day after tomorrow."

"Why so soon?"

Sarah paused for a moment. "I just spoke to Papa. Josh is coming home."

Arnold swallowed. "That's great," he said, sounding as enthusiastic as he could. "To stay?"

"No, he's going to travel with some friend of his, fund

raising, Papa said. He'll only be in New York for a day or two, and I want to catch him.''

Arnold's jaw relaxed slightly. "Of course. I hope we get a chance to see him," he said. "I can't drag Naomi down to Rivington Street.''

"How's she doing?" Sarah asked carefully. Naomi's miscarriage had made them all a little nervous about her second pregnancy.

"Fine—no sign of trouble this time.''

"Thank God.'' Sarah sounded relieved. "We need an heir to the Fursten cosmetics empire.''

"Don't joke—it *will* be an empire," Arnold said. His voice was calm and confident again.

"Who's joking? I'm counting on it. I'll be up to see Naomi as soon as I've seen Josh. Listen, brother darling, I have to get moving. I only stopped off at the hotel to change gears, check my oil, and call you. I have a few more stores to hit.'' She made kissing noises and broke the connection. That was Sarah: impulsive, loving—and as stubborn as he was.

But she was no longer under his control, or his parents'. Little by little she had left her domestic upbringing behind her, moved into a man's world. She used rough language, directed the sales operation with little or no advice from Arnold, and never made a deal that didn't give their interests a clear advantage, one way or another. He wondered what kind of man would want to marry a woman like Sarah.

He wanted her to move away from Rivington Street—"It's no use dressing like Lady Astor if you live in a slum," he told her—but his parents wouldn't move, and Sarah didn't want to live with Arnold and Naomi. She wanted her own apartment! She made that announcement soon after she started going to Philadelphia by herself.

"Lord!'' she said to her worried family. "Philly isn't Sodom or Gomorrah! It's a one-horse town! And I won't lose my virtue if I live alone, either. That's what you're thinking, I can tell.'' And she had smiled impishly at her blushing relatives.

It was amazing she hadn't already "lost her virtue," looking the way she did. But she always said no man had made the sparks fly for her. Arnold wondered again what sort of man she'd choose—even though it made him uncomfortable to think of his younger sister in a sexual situation.

He stood near the telephone, wishing he could express love as Sarah did—but the words never got past the tightness in his chest. Sometimes he thought he would burst with adoration for Naomi, yet he could only try to show it. Speaking it was beyond him, except sometimes when they were in bed. She was always receptive, gentle, and affectionate. But sometimes it seemed she wasn't there with him, that she was off in some distance, only letting him have her. It was at those times that he had to bring her back, that he begged her, "Say you love me, Naomi, please, just once, say you love me."

She would say it, but having to ask made it empty, as though she were not saying it to him but to the phantom presence in the bed with them.

Then the words of love choked in his throat, and all he wanted to do was curse his brother for always being there between them.

He couldn't risk making the phantom a reality by naming it. He had no proof. She never refused him, never seemed to dislike the act. It would have been easier if she disliked it—some women were like that, and she was so innocent. But there was passion in her, he would have sworn it. It was unbearable to him that she didn't give it to him. It was unbearable to imagine her voluptuous little body responding to Joshua in the way Arnold sensed it could respond. Yet he had no proof. He would never have proof unless he asked her—and he would never risk that.

And now Joshua was coming back. He didn't want Naomi upset. Losing their first child had been bad enough for both of them.

She had helped him so much, his lovely little wife. The jars and labels for both lines were Naomi's design. She had a knack for choosing colors and labels, a way with names. And it had taken her mind off the lost child—especially the new perfume line they were planning. She was drawn by the romance of it.

Arnold had a more practical approach to the perfume market, just as he had a feeling about the gold mine in cosmetics. If women could be persuaded that a cream would keep them young or make them look younger, they could be persuaded that a fragrance would make them irresistible. As for Arnold, he could smell a fortune in it. "My son-in-law," Martin Held was fond of saying slyly, "thinks he can sniff out a fortune like a blood-hound." Martin would change his tune before too long.

Martin's financial support had made all this possible, and Arnold had to be grateful for it—but it was his own hard work and Sarah's that had built this business, and he was determined to keep it solely theirs.

He looked around the loft once more, his hands clasped behind his back. *This* would come alive for him. This would respond to every last drop of devotion he gave it. Here, at least, there were no doubts and no phantoms.

It was four o'clock. He decided to go home early, bring some flowers for Naomi to celebrate the new business. Someday he'd come home with clusters of diamonds for her.

He locked the door behind him and walked down the stairs. He still wasn't sure he'd tell Naomi that Joshua was coming home.

Naomi leaned against the living-room window and watched dusk settle on the Hudson, her hand resting on her stomach. She loved this time of day, no matter what the season—and she loved it all the more now that she was safely in her fourth month of pregnancy. She hoped she would really begin to show soon.

Behind her everything was ready to celebrate the opening of the new loft. The table in the dining alcove had a freshly ironed cloth and a bowl of cornflowers between two white candles. The living-room furniture was all light fruitwood, upholstered in a color called copen blue—a far cry from the heavy, practical pieces her mother favored. But even Leah had to agree that the new apartment was beautiful. Moving from the Bronx to River-side Drive had helped Arnold and Naomi get over the miscarriage—and this apartment had a room and bathroom for the new baby, thanks to her father's help.

She drew the sheer white curtains that made the room cozy without blocking the view and settled into her favorite chair. Things were going so well that soon they wouldn't need her father's help. That would make Arnold less nervous, less moody. He hated taking money from anyone. Even her parents didn't know about his ideas for the perfume venture—and that would be the biggest success of all. She and Sarah and Arnold could feel it in their bones.

She sighed contentedly, turned on a reading lamp, and picked up a new book about the history of fragrances. How exotic it was! Pictures of temple priestesses burning scented incense danced before her. She admired the Queen of Sheba, seducing Solomon not for his wisdom but to insure trade routes across his country for what her own kingdom produced—cinnamon and cloves and spikenard. She wondered what myrrh and frankincense smelled like and how the famous beauties of Thebes, with henna'd hair and kohl-rimmed eyes, could soak their hair and their bodies every day with heavy perfumed oils and unguents in the heat of the Middle East.

The book dropped to her lap, and she closed her eyes. She mustn't let Joshua intrude on this special day; it was hers and Arnold's. Most of the time she didn't think of him at all, except when Arab riots and disorders in the Holy Land got into the papers and on the radio. Her life was exactly as she had always expected it would be—except for losing the first baby. She had everything a woman could want: a lovely home, a successful, handsome, adoring husband . . . sometimes too adoring, but a woman learned to put up with that by thinking of other things while *it* was going on. Arnold was never rough, never indecent. There were times when the force of her desire for Joshua on the night he had left her seemed incredible, as if someone else had felt it. She was not the kind of woman who wanted a man to take her in every way imaginable, who wanted to drop every shred of modesty, to be drenched in sensuality, as she had wanted to be by Joshua that night.

But there were still those frightening times when Arnold was not the man stroking her body, opening it, filling it; when it was Joshua who held her and summoned longings from her that took her far from her husband's arms. It only happened once in a great while, and when it did, her anger at Joshua for leaving her was rekindled. Then she would be even more determined to stop thinking of him once and for all. It was growing easier—he had been away for a year, and she had the baby to think of now.

She heart Arnold's key in the door and put her thoughts aside, going to meet him.

"You all right?" he asked, kissing her.

"I'm marvelous." She kissed him back, holding on to him longer than she usually did. "The big question is how *you* are, how Aurora and The Duchess are." She smiled up at him.

Duchess had developed an identity of its own for them; The
Duchess was their dream.

"You have to see it to believe it," Arnold said. "Now that the
workmen are out of the place, you can come and look without
hurting yourself." He handed her a small nosegay of sweetheart
roses and baby's breath. "These are for you."

She wondered why it always embarrassed him to be sentimen-
tal, but her blue eyes sparkled when she took the flowers and
started toward the kitchen for something to put them in. "I have
a special dinner for you."

He watched her, desire roaring in him at the movement of her
hips. But there must be no sex until the baby was safely born.
Even Leah had warned him.

"I'm going to wash up," he said.

She followed him across the living room with a small vase for
the flowers, arranging them in the bedroom, listening to him
describe the loft on Union Square while he washed his hands and
face in the blue-tiled bathroom. "And you had as much to do
with it as anyone—the jars and labels look terrific." He turned
off the water. "Sarah called from Philly."

"How is she? I miss her."

"Coming back in a few days." His voice was muffled by the
towel. "Joshua's coming, and she wants to see him." He'd no
idea he was going to blurt it out like that.

There was silence in the bedroom. He went to the bathroom
door, but she was rearranging the flowers, and he couldn't see
her face. "He's coming with some other guy to do fund raising
all over the country. He'll only be in New York a few days."

"Sarah must be excited," Naomi said. "And surprised." She
started toward the kitchen, and he followed her as far as the
dining alcove.

"I'm surprised too," he said, sitting down at the table. "Aren't
you?"

"I thought he'd never come back once he got out there." The
casserole she took from the oven almost slipped from her hands.
Then she steadied herself and brought it to the table. "Well"—
she laughed—"we have a few surprises for him too, don't we?"

He took the platter she handed him. "There's Aurora and The
Duchess," he agreed.

''And the baby,'' she said proudly. ''You'll have a lot to talk about.''

''If we get a chance.'' She looked down at her plate as he went on. ''Those Fund boys don't sit around. They travel by night and hold fund raisers by day. We might not even see him this time.''

Naomi said nothing. He felt uncomfortable with the silence. ''Maybe it would be a good idea to start a small perfume line,'' he said abruptly. ''For Aurora.''

''But you were going to wait and do something special for The Duchess,'' she said with more animation.

''It would be good experience, though,'' he said. ''And ounce for ounce there's more profit in perfume than in cosmetics.'' He forgot about Joshua. ''I can make more selling less, and that means less money locked into raw materials.'' He took another bite, and she waited until he went on. ''Sarah wants to hire more salesmen soon, and they can sell everything for us for the same draw and commission. But I'll still wait for something special before I put a Duchess label on it.''

They didn't speak of Joshua's visit again during the meal or after it, while he helped her stack the dishes for the maid the next morning. But Naomi went to bed early, and although Arnold tried to do some planning for the next day, his brother's return was on his mind.

How could he act naturally with Joshua after all the resentment he had accumulated against him? How would it affect Naomi? Yet she had behaved as usual; she often went to bed early on the doctor's advice.

She was asleep when he got into bed, as quietly as he could, wondering if he would have to see Joshua. So the Zionists were coming to America to raise money now! From businessmen like Arnold. In the end everyone had to have money, even idealists like his pioneer brother. And they came to get it from dirty capitalists like himself! He turned over to sleep on that thought.

Naomi was awake through most of the night, hoping she wouldn't have to see him again, ever. If she saw him, she would feel humiliated all over again. Abandoned. And the dreams would start again, disturbing dreams that left her aroused and unfulfilled.

She still wanted him. She couldn't forgive him for that.

And he knew she had married Arnold without loving him in the way she loved his brother. She couldn't forgive him for that either.

4

It was a mild night, and the front-step and fire-escape audience was in attendance when Joshua and Lazar arrived at Rivington Street from the pier. Joshua stopped to talk to dozens of people he knew, introducing his friend, and word spread quickly that the Fursten boy was back with a blond Palestinian who didn't look Jewish, spoke a lot of languages, and had seen Jerusalem and the sacred western wall of the Temple.

"It's like a royal progress," Lazar said in Hebrew. "I had no idea you were so popular."

"I wasn't when I left. Maybe they think I've given up Zionism. And you'd better speak English."

Lazar nodded and followed Joshua up two flights of stairs to the Furstens' apartment, right over the small candy store that was their livelihood. Leonard and Manya were waiting in the doorway, looking much older than Joshua remembered, seeming frail and fragile to him when he embraced them both.

Lazar stood quietly, not wanting to intrude on the reunion, but there was a woman in the room behind them, and when his eyes met Sarah's, he was not content to merely look at her. He knew who she was, and he was impatient to speak to her.

He was looking at her in a way that made her want to arrange her hair, smooth her dress. But when he smiled at her, Sarah knew how she looked to him.

He was as tall and deeply tanned as her brother, but his eyes were brilliant blue, and his sun-bleached hair had a reddish cast.

Then Joshua came to put his arms around her, and she laughed with happiness. "You're so tan and strong! Your shoulders are at least a yard wider. You're marvelous!"

"Wait a minute, Whirlwind," he said. "Let me look at *you*. You *have* changed—no wonder you're an irresistible saleswoman. Do you still like it?"

"I love it—and I'm going to get filthy rich at it. But never mind about me. Tell me about you." She looked at Lazar, standing with her parents.

"This is Lazar Kramer," Joshua said. "The friend I wrote you about. And this is my little sister, Sarah."

"You told me about her too, but the description does not match the reality."

He had a musical accent, difficult to place. His voice was not as deep as Joshua's, but he looked about the same age, twenty-six.

"He looks like King Solomon," Sarah said without thinking.

"King David had the red hair," Joshua said.

"Well, welcome to America, whoever you are." Sarah shook hands with him. "Come and sit down—you can leave your suitcases there. I hope you're hungry, because there's a banquet inside, and you're expected to devour it."

They went to the dining room, shining with wax and floor polish. Manya Fursten's specialties were set out on a stiffly starched white cloth: sweet-and-sour cabbage soup, chicken and dumplings, green peppers simmered with mushrooms and onions, a freshly baked loaf of white bread, a homemade sponge cake. They opened the wine Sarah had brought and enjoyed the meal, exchanging news, hearing about the fund-raising tour the two young men had come for.

"We hear such terrible things about the Holy Land," Leonard told his son. "Why is there so much trouble?"

Lazar answered him. "The British made the same promises to both sides—to protect Arab nationalism and to establish a home-land for the Jews. That means the Jews were allowed to buy land, mostly land the rich absentee owners did not want, land that was just sitting there, uninhabited, uncultivated. But the Arabs do not want any more Jewish immigration; they want a

'democratic' system of government in Palestine instead of absolute rule by Britain under the Mandate.'' Lazar shrugged. ''The
trouble is that a 'democratic' system to the Arabs means no Jews
in the government and no more immigration. We cannot accept
that.''

''Will there be more trouble?'' Sarah asked, her dark eyes
anxious.

Joshua nodded. ''The Grand Mufti—as he calls himself—is a
fanatic and anti-Jewish to his toes. He has no patience with legal
solutions. He'd rather stir up the peasants with horror stories
about Jewish plans to desecrate their holy places. He figures if he
gets them to fever pitch, they'll massacre every Jew in Palestine,
and that'll be an end to the problem.''

Manya murmured something in Yiddish.

''Yes,'' Lazar agreed with her in his softly accented English,
''it is a lot like Russia—but there is an important difference. The
Jews in Palestine will defend themselves, and we are here to be
sure they have the means to do it.''

Leonard Fursten was perplexed. ''Then this is Zionism? Keeping them from killing Jews? Who can be against it?''

Joshua took his father's hand. ''Let's say it's Zionism for us,
Pa. This—and rebuilding the state of Israel.''

''The Hasidim and the Orthodox say there can't be a new state
of Israel until the Messiah comes,'' Manya offered.

''They are wrong,'' Lazar said flatly, taking another slice of
bread.

''And our Law?'' Manya persisted.

Joshua and Sarah wanted to hear what Lazar would say. There
had been many explosions at this very table about how Zionists
defied Judaic law—before Joshua had defied his parents and left
for Palestine. Then they missed their son and wanted him back
no matter what he believed.

Lazar did not seem aware of any tension. ''The law will be
there for every Jew to follow as he sees fit—the way you follow
it differently from the Hasidim. The only reason the Jews have
been persecuted is that they have no country of their own; and
they have not got a country because they have been too afraid to
build one.''

''You don't seem frightened,'' Sarah said, watching his strong,
brown hand on the white cloth.

"I was frightened enough as a boy to last me for a lifetime. I will never be frightened again," Lazar said, looking at each of them, his eyes stopping on Sarah.

They were quiet for a moment, then, the dinner finished, Lazar went to answer more of Leonard's questions in the living room while Sarah and Joshua stayed at the table talking

Manya smiled. "Sit and talk, children, just like when you were little." She busied herself in the kitchen.

Brother and sister touched hands briefly again. "Are you all right?" Sarah asked softly.

He took a deep breath. "That letter you sent—the long one, about the miscarriage—was the first one I got. The others were lost. I had no idea until then that they were married. And I had no idea you knew how I felt."

"I waited long enough to tell you everything as it was. I'm sorry it was such a shock. She's pregnant again."

He glanced at his sister, then away. "I'm glad for her, for both of them. I hope she's happy."

"Are you?"

"I'm doing what I want to do. That's about all any man can ask of life. And you?"

"Aside from going out there with you, yes. We're getting wealthier by the minute, and money agrees with me."

"I'll say. It's indecent for a girl of nineteen to look the way you do."

Sarah laughed. "I hope your friend King David thinks so."

"I'm sure he does. He has an eye for the ladies, though, so don't believe a word he says."

Sarah was privately determined to believe every syllable the blond man in the next room uttered, but she only suggested they join Lazar and their father.

"In a minute. There's something I have to know." Again Joshua didn't meet his sister's eyes. "If you guessed how it was with Naomi and me, did Arnold?"

She was glad he wasn't watching her or she could not have lied. It wasn't a real lie—Arnold had never said a word to justify her intuition—but she knew her brothers too well to be wrong. "No, he didn't. They're happy together, and he adores her. And now, with a booming business and a baby on the way . . ."

"Thank God for that," Joshua said. "Arnold and I have our

differences, but I care about him. I couldn't look at him if he knew." He turned to Sarah. "I just couldn't help myself, Shai. Neither of us could."

"I know," Sarah said. "Some things just happen. Some things just are." She didn't say there would always be a suspicion in Arnold's mind that he couldn't face—or that something had just happened between herself and Lazar Kramer that couldn't be helped either. She was ready to go wherever the feeling led her. She hoped it would be straight to his arms.

"There's nobody home but us," Lazar said to Sarah late the next day. He was sitting on the couch with Maresh Skowalski, a man as tall as Lazar and as blond but twice as brawny. "We were both born in Warsaw, so we reminisce."

Maresh lumbered to his feet, smiling. He concentrated hard on manners. Lazar, Sarah noticed, behaved almost exactly the same with women as he did with men. Palestinians cared little for social graces. But social graces or not, a woman was very much aware of being female in Lazar Kramer's presence.

"I hardly got a chance to talk to Josh," Maresh said. "But Lazar's been telling me all about Palestine."

"Maresh has much in common with the Zionists—for a Catholic," Lazar remarked.

"Listen, Poland's been pushed from Russia to Germany and back for years," Maresh said. "Anyone who wants his own country in one piece and in one place"—he thumped his chest— "he's got a friend right here."

"Don't take Maresh off to Palestine," Sarah said. "He's Joshua's best student, and he has a great future in America." She decided to wait for a better time to tell Maresh she wanted him to work for Duchess. If he left now, she'd be alone with Lazar.

Maresh grinned, embarrassed by praise. "If it wasn't for Josh and your mother, I wouldn't have anything. But I have to get going. Anna will be angry if I'm late." He shook hands with Lazar. "I'll see you again before you go." To Sarah he said, "Tell your mother thanks for the baby blanket, will you?"

"Sure will," Sarah said. She turned to Lazar when the door closed behind Maresh. "His wife is half his size and never speaks above a whisper, but he adores her."

She put her briefcase down and took off her loose, hip-length jacket. The sleeveless dress under it was the same dark red silk, simple and straight, but it molded her body, and she was glad she had chosen it. Her face was flushed from the breathless excitement she was feeling at being alone with him.

He was sitting on the couch, a sheaf of papers on a small table near him and what Sarah recognized as the family photo album on his lap. He had chosen the largest piece of furniture in the room, but it was too small for him; the clutter of her mother's crocheted doilies on the back of the couch looked to her like spider webs trying to hold a Goliath. The walls were confining; the ceilings seemed lower.

"Where did they all go?" she managed to say.

"Your parents wanted some time alone with him—and they wanted to go to synagogue too." He grinned. "I have not been inside a synagogue since I was thirteen. I wouldn't know how to behave."

"I don't think Josh was very keen to go either, but he'd do it to please them."

"We are converting your father to the Zionist cause, anyway, and we need all we can get."

She sat down in her father's frayed wing chair, across from the couch. "What did you two find out at Fund headquarters?"

He gestured toward the pile of papers. "All that—each damn page is a town, with names of possible contributors and estimated contributions. We must make them give." His face had changed.

"You hate fund raising, don't you?" Sarah said.

"Yes, I hate it. I hate having to persuade Jews that wanting our own state is not a crime—that a people without a country has no rights; and that donating money to build our own country does not constitute treason to theirs." His shoulders moved restlessly. "And I am not much good at being indoors—I am used to the desert and the hills."

"I wish I could go out there," Sarah said. She wanted to go anywhere he went.

He looked at her, her long, graceful legs in sheer silk stockings, her dress and shoes obviously fashionable, her dark hair bobbed. And he could see her full, strong body in trousers and a work shirt, with that smile of hers that warmed a man's soul, those dark eyes that aroused him, that generous mouth he had wanted to kiss from the first moment he saw her. He imagined her body naked. But it was a hopeless longing—she was Joshua's sister, and she belonged here.

"It will be a while before I can go back myself," he said. "Josh and I have places to go I never heard of."

"What's your first stop?" Sarah said. Why did they have to leave so soon? She wanted more time with him.

He looked at the pile of paper. "Baltimore," he said, accenting the second syllable.

Her face lit up. "I have to go there too! Maybe we can take the same train. I'm on a selling trip," she explained.

"I know—Josh told me about the business. It sounds as though you and your brother have made a huge success of it."

Sarah put her head back on the chair. "Not yet. We have a big job ahead of us. But we're on the way. You know, it's not hard to sell the stuff—it almost sells itself. Our problem is the amount of capital we have to lock into stock to be sure we can meet orders. Arnold hates to borrow money, but everyone else in the business does." She brought her head up again, her face enthusiastic. "I went to see the new factory. It's really terrific!"

"I know how it feels to build something and want to see it finished," he said.

She sobered. "It's better to build a country than a cosmetics factory."

"There is nothing wrong with factories—we could use a few in Palestine. We have to modernize the country if we are ever going to make it independent. And the Arabs do not want it modernized; they are afraid the peasants will get ideas."

Sarah listened, hearing from a distance. She wanted to sit near him. She wanted to touch him. Joshua had written a lot about him, where he came from, how he had been raised, the sort of man he was. A poet who built roads, smuggled Jews into Palestine in defiance of British quotas, and was tireless in raising funds from among the scattered Jews of Europe.

He was Joshua's first real friend. She might have known Josh would choose a man like this.

"How about some coffee?" she asked him. She couldn't sit there so near him and not touch him.

"Coffee is fine," he said. "May I help?"

"There's always a pot on the stove. I'll be right back." She had to get away from him for a moment, so electric was the feeling between them even as they spoke of things that meant so much to each of them. Some instinct told her that his nature was more voluptuous than her brother's. She would have sworn Joshua had finally had a woman out there; she was certain Lazar Kramer had had many. It was strange to be so sure about a man she'd just met. But she knew him, somehow. She knew him.

She brought the coffee back on a small tray and sat next to him on the couch. "Who showed you the family archives?" she asked, pointing to the album still in his lap.

"Josh. He has told me so much about all of you, I had to see for myself what you were all like when you were growing up." He turned a few pages to a photograph of Arnold and Naomi on their wedding day. "A handsome couple. Arnold does not resemble you two, though; he looks more like your great-uncle Abraham. She is very beautiful," he said, looking at Sarah. "Very beautiful."

She could hardly speak when he looked at her like that. "Nobody ever took so much interest in our family album before."

"I never had a family album—or a family. Not like this. I did not know I missed having one." He seemed unsettled by this discovery about his own feelings.

She could not bear his loneliness. She leaned toward him and touched his face, her own expression soft and full of caring. When he kissed her, she made a small sound of avid, ardent pleasure, desire surrounding her like a warm bath.

He turned her body to lie across his chest, her head pillowed on his arm. His hand reached for her breast as naturally as his mouth for hers, but he drew back.

"Oh, please," she whispered, "don't stop."

"You are Joshua's sister, Sarah. You are just a girl. I cannot . . ."

"Can't what? Treat me like a woman? Oh, yes, you can, you must. I want you to." He bent over her again. "I don't care if I'm not supposed to say it. I love you. I've loved you since I was born."

He held her nearer while he said, "No, Sarah, that is not possible, love does not happen like that."

"Doesn't it?" She kissed him again, slowly and sweetly, with an instinctive expertise more compelling than if she had learned it by kissing men most of her life. The innocent eroticism of it overwhelmed him. She drew his hand back to her breast and felt as if she were falling at the touch of it against her.

"Lazar," she said. "It's this—but it's so much more than this. I want to be part of you, part of your dream. I want to help you, share what you have to do. I've always wanted to. Oh, let me, let me. You know you want it too. You knew it that first minute. It's not true that love can't happen like this."

Her hands held his face. Her eyes held his. He kissed her again.

There was a soft abandon about her, a soundless calling, a total giving that moved him emotionally as much as it stirred him sexually.

Long-buried yearnings rushed through him, echoes of the orphaned child mingling with demands of the sensual male and the yearnings of a pioneer for whom Eretz Israel was the only religion.

In a yielding ardor that felt like intoxication, he knew she was his dream of Israel incarnate, her skin the soft golden sands of Herzliya, her passion the burning sun of Judea, her love the glow of Jerusalem. And all at once he knew he wanted to possess this girl not only with the lust of sex but as he lusted to see his homeland born again, as if she *were* his homeland, as if she and his homeland were one and the same.

Holding her, kissing her soft skin, her lovely mouth, he knew he would not take her unless he married her; and he knew he had to have her—and Israel too. He was lonely for them both, and he wanted them both for the rest of his life, by right and in law.

"I still can't believe she's doing this," Arnold said as their hired limousine turned into the street where the wedding would be held. "She just met him a month ago."

"Five weeks," Naomi specified. "That's all it takes—for Sarah. And she's already done it. This religious ceremony is only to please your parents." She was nervous, but this was Sarah's wedding. No one would notice Naomi.

"How can she marry a man who'll let her work?" Arnold went on angrily. "Even if I don't want to lose my partner! He hasn't even got a job you can make sense of. What in hell good is a fund raiser?"

"She says he's a writer too."

"Not good enough to support a wife. She'll be supporting him!"

"I hope you didn't tell her *that*," Naomi said.

"I did—once—and almost got killed," Arnold admitted, smiling a little. "She has a terrible temper." The car had stopped. "Wait a minute," he said. "I'll come around and help you out."

Naomi sat there, feeling like a small whale. She was almost six months along now and glad she was really showing. A pregnant woman should be proud and happy to let the world know she was loved. She was ready to meet Joshua again—she was glad he hadn't stayed in New York long enough for them to meet when he first came home. And she was very curious about Lazar Kramer, the man Sarah had married two weeks ago in a civil ceremony while traveling with him and her brother.

"We're all sales people," Sarah had said merrily on the telephone when she called them with the news. "Except they're selling Israel and I'm selling Aurora and Duchess." She had sounded happy—but Sarah always sounded happy. She sounded something else, deeper and calmer, to Naomi at the time. She sounded joyous, complete, and absolutely sure of what she wanted. Naomi had never felt like that.

Arnold helped her out of the car. It was a sunny May day, and Naomi looked crisp and well tailored despite her bulk in a navy blue sheer wool smock dress and a coat, with white pique collar and cuffs. Her small hat had a white turnback brim on one side. Her white gloves were immaculate. The long rope of creamy pearls she wore was the latest gift from Arnold.

Arnold took her through the side entrance of the building. A tacky, hand-lettered sign said Moskovitz Restaurant—Weddings—Bar Mitzvahs.

"And what a place for a wedding! The woman's got as much money as I have!" Arnold fumed. "Why not uptown?"

"You know how Sarah feels about the people she grew up with."

"I also know how they feel about her," Arnold conceded, making Naomi rest in the middle of the short flight of stairs. "That Maresh Skowalski is doing a terrific job in Philly. Who'd have thought a Polish butcher could run a warehousing operation like that?"

"Did you tell Sarah?"

"She's my partner—I have to tell her everything, even when she's right." Arnold laughed. "Here it is. Go in to Sarah, but don't tire yourself." He kissed her and went back down the stairs to join the wedding party through the front entrance.

Sarah swooped to kiss her sister-in-law as soon as Naomi opened the door to the bride's dressing room. "You gorgeous little thing! You look like a fashion plate even with your tummy— and the pearls are gorgeous. Now sit down. I have a seat for you right here at the back, so you won't have to walk a step."

"You have *never* been so beautiful," Naomi said, admiring Sarah's tall figure in the simply cut white silk sheath, short in front, long in back, and draped in a cowl at the shoulders. Her high coloring and shining black hair were striking against the white cap and veil she had just put on.

"I've never been so happy in my life," Sarah said, suddenly very calm. "Maybe that's why."

There was a knock on the door, and a small man in a tight frock coat and striped trousers looked in to ask if the bride would be ready in five minutes.

Sarah nodded and laughed when he disappeared again. "He looks so uncomfortable. But the bride's been ready since the moment she saw the groom. Naomi, he's beautiful, the most beautiful man I ever saw, even if he dresses like a rumpled bed. Well, I *feel* like one," she exulted. Naomi blushed. "You're shocked, aren't you?"

"I'm learning not to be shocked at anything you say or do."

Sarah settled her veil in front of the mirror. "Well, I don't think it's shocking to have an insatiable passion for your husband— and obviously you don't either."

Naomi was glad the little man in his tight suit came in again, this time with Sarah's mother to take the bride down the aisle and Leah to supervise, as always. Manya was silent and affectionate, stroking Naomi's cheek softly. Leah kissed her daughter. "It seems like yesterday it was you," she whispered to Naomi. "Are you all right?"

"I'm fine, Mama, don't worry. I'll go sit outside now so I can see the whole thing." She hugged Sarah, and they smiled at each other. Then Naomi slipped out and sat in the end chair of the last row. Her eyes passed slowly up the rows of Sarah's neighbors and friends, old and young, the noisy people of Rivington Street; they

could have been transplanted, Lazar had told Sarah, directly to
Tel Aviv without anyone noticing.

Then she saw him. The room was small, and he seemed very
near her. He looked different. Stronger, broader, more rugged—
but as compelling as she remembered, as familiar as her dreams
of him. He was holding one corner of the wedding canopy,
standing next to Arnold, and there was not the least resemblance
between them, she could see that now. Nor the least resemblance
between her feelings for each of them.

Useless, it was useless to pretend she didn't love him in a way
she would never love Arnold, that the tie between them wouldn't
last throughout their lives, a taut thread of feeling as strong as
steel, drawing them together, forbidden, impractical, impossible,
but there.

He saw her, and the smile in his eyes went out before he
looked away. She felt ashamed of her bulk. She didn't want him
to see her like this, dumpy and round and domestic. She wanted
to be beautiful for him, seductive and desirable. She wanted him
to want her, even if he could never have her.

An "insatiable passion," Sarah had called it. But Sarah could
satisfy her passion. Sarah could admit to it.

Arnold must not know. Her eyes dropped to her hands, lying
on the swollen belly that harbored Arnold's child. The pearls he
had given her rested there too, creamy and glowing. There were
a lot of pearls, she hadn't counted how many—but certainly not
one for each time she had accepted Arnold's invasions of her
body when it was Joshua she wanted. She wondered if there were
enough pearls in the world to fill the emptiness she felt, even
with the child inside her.

But Arnold must not know. It would wreck both their lives if
he did. There had always been enough tension between the
brothers about what mattered in life. Naomi thought she knew
what mattered now. She raised her head, her cheeks wet, and
watched Sarah being married to Lazar Kramer through a blur of
silent, useless tears.

It was all right if Arnold saw her crying now. Married women
always cried at weddings and nobody ever asked why.

5

NEW YORK
AUGUST 1929

"I think this calls for a drink, at least," Sarah said, sitting on the arm of a blue brocade easy chair and leaning against Lazar. "We might even reach half a million gross our first year. Then we can throw a party."

She looked at her brothers and Naomi for confirmation. Her extensive travels since Joshua came back in April had borne amazing fruit: The sales of Duchess products, buttressed by the cheaper Aurora line, had burgeoned far beyond Arnold's projections. If they calculated the projected gross sales based on the last five months, it seemed possible to reach the magical half-million dollar gross by the end of their first year in business, still a profitable seven months away. But Arnold was not satisfied.

"Arden is going to gross four million for her wholesale division this year. There's no reason for us to celebrate until we can do better than that."

"We haven't been around as long as Arden," Naomi reminded him. "Wait until next year."

She poured coffee from the tray in front of her. She was feeling uncomfortably bulky. Arnold hadn't agreed to dinner out with Sarah, Lazar, and Joshua, back again from a trip that combined Sarah's selling with the two men's fund raising. Having the three of them in for coffee was all he would allow.

"I wish the Fund was as close to the half-million mark as you seem to be," Lazar said, holding his wife's hand. They traveled together all the time, but Naomi noticed that they always touched when they were in the same room.

Arnold shook his head. "If Arden doubled her gross in the last five years, we ought to triple, the way this country's booming. But now there's talk they're going to make push money illegal."

For a price a salesgirl would push another product instead of the one she was hired to sell.

Joshua leaned forward. "If we followed every law the British make, we wouldn't have a single weapon in Palestine and a lot fewer Jews to fire them."

Lazar agreed. "Pay them more push money than the established lines do. They're not going to refuse it simply because it's illegal."

Arnold's green eyes went from his brother to Lazar with such astonishment that Sarah laughed. "Yes, Arnold, they're as wicked as we are."

Joshua confirmed it. "Gunrunning and cosmetics are both cutthroat operations. You do what you have to do."

"You do what everybody does to survive," Lazar added. "You just do it better."

Arnold felt the first glimmer of kinship with these men. He had always supposed they looked down on his business. Joshua had always called him a materialist—and Arnold assumed it was a criticism, that Joshua considered his own ideals too far above Arnold's to allow for any similarity in their goals and methods.

Yet they were being helpful, advising him to put their own ideas to work in a totally different field. They were right—he would simply pay more push money than the others did no matter what the law was. The profits were more than sufficient for the payoffs. Sometimes the jars cost more than the ingredients inside them! Five cents worth of Duchess cream retailed for two dollars and fifty cents. No one knew the contents or questioned the results promised by the manufacturer.

"It's the mystery that gets them," Sarah would tell her customers and the salesgirls she trained. "Names like Easter Pink and Kiss Coral, instead of light, dark, and medium, will sell lipstick for you—and don't forget that they're coordinated to go with the latest fashions," she would finish triumphantly, borrowing another page from the ingenious Miss Arden's book of tricks.

"And this cream," Sarah would tell the eager women clustered around a counter during a sales demonstration. "It will prevent wrinkles if girls start using it soon enough—and it will take lines away from mature complexions." Sarah never used the word *old*. "Would you think to look at me that I'm almost thirty?" It had been impossible to tell Sarah's age from the day she reached puberty; it always would be. Looking at the tall, full-breasted woman with her magnificently glowing skin, the customers said she didn't look a day over eighteen—and bought.

The retailers listened, used the same techniques, and sold with amazing ease. Then they reordered in ever-increasing quantities and at lower wholesale prices than Arden demanded. Not only that, Duchess sold where Arden would not: off Fifth Avenue and in places where Jews were allowed, those large resort hotels Miss Arden avoided. But Duchess was still a prestige line. Drugstores and chains, small shops and beauty parlors got Aurora—the same product for a fraction of the price, whether they knew it or not.

The industry was booming with the American economy. As social disapproval of cosmetics declined, the amount of money women spent on beauty products climbed. There was no restraint on the claims manufacturers could make for their products to a wildly credulous, infinitely trusting public. "There's just no limit," Arnold always said, "to what a woman will believe. They swear they see a change in their complexions."

It was incredible to Naomi, listening to them, that she could sit pouring coffee in her beautifully decorated blue and white living room as if Joshua were no more to her than a brother-in-law should be. The baby helped. As for Joshua, he seemed completely at ease, but he rarely looked at her directly. And never at her swollen body.

When their eyes met, the secrets in them shouted. As they had shouted at Sarah's wedding when Naomi stood between the brothers, belonging to one and wanting the other. They had been polite, a brother- and sister-in-law exchanging pleasantries, as nice people were brought up to do. Nice people were brought up to hide their deepest feelings; they would never embarrass anyone else or risk disapproval of themselves.

And so she had stood there between them, part of her envying Sarah's frank, tempestuous love for her blue-eyed Lazar Kramer—and part of her hidden, like the moon in eclipse, by the circle of Arnold's arm.

He was proclaiming her *his* wife, she realized. He was proud that her womb was heavy with *his* child.

Arnold had been unusually talkative that day, and Joshua

unusually silent. It was a relief to her to agree with Arnold that she was tired and they must leave the wedding early.

There was no reason to stay. Everything had been said in that first moment when Joshua looked at her and looked away.

But the baby, now quiet inside her, helped.

"When are you going to give The Duchess her perfume?" she asked now, looking from Arnold to Sarah. "Perfume is even dreamier than makeup."

Arnold was firm. "Not until it's the right perfume, the perfect perfume—and not until the American market is ready to pay the same price for a domestic perfume as for a French import."

"Advertising might make them do that," Sarah suggested.

"I know," Arnold agreed, getting out of his chair. "But the product has to be perfect, absolutely perfect. If we strike out the first time up at bat, it'll leave an impression that'll be hard to change."

It seemed to Naomi that Arnold's voice was coming from very far away. The first intimation of pain started at the base of her belly, then expanded downward to her thighs and around her back. She tried to push it away, tried to keep panic from getting between her and the baby. If it hurt her so much, did it hurt him? Poor baby, nothing must hurt him, ever. Go away, she told the pain. Leave us alone. She tried to listen to what Arnold was saying so faintly, something about snob appeal and prices.

Joshua's voice stopped Arnold. "Naomi, are you all right?"

She was very pale, holding tightly to the brocaded arm of the chair. She couldn't answer right away, and Arnold went to her. She looked at him, visibly frightened. "I think something's happening," she whispered.

"But it's too soon," Sarah protested.

Lazar went to the telephone. "What's the doctor's number?"

"It's right there, near the phone," Arnold said. "Tell him I'm bringing her right to the hospital. Come with me, Sarah. And someone call a cab."

Joshua picked up the house phone and spoke to the doorman. "Shall we come with you?" he asked Arnold.

"No, call Leah and Martin first, will you? Maybe it's just a false alarm, but they'd want to know. Meet me at the hospital."

Joshua and Lazar followed them to the elevator. Naomi was quiet but determined between Sarah and Arnold. "I'm really fine," she said to Joshua. Then she stiffened as another wave of pain took over and the elevator doors closed. Her lips moved, but Sarah and Arnold, hurrying to the cab, urging the driver to go as fast as he could, didn't hear her.

She was talking to the baby. The first one had been a stranger to her, barely a fact before she lost it. But this one had been with her for eight months. This one woke and moved, slept and was still. She had been talking to the baby when they were alone together, telling stories, making plans. She had been so happy when she began to show. It was only when Joshua came back that she was ashamed of her bulk.

"But not you," she said to the baby while they wheeled her into a white room. "Baby dear, I didn't mean you."

"No, dear, of course you didn't," the nurse said, using a hypodermic deftly. "Now relax and let this work."

Naomi struggled against the sedative. "No, I don't want to go to sleep. I want to tell him . . ."

Then she felt herself falling and knew, somehow, that when she woke, the baby wouldn't be there to tell.

Joshua and Lazar sat in the waiting room, both of them restless and uncomfortable. They were not accustomed to feeling helpless.

Lazar watched his friend sympathetically. Before Sarah, he could have been so sensible. Now he knew what intense longing could permeate a man even as he possessed the woman he loved. He could never get enough of Sarah. There were no sage words he could offer to Joshua now; wisdom had nothing to do with passion. Only those who had never experienced passion thought it could be reasoned away.

It was early morning when they finally left the hospital, after Sarah had come alone to tell them that the baby was stillborn and Naomi sleeping. Then she had gone back to the doctor's office to wait with Arnold until Naomi woke.

The two men returned to the living room of the suite they shared in a residential hotel when they were in New York. They sat in silence, smoking cigarettes and drinking coffee. One of the best things about Lazar, Joshua reflected gratefully, was that he never talked when there was nothing to say.

At about nine Lazar stirred. "I ought to check in with the Fund," he said, going to the telephone. Although the Jewish

Agency was now the official representative of all Jews, Zionist and non-Zionist, who favored the establishment of new Jewish settlements in Palestine, it was quick to welcome contributions for needy Jews from many organizations.

When Lazar put the telephone down, his blue eyes were blazing.

"What is it?" Joshua whispered. There had been enough bad news from headquarters a week ago when rioting Arabs massacred Jews in Jerusalem and Hebron.

"It's unbelievable. After the rising in Hebron the British, damn their souls to hell, did absolutely nothing, and they wouldn't let the Haganah go in to protect our people in the other towns." His mouth was white with anger.

"Tell me!" Joshua demanded.

"They attacked in Safed."

"My God!" Joshua said. "How many?"

"There are over one hundred and thirty dead now; more than three hundred wounded."

"Safed." Joshua was incredulous. "They've been living together for decades, peaceful neighbors."

Lazar sat down heavily and dropped his head to his hands. "Sweet Lord in heaven, what are we doing here?"

"Sending guns and money," Joshua reminded him.

"Guns the bastards won't let us use to protect our people," Lazar raged. "To the devil with this money grubbing. I should be *there!*" His fist struck his knee in frustration.

Joshua nodded, his jaw rigid. What had happened to the brigade, to Natan and Ben and Isaac? Had they been slaughtered in the desert like the inhabitants of that dreamy little town where Ari had foretold exactly this kind of bloody violence a few short months ago? And what of Giora? What of Shula and Reuven, Aviva and Rachel? Was the kibbutz slippery with blood like the ancient stones of Safed?

"What did headquarters say about us?"

"No change in plans for me." Lazar swore softly. "I have to stay—I make a big impression on American Jews because I'm a Palestinian. As for you, you go to Europe. There's more money here, but you can buy guns more easily there."

"Al Capone can get weapons in America and we can't! There's a conspiracy to block arms sales to Jews."

"There is—take my word for it. But we have no trouble in Europe, so that is where you'll go."

"It's just as well," Joshua said. "I don't belong here." It was impossible for him to stay near Naomi now. What kind of comfort could he bring her, no matter how much he loved her? She was Arnold's wife. He had to accept that, no matter what he could read in her eyes whenever he looked at her.

"You think I do?" Lazar exploded. "I feel like a goddamn fish out of goddamn water—some kind of sideshow spectacle. One son of a bitch told me I'd make a better impression with a pioneer suntan! He even offered to buy me a sun lamp." Lazar paced, unable to contain his anger. "Where in hell's Sarah?"

She came in soon after. Naomi would be all right, the doctor had assured them, but Sarah wasn't so sure Naomi cared.

"It's creepy," she said when she had heard the rest of the bad news. "It's like an evil star. What's going on in Palestine and the baby dying all at once. It feels like the end of the world."

"Well, if it is," Lazar said, "let's not just sit around. Let's go down fighting."

Joshua looked at his friend, sharing his frustration and immeasurably grateful for Lazar's common sense. Evil stars were of one's own making, Lazar contended. " 'The fault, dear Brutus, is in ourselves, not our stars,' " he insisted, "or however it goes." He was ready to fight. It was a better way of living—or dying—than despair.

They were silent now, immersed in their anger. Joshua was glad Sarah and Lazar had each other and even more relieved, in the loneliness he couldn't help feeling at the sight of them, that he was going back where he belonged.

It was ironic: The man in love with Israel had a wife. The man in love with his brother's wife had only Israel.

He must let go of her, once and for all. He must let go.

6

NEW YORK
OCTOBER 1929

Sarah slipped her hand into Lazar's pocket as they left the pier. They had watched Joshua's ship dwindle on the horizon before they turned away. They knew his departure was a prelude to their own separation. As tensions mounted in Palestine, Lazar was rebelling more and more against his work in the States. He would be going back as soon as he could.

Sarah sighed. "How long before you join him?"

He put his arm around her shoulders. "Several months."

"I want to go with you," she said, keeping her voice calm. Lazar was not the kind of man to respond to hysteria. He did what had to be done and expected others to do likewise. Were the women he had known all stalwart and unemotional?

He was shaking his head. "Not this time. We'll be on the move every minute." Even those who objected to the idea of a Jewish state were incensed at the massacres in August. They supported the inherent right of self-defense. Lazar would be going back to help organize stringent defense measures for which, if Joshua succeeded, the weapons would come from Europe.

"I know that," Sarah said, exasperated. "But why would I be in the way?"

"You wouldn't. But there is no hotel to go to when the day is over, only a tent if we are lucky. The Haganah is an underground army, not a selling trip." His arm held her closer. "I'll only be away a few months. We'll need more money."

"Well, I'm not going to fuss over it—I promised I wouldn't." Privately she determined not to let him stay too long without her, no matter what she had promised. "I'll keep busy making pots of money out of pots of cream and send it all to you." They left the pier and crossed the street. Sarah reached up to kiss his ear and rumple his hair. "You glorious creature, let's find a cab and go back to the hotel. I want to make love."

He kissed her as soon as they got into the cab, ignoring the driver's interest and the knots of people gathering in the streets outside.

The hint of approaching evening was there, like the crackle of autumn in the air. But there was something more, a current that passed from one hurrying New Yorker to another as the taxi crossed Herald Square. Elegant women in chemise dresses and cocoon wrap coats, silk stockings, and small cloche hats shopped happily between Macy's and Saks 34th Street, as oblivious as Sarah and Lazar to a growing panic in the streets.

The cab headed north on Fifth Avenue past Arnold Constable and De Pinna, but the sights and sounds of the beautiful avenue were lost on the couple in the taxi.

It was only when they reached the Sherry Netherland, where Sarah insisted they stay now, that they heard newsboys shouting something about a crash. They gave only fleeting attention to what had happened on the stock market that day. They crossed the lobby to the elevator and were in each other's arms as soon as Lazar locked the door of the suite behind them.

"Do it slowly," Sarah whispered. "Undress me slowly."

He kissed her body as he uncovered it, then his hands moved slowly along her thighs, raising them, parting them, stroking her softly. He bent to kiss her; light, quick kisses. He rose to kiss her neck, her breasts, her nipples while his hand stroked her.

"Oh, yes," she said, holding him. "But go inside now, let me feel you inside me, where you belong. I love you so," she whispered when his body entered hers. "I love this, yes." She tightened herself around him. "But I love *you* more. I wish I could turn inside out to take more of you into me."

His mouth moved against hers. "I know, my beautiful love." He moved slowly, murmuring her name again and again. "I want to stay inside you, get lost inside you."

Her body rose to meet his, her hands pulling him down more deeply into her. Their words stopped, and for a few seconds they melted into each other. Then they were quiet, still joined.

They stayed together a long time before he lifted himself to lie beside her, cradling her, pulling the covers over both of them.

After a while she asked him, "What will become of Joshua? He needs someone so badly."

"I know." He frowned, hoping that Rachel hadn't married Ben Horowitz. Lazar had been sure about that match until Joshua's visit to Giora. But surely Ben would have taken advantage of Joshua's absence to marry Rachel before an attraction developed into something more. And there was Shula too. An older woman might be better for Joshua, who would marry more for companionship than love. He kissed Sarah's forehead.

"There were one or two before we left. But something stopped him."

"Naomi stopped him. He's still in love with her."

"And she with him," he agreed. "Does Arnold know?"

"I'm sure he does—but he pretends not to, to himself as well as to her." She stroked his hair. "I could never pretend about a feeling like this." Her eyes filled with tears. "It's such a misery that this baby died too. They're both so . . . stranded, somehow. Like two castaways on the same island who need each other and can't reach each other. Not really. Not the way we do."

"Joshua says the sages consider a good marriage one of God's miracles—like the Red Sea opening."

"The old sages must have known," she agreed. "I just wish Josh could find someone, but even if he does, it'll never be like Naomi for him. We're alike in that way, Josh and I. It's one, in the whole world, just one, that can go this far, this deep."

"That's foolish, darling. In a world full of men and women . . ." He stopped, reconsidering. "I guess you're right. Once you've felt like this, no one else can make you feel quite the same."

She moved to lie on top of him, her head on his shoulder, her mouth against his neck. "Yes, my love, that's what I mean. Nobody else can make either of us feel quite like this. We're going to lead a strange life, Lazar, something tells me. Sometimes more apart than together. A lot of things might happen . . ." She kissed him as he started to speak. "No, don't say it's impossible. Everything is possible. But whatever happens, it won't be exactly like this. In that way we'll be faithful. It's the only way that really matters."

They stayed together, silently reveling in each other while outside, in the crisp air of October 1929, the United States slid toward the Great Depression and Joshua's ship steamed toward Palestine.

7

PALESTINE
NOVEMBER 1929

Joshua's first stop was a meeting with Ari in Tel Aviv. Then he would head for Europe with enough money to buy weapons for the small but growing underground army—and every piece would have to be smuggled into Palestine and hidden once it got there.

"That's if I can restrain myself from using them on those British bastards right away," Ari told Joshua. "They have a new twist to their arguments now: They're telling us they have to reduce immigration because only five percent of the land is arable and can't support more Jews than we already have."

"That's ridiculous! Where are they getting their figures from—the Arabs?"

"I suppose so," Ari said. "The way we figure it, sixty percent of the land can be cultivated. That's if people work it, instead of humping she-goats like our Arab cousins."

Ari's men, silent as usual at these meetings, laughed. They looked even wilder than Joshua remembered them at Safed seven months ago, and there were more of them. "Don't knock she-goats," one of them said.

Ari was still giving instructions. "While you're in Europe, see if you can get any idea of what's going on in Germany. We hear rumbles."

"Germany's in bad shape," Joshua agreed. "When a country's flat broke and ailing, anything can happen."

"And will. Your own country's suffering. If this lasts, it's bound to affect the whole world. It's lucky most of us can live on stones and gnats' piss or we'd have been finished. Anyway, you ought to be able to pick up weapons cheap—especially from the Czechs—and smell out the political situation at the same time." He scrutinized Joshua. "How was it, being back home?"

Joshua shook his head. "You've got it the wrong way: I'm back home now." He acknowledged the men's appreciative cheers. "Where's Lazar's old brigade?"

"Pretty well scattered these days. You can't build roads while people are being slaughtered. They carry shovels on their shoulders and guns in their bedrolls. More of them are Haganah than labor brigade now."

"And Giora?" Joshua said. "Was anyone hurt?"

"Not there, but nearby. Giora took in the wounded. They told us it wasn't a pretty sight."

"Any objection to my going to Giora for a day before I leave?"

Ari shook his head. "Go ahead. They could use something to raise their morale." He put a square hand on Joshua's shoulder. "Have a good time—but get your ass back where it belongs in time to meet your contact, right?" He extended his other hand.

"Right." Joshua shook his hand. Ari was a man he admired tremendously, whether or not he agreed with his violently anti-British stand. Joshua thought the British were up against a problem that was totally insoluble; either the Jews or the Arabs would be hurt, no matter what they did.

He took the train from Haifa, across the Plain of Esdraelon, the heart of the grain-rich Emek Yizre'el, now neatly parceled into villages and kibbutzim. What opposing views of this Holy Land there were! To the British, Palestine meant shepherds and flocks, a land biblical and beautiful but primitive, part of the white man's burden and, since the League of Nations approved the Mandate in 1922, part of the Empire. More wogs to be governed benevolently.

To the Zionists it was a land devastated by years of neglect, a land to be redeemed by their labor. Aside from those who regarded it as their religious home, most of the hundred thousand Jews who had come here during the twenties saw it as a heritage that had to be reclaimed by their own hard work.

For non-Zionist Jews scattered throughout the world for two

thousand years it was a problem. They were torn between supporting their fellow Jews and objecting to some of the political and social views of the settlers. The creation of a Jewish state was considered an impossible, even dangerous, dream, dangerous because it would call more attention to a people already isolated, alienated, segregated. People who were "different." They did not agree that a people without a nation was a victimized people.

To the Arabs it was paradise, even in the midst of grinding poverty. They knew no other life but this, a life that was familiar, orderly, and undisturbed for centuries, where each man knew his place and was comfortable in it, where nothing changed. The vast numbers of Jews coming into the country constituted a threat to that order, to that idyllic existence, lazy, antiquated—and serene. Above all the wealthy Arab effendis wanted to keep the peasants serene.

Joshua saw all sides of the problem, but he was aware that he could fight for only one. He had made his choice years ago.

It was a slow ride, even across that narrow northern section of Palestine loosely assigned to the Jews by an arbitrary division at the Jordan River; on the river's east bank was the Kingdom of Transjordan, created out of the air by the British, ever seeking cordial relations with the Arabs while they approved in theory the creation of a homeland for the Jews.

Joshua got a ride from Bet She'an, where the railroad ended. On the last part of the journey he delighted in the sights and smells of an early evening in the peace of the open countryside, so removed from the bustle of civilization yet holding all civilization in the minds and pasts of the settlers—a civilization waiting for a state. He saw no one he could ask about the brigade's whereabouts. How could he locate men whose address was a kilometer marker on some road yet unbuilt?

It was dusk when he reached Giora. The watchtower sentry was nervous enough to keep him standing outside the stockade at gunpoint until Reuven came out to see what madman was wandering in the fields at this hour.

"It's the Rabbi!" Reuven called back to the guard. "One of Lazar's maniacs." He grasped Joshua's hand. "Welcome, Rabbi. You're too late to say the blessing but just in time for dinner. Didn't anyone tell you a man can get shot walking around the

fields?'' Since the massacres at the end of August there was far
less freedom of movement from one settlement to the other.
Anyone who could not identify himself immediately was suspect
to every watchtower sentry. They worked in shifts around the
clock to guard against surprise attack. After dark the stockade
was patrolled by pairs of men, and pickets were stationed in the
fields and orchards.

"But no one here was hurt?" Joshua followed the big, grizzled
man toward the dining hall.

"No, not here. We had some from outlying settlements."
Reuven stopped. "We won't forget that. Rachel heard them
screaming before she saw them.'' He shook his head sadly.
"Covered with blood, one with an arm blown off, some others
dragging a man with no legs. Rachel gave the first alarm.'' He
shook his head again. "We did what we could for them, but the
one without legs died. Probably better off. We didn't know if we
would be next. We didn't even know about Safed—the Arabs
had cut the lines. We only found out when Ben came through
with a Haganah patrol—and we damn near shot them, just like
you.'' Reuven shrugged, resigned to remembering the panic of
that night; then he resumed walking.

"Is it true the British did nothing after Hebron—and wouldn't
let the Haganah in to prevent Safed?" Joshua asked.

The big head nodded. "We won't forget that either.'' Reuven
was grim, but his face changed as he entered the hall. "Look
who's here, everybody! The Rabbi, back from America. How
long are you staying with us? For a night?''

There was a rousing welcome from the people eating their
evening meal. There were empty places—some of them were on
guard outside. Someone set a place for Joshua at a long table,
and he said hello to all of them, looking for familiar faces.

He saw Rachel first and smiled at her. She looked as if she had
grown up since his last visit. Her face had put off girlhood
forever since the massacre. Ben was sitting next to her. He raised
one hand to wave at Joshua, saying "later" with his lips; his
other hand rested for a moment on Rachel's shoulder. Turning,
Joshua found Shula and the platinum blond Aviva and waved to
them. Then he ate his dinner. Once this shift had finished, they
would relieve the guards outside. There was no time for small
talk now.

It wasn't until the shifts changed that he caught sight of Dr. Levy.

"Isaac!" he shouted, running to embrace the small, wiry man. Isaac hugged him back.

"Where's Lazar?"

"In America. Where's Natan?"

"With the Haganah, pretending to build roads. God, it's good to see you!" Isaac beamed.

"I almost didn't recognize you, with that beard," Joshua said. Isaac had grown an impressive beard, square-cut and as brown as his hair except for a rim of white at its edge.

"It was something to do," Isaac said with a laugh. "It looks like the beard of the prophet, I'm told."

They sat outside while they talked, joined by their friends, except for Ben, who was on watch and only had time for a handshake before he went out to the stockade. Reuven told Joshua the Jews had abandoned long-established homes in mixed communities to group together in all-Jewish settlements where they felt safer. The Doctor talked about the new British commission of inquiry to be sent in following the massacres. "They'll issue another white paper," he said, cynically. "And you know what those are good for!"

Shula and the two younger women agreed. "They're going to say the massacres were protesting Jewish immigration—but they were political, and the peasants don't understand politics. It was made to seem religious. The Mufti incited them to kill their own neighbors."

Reuven interrupted. "Enough talk of killing. Tell us about Lazar in America. Did he capture as many hearts there as he did here?"

Joshua smiled. "No, he got captured himself." He paused to make his announcement more dramatic. "Lazar's married!"

They hardly believed him at first. Looking around the circle, it occurred to Joshua that any one of the women there might have been one of Lazar's paramours—but he had a feeling the most likely one was Shula. He was sure Rachel and Aviva were virgins, and Lazar had always avoided virgins.

"What's she like?" Aviva wanted to know. "Is she a rich American debutante?"

"No." Rachel was sure. "Lazar wouldn't."

Shula laughed. "Lazar would do almost anything for the Yishuv. Maybe she's a rich widow."

"So, *nu*?" Isaac said. "Tell us about her. There'll be enough broken hearts as it is; I don't want them to die of curiosity."

Joshua was very serious. "She's twenty, very beautiful, and on the way to being very wealthy, though she doesn't really care much about money for its own sake. She's a Zionist—but for the moment she's a saleswoman, so she can travel with him most of the time."

"What does she look like?" Aviva asked.

"She has very dark hair, and her eyes are almost black. She's very tall for a woman, very striking. She has a sensitive mouth, and she laughs a lot."

"Except for the money and the laughter," Rachel said, "she sounds a lot like you."

He smiled at the dark-haired girl. "She is. She's my sister, Sarah."

They cheered then, pounding Joshua on the back for keeping them in suspense, congratulating him, demanding to hear all the details of Lazar's whirlwind marriage. He obliged, glad to take their minds off the terror they'd been through. Shula and Isaac noticed that he was much more animated, far less withdrawn than he had been.

Rachel had the feeling that more than his personality had changed. It seemed to her that he had moved from one stage of his life to another, and she watched him intently, trying to discover more. When Ben approached after his two-hour guard duty, his blue eyes saw everything in the circle around the fire: Joshua's animation, Rachel's rapt attention to him.

Ben stopped for a few minutes before joining the circle. Joshua was his friend, but he would have done anything to keep him in America for a few weeks longer. Rachel might have been "sure" by then. She had been too young to make up her mind when he first met her and fell in love with her; now she was eighteen, and the reason for her hesitation was sitting there next to her.

But Joshua was the wrong man for Rachel. She deserved the kind of love that had sought no harbor and found none before her. No other girl had remotely interested Ben Horowitz and never would. Ben's happiness was threatened by a man he liked and admired but wished he'd never seen.

He knew Joshua loved someone else, but telling Rachel about that had never crossed Ben's mind. A man of honor kept his friend's confidence.

Ben took a deep breath before he stepped into the firelit circle of excited people, who made Joshua tell him about Lazar all over again.

Ben smiled at the idea of Lazar as a husband. "Any prospects for you?" he asked Joshua.

"I'll be moving around too much to settle down," Joshua said. He began to talk about his European assignment. It would take him back and forth from Europe for several years to come. "Someday I might be able to do what I've always wanted," he finished ruefully.

"And what is that?" Rachel asked him.

"Just stay in Palestine," he said. "Just live here."

"There's a lot to be done before any of us can just live here," Isaac said, and the settlers silently agreed. Their dreams of a state were far in the future; the question at this moment was survival itself.

When the group broke up for the night, Joshua went with Ben and Isaac toward the men's dormitory. It seemed tactless to go directly to Shula's little room, although she clearly expected him; she had let him know it in that wordless way women have. He was beginning to understand the language of women—but Shula had been the first, and he had a special affection for her. He slipped out when the men were quiet, unaware that the wakeful Ben saw him go and was still unable to sleep.

Joshua spent the night enjoying Shula's warm, welcoming body once again. This time thoughts of Naomi did not divert him from the sensations he felt. He had left romance behind him forever. Between Joshua and the women he would know in the future, there would be respect, friendship, understanding, lust— sometimes all of these—but never that passion for total possession which is called love.

When he left for Haifa and Europe the next day, he embraced them all, this new family of his. Only Rachel, slim and brown, her black braids shining in the sun, said good-bye without letting her lithe body touch his. And it was of Rachel he thought more and more in the months that followed.

*   *   *

As she was thinking of him. It seemed to Ben that even if Joshua's visits were infrequent, he was always at Giora—in Rachel's mind. She slipped further away from Ben as the months stretched into a year and then another, while hope faded in Ben's heart. And then a new hope flickered: It might be just a physical attraction. Once satisfied, Rachel might come to her senses and marry a man for whom she was more important than anything else, even a state. For Rachel, Ben would go back to England, to his family. Her life would be one of ease and luxury, not hardship and danger.

He was not prepared for the jealousy that cut through him when, finally, Rachel and Joshua became lovers. He thought he could not bear it when Rachel went to Haifa one day to see Joshua off and didn't return that night. He waited for her until dawn, his imagination fed from some unknown, savage depths, painting things against the black velvet sky that made him want to kill Joshua.

At midmorning she came into view from the crossroads, oblivious to his scrutiny, a half-smile on her beautiful face and in her walk a rhythm that in Ben's mind was different from the way Rachel had walked before last night.

She stopped when she saw him waiting like an angry angel at the gate. "Ben? Is anything wrong?"

"What happened last night is wrong," he said coldly, sounding proprietary, surprising even himself by his feeling that she belonged to him, had no rights he was not ready to give her.

She flushed angrily and almost answered him. Then her hand touched his shoulder gently. "Don't, Ben, please don't. I love him."

He turned away to hide the tears in his eyes. "And I love you. If love were all . . . but it isn't." He turned back to plead with her. "Rachel, he'll never marry you. Even if he does, he'll never be in one place long enough. It's not what he wants."

She shook her head. "I wasn't even thinking about marriage. I was just thinking about—loving him."

"But you deserve more than . . ." It was hard for him to say it, but he had to. "You deserve more than just sleeping with him whenever he's around."

"Oh, Ben." Her eyes were troubled—not for herself, he

realized suddenly, but for him. "I don't care about what I deserve. I only care about what I want."

"And you want him."

She nodded, wanting to take his hand, afraid to touch him.

He turned away again. He almost told her about Naomi, but that would only make her angry. "You might change your mind after a few years of this."

"I don't think so," she said softly.

He started toward the lakeshore. "I'll be here if you do."

"Yes, Ben, I know." She watched him go with a feeling so close to love that it was a reflection of it. Then she went on along the path to Giora to wait until Joshua came back again.

Book
Two

8

NEW YORK
JANUARY 1933

"Adolf Hitler new German chancellor!"

A newsboy shouting on the corner of Sixth Avenue slowed Naomi's brisk walk to her mother's apartment on Central Park West.

She knew a lot about Hitler, more than most Americans did, because of Sarah and Lazar. It was a name that meant trouble for the Jews, Lazar said, "and war for the whole world." But Naomi thought the world had enough trouble already without wanting a war. What harm could some nasty little anti-Semite in Germany do?

Naomi walked on, glad to be out again in the bracing air. For once there were hardly any of the ragged, shabby men with reproachful eyes who had haunted the city since the stock market crash four years ago. Today Naomi was feeling better, and she didn't want to feel guilty because her family hadn't suffered any of the financial difficulties the country had been experiencing since 1929. On the contrary, Arnold's profits had exploded year after year. He had taken Naomi's father and her two brothers into Duchess with him, moved them and his own parents to Central Park West, kept them all in comfort, even luxury, with his phenomenal success.

Arnold's success was a mixed blessing for Naomi's father. Martin Held's business was not large enough to compete with the really major manufacturers; it had relied on excellence rather than volume, and craftsmanship was a marginal commodity when an economy was in trouble. He was ashamed when he was forced to turn to his son-in-law for help. It was even worse when Arnold was first generous and then, when it was obvious that nothing would save the business from ruin, magnanimous in offering executive posts to Martin and his sons.

Naomi thought she knew how her father must feel. Gratitude was not the most savory of dishes. She had enough cause to be grateful to Arnold herself. He was good to her, even when occasional outbursts of nervous temper made her speak sharply to him and lock herself into the den for the night. Naomi's mother, scenting trouble like a bloodhound, would be there the next day to console her daughter and counsel prudence.

"We owe him so much," was Leah's constant reminder. It annoyed Naomi as much as it did Martin.

"I'll be goddamned if I'll ever understand why an industry of paint and powder puffs makes money," Martin would say. "People don't *need* face cream and lipstick—they need where to sleep and what to eat and something to keep them warm."

"It's because I sell dreams," Arnold always insisted, "and in bad times people need dreams more than ever."

He was right. The country was drunk on dreams, a lot of them broken but most of them mended or made in dark, quiet, secure movie houses where the flight from grim reality was complete. The romance on the screen was so much better than life that life was now being modeled on celluloid romances.

Women especially, harried and worried or idle and bored, wanted to be swept off their feet the way Valentino had carried off his heroines, to ecstasies more wild in the imagination than any explicit portrayal could have been.

"It's simple," Sarah once said. "Dr. Freud tells them what they really want, the movies show them what it's like to get it—and we show them how!"

This cream, that fragrance, this dress, this shade for the lips, that shape for the body. Yes, it was true, dreams made money. Now that Roosevelt had been elected and there would be new prosperity, Arnold said, they would make even more money.

Sometimes Naomi felt guilty about all the money, but not today. If there were some kind of ledger to balance in life, Naomi felt she and Arnold had already had their share of trouble: four children lost in nearly five years of marriage, the last miscarriage just one month ago.

Sometimes she thought it would be better if they could talk about it instead of pretending it hadn't happened. But it was difficult to talk to Arnold about how she felt, about their marriage. They both seemed afraid to start a trickle that might become a flood. All he asked of her was to be brave and beautiful, as befitted the wife of a young millionaire. He showered her with gifts she had no idea she wanted. He moved her to ever more luxurious apartments, the newest on Fifth Avenue, across the park from her mother.

It was his way of showing love, the only way he knew—except for sex, and she could have done without that. More and more she felt like screaming when he touched her, and wrong to feel like screaming. He was her husband, and she loved him. She simply didn't like sex. Maybe there was something wrong with her, but what woman would like it after losing four children? Every time he turned to her in bed, she was half-afraid, half-hoping that she would conceive. But with so little hope of carrying a child to term, why must she submit to the whole performance? And to what happened after it, in her sleep.

She shook her head. She didn't want to think about that today. Today she was going to see Sarah's children, two-year-old Rebekah and one-year-old Seth. They were staying with Naomi's mother while Sarah and Lazar were in Europe.

What had Lazar said a few weeks ago? "If that little bastard takes power in Germany, we're going to risk everything to get our people out fast."

We. That meant every Jewish organization in the world—and that meant Joshua too, risking his life to bring Jews out.

Suddenly she felt too weak to walk on. Her hands were damp and beginning to shake again, and the knot in her throat was tightening. She couldn't arrive at her mother's apartment in such a state. The family fussed enough already about Naomi's moods, Naomi's frequent crying spells. Why couldn't they leave her alone?

She crossed the street and sat on a bench just outside Central Park, oblivious to the sharp wind. Where was he? What was he doing? Did he ever think of her? Joshua was always with her, in fleeting moments of thought like this one—and always in her dreams. She couldn't help herself. It was wrong, it was unfair to Arnold. It was unfair to have married him in the first place. At least Joshua hadn't married someone unfairly.

She loved him, she had accepted that. But not in the earthy way Sarah loved, not that way. She had romantic daydreams of him, the same that other young women had of Valentino, Clark

Gable, Ronald Colman, or Gary Cooper. Naomi didn't sigh over
matinee idols. She had a real man who was always with her and
no more unattainable than movie stars were for other women. No
movie star had ever said he loved any of *them*. Her daydreams
were based on reality.

But she was dreaming about him at night too, after sex with
Arnold. Then she dreamed it was Joshua who kissed her avid
mouth, who entered her welcoming, open body while she held
him with her arms and legs and begged him not to stop, never to
stop. Shameful dreams that seemed to last for hours and never
lasted long enough. Degrading dreams that made her feast on his
body in ways she hadn't realized she knew about, desires that
raked her until she woke, wet and throbbing, unable to sleep until
the throbbing stopped, unable to face Arnold in the morning.

There was no one she could tell, although she was often
tempted to confide in Sarah. She kept all of it to herself, along
with the conviction that Arnold deserved better, that she had
cheated him without meaning to. Arnold no longer asked her to
say she loved him—even though she did love him in a way that
had nothing to do with desire and fulfillment. She had just asked
for her own bedroom, saying she was so nervous she had to sleep
alone for a while. She had to escape from the apprehension that
clutched her every night at bedtime.

Sometimes she thought she would start screaming and never
stop. . . .

She pulled her new fur coat more tightly around her, shook her
head, and rose from the bench. It *must* stop. She would make
it stop. She would find something to do, something that mattered.
She breathed the cold air deeply as she walked. When her mother
answered the door, she was smiling.

9

PALESTINE
MAY 1933

" 'Thou art fair, my love, thou art fair,' " Joshua said softly, kissing Rachel.

She laughed. "And thou art mad! I'm brown as a berry, not fair—except for here and there."

"I know—you still look like you're wearing white shorts and a shirt. Very erotic, in a prim kind of way."

They were in the bedroom of a small house on the beach south of Tel Aviv, lent to them by a friend for a few days. Then Joshua would go on another arms-buying mission to Europe and Rachel back home to Giora.

"Am *I* erotic—even in a prim way?" Rachel wondered if he loved her as totally as she loved him, or if the shadow of the past was still with him.

"*You* aren't prim, darling. In fact, you're a surprising package."

"In what way?"

Joshua rolled onto his back and lit a cigarette. "You're such a mixture of contrasts: romantic and practical, passionate and disciplined, compassionate and incredibly brave."

"Thank you," Rachel said. "But for which of those qualities am I here with you?"

"All of them," he said, taking her hand. "And now that you've brought it up, why am *I* here with you?"

"Because I love you." She said it simply, but to Joshua it was a reproach. She had not listed his qualities and decided they made him a good mate. She loved him, as openly and simply as she had been raised, on a kibbutz reclaimed from barren land and pestilent swamp, where life was hard and precarious and simple, uncomplicated by manners or fashions or philosophies.

He had seen her four years ago as a perfect Sabra, but she was more than that. She was a woman with a mind of her own, a strong woman with a body like a young huntress, an independent person who was with him because she loved him, without any mention of marriage and even though he spent most of his time away from her. Yet he could not honestly say that she was his only love. There was the shadow of Naomi in his past and the utter dedication to his task in his present. Ben was still desperately in love with her—but she was not somewhere with Ben; she was here with Joshua.

He put out the cigarette and turned to her again, brushing her long black hair from her face. His dark eyes mirrored her. His arms went around her sweet, strong body, and he held her close against him.

"And I love you, Rachel," he said. "Don't ever doubt that. From the first time I ever saw you, there was something that kept me coming back, hoping each time that you hadn't married Ben." He kissed her. "I just had to find out what life was about out here, what I could do. I had to hope you'd still be free each time I came back. Thank heaven you still are."

It was enough for Rachel. She was all the things he had said: practical, sensible. Love to her was only part of life, not all of it. But the passionate side of her nature was drawn to the hidden, somber depths of Joshua. Someday he might open to her, tell her about the woman in his past.

She had come closer to marrying Ben lately than Joshua knew, because of that past and its unknowable effect on their future— but it would serve no purpose to tell that to Joshua. She was here with him; that was proof enough, if proof were needed, that she loved him more than Ben, no matter what part of him he kept hidden from her. It could only be a woman. She knew him well enough by now to be sure of that.

"Rachel?" Joshua kissed her again. "What are you thinking?"

She tightened her arms around him, her mouth against the smooth, tanned skin of his shoulder. "That I'm very happy. That I want to go swimming with nothing on. That I feel like a princess, like Salome or Esther or even Lilith." She laughed, a sensuous little laugh.

Passion overwhelmed him. The words she said, the way she was moving against him, the simple, straightforward nature of her, as open and intoxicating as a desert night, touched and aroused him, and he let desire loose.

Here was no goddess to be adored. Here was no past to haunt him with regret, no present to divert him, no future to distract him. Here was a dark-haired woman he loved in this moment as she loved him, a woman he desired now, now, this very minute, with every fiber of his being. But even as he held her, possessed her, moved with her, the moment was ending and he was suddenly terrified that it might never come again.

"Rachel," he implored her, close to the end of this fleeing, shining, all-consuming moment. "Rachel, marry me, please say you'll marry me."

Her eyes were closed, but her mouth smiled and took his. "Yes," she whispered into him. "Yes, yes."

There would be other matings between them, but none so profound as this one, none so liberating in the bond they had just made, none so startling in its naked sensuality or so free from all that had gone before and all that might come.

They slept again when it was over. They swam naked in the Mediterranean. They walked on the beach at night. They said very little to each other in those few days, until the last night when they sat on the veranda of the little cottage, watching the moonlight on the sea.

"When shall it be?" Joshua said. "How about tomorrow in Haifa?"

Rachel shook her head. "I want to be married at Giora. I want to be married in a dress—and I don't even own one yet." She laughed softly. "I'll be ready the next time you come back. But I'll go to Haifa with you tomorrow and take the train from there."

His hand reached out for hers. "I remember the trip to Giora in 1929 when I came back from America. How beautiful the fields of the Emek Yezre'el are. And at the end of the trip—you."

"How long will you be gone this time?"

"No way of knowing. I have the usual purchases to make, and we have to find some way to convince the German Jews that they must get out—now. If they won't do that, we have to find routes for smuggling them out if the gates slam shut."

"But so many have come this year already," Rachel reminded him. "What makes your people think there won't be more?"

"Nobody believes Hitler means what he says. A lot of German

Jews were furious with Isaac on his last trip for suggesting that their loyalty to Germany would ever be questioned—they were Germans first and only Jews by the way.''

"What does Lazar say?"

"Lazar always believed Hitler meant every word. He's back in Europe again with Sarah—someday you'll have to meet Sarah, you'll love her—and what he's seen hasn't changed his mind.''

"The book burning?"

"That—and new restrictions against Jews every day. Lazar wrote there's an atmosphere of violence you can cut with a knife. He shouldn't go back too many times either. My sister's American, but Lazar's a Jew on a Palestinian passport.''

"Will you ever be a Palestinian?" Rachel wondered.

"I'd be one already—but headquarters says my American citizenship gives me better protection and might give me more entry if things get worse." He looked at her. "Will you mind being married to a foreigner?"

She laughed. "Almost everyone in Palestine is a foreigner. Ask if I mind being married to a rabbi!''

He laughed with her. "They want me to keep that profession too. Who'd suspect a rabbi of running guns?"

"Anyone who's met you," she said, moving to sit on his lap. "You might have to grow a beard, you know.''

"Would you mind?"

"No. I've never kissed a man with a beard.''

He held her close, listening to the gentle lap of the water, the night sounds of small animals in the reeds. He had no idea how many weeks would pass before he would see her again, before he could luxuriate in the peace and quiet of her and of a night like this. But she would be his wife; wherever she was would be home. They sat for a long time before he went into the cottage for some blankets. They went down to the beach, made love, and slept soundly on the sand until morning.

They said good-bye in Haifa, and he watched the train pull out, taking her away. Then he turned and walked briskly through the sunny streets to a small house at the foot of Mount Carmel.

It was Ari who answered his knock. Some of the faces in the small parlor were familiar: Ben Horowitz, Isaac Levy, Natan Markevitsch—only Lazar was missing from the group of five who had worked and lived so closely together in the brigade. There were seven of Ari's senior lieutenants and two men Joshua had never seen before.

They wore rumpled business suits. Their pale complexions and their accents told him they were new immigrants from Hitler's Germany, part of a wave of doctors, lawyers, technicians, and engineers flooding in as a result of the restrictions in Germany. Ari had been undisturbed by the influx of urban citizens to an agrarian country. "We'll teach some of them to plow and the rest to shoot," he said. "The engineers can maybe fix up our miserable weapons—or design new ones."

"Hail, the Rabbi cometh," Ari said, following Joshua into the room. "Rachel go back?"

Joshua nodded, waving a greeting to the others, avoiding Ben's eyes.

"Beautiful lady," Ari said. Then his voice rose. "Now we have serious business. On this trip you have to buy more guns for less money. The Depression makes it harder for Lazar to raise money in America—although everybody says this Roosevelt will do something for the economy soon. For the moment, *you* must do something. Lucky you have an American passport. Soon you'll be one of the few who can move around Germany freely."

"Is it that bad?" Joshua asked the two newcomers.

"Worse," one of them said.

Ari said, "Nobody else is going to help us—we have to help ourselves."

"We have to help ourselves *here* first," Natan objected angrily. "The Arabs are still attacking Jews *here*."

Ben Horowitz put a hand on Natan's broad shoulder. "Natan, the Haganah can cope with the Arabs, even if we have to stay underground. But nobody's ready to deal with Hitler."

"The Arabs will always be a problem," Natan insisted. "Who knows how long Hitler will last in Germany? I have a pregnant wife at Giora right *now*." He had married his adored Aviva a year ago, and their first child was expected soon.

"I know how you feel about Aviva," Joshua said. "I just sent Rachel back there." His eyes rested briefly on Ben. "But if what we hear about Germany is true, we have to do something about it."

"It's true," one of the Germans said.

Natan lapsed into surly silence.

"All right," Ari said, speaking in his usual explosive phrases. "Here it is. The Rabbi and Dandy Ben—now, he looks 'Aryan,' you should know, a new word Hitler dreamed up—go shopping in Czechoslovakia first, then to France, where they'll meet up with Lazar. Natan goes to Romania, Hungary, wherever there are arms to be dumped cheap. And you all keep an eye open for smuggling routes—people as well as guns. Isaac, you're needed here, there's a typhoid scare again—anyway you look too Jewish for Austria. You all have money. You all know your contacts. Don't stay too long. Buy guns. Buy information—precise information. Smugglers can't be sloppy. That's it. Any questions?"

No one spoke. They split up, leaving the house in twos and threes. Joshua and Ben walked toward the center of Haifa.

"Natan speaks for a lot of us," Ben said. "The militants are getting fed up with the Haganah's policy of restraint. It could lead to a deep split."

"I know," Joshua said. "I don't want to be in opposition to old friends." He could feel the tension between them as they walked along.

"Rachel," Ben said very suddenly, as if he had been keeping her name inside too long to control himself.

"I wanted to tell you alone, Ben. We're going to be married the next time I come back."

Ben kept walking, his shoulders stiff and square.

"It was hard for her to choose between us," Joshua said, "if that makes it any better for you."

"No," Ben said shortly. "It makes it worse."

There was a silence between them. Joshua wanted to tell him that love was not a thing anyone decided to feel; it simply happened. It seemed to him he'd said that before, he couldn't remember when. And Ben didn't need to be told.

He tried again. "Ben, I know how you feel, but we're friends." He stopped. "I wish there were something I could say."

Ben kept his eyes on the street ahead of them. "You might say she's the only one you love."

Joshua nodded, remembering dreams of Naomi shared with his friends when he first came to Palestine. "She's the only one," he said. "I waited this long to be sure of that."

Ben's shoulders relaxed. He turned to look at Joshua, his

expression less tense but his eyes still sober and searching. "I'm glad about that," he said finally. "It's what she deserves." He put a tentative hand on Joshua's arm, as if it were still hard for him to do. "Come along, I'll buy you a drink."

They walked together on the sun-flooded street, quiet again. It was almost the old, companionable silence they hadn't felt with each other for many, many years.

They never mentioned the subject again. Joshua had told the truth. Rachel was his wife, Palestine his country. And they were both struggling to survive.

10

NEW YORK
JUNE 1933

Even from his corner office, well removed from the elevator doors opening onto the entire floor Duchess occupied on Park Avenue, Arnold heard the voices and the laughter. Sarah was back! He got up from his desk and went to the door to meet her.

She came down the carpeted corridor, electric, free-striding, her dark hair topped by a Parisian hat that would have looked foolish on any other woman, her figure draped in gray silk jersey under an unlined sheer wool cape of the same color.

"Angel!" She gave her brother a bear hug. "How are you?"

"I don't have to ask how you are! When did you dock?"

"Yesterday at three—as you know perfectly well. For not calling me at home, you get an extra special gift." She handed him a box. "God, did we miss Rebekah and Seth! That's the last time we go anywhere without them." She sat down in the burgundy leather chair facing Arnold's desk, tossing her cape aside. "Go on, open your present."

It was a perfume flask about seven inches high, of dark green glass almost totally covered with a web of golden fretwork. Arnold whistled when he saw it.

"Eighteenth-century French," Sarah smiled. "Gorgeous, isn't it? The best thing in your collection."

"You must have spent a fortune." He held it lovingly.

"Never mind, we'll make enough on the ideas I brought back—the French are full of ideas you wouldn't believe." Her face changed. "How's Naomi?"

"Better. Less . . . emotional. She's working with Rabbi Wise and forming a group to place refugee children."

"Oh, Arnold," Sarah said, a little sister again. "It's not fair."

"It's not fair to Naomi. I don't care if we never have a child—if only she could be happy." He looked at his sister, things locked inside him that he could never say, not even to her.

"I'll go over to see her as soon as I've finished here." She took off her hat and rummaged in a soft leather handbag so he wouldn't see the tears in her eyes. If only he would *talk* to her! "Damn, I can never find anything in here—I'll have to design one for myself. Ah, here they are." She lit a cigarette. "How's business?"

"Better every month—every week. Your friend Maresh is handling warehousing for the whole east coast out of Philly— we've built two more stock hangars."

"I told you about him." Sarah beamed. "We'll be going to Philly next week. You can't buy devotion like his."

"I know. I never have to go near the place. But does he ever say more than three words at a time?"

"Sure—if he has something to say. He talks to Lazar the way he used to talk to Josh." She was suddenly very busy with the papers in her briefcase. "But I have lots of news for you. First of all, you were right: It's cheaper to import the floral absolutes ourselves and do the perfume blending right here. We eliminate the brokers and buy directly from the growers in France and Italy—or deal with spot brokers if the stuff comes from places we can't get to easily: Russia, Madagascar, North Africa, China."

"Good enough. But we need a perfume that will outsell Chanel Five and L'Aimant. And we haven't found one yet. We still need an expert blender, a 'nose.' "

"That's my news! I have one. A young Polish Jew I found shivering in a café in Paris."

"Another one of your drowned rats?"

"Never mind, my rats are your best workers, and you know it.

This one—his name is Otto Einhorn—has a degree in chemistry, but he has a nose for fragrance. Couldn't get work in France— the French think nobody can do it like them." She sniffed. "But Otto is a perfume maven."

"How do you know?"

"Bought him a swanky suit and took him up to Lanvin with me. Said he was my secretary—they thought he was my lover too." She laughed. "Such a peanut, my lover—well, they never saw Lazar. Anyway, they store their attars blind—no names on the tester bottles, only numbers. He identified every one—even knew what altitude the lavender was grown at! The Lanvin fellow nearly fainted. And"—she paused dramatically—"he got a good whiff of something new they're working on. So did I—it's sensational! He knows what's in it too—rose, jasmine, something called vetiveryle and a few other synthetics. Anyway, we can get close to it—we can do better! Then you'll have a perfume worthy of the Duchess label. Made here, bottled in France."

"Bottled in France? You're nuts, Sarah. What's the use of importing everything to make it here, then shipping it back for bottling there?"

"First, only we will know what's in it—the proportions, I mean. Second, you can sell it for three times more if it comes from France. You know the carriage trade still isn't ready for domestic perfumes. Third, plush packaging is a must, and that's a French specialty—cut glass, velvet boxes. It's cheaper to do it there—labor, materials. Make sense?"

"So far. But I'll want to check freight costs."

"I did. But you have to advertise it, Arnold. A lot. *Vogue, Vanity Fair, Harper's Bazaar.* Just one picture and the name— Duchess. The picture has to tell the story—sexy but high-class. It'll cost a fortune."

"We can afford it." With the cosmetics they had a 25 percent net profit on the wholesale; perfume, Arnold knew, would net at least 35, probably more. He nodded approval. "That's good enough for me—if the fragrance is okay. Now, where's this Einhorn?"

"At the Waldorf. You can't put the best perfume blender in the world anywhere else—it'd make a bad impression when we start publicity on him." She put one sheaf of papers aside and picked up another, looking at Arnold with a mischievous smile.

"All right, what is it?" he asked, as if she were a little girl with a secret.

"A spa."

His smile faded. "What?"

"A beauty retreat for women. In California." She leaned forward, enthusiastic. "You feed them on lettuce leaves and lemon juice, you give them facials, massages, high colonic enemas. You exercise them till they drop. When they leave, they take a complete line of your products with them." She started to list the costs on her fingers.

"Food for the clients costs you next to nothing. You only need a few operators to start—one facial, one exercise, one masseuse, one colonic nurse, one makeup/hairdresser. Or maybe the facial can do the makeup. About seven thousand salary each a year makes thirty-five thousand. You can buy an old farm cheap since the Depression—about fifty thousand, maybe seventy-five with a lot of land." She laughed. "With enough land you can grow your own lettuce leaves and lemons in the bargain. You fix it up for twenty, twenty-five thousand. Another thirty-five for advertising. That's an investment of one hundred seventy—two hundred thousand tops."

She lit another cigarette while Arnold listened, his objections fading as he spoke.

"You charge the women five hundred a week—less won't work, the society set doesn't want to mingle with riffraff. You sell them at least one hundred dollars worth of your stuff when they leave. Figure on twenty-five women at six hundred per week—that's almost eight hundred thousand a year. Your original investment is paid off in about three months, and the rest of the first-year income will be clear profit, not to mention equity in the land and the renovated house. You can't lose on a deal like that."

"What gave you the idea?" Arnold asked, marveling.

"I went to a spa in France! There they drink those lousy waters and eat like horses. Here the women are diet conscious— they all want flat titties and no behinds. So we'll give them plain water and hardly any food. It's great for relaxation too. After a social season, those women need it."

"But based on what you said, we'll have to keep the place full year round."

"We will. They always knock off a few weeks a year to recharge their batteries. And we'll be right near the Mexican border—you can get a fast divorce in Mexico and rest up after it. Also an abortion."

"No abortions at our place!"

"Of course not. They'll just have a place to go for cover and to recuperate when they come back. Okay?"

"Okay. You dream up any other ways to spend our money?"

"Make more, you mean. We need more products in the line."

"We already have twenty-five!"

"Arden has one hundred and eight in five hundred ninety-five shapes and sizes."

"Arden isn't going into the perfume end in a big way—and she's not running a spa."

"Oh, yes, she is—the spa's on the boards. My chauffeur sleeps with her maid. Maybe not the perfume, not imported like ours. But I still think you need a few more items for Duchess."

"Such as?"

"Shampoo. Hair rinse. Bath oil to match the perfume, soap to match both. Why not a body lotion to go with the fragrance? We could do gift packages for Christmas, Valentine's Day . . ."

"All right—enough! You make me dizzy."

"Well, I know you'll agree on everything—even if I have to use persuasion." She smiled at him lovingly.

"Blackmail is more like it." He smiled back.

"Bullshit," Sarah said.

Her brother looked shocked. "A woman shouldn't use foul language."

"It's not foul—it's expressive. If I had to think what's proper every time I opened my mouth, I'd never say anything. Think what you'd miss!"

He laughed. "I give up. What's in the other case?"

"Bottles, jars for you to look at. Incidentally, no more square jars. It takes less product to fill a round one. Also samples of packaging, so when the time comes, you'll know why ours has to be extravagant."

"I already know—nobody wants to think about rags, only riches."

Sarah nodded. "And because of that, I have everything I ever wanted." She hesitated. "I hope you do."

"Of course I do," he said, looking ɑ the photograph of Naomi on his desk. "Did you see this one in *Vanity Fair*?"

"And how! 'The exquisite cameo beauty of Naomi Fursten, wife of Duchess Limited's dynamic young president,' " Sarah quoted and wondered if anybody in Palestine ever saw the magazine. She had decided not to tell Arnold about Joshua's marriage before breaking the news to Naomi—alone. "I just thought— maybe Naomi will have an idea for the advertising campaign. Come on," she said, briskly. "I'll go to the Waldorf and introduce you to your new 'nose'—the little Einhorn. Treat him gently, Arnold. He's a frightened young man. The things he says about what's going on in Germany . . ."

"I'm interested in his nose. Germany has nothing to do with us."

"If Hitler starts a war, it will. I just hope you're right and Lazar's wrong," Sarah said dubiously.

"This time Lazar's wrong. Roosevelt's just been inaugurated, and there's a new feeling in the country already. He's not going to mess things up by taking sides in another European squabble." He held Sarah's cape for her. "Why don't you have lunch with Einhorn and me?"

"Because I'm having lunch with your exquisite cameo wife." Sarah smiled.

"How's Lazar?" Arnold said as they went down the corridor to the elevator.

"Worried," Sarah said. "He has only one concern, as you know. When a country starts to burn books, something is terribly wrong, and it isn't the books. Do you know they can't print any book in Germany now without approval from a slimy little character called Goebbels? There's a swastika flying from almost every building—and the prisons are loaded with everyone who objects." They got into the elevator. "The whole country's gone crazy."

"It's not the whole country," Arnold said. "It's a handful of bullies."

"That's probably what they said about Attila the Hun," Sarah said as the elevator doors closed behind them.

"It looks like a movie set—all white and stunning," Sarah said, pretending interest in the decor of the Fifth Avenue apartment. She watched Naomi chain-smoking, moving her hands nervously, laughing too brightly. There was hardly anything left of the sunny, gentle girl she had followed down the aisle five years ago, of the young wife so proud of her pregnancy at Sarah's own wedding. She had thought Naomi had come to terms with things—but Sarah realized now that she had been too wrapped up in Lazar and her own two children to see the gradual change from the quiet, warm-hearted young woman to a brittle, high-strung fashion plate,

Arnold had said she was less emotional! But Arnold saw only what he could bear looking at. Was the trouble because there were no children in this marriage—or was it still what it had always been?

"I think you've done a magnificent job," Sarah said, rumpling her short hair in the way she had when something worried her. "They'll be photographing the apartment for *Vogue* next. I wouldn't dare let them see *my* zoo."

"You have better things to do with your time than decorate apartments," Naomi said. "And you always look absolutely perfect."

"I have to—for The Duchess," Sarah said absently. The separate bedrooms hadn't escaped her notice, never mind that there was a communicating door. Couples who had to go through a door to communicate didn't do it very well or very often. She wondered how in hell she was going to tell Naomi about Joshua—but maybe he wasn't the reason.

The two women went into the living room from Naomi's all-white bedroom. "This is still blue," Naomi said. "Ultra modern but blue. I liked the view from the Riverside Drive apartment better, didn't you?"

Sarah took a deep breath. "I don't give a tinker's curse about your view," she said.

Naomi looked at her, startled.

"Yes, that's what I said. I'm interested in you. You look like a string on Menuhin's violin. Now what is it?"

Naomi shook her head. "Nothing."

"Bullshit," Sarah said. "You smoke like a chimney, you're thin as a broomstick—and what's the story on the separate bedrooms?" She sat next to Naomi on the blue velvet couch. "For heaven's sake, talk! You know you can trust me."

Naomi's voice was still brittle. "What's wrong with separate bedrooms?"

"Nothing—unless you don't like sleeping with your husband."

Naomi looked away. "I can't stand sleeping with my husband," she whispered. "All I get from that is dead babies."

"Jesus, Naomi! Love doesn't have to mean babies. Arnold doesn't care about babies—he loves you."

"Well, I care about babies," Naomi said, starting to cry. "What's the point of marriage without them?"

Sarah shook her head. "You know better than that. You sound like some pious moralist—and that's not you. You have too much life in you to feel that way—or you used to. Is it Arnold? I know he isn't the easiest man to get close to, but he'd do anything for you."

"I don't want to hear about Arnold and what he'd do for me!" Naomi's voice rose. "Do you think I don't know how much I owe him, how much my whole family owes him? They remind me of it all the time. Do you think I don't know how unfair I'm being? I'm sick of thinking about it. If I had my own way, I'd divorce him tomorrow for his own good." She looked at Sarah defiantly. "Yes, I would—no matter how much he does for me. I don't want him to love me. I want him to leave me alone!"

Sarah put her arms around her sister-in-law. This was no time to ask her pointblank if it was Joshua she still wanted. She would probably deny it anyway. Children would have helped. Sarah thought of her own children.

"My poor baby, go on and cry," she said, holding Naomi close to ease the shaking. "Only a woman who's lost children knows how it feels to be you. But I don't think divorcing Arnold would solve the problem, even if you had the courage to do it. I think you have to get your mind off your troubles and onto something else before you go getting divorced." She held Naomi at arm's length. "Perfect cameo beauty, my ass. You look like hell on a stick."

Naomi's laugh was shaky. "You're the only person who can say things like that without hurting a girl's feelings, Shai. But what can I do? Arnold won't let me work. He even objects to the work I'm doing with Rabbi Wise—and it's all I know how to do."

"He'll let you do what I have in mind. Wait till you hear,

you'll love it. But let's go inside and fix your face first. Arnold'll be home soon, asking questions. Go on, I'll make us both a drink and bring them to the bedroom.''

Sarah went to the mirrored bar and poured two brandies, adding ice and a little soda to hers. She carried the glasses to Naomi's all-white bedroom and set the straight brandy on the dressing table. It was now or never—and Naomi was cried out.

"Joshua had a surprise for us," Sarah said, "when we saw him in Paris.''

"What?" Naomi finished creaming off the smudged mascara.

"He's married." Sarah turned her back on Naomi and studied Fifth Avenue, eleven floors below. "It's high time too. Josh is thirty, and a man needs a wife, especially out there.''

"Did you meet her?" Naomi patted her face briskly with Duchess astringent.

"No, but I heard about her—Lazar knows her. Twenty-two. Born at Giora, one of the oldest settlements in Palestine. She has dark hair, dark eyes. The first dress she ever wore was at her wedding—with her hair in long braids. She's a real *chalutza*, a pioneer. Her name is Rachel—and Lazar says she's special. Anyway, Josh is married, and that's a comfort to all of us, don't you think? She'll be alone a lot, though; Josh travels all the time.'' Sarah heard herself talking too much, but she was giving Naomi a chance to steady herself. The brandy glass on the dressing table was empty when Sarah turned back.

"Does Arnold know?" Naomi asked, her voice thin.

"No, I forgot to tell him, we were so busy talking business.''

Naomi finished applying her makeup. Sarah was a bad liar but a good friend to tell her the news before Arnold got home. "I hope they'll be happy," she said. She looked at Sarah, her face smooth. She got up and led the way back to the living room, poured more brandy for both of them, and sat down with Sarah. "I think you're right about me. I need something to do. What's your idea?"

There were to be no more confidences, Sarah could tell, but Naomi seemed steady enough, and she followed her lead. "We're finally going to have a perfume worthy of The Duchess, and we need something sensational in the way of advertising. I already told Arnold, just the name Duchess and a photograph or a painting, something very sexy but very high-class." She smiled.

"If I had my way, we'd use Goya's Naked Maja—she was the Duchess of Alba. But America's not ready for naked women yet."

Naomi agreed. "A lot of them wouldn't buy a perfume advertised with a naked woman, no matter how much they wanted to. And men wouldn't give it to their wives—only their mistresses." She smiled. "We'd lose almost as much business as we'd gain."

"Okay, then. Find something dreamy and provocative, sexy enough to suggest what will happen when a woman wears this perfume. You know what I mean."

"I know just what you mean," Naomi said, livelier by the minute. "I'll try the museums first, paintings, engravings. It'll be fascinating." She looked as interested as she sounded, Sarah was relieved to see. "When do you need it?"

"Take your time—we haven't got the perfume yet. Arnold's just been meeting the man I found to blend it—our 'nose.' But we'll start the advertising a few months before we put it on the market."

They were still talking about it when Arnold got home. He kissed Naomi, surprised by her animation, her enthusiasm for the new project. Sarah was right—she did need something to do. Her choice of jars and labels years ago had proved her sense of design—if he needed proof of her good taste. Maybe if she were involved in the business again, as she had been at the beginning, the coldness between them would disappear. . . .

"What have you done with tiny Otto?" Sarah was asking. "I hope you didn't scare him!"

"Stop carrying on. We just sat and talked perfume. He knows his business, as far as I can tell. We can work together. He just wanted to walk around, see the city on his own." He didn't add that he had given the pale young man more than enough money for whatever he might need. He suspected Sarah had done the same thing, the way Einhorn had tried to refuse it.

Sarah was mollified. "Just be kind to him. He's been kicked around enough. And he's a ghetto Jew—it's another mentality."

"What am I, some kind of monster, for God's sake?" Arnold demanded, fixing himself a drink.

"Of course not," Sarah beamed. "You're a pussy cat."

"He only makes believe he's a monster sometimes," Naomi

said, "so nobody will guess the truth. I'll be right back—I want to see what's being done for dinner."

She stopped in the pantry, leaning against the door. Joshua was married. To a "special" kind of woman. She closed her eyes, imagining the unthinkable: Joshua and a woman together, in the way she had dreamed so often. But the woman was not herself. The woman had black hair and dark eyes, dark like Joshua's, full of desire like his.

She opened her eyes; her sweet, romantic revery of love was shattered forever, and only her erotic dreams of him were left— dreams that did not come without Arnold to spark them. She would see the doctor tomorrow about preventing conception—that was something she wouldn't tell anyone, not even Sarah—and then Arnold would take care of her nights, the way Rachel would take care of Joshua's.

It wasn't what might have been, but it was better than nothing.

She went to speak briefly to the cook. She returned to the living room in time to hear Sarah telling Arnold about his brother's bride.

11

The main warehouse for Duchess Limited was a few miles from Philadelphia. Sarah and Lazar hired a car, leaving their children with Maresh's wife and her own brood.

"It's a gorgeous day," Sarah exulted. "It's too bad we didn't bring the kids."

"They might see something they shouldn't talk about."

"Seth can barely speak," Sarah protested.

"But Rebekah talks as much as you do—and when you use a cosmetics warehouse to hide guns, you don't take chances. What if Rebekah told her Uncle Arnold about it?"

"He'd have a heart attack," Sarah said, dejected. "I hate

doing this behind his back, but he'd never agree. He *still* won't believe there's going to be trouble.''

"Well, it won't be long before we've made other arrangements.'' Lazar patted her thigh under her pleated skirt. "I don't like it either, but we had no choice.''

"Maresh is a gift from the gods,'' Sarah said.

"He's doing it for Joshua. He'd do anything for your brother.''

"You too. He'd do anything for you too.''

"That's all to the good. Who knows what else we might have to ask him to do?''

Weapons were harder for Lazar to find than money since the Depression. Antiquated pieces from the Great War were the best he could go, but delivery was on a haphazard schedule, and shipments had to be hidden until they could be smuggled out. They needed someone who was always on hand and completely reliable.

Maresh took personal charge of all receiving at the Duchess warehouse, and he could be trusted to keep such shipments hidden as long as necessary.

Sarah broke into Lazar's thoughts. "Tell me about Rachel. We're all curious about her.''

"She's an independent soul, always was—and not political anymore. For a while she followed Ben Gurion's Poale Zion Marxists.''

Sarah held up a hand. Any discussion of the Yishuv's political factions confused her. The settlers came from many different European countries. Where they were not permitted to assimilate, they had joined protest groups, all of them different. Now, in Palestine, they were still protesting, often against each other.

"You know I can't tell one from the other,'' Sarah said. She eyed her husband carefully. "Did you know her very well?''

He laughed, understanding what she meant. "No.''

"Well, I'm glad to know that. It would've been awkward if you had—she's my sister-in-law now.''

"What do you think we were doing out there in that labor brigade? All right, I know what you think *I* was doing, but our aim was to increase the population more by immigration than fornication.''

"I'm sure of it,'' Sarah said. Then, seriously, "I hope Josh will be happy. Naomi's not very well. She still has . . . feelings for him.''

"Well, he's married now."

"My poor innocent, do you really think being married means never wanting someone else?"

"Do you?" He turned his eyes from the road for a second. "Want anyone else?"

"No, but we're different. Sometimes I'm afraid it's too good to last." She crossed her fingers, still serious.

His hand moved higher on her leg. "It'll last. You see too many movies about star-crossed lovers." Sarah relaxed, sighing softly. "Do you want to stop for a while? The grass looks as lush and velvety as you feel."

"Yes," Sarah said, her eyes closed. "Oh, yes."

They were late in reaching the warehouse, but Maresh was still on the floor of the huge, hangarlike building when they did, his powerful frame covered by a blue smock, checking shipments with his men. He had given up trying to dress like an executive—it was too uncomfortable. His big, square face wore a wide grin when he welcomed them.

"So Joshua finally got himself married! He wrote us. Anna and I had a bottle of wine to celebrate." He led the way to his small office. "Come on and have some coffee," he said, pulling out chairs for them. "How are the kids?" He sat down once he had poured the coffee, and they exchanged family news briefly. Then he closed the office door. "What do you want to talk about first?"

"The guns," Sarah said.

He nodded, removing a file from the wall safe. They were soon absorbed in making arrangements to send the small arms Maresh had hidden in the warehouse to Boston for transshipment by rail to Canada and then by ship to selected points in Palestine.

"Let's hope more of them will get through this time," Lazar said.

"The British taking a lot?"

"They aren't stuipd. They know the coastline as well as the Haganah."

"Josh wrote it's bad in Europe, going to be worse for everybody."

"It is, Maresh," Sarah said glumly. "Hitler thinks Russians,

Poles, and Gypsies aren't much better than Jews. All inferior—only fit for slave labor.''

Maresh stood, his massive shoulders straining under the blue smock, his face puzzled. "I don't like going behind Arnold's back, but I know he'd never let me do this if we told him, and it's the only way I can help. Maybe I ought to go back to Poland—or even Palestine—and do something instead of letting the rest of you do it.''

"I feel the same way you do," Lazar said. "But both of us are helping from here. If Josh needed us more over there, he'd let us know.''

"Yeah," Maresh agreed. "He said he would." He looked at Sarah, still frowning. "You want to see the shipping figures?''

"No, just mail them to New York as usual. I want to know if you have enough room here to stock a big new item for Duchess.''

"I'll make room," Maresh said.

"Well, get ready, kiddo. We're going into perfume, and we're going to be wading through money by next year—and we need all we can get.''

It took eighteen months to turn Sarah's ideas into profitable reality. To Arnold's delight Naomi's father volunteered to find a property for the spa in California, and Arnold was relieved to let him do the time-consuming search. Martin was often difficult to handle. He still thought there were a lot of things he could teach Arnold about business.

Once the estate was bought, it seemed a good idea to let Martin supervise the extensive renovations—and only logical for him to move out there with Leah to supervise the spa from behind the scenes. As annoying as Martin was, Arnold could trust him implicitly. It solved the problem of Arnold's parents too: Los Angeles had a better climate for them than New York.

In early December 1934 the wrought-iron gates to the Domain were opened, crested with the five-pronged Duchess coronet. After an opening celebration Arnold and Naomi returned to New York with Sarah and Lazar. The Domain was filled with clients from the start.

"I started out a tailor," Martin said to Naomi on the telephone that Christmas, "and I end up a gentleman farmer. And your mother is governess for a bunch of Simonized *nafkas*.''

"Papa." Naomi laughed at him. "Just because they diet and exercise doesn't mean they're whores!"

"Who cares as long as the money keeps rolling in? We're open only three weeks, and we're booked solid for the next six months! The climate is marvelous, Leonard and Manya feel like spring chickens. The only thing is we miss you children. When you are coming to stay in this palace?"

"As soon as we can, Papa—after the new year. We're starting the advertising for the new perfume then."

"And my little girl found the perfect picture for it. Arnold told me the last time he was out. I'm proud of you."

Naomi was proud of the picture herself. While Otto Einhorn produced his formula, similar to the fabulous new Arpege but with a subtle difference—"another base note," he said, in perfumers' jargon—and Arnold began its production, Naomi had searched everywhere to find the right image for the advertisements. Dozens of drawings and portraits were turned down.

"Too cold," Sarah said. Or: "Too haughty—she looks like she never takes her drawers off except to pee." Naomi finally turned to her own imagination for what she wanted. She commissioned a painter, described the scene to him, and had him submit dozens of sketches until she was sure the painting would have the romance, the golden glow she wanted.

It was of a young woman, her blond hair topped by the Duchess coronet, who had been sitting for her portrait in a white Empire gown. She had just been lifted from her chair into a delirious embrace by the dark-haired artist. He held her to him with one strong arm, his palette raised in his free hand to be thrown aside in the next moment, the almost-finished portrait quite forgotten in the background as they both gave way to passion and her body curved toward his.

There was a sweep about it, a taking up of the female by the male, that fascinated everyone who saw it. The contrast between the young woman's cool poise in the almost-finished portrait in the background and her utter abandon in the artist's arms was more than suggestive.

"It's outrageously sexy!" Sarah said. "There's no doubt about what's going to happen next—it's almost happening while you watch. It's perfect, Naomi." She turned to Arnold. "This would sell a million gallons even if the perfume weren't as good as it is.''

Arnold agreed with her, baffled by something in the portrait and by the change in Naomi since she had started the project. She was always busy now but less strained. Almost her old self. It was a joy to be welcome in her bedroom; sometimes she even came to his.

He had always been certain Naomi had the kind of passion in her that was smoldering in that portrait—passion she had never given to him. It would have been even more fulfilling to him than his success.

The original painting hung over the fireplace in their living room, and he often studied it, trying to get to the bottom of it. It was symbolic, in its rich textures and soaring romance, of the nature of his business and its phenomenal rise. He wished it were equally symbolic of his marriage.

But at least he had the warmth of her affection again, if he could not have the heat of her desire. The affection had returned at a crucial moment, after months of abstinence—just when he was on the brink of an affair with Annalise Becker, one of the junior chemists at Duchess, a quiet young refugee who seemed as much in need of someone as he was. But he had never wanted mere sex. He was attracted to Annalise, but it was Naomi he wanted, and the feeling in her she withheld from him. He could no longer blame his brother for that withholding. Joshua had been far away for years, in touch only by occasional letters, married to another woman. Arnold had no one to blame—no one but himself, for wanting something he could not have, that might not even exist. He resolved to be content with what life offered.

And as 1934 ended, it offered a lot. He had decided to let Christmas pass and launch the new perfume when people weren't distracted by other gift items. It was a luxury, anyhow—and the rich were always there, as secure as The Duchess's now-famous golden coronet.

''Just wait till the perfume comes out,'' Sarah said to Lazar with happy satisfaction. ''I'm going to wear a coronet myself.''

They were on their way to Arnold's for a New Year's Eve party. Lazar looked at his wife, sitting next to him on the back seat of Arnold's limousine. Sarah was wearing a close-cut black moiré dress with a low neck and long sleeves. Her hair had grown and was pulled back in a low chignon. A long, fox-trimmed black wool cape fell around her shoulders.

"You don't need a coronet," Lazar said. "You know how black looks against your skin—especially your hair when you're naked. Don't ever cut it short again."

"You're beautiful too," she said. "And you wear evening clothes now as if you were the Dandy Ben you're always telling me about. When am I going to Palestine with you?"

He had made many brief trips without her, always hoping he could stay there and send for her and the children. But he did his job too well; he had made a science of fund raising, and the money he collected, even during these tight Depression years, was absolutely essential.

"Soon enough," he said.

"It can't be too soon for me," Sarah insisted.

The car stopped, and they went through the tinseled foyer and up to Naomi's apartment. It was predominantly a family party; Arnold socialized only for business purposes and never at home, preferring the publicity of large parties and charity balls and dinners. There was a smaller group this year than usual: Leah and Martin and the elder Furstens were absent. But Otto Einhorn was there and Naomi's brothers, Simon and David, with their wives, two pretty young women who, it seemed to Naomi, talked about nothing but their clothes and their babies. Maresh and his Anna had come from Philadelphia. It was a tradition, even if Maresh was always terribly uncomfortable amid all this grandeur unless Sarah was around.

They were a comely group of people, aware of their good fortune as they moved into 1935. They had all worked hard to get ahead, even if it seemed frightening to be so successful in the midst of a depression. They treasured their success but tended to keep their enjoyment of it to themselves. Even with each other they celebrated quietly, and because the business absorbed most of them totally, they usually ended up talking about Duchess, as Arnold was doing now.

"That bill will never pass," he said.

"What bill?" Simon's wife asked. She always displayed her interest in Duchess when she was with Arnold.

Sarah laughed. "They want to limit what they call 'overromantic' advertising of clothes and cosmetics. They say it's bad for women, gives them an unrealistic approach to life."

Lazar shook his head in disbelief. It astounded him that Congress was interested in romance while Hitler withdrew from the League of Nations to start rearming and Churchill warned the House of Commons that Germany's air force would surpass Britain's in a year. But even Lazar had to admit that love, as represented in American books and movies, was strangely antiseptic: in Sarah's words, "No sounds, no sweat, no heartaches, just waves breaking on a shore and happy endings." Well, his own story was the only happy ending Lazar had seen in his special circle of friends. Joshua had suffered through years of indecision until he finally married Rachel. And Joshua's gain was Ben's loss.

"You'd think the United States Congress had better things to worry about," Naomi said.

"Americans have enough to worry about," Arnold agreed, glancing at Lazar. "They aren't interested in European squabbles— and they're right." It was the only subject he and Lazar argued about.

"They are wrong," Lazar insisted. He rarely raised his voice; when he did, people listened to him, as they were doing now. Naomi gave Sarah an anxious look, but Sarah only shrugged slightly. If the two men were determined to have it out once more, there wasn't much she could do about it. Arguments upset Naomi. Sarah didn't mind them.

Arnold dismissed Lazar's opinion as he would an unprofitable business scheme. "There's no point in discussing it," he said loftily.

"Do you think you can change the facts by not discussing them?" Lazar was impatient, even derisive. "You bury your head in sand like—like . . ." Lazar searched for the word in English.

"An ostrich," Sarah said, raising a warning eyebrow at Arnold. It was one thing when he was high-handed with his business subordinates, but he couldn't dismiss Lazar with such majestic authority—not on this subject.

"And your brother?" Lazar said sharply. "Are you forgetting him? What do you think he's doing, running back and forth to Europe, smuggling guns into Palestine like a thief?"

Arnold grew very still, and his voice was chilly, as always when he was really angry. "Just because Joshua chooses to do that doesn't make it a necessity. He isn't God!"

Maresh stirred. "But it has to be done, Arnold. Josh wouldn't lie."

"Of course it must be done," Einhorn added.

The others were quiet. Arnold always treated these two with a consideration he did not extend to Martin Held and his sons.

"Even if it must be done—and I'm not agreeing with you—I don't want anything to do with it," Arnold said.

"You can't mean that," Sarah burst out, looking anxiously at Maresh's flushed, troubled face. "You'd help if you could, I know you would. Oh, for heaven's sake, let's talk about something else. This is supposed to be a party!"

Arnold looked steadily at Lazar, the way he sometimes looked, Naomi thought, when people talked about Joshua. "I don't want anything to do with it," he repeated.

Lazar hesitated only a second, then Maresh's face decided him. "You already do," he said—and told Arnold that the Philadelphia warehouse had been a transit point for gun shipments.

The stillness in the room was absolute.

"It was my idea," Lazar said. "I should not have persuaded Maresh that you would want to help—but I will do anything I have to do, even if it is against the wishes of a man whose ability I respect."

Arnold's face was frozen with fury and disbelief.

"Yes, I do respect you," Lazar said. "Except for this one thing that you refuse to recognize, heaven knows why." He stood up, his tall body defiant. "Do you want us to leave?"

"Oh, Arnold, please," Naomi said. "They'll stop using the warehouse from now on. Won't you?" Her eyes begged Lazar to agree.

"We made other arrangements long ago," Lazar said. "But I'd do it again tomorrow if I had to."

Arnold managed to swallow some champagne to clear the constriction in his throat. He couldn't risk an open rift with Sarah, with Maresh, with Otto, because of Lazar! He liked Lazar, even if he was crazy; he could even believe the feeling was mutual. What he could not accept was the influence Joshua had on all of them—Maresh hadn't seen him in years, and

Einhorn had never met him. Must he be eternally subject to his brother's influence, direct or indirect, even to the point where it affected his business? It was the one thing in Arnold's life he had believed was solely his own.

He looked over the rim of his glass, controlling the impulse to shout at them. If only Joshua were here, the real target of his rage, he could have done it. But these people were as much under Joshua's thumb as he was. They were all victims, hostages to some force of will or character or personality in a man who didn't care enough about any of them to stay in America where he belonged.

"Well, you're honest," Arnold said to Lazar. "I'll say that for you." He kept his voice low so no one would hear it shaking. "And what's done is done, so to hell with it." He could feel the roomful of people relaxing. "Now that you know how I feel . . ."

He felt Naomi's hand on his shoulder, calming, appreciating. She bent to take his glass, kissing his cheek. "Everybody, please," she said. "There's lots of champagne."

12

GIORA
NEW YEAR'S DAY 1935

Natan Markevitsch looked up eagerly from the fire he was stirring when Isaac came out of Rachel's room. "What is it?"

"It's a boy!" Isaac said with a mighty smile. "A marvelous creation, an infant." He shrugged into a heavy jacket and squatted near the fire. His white-bordered beard bobbed as he puffed on his pipe.

"How's Rachel?" Ben Horowitz wanted to know.

"Another marvelous creation. It's a wonderful thing to see a strong, healthy woman produce a strong, healthy child."

"She hardly made a sound," Natan said, thinking of his fragile wife, Aviva, soon to be delivered of their second child.

"I promise you Aviva won't have a hard time," Isaac said, patting Natan's arm. "You treat her like china, but she really won't break."

Dandy Ben stretched out on his back, looking at the stars. He had lost some of the brand-new polish of youth, but he still had the chiseled features and the well-pressed look that had earned him his nickname. "We're getting on," he said. "Lazar has two, Natan has almost two, and now the Rabbi has his first. I really feel old."

"Get married," Isaac advised him. "You'll feel young."

But Ben did not seem to hear. "Where's Josh now?" he asked.

"Who knows?" Isaac said. "Somewhere in Europe trying to make blind men see. He and Lazar are always on the move. Joshua sent out a lot of stuff, though. But he says Germany is producing a fantastic amount of arms—and Ari wonders where Hitler will try them out first."

"I'll be glad to try them out for him right here," Natan said.

"Things have been relatively quiet lately," Ben remarked. "Maybe the trouble is over."

"Come on, Ben!" Natan said. "More Jews are coming in every day from Germany and Poland, and the Arabs get angrier with each one."

"But prosperity talks," Isaac insisted. There were fourteen thousand Jewish businesses in Palestine now, tripled in seven years. The recession was over. The Arabs had work. "When you have prosperity," he went on, "people don't run around killing each other."

Natan didn't agree. "There are Arabs working for those firms— making money, getting ideas. The effendis won't want the peasants getting ideas. Anyway, if what you say is true, why are we smuggling in arms?" Natan was disgusted, angry. "You're all dreaming."

"I think we should all have a drink to Joshua's son and then get some sleep." Ben offered a flask of brandy he produced from under his blanket. "I propose a toast to young Benjamin Fursten and his mother!"

"Benjamin?"

Ben nodded. "After Rachel's father." He passed the flask around the small circle.

"Who's going to cable Josh?" Natan asked.

"Ari will," Ben told him. "I'll be seeing him in Haifa in the morning. He'll know where Josh is. Anybody else moving out tomorrow?"

They shook their heads. "There've been no orders from Ari," Isaac said. "Natan wants to stay here until the baby's born if he can. And I'm stuck. That's what I get for being a doctor."

"You know we need a central point for anyone shot by a British patrol," Ben said.

"Or sliced by an Arab," Natan added.

"Anyway," Ben went on after a pause, "you get a kick out of delivering babies."

Isaac smiled. "I do, at that." He got up, shaking out his pipe. "I'm going to have another look at my patients. I'll send Aviva out. Take her home, Natan, she needs rest. I'll stay with Rachel for the night." He went back into the room and closed the door.

Ben got to his feet. "Take it easy, Natan," he said. "We can't fight the British and the Arabs and Hitler all at once. We have to protect our people from the nearest danger and get ready to fight the biggest."

"I know." Natan sighed. "But someday we'll have to fight them all. I just can't forget what happened in Russia—in Kishinev, in Odessa. I can't forget what happened here in Hebron, in Safed, and just a mile away. I think I was born with the memory of raids and rapes and butchery in my bones. It's why I came to Palestine—and I still feel it here. Do all Jews feel it? Did you feel it in England, where there never was a pogrom? Did Joshua feel it in America, where he was safe?"

"I don't know," Ben said. "I just know that until we have a country of our own, it's something to fear. So save your anger and your strength, Minotaur. You'll need it." He put his hand on Natan's heavy shoulder for a moment, then left him near the fire.

Natan's face was dark with worry, until Aviva, heavily pregnant, came out of Rachel's room. Then he got to his feet, and his face lightened with unbelieving love. He still could not accept that this beautiful creature, her face flowerlike, her pale blond hair long and silky, was his wife, loved him. She smiled when he embraced her carefully, buttoning her jacket for her against the chill.

"Wait till you see him," she said. "He's lovely."

"You're lovely," Natan said, his big hands framing her face. Then he kicked sand onto the fire, smothering it carefully.

They walked toward their own room in the line of married couples' quarters. His powerful left arm held her gently. His right hand held a rifle.

From the darkness Ben watched them together, wanting Rachel. He had learned to bear her wifehood; he had never stopped wanting to take care of her, wanting to love her.

Joshua should have been here. He should have moved heaven and earth to be here when Rachel gave birth to his son.

Benjamin.

It seemed right that Rachel's father and Rachel's son should have Ben's name. She had never known a father's love—and Ben was with her more than her husband was. If he couldn't live with her, at least he could be near her. It was better than nothing.

13

NEW YORK
JANUARY 1935

This dress had to be perfect, Naomi knew. The fund-raising dinner would provide another setting for Rabbi Stephen Wise to speak out, in that thunderous voice of his, against Hitler's rabid anti-Semitism, which was spreading over Germany like a foul-smelling fungus. It would raise funds to help those who were trying to escape Europe, especially the children. Naomi wanted desperately to head that committee, and the society women who decided such matters based their decisions on appearances.

She had just brought the dress home after a final fitting, but she wanted to be sure. She stood in front of the three-way mirror in her dressing room, looking at it from every angle. It was layers of pale-blue chiffon over a fitted slip of deeper blue satin, the color of her eyes. Satin shoes had been made to order. She would wear elbow-length white kid gloves, the pastel beaded bag Sarah had brought her from Paris, and her sapphires.

She heard the maid greeting Arnold. He was home early. "Come in for a moment, will you, dear?" she called. "I want you to see what I bought for next week."

Arnold came through the all-white bedroom, past the bed strewn with pillows of all shapes and sizes in hand-embroidered organdy slips. The bedspread was foamy white lace over white satin. Silky white bearskin rugs were scattered on the white marble floor. It was like a movie set, but he had always found it a cold, forbidding room.

He stopped in the dressing-room doorway as she turned to him, looking exquisite in the wispy, floating blue chiffon, her body chastely revealed by the clinging satin sheath-slip.

He nodded his approval, almost too overcome to speak. She looked as young, as beautiful, as golden as she had at their wedding. She had said then she could never love him more than she did that day. She never had. He ought to accept that she never would. Then why this ache in him for what he could never have?

"It cost a fortune," Naomi was saying. "So I hope they like it. If I want to head that committee, I have to look exactly right." She smiled. "No matter how much money you contribute."

"This is really important to you, isn't it?" He had never thought of Naomi apart from her life with him.

"It's a chance to do something important. I have to *do* something of my own." She raised her eyebrow. "Sarah said it was dumb to have to look fashionable in order to help orphans, but that's how things are."

"That sounds like something Shai would say." He had just had some other news from his sister that made him uneasy. He wondered how to tell Naomi without making it seem too important. He stood looking at her. He was impeccably dressed, as usual, in a gray pinstripe suit tailored to compliment his slim frame and his average height. His shirt was immaculate white-on-white; he kept a supply at his office and changed several times a day. His tie was deep garnet. His face was still handsome, the changeable green-gray eyes the most striking feature; but his expression had a cast of authority now. Anyone who looked at Arnold Fursten knew he was a man who made decisions and gave orders.

Naomi felt his eyes on her. "Why don't you go and fix us both a drink? I'll change into something more comfortable for dinner." She wasn't sure she was in the mood for lovemaking tonight.

That he desired her didn't displease her. It was a comfort. But she was glad their intimate relationship had settled into a friendly kind of thing, and glad too that he was willing to leave the frequency and the atmosphere of it to her. Sometimes the techniques he tried in order to arouse her were unappetizing, but he never insisted.

She had overcome the emotional battering of all those lost infants, and she used something now to avoid risking any more. Her inner life was almost as calm as her outer one. Even her reveries of Joshua had changed. They had become small, innocent treasures to be taken out in quiet moments, like seashells on rainy winter days. They were no longer erotic etchings to furnish her secret life.

No, she decided, she was not in the mood for lovemaking tonight. She changed quickly and went through her bedroom, buttoning her severe black house gown, unaware that her ivory skin and red-gold hair against the velvet made her even more desirable to him.

They talked quietly over a glass of sherry about what the first reaction to the Duchess ads, just released in all the glossy magazines, was likely to be; about their parents out in California and when they might go to visit the Domain together. The Helds seemed perfectly happy running the place; Arnold's parents were content, although they still missed Rivington Street. Arnold knew they only hungered for Joshua, always Joshua. He cast a more powerful shadow in his absence than Arnold did when he was right there in California with them. What would his parents say about the latest triumph of their prodigal? A son. He glanced uneasily at his wife.

When the maid announced dinner, they went to a small table in a windowed alcove overlooking Fifth Avenue; the large dining room was only for company or family dinners.

"I hope you feel like soup," Naomi said when the maid placed a silver tureen on the table and returned to the kitchen. "It's been so cold today, I thought you'd like it." She ladled it into Wedgwood bowls, a pretty blue against the white damask cloth. Arnold poured the wine. Naomi always had wine on the

122 *Leona Blair*

table along with flowers and candles, even when they dined alone.

He wondered what the table at Giora looked like and the one small room Joshua shared with his wife. He had asked Lazar only once and received a reply typical of his careless brother-in-law.

"The table's wood, and the room has four walls and a window—if you're lucky. Otherwise the whole thing is a straw mat on the ground." Lazar still longed for the rough wilderness; the years of luxury in America hadn't changed him. He was as unknowable to Arnold as Joshua was.

"Arnold, are you all right?" Naomi had taken a few spoons of her soup, but she was looking at him now with concern. He hadn't moved since he had poured the wine.

"Sarah had a cable from Joshua. He has a son—born about ten days ago."

She stopped eating, and they stared at each other as if he had announced some event of cosmic importance. The silence stretched too long between them.

"You ought to be happy to have a nephew," Naomi said finally, trying to speak normally through her constricted throat. What filled him had to be a mixture of family pride and anguished envy.

"Of course I'm happy—for them," Arnold said, playing with the stem of his wineglass.

"You don't sound happy." Naomi knew this was dangerous ground. Was she trying to hide her own turbulent feelings by talking about Arnold's—or did she want to share them with him? It was true that, outside of her interest in Duchess, she couldn't share much with Arnold, as withdrawn as he was. Certainly not her forbidden feelings for his brother. But what else *could* they share? *They* had no child.

The stem of Arnold's wineglass snapped, and Naomi looked at it, too shocked to move or call the maid, watching the red stain spread on the white cloth like a pool of blood.

"I'm jealous of him!" Arnold's voice was low but violent, and he stared down at the spreading stain, feeling the old conviction that he would never be his brother's match, feeling all his dormant suspicions about Joshua and Naomi spreading with the wine stain. He looked up at her accusingly, a jumble of feelings in his chest, unable to read her face. "He always gets what I want."

He had begged her often enough in the past to say she loved *him*. But he had never named the barrier between them.

She was afraid he would mention it now, and she simply could not hear that name and feign indifference. In panic she deliberately turned his words into an attack on herself.

"You're so cruel!" she said, watching his expression change from closed suspicion to open astonishment. "You know I want a child as much as you do. Why must you remind me that I can't . . ."

He stood. "Naomi, I never reminded you. I never said a word about it except that I was sorry . . ." He came toward her.

"Leave me alone!" Her voice stopped him. "Don't come near me. Don't touch me. You're not sorry, except for yourself. All those years when I lost one baby after another and all you did was keep on, making me . . . If that's how you feel about it, why don't you divorce me and marry someone who can have children like a cow?"

His face was white. "Divorce? What are you talking about? You're hysterical. Naomi, please." He put out his hand, but he didn't touch her. "You know how I feel, how much I love you. If we can't have children, that doesn't change how I feel. Do you think I like sleeping in another room most of the time? It only makes both of us more unhappy."

"Then shut up about it," she said, her voice shrill. "Stop talking about it."

Anger overcame him. "I wasn't talking about it, damn it. I was only telling you my brother has a son. What's so terrible about that?"

She picked at her napkin, tearing the hand-rolled hem. "You said he always gets what you want, sitting there, looking like it's the end of the world. You said you were jealous of his son. How do you think *I* feel?" She caught herself. "To hear you say that, I mean?"

His eyes, an angry gray, watched her carefully. "How *does* it make you feel to hear he has a son?"

Her face flushed with anger and a swarm of other emotions she did not want to name. The napkin tore. She put it on the table and rang a small crystal bell, her eyes still on his. When the maid came in, Naomi's voice was as cool and clear as the bell.

"I'm not feeling well, Maida," she said. "Mr. Fursten will have his coffee in his study, as usual. You can clear away after you bring it. Good night."

The maid, a neat figure in her black uniform, said good night and went for the coffee, leaving them alone again.

"You didn't answer me," Arnold whispered. "How does it make you feel to hear they have a son?"

"I don't want to talk about it. I'm going to bed."

"Alone, of course. That's not the way to have children, is it?"

She turned away without answering him and went back through the bedroom, past the dressing room, and into her bathroom. She closed and locked the door, her hands shaking with fury.

How could he? How could he be so callous? Hadn't he said he would love her all his life? It was the ultimate betrayal. She could accept his marriage, but a child by another woman! Her own pregnancies weren't her fault. She had to submit to her husband, it was a wife's duty.

But he! Bad enough to marry for sex—and for some strong, dark woman to clean his hut and carry water from the stream and God alone knew what else. Was it her fault she wasn't brought up to live like that? He could have stayed right here in America if he really loved her. She might have had children with *him*!

She looked at herself in the mirror. She was just as much a woman as the one he had married. She wasn't tall, she wasn't strong, but she was just as much a woman as *his* wife—his *wife*! She thought of his wife lying under him. She thought of the woman with his baby in her arms.

Silently she undressed. She filled the tub with hot water and got into it. She remembered the night he had kissed her as if he would never have enough of her, as if he wanted to carry the imprint of her on his body for the rest of his life—the night he begged her to run away with him, when his hands moved over her body so hungrily. Oh, yes, she was as much a woman as that other one. She would prove it to him—to everyone. She knew how they all looked at her, pretending to pity her because she couldn't have children, making her feel she was somehow unfinished, incomplete.

She dried herself, smoothed creamy Duchess lotion over her

body, and reached for a filmy nightgown. She would use no contraceptive tonight. She brushed her hair, not so short now, a cloud of amber waves in the light. She walked back through the bedroom and opened the door. Arnold had changed to slacks and a pullover and was putting on his coat in the living room.

"Where are you going?" she asked, too surprised to let him speak first, as she had planned he should.

"Out for a walk," he said, not looking at her. He was going to call Annalise and ask if she would see him. He was sure she would. There was a look in her eyes whenever he saw her, exchanged a few words with her, that told him she would. She wanted nothing in exchange either—he could not have borne it if she had. She just wanted to be with him, and he needed someone who wanted him.

"Don't go, Arnold," Naomi said, willing him to look at her. He turned, his eyes moving from her face to her body, her breasts and hips clearly outlined under the chiffon as she stood against the light from the bedroom. "Stay with me." She held out her hand.

"Naomi, please. I don't want to argue anymore."

"Neither do I." She walked toward him, put her arms around him, and kissed him, as she had never done before. "I'm sorry for what I said. Come and stay with me." Her meaning was unmistakable.

His arms tightened around her, and he kissed her with a mixture of passion and fury that both frightened and excited her. He dropped his coat. He held her as they walked toward the bedroom.

Her eyes were closed when he put her on the bed, closed when he began to take her nightgown off, closed when it tore. She felt his tongue inside her mouth, his hands all over her, his fingers touching her, probing, pushing. Her eyes were closed when he held her outstretched hands while his head moved down to her breasts and his mouth caressed her nipples; closed when he pushed her thighs apart with his knee, when he put himself inside her, when she felt herself move along with him.

Oh, God, she thought, let me conceive. Please, please let me conceive and let me have a child this time. Let me have a son.

He was panting now, as much as she was. She moved faster until the sound he made told her it was over. A vast shudder of

triumph and rage and perverse excitement shook her body at the
same time release shook his. He mistook it for the first answering
passion of his marriage, and he kissed her again, gratefully,
adoringly, his hunger for her fed at last, his thirst for her slaked.
She let him. She might have to do this again before she conceived.

Finally he moved away to lie next to her, stroking her. She
stayed there, not going to the bathroom as she usually did to
wash herself clean of the sloppiness. She kept her knees bent.
She wanted to put a pillow under her hips to make conception
easier—her mother had once told her that—but she didn't want to
move too much.

He stirred—and she tensed. Not again, not tonight. She could
not do this again tonight. But he only leaned over to kiss her.

"I love you, Naomi. I'm sorry for what I said." He wondered
what he had said.

"It's all right, Arnold. Forget about it."

"Naomi?"

"Yes."

"You do love me?"

"Yes, Arnold." She patted his arm. It was all she could say,
but after a response from her such as he had never known, he
was content. Soon he slept.

She smiled in the dark, a tremulous little smile that had more in
it of anger than of either triumph or relief. She had never dreamed
she could do this, but there were some things that were unbearable unless you did something about them, unless you fought
back with whatever weapons you had.

I hate you, she thought. But whether it was this brother she
hated or the other one—or herself—or all the people who expected more of her than she could give, she could not have said.

14

GIORA
NOVEMBER 1935

Palestine at last! Sarah looked around the small room she and Lazar occupied during her first brief visit to Giora. Lazar had made many trips before, but he had just been reassigned to Palestine by the Fund, much to his relief and her apprehension. The room was as bare and rough as he'd said it would be; yet she would have lived in it happily if she and the children could only stay out here with Lazar.

"Not now." Lazar was adamant. "Not until we've brought in every European Jew we can, not until Hitler's out, not until we're secure against the Arabs."

There were rumblings again among the Arabs. With the announcement of the Nuremberg Laws in Germany two months ago, formally depriving Jews of civil rights, education, admission to any professions or the military, the rising tide of immigration from Germany had become a flood. Arab hostility mounted with the Jewish population. Palestine's small boomlet of prosperity had evaporated, and the Arabs argued again that the territory could not support any more settlers. A six-fold increase in Jewish population, they said, was too much. They demanded an end to immigration, an end to land sales to Jews, and a self-governing Arab state.

The Jewish community insisted that more settlements could be established in the barren desert, more swamps reclaimed, without depriving Arabs of any land they occupied or cultivated. If no other nations were willing to increase their immigration quotas in the face of Hitler's sinister actions, the British must let the Jews come to Palestine. The Balfour Declaration had guaranteed a national homeland for the Jewish people. They needed it more now than ever.

"But nobody believes Hitler will do what he threatens," Joshua had said in despair just last night. "Even most of the Jews in Germany think it's just another anti-Semitic bubble that will burst."

Yet Hitler did not appear to be making idle threats. As 1935 drew to a close, almost sixty thousand Jews had come to the Holy Land because they believed they were in danger; but the danger they left behind was now threatening them in Palestine, waving the crescent of Islam instead of the swastika.

Sarah sighed. She knew she must soon return to the United States with the children, that she would be separated from Lazar longer than at any time since their marriage. But there was no other way. No woman with safe haven in America had the right to deprive another woman, two other children, of space and food and escape from Germany, where the danger was far greater than here.

She reached for a letter and read it several times to be sure her first impression was right. The birth of a daughter had done more for Naomi than heal old wounds. It had prevented new ones.

There was nothing specific in what Naomi wrote, but the frantic, brittle nervousness was gone. Sarah was sure her sister-in-law was not only happy with her baby but content with her life, something she had never been since Joshua's first departure for Palestine almost eight years before.

She put the letter down and started dressing in cotton twill trousers and a work shirt—standard here. She could not complain. The years Lazar had been able to spend with her in America were a gift, not part of the bargain she had made when they married. She could not complain when a woman like Rachel accepted her own long-distance marriage as a matter of course. Zionist wives knew what to expect. They worked as hard as their husbands for a homeland, and if the work separated them, they accepted it as part of the price.

Sarah admired Rachel. They were about the same age, yet Sarah often felt Rachel was years older, even though she looked like a girl with her long black braids pinned up when she worked in the dairy. When she held her son, she might have been his older sister.

It was only Rachel's dark eyes and her firm, strong jaw that showed she was a woman. And it was when she looked at Joshua that her respect for the man she had married became a woman's love. It was very different, Sarah had to admit to herself, from the storybook romance she herself lived with Lazar, would always live with him no matter how many years they had together. Rachel's was a calm, strong, steady love.

But there was rapture in it too, Sarah was sure. A sensual woman herself, she could always tell when there was that electric flow between a man and a woman—the kind of flow, obvious and doomed, she had seen between Naomi and Joshua, trying to be polite at Sarah's wedding, the kind there had never been between Naomi and Arnold.

She picked up the letter again. At least Naomi was serene; better serenity than the emotional wasteland of that marriage up to now. If only Naomi and Arnold would talk to each other, even scream at each other. But that was asking too much of people who couldn't even talk truthfully to themselves.

As for Sarah, she had always sworn she would rather have a brief taste of ecstasy than a lifetime of serenity. She thought it now as she brushed her hair and tied it back with a ribbon, shivering slightly although the November day was mild and pleasant.

Then she went outside to find Joshua and Rachel.

Joshua watched her coming toward the citrus grove where Rachel and the baby sat on a blanket in the shade of an orange tree.

"She looks marvelous," Rachel said, echoing his thoughts. "I can understand why Lazar didn't let her get away."

"She's always been like a tonic," Joshua agreed. "And now that Lazar isn't caged up in drawing rooms, he's—the way he was when I first met him. And you." His hand stroked her dark, glossy hair, and he smiled down at her.

"You're not the same," Rachel remarked, taking a pebble out of Benjamin's chubby hand. "You're different."

"Sarah said the same thing last night. I'm not aware of having changed that much—except that I'm doing what I want to do. And I'm where I want to be. And I have you and Benjamin." He bent to kiss them both. "On second thought, that's enough to change a man completely, isn't it?"

Rachel made no comment. She was often silent when another woman would have said more, asked more. There was a lot about

Rachel that Joshua felt she would not share with anyone, not even with him. He had no idea that she felt exactly that way about things he didn't say.

Sarah reached them and bent to pick up the baby, holding him till he gurgled with pleasure. "He's really too funny to be real," she said. "He's as steady as his mother and as wise as his father—and at eleven months, that's funny." She cradled the baby's head against her cheek. "Where's my crew?"

"Lazar took the kids to the dairy to see the cows," Joshua said. "Come and sit down—Benjamin's heavy."

Sarah sat down and put the baby on the blanket. "I had a letter from Naomi," she said. "She sends you three her blessings—says she still can't believe she has a baby, and neither can Arnold."

"It's a pity she can't have any more," Rachel said, bending to kiss Benjamin's ear.

"Neither of them cares. Julie is matchless, so it's quite normal that she'll be an only child." Sarah laughed. "She says Arnold's already spoiling her—at six weeks!"

"They must be so happy," Rachel said.

"Lord, I hope so," Sarah said. They both looked at her attentively. "I mean after all those miscarriages," she added hastily. She had never talked to Joshua about his feelings for Naomi since the night he had brought Lazar home to Rivington Street. She glanced at her brother now. He was playing with his son, but there was a tension about him that had not been there before. She tried frantically to think of something to say to change the subject, to fill the silence.

Her eyes met Rachel's, and the two women looked at each other for a split second, in the kind of female code that says more than hours of conversation.

The moment passed, and Joshua stood up. "I'll go find Lazar and the children. If we're going to Tiberias, it's time we got started."

He gave the baby to Rachel and walked toward the dairy, with the same long stride Sarah remembered from her own girlhood. Nothing was said until he turned the corner and was out of sight.

"He sent a picture of us to your brother in New York," Rachel said. At last she knew who, but she wanted to see why. "I hope they'll send one back."

"I'll make sure you get one," Sarah said. She looked at Rachel again. "Josh is very happy, you know."

Rachel nodded. "He was just telling me the same thing." But that was before mention of Naomi's child had made him tense, remote, the way he used to be.

Some feelings, Sarah thought, never disappear. They just move to another place.

15

NEW YORK
NOVEMBER 1935

Naomi held the baby, still marveling at this creature who had crossed the great divide from nonbeing into being only six weeks ago, a creature with thoughts, made of her thoughts, made *because of* her thoughts.

The jealous anger and perverse sexuality that had driven her to the making of Julie seemed very remote now. The whole torrent of loss, guilt, and frustrated motherhood, the whirlpool of misdirected love that had threatened to engulf her, were far in the past. She was done with feeding on dreams; she had been like the survivor of a shipwreck slaking thirst with seawater—the thirst only increased.

The moment the baby began to move inside her, she had moved into reality. She knew now what she felt for Arnold: trust, pride in his achievement and the life he gave her—and pity for a kind of love she could not return. She was resolved to make him believe she returned it. Anything else was selfish and unfair to both of them—and to their child.

She held the baby closer. The things this tiny head would learn! Feathers and snowflakes and trains. The feelings too. Softness and anger, pity and pride. She would protect Julie from the worst of it as long as she could.

The nurse came to take the baby away. Recovery from a Caesarian delivery was very slow, Naomi complained. Particularly since she had been forced to spend almost all her pregnancy in bed to avoid a miscarriage. But Arnold had insisted she follow the doctor's orders.

She smiled, thinking of him. He was so amazed at this tiny center of their universe. Both of them accepted the fact that Julie would be their only child. They felt so lucky to have her.

Naomi dozed off, still smiling. Arnold didn't disturb her when he came home but stood watching her for a moment before he went on to the nursery to see his baby.

She was so many things to him, this tiny girl, so small and helpless and perfect. But she was something more than a daughter. She was living proof, the breathing memory, of the first and only passion of his life. More than anything, more than the success of Duchess perfume, launched about the same time Julie was conceived, more than the extraordinary profits the Domain brought in, this infant was Arnold's proof that he had succeeded: Naomi loved him as he wanted to be loved. He had been right to keep his suspicions to himself, to hide his hurt from her. Time had done its work.

He no longer pondered the sequence of events on the night she had first argued with him, then seduced him so ardently. He decided they had both been on edge, and he was grateful he had not gone to Annalise Becker for counterfeit comfort. He no longer brooded over the Duchess painting either. He had always known that the sensuality he felt in the painting was there in Naomi, and at last she had given it to him, like a sleeping beauty, wakened from a spell. He was not going to question why she had slumbered so long. He was certain that, once she had recovered, their intimate moments would be as soul-satisfying as he remembered. The memory was on the fringe of his consciousness every time he looked at his baby daughter. A love child—he thought he knew what that really meant.

The old suspicions about Joshua were gone. He and his brother would never understand each other, but that was no reason for distrust. They were too different for any rivalry to be significant. Sarah had said it once, in that apt way of hers: "Can a peach outdo a geranium? You're two different species."

The news from Sarah and Joshua lately was frightening. If war should come in Europe, there were steps he had to take now to insure the health of his expanding empire. The supplies of attars and essential oils needed to make perfume came from all over the world. Even if the war were contained inside Europe, shipping would be disrupted. He was already shifting to South American sources, and he was starting some floral cultivation of his own in the southern United States.

He stroked the baby's cheek gently with his finger, frowning. Sarah should come back from Palestine. In the first place, it wasn't safe. And there were business decisions to be made by both of them. She had written a lot about Palestine, and there had been a warm letter from Joshua too after Julie was born, with a picture of Josh, Rachel, and their baby. Now they were both fathers. It was a line they had both crossed, fine but significant, which redefined both of them. He could think of seeing his brother again with anticipation, pushing his resentments to the background, forgetting he had ever harbored them.

He went back to Naomi's white bedroom. She was awake, and he bent over to kiss her. "How are you?"

"Fine—but disgustingly lazy." Naomi smiled happily. "I've just had another nap. I wish the doctor would let me get back to work on my committee."

"And the baby?"

"It doesn't take that much of my time, Arnold. And you know how important it is to me—even more so now that we have a baby of our own. If ever she were to be left like some of those children . . ."

"She won't be—not ever."

She held his hand against her cheek for a moment. "Anything exciting happen today?"

He shook his head. "But I wish Sarah would come back. We have things to do."

"She won't leave Lazar before she absolutely has to." Naomi nestled into her pillows. "I wonder if Julie will ever meet her cousin Benjamin."

"We might make a trip there sometime, when things are safer." He kissed her hand. "I'm going to shower and change for dinner." She watched him go toward his own bedroom, his posture making him seem taller than he was. Until recently he had rarely mentioned his brother. Now he was thinking of going to Palestine to see him!

Naomi opened her night-table drawer and took out the picture

Joshua had sent. He looked the same, but it was hard to tell if he had really changed. Joshua was three-dimensional. His essence was in the way he moved, in his voice, his ideas. They made him larger than life.

She wondered what the girl was like. She was about Naomi's age, but she looked too young to be a mother, far too young for Joshua. It was difficult to imagine her as his wife. What on earth would they find to talk about if they ever met, she and this Palestinian girl? They had nothing in common at all. Nothing but Joshua.

Naomi shook her head, put the photograph away, and got up to get ready for dinner.

Book
Three

16

GIORA
NOVEMBER 1940

Violence. Palestine was a land where violence flourished instead of wheat. Rachel held her five-year-old son with one hand and a repeater rifle with the other, watching until the trail of dust from the truck taking Joshua toward America had disappeared.

Her eyes scanned the area automatically every few seconds. They were always on guard these days, even though the three-year Arab strike was over and the anti-British riots quelled. At any moment a white kaffiyeh might appear over any small rise and the words *"Aleihum! Thah el Yahud!"*—"At them! Death to the Jews!"—ring out.

Rachel looked down at Benjamin, who had never known anything in his little life but love and violence. "It's time to go back to school, darling. Abba's gone."

The child listened, as quiet and self-contained as his father. He looked at her with Joshua's eyes. The rest of his face was hers, the mouth less wide, less sensual than Joshua's, the chin as square and sturdy as her own. But the eyes were his father's.

Joshua's might have been Arab eyes, so deep and dark, flashing fire when he was angry, flashing desire as they had last night. Last night left eddies of erotic memory in her body even as she answered her little boy's piping questions on the walk from the road to the new outer fence of barbed wire outside Giora.

Joshua had undressed her gently while she stood near the bed. He stroked her back and buttocks lightly, lifting her up while he kissed her. Then he lowered her body, letting his mouth travel the length of her and come back again to the place he opened between her thighs, first teasing her, then insisting with lips that knew exactly how to bring her pleasure. He put her on the bed after the first wave of hot sensation shook her, to move once more over every inch of her, refusing her attempt to make love to him, wanting only to make her peak again and again, reveling in the body of his wife of seven years, a body he knew as well as she knew his.

There was so much about him she still didn't understand. What were the wellsprings of this sensuality that was always present in him but sometimes exploded from his depths, as it had done last night? She wanted him again, right now, even as she went into the stockade with her child and led him to the children's house. She had no idea when she would see him again. He was going to America to see his family; he would then take Maresh with him to England, a country holding on by sheer grit from Dunkirk, the incredible Battle of Britain, and the expectation of a German cross-channel invasion that never came. Heaven alone knew why: England would have fallen to the Germans overnight.

Joshua chose to enter England from America; he would have been immediately suspect if he went in from Palestine. He risked losing his American citizenship if he put on the uniform of another country, but there were many men in the beleaguered Isles of Britain who were not her sons, and governments were looking the other way to they might fight for her, as Joshua was determined to do.

"The Brits won't let Palestinian Jews form a brigade—all they can do is dig trenches," he had said a week ago in the dining room. "They wouldn't let Palestinian Jews fly RAF planes, not even during the Battle of Britain! But they won't stop an American rabbi from giving aid and comfort. That way, I'll be able to *do* something."

He had looked around at the people in the hall: Lazar, Ben, Isaac, and Natan, Ari and his Haganah boys. Rachel knew that only these men could convince Joshua to stay in Palestine and wait for the war to come to him, as, sooner or later, it must.

"You can do something here," Ben insisted. "There'll be fighting in North Africa. Hitler's taken Austria, Czechoslovakia, Poland, France, the lot. He has to secure North Africa or he's threatened from the south through Italy."

"We finally got official permission to carry arms," Natan pleaded. "And you want to leave! Why?"

"Because that maniac is going to kill every Jew in Europe," Joshua shouted. "He has said so. His SS was set up in 1929 to kill Jew-Bolshevik subhumans! His Gestapo has been slaughtering since 1933. Someone has to do something about it!''

"And what are you going to do?" Lazar demanded. "More than we're already doing?" They were bringing Jews out on cattle trucks, through the Balkans, from Russia to Istanbul, across the Black Sea. They were publicizing every bit of evidence they could smuggle out to let the world know what was happening inside Germany and the occupied countries that had fallen to Hitler like ripe fruit.

Joshua shook his head fiercely. "I'm not sure. I just have to go. Maybe it's because I've spent so much time in Europe, seen so much already, that I can't wait. You're armed, you're legal now." He didn't say that the arms were there to a great extent because of him.

Lazar disagreed. "We're legal only as a police force, not as an army. We can carry arms—but look at the arms we're allowed to carry." He kicked an old rifle with disdain. "The British are too busy surviving to keep a significant army here. We're surrounded by hostile Arabs, and we need every man we have."

"I'll send you more men, I swear I will. That's why I'm going, to send out more than a trickle of Jews." Joshua looked from Lazar to Ari. "You can't ask me to stay here when I *know* I can be of more use elsewhere."

There had been a silence among the men while Rachel and the women waited. It would be so dangerous if he crossed over to Europe from England, and she knew that was what he had in mind.

For him it wasn't enough that new settlements were springing up almost overnight—despite British attempts to stop them—in order to receive and house whatever refugees could reach Palestine, legally or otherwise. There was no other place for them to go. Someone had said it for the world: Nobody wanted to import a racial problem. A ship that left Hamburg with almost one thousand aboard had been turned away by Washington and Havana just last year and returned to Germany.

"You think they'll die a natural death?" Natan had said bitterly. "Over two hundred of them were children. *Little kids!* You going to tell me no country has room for two hundred little kids?"

And so the watchtower settlements mushroomed, many of them springing up on Saturdays. The British still thought Zionism was a religion and that no Jews work on their Sabbath. But work they did. All that was needed was a fence and a watchtower, and there was another settlement, room for more refugees on a patch of rocky land.

The Haganah trained feverishly under Orde Wingate, a British officer who viewed with contempt his country's feeble effort to put down the Arab protest rebellions of the last three years. The strikes and riots were as much against the British as the Jews—and at last the Jews were permitted to carry arms for self-defense.

In Wingate's opinion the only defense against the silent, slinking Arab raids that left villages strewn with hacked up, fly-blown bodies stinking in the sun was to raid the raiders and clear out the militant Arab camps. Wingate was eventually recalled but not before he left a legacy of trained commando units which would grow into the elite Palmach strike force. Some of the youngsters, not content with the rescue efforts made by Jews in Europe, talked of going to the Continent to bring people out.

But none of these measures, some of them dangerous and desperate, satisfied Joshua. He was convinced that the entire Jewish population of Germany and Poland—those who had not fled to the area Russia occupied in 1939—would be decimated. Hitler had said so.

Ari had said nothing during the argument. Now he spoke, his iron-gray hair stiff as bristle. "You're not going over there to be rabbinical or to buy arms—that's impossible. You want something else, and you think your contacts in Europe will be of help." He held out his hands. "Conclusion: You want to get in touch with the resistance movements in France, Denmark, Norway and the Polish underground to organize escape routes." He squinted at Joshua. "You probably want to go in and organize a Jewish resistance."

The rest of the men looked up. Ari shook his head at them. "We need every one of you here, so don't get ideas. The Rabbi might be able to do it. If he can't go in, he can organize. And a man of the cloth is a good front."

"I speak Polish," Lazar said, his blue eyes alight with interest. "There are more Jews in Poland than anywhere else."

Joshua was negative. "It's too dangerous for you. You're well known in Poland now." Lazar started to object, then changed his mind. He had plans of his own about Poland he was not ready to reveal.

"Who, then?" Ari asked, anticipating. "You obviously have someone in mind."

Lazar smiled, understanding who Joshua had in mind before he spoke.

"A man who works for my brother, Maresh Skowalski. He was born in Warsaw. Lazar knows him—he's been helping us smuggle guns for years. And he's a Polish Nationalist. The only reason he hasn't joined the underground already is my sister Sarah; she knows I want him with me."

"So you want to organize an action in Poland," Ari said, smiling. "The British are in trouble. They're not going to be generous with help."

"They're great with words, though," Isaac remarked. "The slaughter in twenty-nine were 'incidents' because only Jews got killed. The Arab riots were 'a state of emergency' because their soldiers got killed. And now they find out you can get killed by Germans even if you're blond with blue eyes!"

"Screw the British," Natan said angrily. "Why do you even want to help them? They deserve killing."

"Natan, be fair," Joshua pleaded. "They fought like lions in the air after Dunkirk. They refused Hitler's peace offer when they could have bought time that way, as the Russians did, with their rotten nonaggression pact."

"Screw the Russians too," Natan said. "How many of us have *they* killed for no reason?"

"The trouble with you, Josh, is that you always see both sides," Ben said.

"Because Lord Peel was right about us and the Arabs: it's a conflict of right with right," Joshua answered. "But I only fight for one side."

Ari was doubtful. "Someday you'll have to see only one side or you won't be able to fight. What do you think—we're all saints just because we've been persecuted? Noble pioneers? We don't fight and kill?"

Isaac said, "Ari's right—we've learned from the boot that squashed us. Take his advice, Josh: Don't look at both sides. Look at our side, or you'll crack."

"I still say that until America gets into this war, we have to cooperate with the British, hold our tempers."

Some of the men murmured agreement, but Natan's mighty fist crashed down on the wooden table. "You Haganah people drive me nuts with your goddamn restraint. Who ever used restraint on us?"

"You're talking like an Irgun fanatic," Ari said.

"I may turn into one," Natan told him hotly, "if that's what I have to do to protect my family from the Arabs. The English wouldn't when they could—and now they have their own war to fight."

"All *right!*" Ari's voice stopped the discussion. "We can't decide that tonight." There was tension in the room. Some of the men had had enough of cooperating with the British, of Ben-Gurion's insistence on *havlagah*—restraint—by the Haganah. They preferred the no-compromise position of Menachem Begin's Irgun. If the British would do nothing to solve the problems in Palestine, let the British get out—or suffer the consequences. The two factions were spliting wide apart.

Ari went on. "We're here to decide if the Rabbi goes or not. I'm a fine general—I ask my troops for decisions." The men laughed, easing the tension.

After a moment Ari shrugged. "You go. If you can do anything, you stay. Otherwise you come back. We do need every man." He looked around the hall at the settlers gathered there. "Every woman. Every child old enough to shoot a gun. Just because the Brits killed a lot of angry Arabs over the past few years doesn't mean there aren't a lot more out there. And they hate us more than they hate the English for having let us in." He stood with a grunt. "I'm for bed. To train kids for commando units I have to look healthy at least, since young I'm not."

That decision had been made a week ago—and last night had been just last night, although it seemed years away to Rachel. She went into their room and stretched out on the bed. Joshua would be in New York soon. He would see his family, his brother, Arnold. And *her*.

After eleven years he would see her again. There was still something lingering, something more important than what Joshua had with other women, women like Shula before she'd moved to Tel Aviv—maybe still, for all Rachel knew; women in Europe on his long trips, women who didn't matter. There were often men and women on the sidelines of a marriage who didn't matter. The danger came from those who did—like Ben Horowitz for her. The feeling that had almost made her choose Ben as a husband warned her not to seek comfort from him while Joshua was away so long. Part of the time in New York with a woman who mattered to him.

Rachel sighed. Was there anything to the Hasidic legend of the *bashert*? Those pious Jews who worshiped God with a dancing merriment that shocked the Orthodox insisted that it was so. Certain souls were destined to be joined and would struggle from the corners of the earth to find each other. It didn't matter if circumstance made them totally unsuitable. The power that drew them together was stronger than the barriers that kept them apart. One would never feel complete without the other if they never met. Both would always be searching.

Superstitious nonsense, Rachel told herself. And yet, why did that one woman still cast a shadow on Joshua's spirit? They had nothing in common, not their lives, their ideals, their minds. Joshua's life was here in Palestine, working for the same cause Rachel had been born to, working for the safety of his wife and son and the family of the entire Yishuv. He loved her, she knew that. He desired her—last night was proof of it.

Unless it had been some kind of anchor for him too, as if he were seeking safe harbor in Rachel's body, so that he would not be tempted by someone else, someone he could not resist and would never forget simply because she was his One, the destined, the *bashert*.

Rachel's eyes closed. Her hands, guided by the memory of his, traveled from her breasts to her belly. If there was any connection between last night's passion and Joshua's anticipated meeting with his brother's wife, Rachel did not want to know what it was.

17

NEW YORK
DECEMBER 1940

Arnold looked out of the window of his office at the city bustling below, nervous about seeing Joshua again, not understanding why but determined not to let it show. Eleven years! So much had changed for both of them. Both husbands and fathers—and their parents gone too, within a year of each other. It meant something to lose parents. It was a hint of mortality, a very clear reminder that no one lived forever.

Arnold shook his head. Thoughts like these rarely troubled him. He was too busy with work. But now his older brother, the god of his babyhood and the bane of his young manhood, would soon be here, in this very office. Armored with success, he should be feeling confident, happy at the prospect of the meeting. He was not.

It had nothing to do with Naomi. They had a happy life together. They had moved to a beautiful home at Sands Point, built after Julie was born. Naomi was very busy with Julie, with Sarah's children, with her work for refugee orphans, with the social life that was part of Arnold's incredible rise in the industry. The company had gone public and although the family was still the majority shareholder, Duchess stock was always solid, its dividends consistent. If not the biggest, Duchess was prestigious enough for the slick magazines and newspapers to gossip about the handsome young Furstens, their lovely child, their imposing home. He knew Naomi was happy. If the heat of those nights when Julie was conceived had not returned in quite the same intensity, she gave him warmth and pleasure.

Then why this apprehension over meeting his brother? He would never understand why Joshua had chosen such a life—a waste of brilliance, in Arnold's opinion—but he wished him well. It no longer mattered that their parents had always idolized

Joshua and took Arnold for granted. Joshua had represented escape, rebirth, and renewal to them from the moment he was born. Arnold could remember with affection all the hours his big brother had lavished on him, the stories, the little excursions, the lessons when he was Julie's age and unaware that Joshua's magic wasn't confined to the family, that it reached out and encircled everyone he met, eclipsing his younger brother whether he intended it to or not.

Arnold went back to his desk and concentrated on a thick memorandum from Duchess's legal department. The Federal Trade Commission was always poking its nose into the cosmetics business these days. Arnold insisted that the American Medical Association lobby was behind it, using the industry to divert Roosevelt from the ogre of socialized medicine.

It was the AMA that had lobbied for passage of the Wheeler-Lea Amendment in 1938, extending government control to cosmetics as well as food and drugs. Now claims would have to be substantiated. Tissue cream could be discontinued for not renewing skin tissue or fresheners because they did not really freshen skin.

With the passage of the Food, Drug, and Cosmetics Act dangerous ingredients would have to be eliminated. New formulas had been incredibly costly—yet the profit was enormous enough to defray the cost easily.

Aside from that Arnold wanted no trouble with the Federal Trade Commission, empowered to implement the new laws. The FTC had already called Pond's to court for its New Skin Vitamin Cream, supposed to provide a more "scientific" way to nourish America's complexions. Arnold was determined to avoid that kind of notoriety. The idea of a seizure judgment such as those against Lash Lure mascara and Guerlain lipstick horrified him. He knew there were ways to avoid such judgments: pleas of no contest led to insignificant fines; legal tactics stalled off consequences until all incriminating merchandise was sold and new, acceptable products were on the shelves. But Arnold wanted no such bend sinister in The Duchess's unsullied pedigree. With Einhorn and his own legal department he intended to avoid confrontation with any federal agency.

But as in the rest of the industry Duchess's claims were no longer made on Duchess labels. The magic effects of the prod-

ucts were touted in very subtle, ever increasing advertising instead. The company's balance sheet was still amazing.

Even the war in Europe hadn't stopped Duchess. Arnold had
arranged long ago for alternate sources of supply in South America and elsewhere. He had increased floral production in the
southern United States, putting Maresh in charge of the planta-
tions. And his decision to branch into pharmaceuticals was a
sound one: it would be an essential industry if the country got
into the war. But he hoped America would not be involved. Why
Joshua wanted to go to England to get into the fight was beyond
him.

He looked up. Joshua was standing in the open doorway,
looking at him with an expression he remembered from his
boyhood, a combination of pride, love, and interest in whatever
his little brother had to tell him about the day's events. He came
from behind his desk, his nervousness forgotten. The brothers
embraced, a fiercely affectionate hug that bridged the years.

"My God," Arnold said, past the tightness in his throat.
"You're so thin! Are you all right?"

"No thinner than I was at Sarah's wedding." Joshua sat
down on the other side of Arnold's carved mahogany desk,
neatly arrayed with gold-tooled leather accessories. "You look
marvelous—but then, I've seen your picture often enough."

"Where?"

"In *Vogue*, *Bazaar*—the fashion magazines. Oh, yes, we have
them, even at Giora. Rachel eats them up. She says it's the only
way she gets to see her American family."

"How is she? How's Benjamin?"

"She's wonderful. And Benjamin is fantastic. He doesn't say
much, but he sees everything. Sarah says your Julie is quiet
too."

"You'll judge for yourself when you see her tonight. You're
coming? Naomi's making a special dinner."

"I have to go to the Jewish Agency office, but Sarah and I will
drive out with Rebekah and Seth in plenty of time. Sarah stopped
off down the hall somewhere. I think she wanted to give us some
time together. I'll only be here a day as it is."

They looked at each other. "I'm glad to see you," Arnold
said, meaning it. "I wish you could stay longer."

"I want to get where I'm going. It's only because it's better for me to enter England from America than Palestine that I got this chance to see all of you.''

"Sarah told me. If what they say is true, though, you'll be in more danger over there than you've been throughout the Arab riots.''

Joshua moved nervously in the luxurious leather chair. "What they say *is* true, Arnold. And the danger will be the same everywhere if it isn't stopped.'' He sounded impatient, as if he didn't want to discuss the situation, only act on it.

"Is there anything I can do to help?'' Arnold asked.

"Yes. Make sure Rachel and Benjamin don't starve if anything happens to me.'' His dark eyes held Arnold's.

He had said it softly. No, he had asked it, as a favor. Yet Arnold felt vaguely reduced. There he sat, president of a multimillion-dollar corporation, surrounded by the evidence of his success—and somehow it all seemed unimportant in comparison with what Joshua, in a cheap suit years out of date, was about to undertake. Joshua was risking his life. All he expected of Arnold was money for his wife and son if he died.

"Of course,'' Arnold said. "If you really have to go.''

"Somebody has to go,'' Joshua said shortly as the door opened and Sarah came in.

"Well, what do you think of each other after so many years?'' She looked from one to the other. "I hope Josh is suitably impressed! Josh, why is it you look like a ragamuffin here and perfectly okay in Palestine?''

"Everybody's a ragamuffin in Palestine—I blend in there.'' Joshua smiled. "And, yes, I'm impressed. Arnold, you've done everything you said you'd do and more. A man can't ask for better. I wish I could claim as much.''

Arnold relaxed. Joshua had never denied his achievement, that was a fact. Neither had Lazar. They had only made him feel it was not something that really mattered.

"Hey, what about me? I'm half of all this,'' Sarah said.

"You've been dividing your energies lately,'' Joshua reminded her. "Arnold, you let her get away with a lot—but then, we always did, didn't we?''

A wave of nostalgia swept over the three of them. "Who would have dreamed all this,'' Sarah said softly, "on Rivington Street?'' Since their parents' deaths there was very little to remind them of Rivington Street unless they were all together like this.

Arnold cleared his throat. "I was just asking Josh if there was anything we could do to help."

Joshua and Sarah exchanged a glance.

"Arnold, dear, you're going to be terribly angry," she said.

He waited, looking at Joshua.

"Maresh is coming with me," Joshua said.

Sarah broke in with a rush of words. "For over a year he's wanted to join the Polish underground in England and from there to get into the resistance inside Poland. I managed to keep him here this long with Anna's help, but he's made up his mind to go with Josh."

Arnold was astonished. "With Anna and all those kids to take care of? The best quality controller in the business?"

"I remember when you didn't want to hire him at all," Sarah said, trying to make light of it.

But Arnold didn't smile. "I was wrong. Even if he'd rather grow potatoes than jasmine. He's one of the few men I can trust. Why does he want to go?"

"He is a Polish Nationalist, Arnold," Joshua said. "His country's been invaded—again. Poland's been cut up like a pie for centuries."

"And he can be trusted," Sarah added. "You just said it yourself. Most Poles are more anti-Semitic than the Germans, but not Maresh. Where Josh is going, he'll need someone he can trust."

Arnold swiveled his chair to face the tinted window looking south on Park Avenue. He was caught in a trap. He needed Maresh for his business. If America got into the war, he would need him more than ever. But Joshua needed him to save lives—possibly Joshua's own life. Between the needs of his hard-won empire and his brother's life, there could be only one choice. Joshua's purpose had always been more important than his.

And yet, when men like Joshua and Lazar needed money, to whom did they turn? To men like Arnold, money-grubbing capitalists supposedly without ideals who kept the world turning nevertheless. The hypocrisy of it! That man who ignored and despised money should be admired more than men who made money. In the end money was what they all needed and wanted. Parasites, all of them.

"Maresh is his own boss," Arnold said, turning back. "I can't keep him if he wants to go."

"He'd want your approval," Sarah said. "He's as loyal to you as he is to me and Josh and Lazar."

"To Lazar?" Arnold questioned sharply. "What's he got to do with Lazar now?" The memory of the guns stored in a Duchess warehouse still rankled.

"He's my husband, remember?" Sarah said. "And when Lazar joins Josh, I'd feel better if Maresh were along."

Arnold nodded, satisfied. Easing his sister's mind was acceptable; Joshua's heroics were not. He stood when Joshua got up to go, walking with him to the office door. Joshua put his hand on his brother's shoulder. "Thanks, Arnold."

"What for?" Arnold said, trying to hide his anger.

"For everything. For understanding about Maresh. For Rachel and Benjamin. Rachel knew she could rely on you."

A mix of feelings gripped him. His brother was a parasite, a hypocrite, a crazy idealist—but his brother might be killed, and he loved his brother. Damn him, he loved his brother.

"How could she know? She doesn't know me," he said gruffly, completely confused.

"But I do—and I told her what you're like." There was an awkward pause. Then, "I'll see you tonight," Joshua said, closing the office door behind him.

Arnold went back to his desk, avoiding Sarah's shining eyes, as uncomfortable with her approval as with Joshua's. Yet everything seemed all right again, the way it had been on Rivington Street when he worshipped his big brother and protected his little sister. Where had he lost it, that wholehearted love?

"Well," he said to Sarah, "let's decide who's going to replace Maresh."

18

She moved around the luxurious drawing room at Sands Point, shining with a glow he had not seen since she was a girl, since he had fallen so hopelessly in love with her that he could never want anyone else. This was the Naomi everyone adored, the one who lit up a room like sunshine when she came into it, who did things to make people happy.

Watching his wife, Arnold knew she had not simply mellowed with maturity, was not calmer because she was content, and did not return his love measure for measure. He had been a pitiful fool to think any part of that girl could simply vanish into womanhood. She was still there, only needing the right spark to set her off—and the right spark was his brother, sitting on a beige silk sofa and talking animatedly, hpynotically to Sarah's children, one on either side of him, the way he used to talk to Arnold and Sarah. The streak of desperation in Joshua because of the war only increased the intensity of his personality, the impact of his charm, the effect he was having on Naomi.

He watched her watching Joshua, her eyes shining, her lovely pale red hair like a halo. He knew the scent of it when he held her in his arms, knew how it curled between her thighs, how it felt to be inside her small, perfect body. And knew she didn't really want him there, had never wanted him there. No matter how often he had told himself before Julie was born that an innocent girl like Naomi could not have responded fully to a husband's embrace; no matter how often he had told himself since Julie that at last, at last, she desired him, another thought had always followed somewhere far back in his mind: Would she have desired his brother more? And when she let him lie there, stroke her breasts, whisper her name, pour himself into her, that question had always been with him.

It was with him now, while he watched her. And now he was sure of the answer.

Beyond the mullioned Tudor windows of the drawing room it was night, blacking out the lawn that was velvet green and splashed with flowers in summer but as winter-sere and fallow tonight as Arnold felt. The room was warm, furnished with clusters of chairs that made conversation easy even at large parties but allowed a small group to congregate in one area, as the family was doing tonight.

Enormous as the room was, Arnold felt smothered in it, as if no room were big enough to hold his brother and himself when Naomi was in it with them, a streak of laughter and color in turquoise crepe hostess pajamas against the beige and white room. The only other color was the Duchess portrait hanging over the huge fireplace, with its beige marble mantel and surround.

Joshua was telling stories to ten-year-old Rebekah and nine-year-old Seth, stories of their cousin Benjamin, their aunt Rachel, their father still in Palestine. Their last visit there had been three years ago, before the Arab riots became so dangerous, but they remembered all Lazar's special friends from the days of the labor brigade: Dandy Ben and Natan the Minotaur and Dr. Isaac with his funny, white-rimmed beard. They clamored for stories they had heard a dozen times.

"But what's taking Sarah so long to bring Julie down?" Joshua asked. "I want to see my niece!"

"She's a little doll," Rebekah said, looking more like her father than ever. "She likes my mother to tell her all about Daddy. She's crazy about my father."

Seth, as dark and exuberant as Sarah, agreed. "We taught her to talk—and it wasn't easy either, let me tell you!"

Naomi laughed with Joshua. "You sound just like your mother, Seth. Even Julie says so. But here they are now—come on, darling, say hello to your uncle Josh."

Julie left Sarah in the doorway and ran first to her father. Arnold picked her up, feeling her little arms around his neck like soothing ribbons of love, love that was unalterably and completely his. She smelled deliciously of baby soap and talcum. Her hair, the same red-gold as Naomi's, had been shampooed that afternoon and hung in long curls around her face, held at the temples by two silver barettes. She was dressed in a miniature

---

hostess gown of taffeta, the same color as Naomi's. Her face was Naomi's face, but *she* was Arnold's. He held her for an extra moment before he put her down and turned her toward her uncle.

"There," Rebekah said to him triumphantly. "Didn't I tell you she was a doll?"

"This is Uncle Josh," Seth said. "He tells almost as good stories as my father."

Joshua watched the little girl approach. She studied his face carefully, in the quiet, self-contained way she had with strangers. Then she held out her hand, and Joshua took it gravely.

Sarah came to join them, laughing. "Well, that's all you get for now, Josh. If you mind your manners, you might get a kiss by bedtime." She knelt to hug her niece again. "I'm glad you know *me*, Julie," she said. "I wouldn't like to get a once-over like that."

"Darling," Naomi coaxed gently, "can't you say something to your uncle Josh?"

Julie put her hands behind her back and shook her head.

"Never mind," Josh told her. "It's a treat just to look at you. The last picture of all of you in *Vogue* didn't do her justice," he said to Naomi. The full-page picture of Duchess's president with his beautiful wife and their angelic five-year-old had made the rounds at Giora, where the glamor of Joshua's family was legend. "I have a little boy not much older than you," he said to Julie.

"That's our cousin Benjamin," Seth said. "*His* mother carries a gun."

"Seth, that's not important." Sarah glanced at Arnold apologetically. Arnold didn't want Julie to know anything about guns or danger. He criticized Lazar often and openly for refusing to pretend to his own children that he lived an ordinary life in an ordinary country.

"I think it's time for dinner," Arnold said. "We don't want to keep the children up too late." He looked at Naomi.

"Ready whenever you are." Naomi smiled at him, her face so lovely he wanted to shout at her in front of all them, *Why not for me? Why for him and not for me?* But he had never asked her, and he would not ask her now. That would give the phantom life by clothing it with words.

*   *   *

It was a simple meal, but it seemed to Arnold that it went on forever, that hour faded into endless hour before Sarah and Joshua were finally dressing the children for the ride back to the city while Julie watched, leaning against her father's legs as he sat in his beige leather chair near the fire.

"I'll see you tomorrow," Joshua told Arnold. "My flight's at seven. Naomi—" He turned to her. His hands held her shoulders, his mouth grazed her cheek. He had done the same thing when he first saw her that evening. "Keep up the good work with your refugee committee."

Arnold watched her look up at him, obviously glad of the work they had in common. "I will. You be careful over there—and give me more children."

Arnold flushed at the sound of her voice. It was intimate, suppliant, as if she were asking him to make her more children, literally. He sat silently in his chair, watching, while his chest turned to stone.

Joshua knelt beside Julie. "Good-bye little niece," he said, his hand on her hair, so like Naomi's hair. "I'll think of you when I need to think of something beautiful."

Of course he would think of her. She was the image of Naomi.

Julie studied his face again. Impulsively she put her arms around his neck, her cheek next to his. Then she leaned back against her father.

"I'll go to the garage with you," Naomi offered. "Arnold, will you take Julie up? It's awfully late for her."

They left in a babble of children's voices and good nights. Arnold stood and lifted Julie, cradling her in his arms. "Come on, Princess, it's time for bed."

Julie yawned. "Daddy, why does Uncle Josh have to live so far away to paint?"

"Paint? He's not a painter," Arnold said absently, starting across the drawing room with Julie in his arms.

"He's a painter there," she said sleepily.

He followed the direction of her arm to the Duchess portrait over the fireplace—and stopped walking. The artist's face was half-hidden as he bent to kiss his duchess, his embrace fierce, demanding, hers eager, yielding. Only his profile was visible—

but of course! That profile was Joshua's. And the dark hair, the height, the long, graceful hands, the slim body. The painting Naomi had commissioned out of her own imagination had puzzled Arnold for years. At first he had looked to it as proof that there *was* a chord of passion in his wife if he could only touch it. For years, since Julie, he had been sure that he had. But after watching Naomi tonight the meaning of her famous fantasy painting was obvious to him, as it must have been to her, to Joshua, to Sarah and Lazar, probably even to Rachel—and God alone knew how many others who had seen Joshua after seeing the Duchess ad.

"Arnold?" Naomi had come back through the rear corridor that led to the garage from the house. "You still here? The baby's asleep."

He looked at Naomi. For the first time in his life he hated her for cheating him, as much as he hated his brother for stealing what was his. He hated her for ridiculing him with that portrait. He almost said so, but he was too proud. There was Julie to protect too from the only result of such an accusation after all these years of pretense: divorce. And he could never prove that the meaning of the portrait was what he now knew it to be. He would see it a hundred times a day, and each time it would be a slap in his face.

"Arnold?" Naomi said anxiously. "Are you all right?"

He nodded. Unable to speak, he moved toward the two-story-high entrance hall and the curving staircase to the upper floor, carrying his sleeping daughter.

"I'll be up as soon as I turn out the lights," he heard her say. "Don't wake Julie—we can cheat on the tooth-brushing just this once."

Cheat.

He carried Julie to her room, took off the turquoise dress, and put on her nightgown before he tucked the sleeping child into her canopied bed and opened the window. She had been more than precious to him from the moment he saw her. Now she was everything to him—the only creature on earth who loved him without guile or restraint.

He heard Naomi going into her room, moving around, undressing. Suddenly he wanted her—and he wanted to humiliate her in

some way, to take her without the tenderness he had always
shown no matter how ardently he made love to her, to possess
her as his painted brother possessed her, violently, whether she
wanted it or not.

After an evening with her living dream she would certainly not
want it. But she would not say no. She had never said no.

He crossed the hall to her room and opened the door without
knocking.

19

Faded winter sunlight splashed Naomi through the naked trees.
She turned back toward the house, pulling her coat closer
against the crisp air. She was lost in the silence of a small wood
on one corner of the estate, the only noise the sound of her own
footsteps on loamy, fallen leaves and small, snapping twigs.

No matter how she tried, she had no explanation for what drew
Joshua and herself together, so deeply and powerfully that neither
of them needed words to say it was still there. She simply felt
ablaze from within when he was near and like a sculpture of a
woman, as cold as marble, when he was not. It was foolish;
worse, it was illogical because of the love she had for Arnold.
Even if it was another kind of love.

Illogical or not, it was how she felt.

What was it about this wire-thin, wire-tense man, preoccupied
with dangers to his family, his country, himself—what was it in
this man and no other that electrified her so, made her aware of
his body and her own, made her want to touch him, kiss him,
hold him in a way that was frankly erotic but so much more than
that. She wanted to spend hours talking to him, even though she
had no hope of ever really understanding his mind. Just to see
him changed her.

He was older. His wonderful eyes, avoiding hers so carefully, were couched in fine lines of age and worry. It didn't matter. His wonderful mouth spoke only of his wife, his son, his country. It didn't matter. Naomi had never seen him as another woman's husband, another child's father. To her he was still the man she loved fiercely for reasons that were still as mysterious to her as they had been at the start.

Such things shouldn't happen to ordinary people like herself. Hopeless lovers lived in books and operas, not in real life. In real life people stopped yearning for what they couldn't have, shouldn't want, mustn't risk. Or so she had believed.

Now she thought that ordinary mortals were behind those legends of desire and tragic fulfillment. They became extraordinary only because they chose to gamble, with their own lives and others'. None of them loved any more than she did, would have felt any more remorse than she would. They were different only because they took risks and accepted consequences. It was as simple as that. People were made of the same basic material; it was what they did with it that made them different.

But there had to be two who would take the risk. She knew now that Joshua never would—not for love of her or anyone else. It was only for something bigger that he would risk everything.

He had always said his life was a new Israel. Their love for each other was secondary. He was a man to whom love of home, child, woman—herself or any other—would always be secondary. That was what she had not understood. He had not measured her against his life's work and found her less desirable than it. It was a thing apart, and he took into his life only what contributed to the ultimate achievement of his goal. The girl she was had been unprepared to help him toward a dream, to which she was secondary; she wondered if she would be prepared to help him even now, given the conditions of life with him, both material and emotional. And so she had hurried into marriage to prove to herself that someone wanted her.

Anyone who loved Joshua could expect only a half-love in return. She had just realized how painful that was to endure. Now, suddenly, she thought that Arnold had endured it throughout their marriage.

She stopped at the edge of the wood, and a deep compassion for her husband overwhelmed her, a realization of how it would have been for him if he'd known the truth. That was how it was for her now: wanting someone who was possessed by a dream. Fighting a dream was a sad battle, no matter how much one loved the dreamer.

She walked on, knowing that life for her would never be the same. Awareness and compassion shaped a woman as much as love and sorrow, as much as jealousy and triumph. Perhaps more, since awareness and compassion concerned others beside herself.

From the bottom of the long lawn that sloped up to the house from the water, she saw Arnold's car pull into the drive. He sometimes came home this early in the day to see Julie if he had to stay in the city late that night.

She thought about last night. How long ago it seemed since she had been in the same room with Joshua once more, since she had felt it again, that reaching between the two of them that had burst into life so suddenly years ago and would never be satisfied—and never go away.

Last night.

How unlike Arnold to come storming into her room and her thoughts like that last night, silently insisting on taking her to bed as if it were some ritual that could not wait another moment, making love with a demanding violence that surprised her as much as it helped to satisfy the desires Joshua aroused, then leaving her immediately afterward, when he always spent the night with her after sex. She had put it aside, thinking of nothing but Joshua while it was going on and for most of the sleepless night that followed.

Now she realized, with that new awareness that illuminated so many things, that Arnold had been *punishing* her, asserting himself, that Arnold knew exactly what her feelings for his brother were, that he had always known!

She stopped again on the driveway near his car, apprehensive, confused. All these years—and he had never said it, never. All at once she was angry that he had never said it. Then remorseful for having withheld from him what he wanted as desperately as she wanted Joshua. For all these years he had had only an echo from her. If he had only said it, she might have realized sooner how much she was hurting him. Or she might have gone to Joshua before her wedding, before there were Rachel and Benjamin and Julie to stop her. She had lied to herself when she married Arnold; she could never have lied to him.

They were equally guilty then, she for not telling, he for not demanding to be told. They had both accepted less of life than they wanted. Now all they had left was each other.

She went quickly through the entrance hall and up the stairs, hearing voices from the playroom. She could see him and Julie even before she reached the landing, watching their daughter with the same look on his face that had always been there for Naomi. She composed herself. Julie mustn't see how upset she was. But there was so much she had to say to Arnold that had never been said, that needed to be said. She had to tell him how much she had never known before, how, suddenly, she had grown up.

He turned. His eyes were cold. The glow of adoration had faded from his face.

"You're home early," she managed to say, uneasy at the way he looked.

"Yes, to see Julie. I have to go back to the city to see my brother off—and there's a meeting that can't wait." He turned back to help Julie arrange a room in her doll's house with the new pieces he had brought her. "It'll be too late to come home, so I'll stay in the city tonight."

See Julie. See "my brother" off. Stay in the city. It was something they often did—but together.

He was unapproachable. For the first time since they had known each other as children, he was cold and forbidding to Naomi.

She went to kiss Julie, holding the child close, a tie and a shield between them. Arnold had always told her the details of his business—she could talk about that.

"What's the meeting about?" she asked over Julie's head.

"A lot of complicated things," he said vaguely, getting to his feet. "Come and kiss me, Princess," he said to Julie. "What shall I bring you tomorrow?"

Julie ran to him, and he lifted her, listening to her little-girl needs as if she were one of his vice presidents. When he put the child down, there was an awkward silence. Then he kissed Naomi briefly on the cheek, as he would have kissed a lady acquaintance at a charity ball. "I'll see you tomorrow," he said.

How could she talk to him now? He was as closed, as forbidding, as an angry god. She could not reproach him for years of silence—not when the answer to his inevitable question, "Do you still love Joshua?" was yes.

He would be deaf to the fact that she loved him too. He would never accept that there were different kinds of love and she could not give him the kind he wanted. It had nothing to do with the way he was, nothing to do with Joshua. It had to do with Naomi herself.

She watched him go, hardly hearing Julie's prattle. Something irretrievable had been lost between them, something she had never been aware of until it was gone.

Arnold went down the stairs, knowing he would turn back if she called him. But there was no call. He got into his car and went down the drive and through the gates. He would see his brother off, and then he would go to spend the night with Annalise Becker. Annalise had lost everything when she fled Europe six years before. She had no one else, and she wanted him. He simply had to be with a woman who wanted only him.

20

NEW YORK
SEPTEMBER 1941

The men stood when Arnold came into the conference room. Naomi's brothers, Simon and David Held, nodded without speaking. Neither of them knew how to address Arnold, although they had been working for him for more than ten years. Surely not as "Arnold"; and "Mr. Fursten" seemed ridiculous for a brother-in-law. They were more uncomfortable with him lately; he had changed so much over the past year. They knew they were doing a good job, because Arnold never kept anyone who didn't—and lately never praised anyone who did. Simon, in production, and David, in sales, had different personalities when Arnold was around, along with a lot of other people.

Ellis Trent, the only non-Jewish vice president of the company, called Arnold "Mr. Fursten." He had advised Duchess since the government had begun tightening its control on the cosmetics industry. Arnold had brought Trent away from the legal firm which had represented Duchess until three years ago, and created his own legal department with Trent as its head.

"With the Federal Trade Commission breathing down our necks, we need constant legal advice to stay out of trouble," Arnold reasoned. And with Trent's guidance they had kept out of trouble.

Arnold didn't really like Trent. "Too smooth," he told Sarah. "You never know what he's thinking behind that smooth expression. But he does the job, and that's all I care about."

Such confidences were kept for his sister, his chief chemist, Otto Einhorn, and his advertising director, Joseph Morgen, who had dropped the *stern* from his name when Arnold bought him away from Arden. Arnold liked Joe Morgen. Both men had started as clerks at Arden. His devotion to Arnold was a joke in the industry but a joke that stayed outside the bronze doors of the Duchess building on Park Avenue. Arnold was too important now for anyone to risk making jokes about him. He was too short-tempered as well.

Arnold looked around the paneled conference room for Einhorn.

"He'll be a little late," Simon Held said, interpreting his brother-in-law's questioning glance. Simon was supposed to know where every important man at Duchess was at any given moment. "He said he had some important test going that would take another ten minutes."

Arnold nodded briefly. "Anyone like some coffee while we wait?"

They all moved to the sideboard, where tea and coffee were set out in thermos jugs. There was never any alcohol served at Duchess executive meetings. The men who ran Duchess—Simon and David Held, Ellis Trent, Joseph Morgen, and Otto Einhorn—deferred to the man who, with his sister Sarah, owned the company. That included respecting his aversion to dirty talk and his demand for "precision, punctuality, and enthusiasm in your work." He expected his executives' lives to belong to the company as totally as his did.

Simon and David Held had accepted, however uncomfortably, the change in Arnold. He had never been an easy man to know.

They decided his new severity was a hardening of traits that had always been present in his personality, traits reinforced by his success, his power in the industry.

Sarah had different ideas about the change in Arnold, but she kept them to herself, as she did her other observations about his relationship with Naomi. Even Lazar knew nothing of Arnold's precarious marriage to a woman he still adored, no matter how bitterly he resented her, no matter what he did to find comfort elsewhere.

It was a worry to Sarah. Arnold was discreet about his affair; but it troubled her to see the grim, set lines his face wore now and to know how unhappy her brother was. Lazar's safety was a greater worry. She knew that whenever he wasn't in Palestine, he and Maresh were with the few thousand Jews who had escaped to Russian-occupied Poland. Stories were coming out of Europe, not only of Nazi horrors too infamous to be believed but of ragged bands of Jewish partisans, wild as mountain lions and as much pursued by Jew-hating Poles as by Jew-murdering Germans. She and Lazar had been together only a dozen times in the three years since her last trip to Palestine, and the moments she'd had with him were too precious to be wasted on anyone but themselves and their children—not even on people Sarah loved as much as Arnold and Naomi. She had withdrawn to her own preoccupations, letting Arnold run the company as he wished, no matter what his demands on his executives.

"But he pays well for it," Joseph Morgen had defended him to Ellis Trent on one occasion.

"He has to," Trent had replied, enigmatically as usual, leaving Morgen to wonder exactly what he meant. As far as Joe knew, Arnold tolerated no shady practices. Morgen decided that Trent was talking about Fursten's personality, which had changed a lot in the past year or so. A cold man, Arnold Fursten. Even his anger—always provoked by inefficiency or failure to keep two steps ahead of competitors—was cold. As for the woman chemist who was supposed to be Arnold's mistress, Joe had seen him with her in the lab a number of times, and he was as distant with her as with anyone else. If he had any feeling for her at all, he reserved it for the bedroom, wherever that was. No one knew for sure.

"Anything new?" Arnold said to Trent, adding a slice of

lemon to his tea. He liked Earl Grey in the afternoon and Twining's Breakfast Tea in the morning; his personal steward made sure he was never offered anything else.

Trent shook his head. "Not for the moment. They're resting on their laurels after the Food, Drug, and Cosmetics Act—and people are wondering when we'll get into the war. Not much time to think about beauty."

Arnold smiled thinly. "They'll think about it once we *are* in the war—you can make book on it. When there's trouble—depression, war—they think about it. In the meantime we'll be branching out."

"Branching out?" Joe Morgen repeated, stirring his coffee. "I thought you decided to sit tight until we absorbed the expense of new labeling after that damned law."

"It's taken a fortune to reformulate and relabel all our stock," Simon agreed, surprised that Arnold was thinking of expansion after the trouble Duchess had just been through to conform to the new regulations.

Arnold said nothing. He would make the announcement in his own good time. His thin smile broadened when Otto Einhorn came into the room, his white smock flying, his wiry hair gray-streaked and disheveled. He was the only person at Duchess permitted such latitude in dress and appearance. But since Einhorn had no idea he was enjoying special treatment, none of the others resented the place he held in Arnold's little kingdom. They admired the man for his chemical wizardry, and they liked him for the way he stood up to Arnold, all the more because standing up to Arnold wasn't Einhorn's intention.

"He has no intentions," Sarah had told them all once, while they were waiting in this very room for both Arnold and Otto Einhorn. "He's a dreamer of sorts, a poet of chemistry. He lives in a world of his own, and he's totally unaware of anything outside his formulas and his test tubes."

Sarah followed behind the chemist now. At thirty she was as ebullient as ever, although there were signs of strain around her eyes, and her hands moved nervously. She was a beautiful woman. Her tall figure was perfect for the Adrian original she wore, a wide-shouldered, belted black silk dress, splashed with sad-faced surrealist lions. A wide-brimmed hat, it narrow, high crown trimmed with black ruffled netting, was tilted forward on her head. She carried elbow-length black gloves. The men admired her silently. Her brother had not asked where Sarah was. Sarah's whereabouts were not for public discussion—any more than Arnold's were.

"Sorry we're late, fellows," Sarah said. "Otto got caught up in ammoniated mercury."

"Sit down, sit down," Arnold said, pulling a chair out for Sarah. "Unless you want some coffee?" She shook her head. "What about ammoniated mercury?" he asked Otto.

Einhorn, at the sideboard, had already poured coffee and added heavy cream and sugar. He rummaged in a cabinet for his favorite "biscuits"—a ginger cracker Arnold imported from Vienna for him, now via Brazil—and sat down at the table with a cup—no saucer—and a handful of cookies, nodding to everyone at the table.

"It's dangerous," Einhorn said, popping a ginger cookie into his mouth. "You have to stop making Pale Hands." A few crumbs fell on the polished mahogany table.

"Stop making Pale Hands?" Simon objected, his dark brows curled into a frown. "It's the most effective bleach cream on the market."

"And one of our best sellers too," David put in.

Einhorn repeated, "It's dangerous. You have to pull if off."

Arnold put up a hand, silencing his production and sales men—he had never thought of them as brothers-in-law. "What harm can it do?" he asked Einhorn.

Einhorn put his cup down on the gleaming table, and Arnold forced himself not to flinch at the ring of moisture it would make. Sarah smiled faintly at the scenario; Arnold controlling his imperious nature for a greater cause always amused her.

"Depending on the quantity, it could cause anything from skin discoloration—which is what we sell it for—to death," Einhorn said.

"What quantity?" Ellis Trent demanded.

"Of course! We'll just reduce it below the danger level. It'll take a little longer to fade skin spots," Arnold said. "That's no problem."

"Oh, yes, it is. You would have still to test every woman who buys every jar, because the danger level is for every woman different." Einhorn's English syntax still lapsed occasionally. He munched his cookies, sweeping the crumbs onto the thick, sculptured, moss-green carpet. "Pull it off the line. Today." He picked up his cup, noticed the stain, and rubbed at it with the tail of his smock, adding to the spots, looking apologetically at Arnold. He was apologizing, they all knew, for the dangerous cream, not for the ring on the table.

There was a momentary silence. Then Arnold shrugged. "Pull it off," he said. "Joe, do a press release. Say that Duchess doesn't wait for government restrictions, that we always test our own products, and we are voluntarily withdrawing this one because of its potential risk. The other companies will have no choice but to follow suit, but we'll be the first, and we'll profit from the publicity. Otto will find some use for all the stock and returns. Agreed?" It was a rhetorical question, and he barely paused for a reply. "Anything else?"

"We're still not getting the same quality floral absolutes from our own domestic crop as we got from the imports," Simon said. "They're going to try different fertilizers, but if that doesn't work, our import stock will be exhausted before 1941 is over—and who knows what we'll get from anywhere abroad if we get into the war."

"Maresh could have improved the quality," Arnold said pointedly, glancing at Sarah.

She answered him sharply. "Even Maresh would need time. It takes eighteen years for an orange tree to mature."

"Well, we haven't got time," Arnold said more quietly. He was not about to quarrel with his sister, and she seemed more nervous than usual today. Sarah's temper rarely surfaced, but when it did, it was titanic. "Anything you can do?" he asked Einhorn.

"I think so," Otto said. "Don't forget, some of the greatest perfumes are mostly synthetics. I have some ideas in mind about changing the layer blending—reversing the order, even the fixatives, to get more out of the essential oils. The trace elements also we have neglected, even with NMR spectometry . . ."

"Don't get technical, Otto dear," Sarah protested. "Just tell us if you can or if you can't."

Otto nodded. "I think yes."

Arnold sat back. If Otto thought yes, it was a virtual certainty. "How long?" he asked.

"In a month or two."

"Time enough?" Arnold asked Simon. The chunky, dark-haired young man who so resembled his father, Martin Held, agreed. "Then," Arnold went on, "if there's nothing further today . . . I wanted you all to know we've gone into pharmaceuticals."

They absorbed this quietly. It was Joe Morgen who spoke first. "That's a good move with a war on—but where in hell will you find the plant you need? Every pharmaceutical company in the country has doubled in value already. It'd cost a fortune to buy even the smallest factory, and if there's war, there'll be no building material available."

"Unless . . . ." Sarah began, looking from her brother to Otto and Ellis Trent.

Arnold nodded. His sister was a smart woman. "Exactly. Unless we had already bought some factories—and converted part of our own." He leaned forward in his enthusiasm. "The equipment is very similar. We already produce under controlled conditions of quantity and mix. Otto assured me it's easy enough to make the conditions sterile. We'll just stick to substances most like our own: salves, antiseptics, powders, all of that. And we've been buying up small factories and taking over companies for some time now."

"Good for you!" Sarah said. "Why didn't you tell me?"

"You've been away more than you've been home." Again the hint of reproach in his voice. "In the meantime Trent's been busy—and not only in expanding plant. He's been lining up government connections for the contract awards."

Ellis Trent smiled. "All it takes is money in the right places."

"Almost always," Sarah said. "Arnold, I'm proud of you. When we get into this war, I'll feel better if we're producing medicines, giving more to the battle than morale boosters."

"And I also," Otto said, "as long as we sell to the right side."

"As long as we sell, does it matter?" Trent observed.

"You bet your ass it matters," Sarah said hotly, while Arnold winced at her language. "You know damned well this country is going in with the Allies. Any sales to the Axis would be treasonable offenses."

"You'd be surprised how much business will be done between

companies on opposite sides of the battle,'' Ellis said, unperturbed. ''Don't believe all the propaganda governments spread around in a war. Materiel—pharmaceuticals included—will go where the bid is highest, directly or indirectly.''

All eyes turned to Arnold. Einhorn leaned forward, waiting. ''No,'' Arnold said, brushing their fears aside. ''This company will never sell to the Axis.''

''Or to any neutral country that might supply the Axis, no matter what the profit?'' Sarah said, challenging her brother to close any such possibility once and for all.

''Of course not!'' Arnold said, amazed at his sister's inference. ''Do you suppose my sympathies are with the Germans?''

''Mine are with the Jews,'' Einhorn said. ''I make nothing— not perfumes, not medicines—that does not fight my enemies.''

''You have my word, Otto,'' Arnold said, staring down Sarah's suspicions. ''There was never any question. Now let's get down to cases.''

They began to discuss the new project, deciding which of their factories would be converted if they were awarded the contracts they had bid on, channeling various phases of responsibility to different department heads.

''Hire women,'' Sarah said when they discussed extra personnel. ''The men will be drafted.''

They considered the pros and cons of publicizing the company's new venture. Arnold and Joe Morgen were in favor, Ellis Trent against. ''We might have to do it later,'' he said. Arnold conceded.

They divided operations between subsidiary sales and production men under Simon and David. The groundwork had already been laid by Arnold and Ellis Trent; the details were a group effort.

The meeting broke up when Arnold looked at his watch. ''We have to go,'' he said to Sarah and the two Held brothers. ''Julie's party is at six, and we have to pick up the wives and kids. We'll go on with this in a few days,'' he said to the others. ''But with a pharmaceutical cushion Duchess has nothing to worry about, war or not.''

''That man's so damned smart,'' Joe Morgen said when the four members of the Fursten family had left after brief good-byes to the others. "And he's still not going to miss his kid's sixth birthday party." He shook his head in silent admiration.

Trent shrugged. "Anyone could see that drugs were the obvious alternative, the obvious collateral line."

"Yes, but he saw it years ago. And look how he's taking the bleach-cream catastrophe and turning it to our advantage." He turned to Otto. "You have to admit that medical supplies are patriotic."

Einhorn looked troubled. "Smart he is," he acknowledged softly. "Patriotic I am not so sure. Maybe he doesn't do this for the war. Maybe he does it only for the company."

Joe got up, still beaming. "What's it matter why he does it? The result's the same. Well, it's late. I have a press release to prepare on Pale Hands and a meeting with the agency boys to set up. See you."

He went out, leaving the two men, one fashionably tailored and calm, the other agitated and unkempt, in silence at the large table. They looked at each other.

"It is really true," Einhorn said, "that a company could sell goods to the enemy in a war?"

"Happens all the time," Trent said. He found Einhorn offensive in many ways, no matter how good a chemist he was.

"Not with this company. He gave his word."

Trent was silent.

"He gave me his word!" Einhorn insisted.

"Then we must suppose he'll keep it," Trent said lightly, as if he were humoring the chemist. "There'll be enough money in government contracts. He won't even be tempted to break his promise." He gathered his papers. "So it doesn't matter."

"It matters," Einhorn said. "To him it will matter. Even to you it will." He went out, leaving Trent by himself in the fading September light.

Very soon it would matter to all of them. Very much.

LONDON
NEW YEAR'S EVE 1942

London was boisterous, rowdy, living on its nerves. Years later the survivors would say the war had been an adventure without parallel, a time of excitement and camaraderie. Ashamed of themselves, they would confess that it was the high point of their lives.

Lazar Kramer and Maresh Skowalski sat together in a pub on Baker Street, not far from where the ingenious Sherlock Holmes was said to have lodged. Stubborn, frightened London was celebrating the onset of 1943 with the lunatic gaiety of war.

The war had gone badly. America's entry a year ago had given the Allies heart; what they needed was power to hold back a tidal wave of German victories. Europe was Hitler's playground, the scene of fiendish games. Most of Russia seemed ready to follow the fate of Stalingrad—unless the tide had turned and the Red Army's incredible offensive succeeded. The German army had occupied the entire Crimea since the fall of Sevastopol in July. In Africa, Rommel had taken Tobruk and broken through into Egypt as far as El Alamein; Montgomery had only just forced him to retreat last month.

In Palestine the Haganah worked openly to help the British, even though British immigration policy for the tortured Jews of Europe had not changed. A group of Jewish extremists hardened their position; they would never forget that Palestine stayed closed while the gates of Auschwitz yawned open. But for the moment there was no question of the Yishuv's loyalty to Britain.

The world began to think there might be some truth in all the stories coming out of Nazi Europe, particularly when reports of a conference at Wannsee, specifically called to design a "final solution of the Jewish question," emerged. Someone ought to rescue Hitler's victims, the world said, before it was too late.

There were no volunteers. Some would accept only experienced agricultural workers—and the Jews of Europe had long been forbidden to own or work land. One country wanted only baptized immigrants. Three other countries said merchants and intellectuals were undesirable citizens.

There would be offers from a Nazi named Adolf Eichmann to sell Jews for money or barter them for drugs and other war materiel, but the flesh trade would never take place.

The civilized nations would shudder later over film footage of the death camps, would piously participate in the war-crimes trials at Nuremberg when the massacre was ended. At present they left the Jews to their fate.

From Palestine, the only place where a part of the populace wanted Jews, would come Palmach commandos, flown to Europe to organize resistance and escape. Most of them would die. In London, Charles de Gaulle now led the Free French and plagued the British for more authority; Churchill would say later that of all the crosses he had to bear, the Cross of Lorraine was the most difficult. In London there were escaped fighters from Belgium, Denmark, Holland, Norway. And in London the Polish government's Interior Minister was Stanislaus Mikolajczyk. It was to this headquarters that Lazar Kramer and Maresh Skowalski were loosely attached.

The pub this New Year's Eve was thick with smoke. The talk and the laughter were deafening, but Lazar and Maresh sat quietly over two pints of ale, watching the door, waiting.

There was a resemblance between them. Both were well above average height, although Maresh was by far the broader, his powerful body oddly at variance with the gentle, anxious expression on his square face. Lazar's hair, bleached by years of Palestine sun, had a lot of natural white in it now; his eyes were a deeper blue than Maresh's but as penetrating, as watchful. He moved his well-muscled body with trained ease but quietly. They were different, yet their attitudes were alike, a kind of constant wariness. Out of habit both of them knew how many men were on either side of them, where the exits were, how they could get out quickly in case of emergency. They spent a lot of time on the Continent, every moment of it dangerous.

Their faces, weatherworn and strained, broke into smiles when Joshua pushed his way into the door of the pub. He wore a

United States Army uniform now, in place of the Red Cross uniform he'd used until December 1941 to work with the underground in Poland. There were captain's bars on the shoulders of his jacket. There was a "U.S." insignia on one lapel, a Star of David on the other. His dark hair, when he took off his hat, was heavily streaked with gray. The gray was more apparent on him than on blonds like Lazar and Maresh—but his smile mirrored theirs as he pushed his way to their table. The three men held one another in a boyish embrace.

"How much time you got?" Maresh asked.

"An hour."

"You made it!" Lazar shouted. "We were beginning to give you up."

"Not me," Maresh insisted. "He never broke his word to me from the time we were five years old." He started toward the bar. "I'll get the drinks. What'll it be, Josh?"

"Same as you." Joshua sat down next to his brother-in-law and studied him carefully. "You look in pretty good condition. I have to report to Sarah, you see." His face became more serious. "Is it true—that you and Maresh have been going in and out of Poland like tourists?"

Lazar nodded, his face reflecting Joshua's. "The sights we see aren't in any guidebook, though. Thanks, Maresh." He helped the big man set the mugs of ale down.

"How many Jewish partisans are there in the Polish countryside?" Joshua asked, taking a deep swallow of his ale.

"About one thousand," Maresh said.

"Can they help sabotage the deportations from the Warsaw Ghetto—the rail lines to Auschwitz—anything?"

Lazar shook his head. "They do what they can, but their main interest is in staying alive until it's over. I don't like to shock you, Josh, but funny things happen to hunted men who live like animals." He glanced at Maresh, who looked glum.

"Tell me, Lazar. What's been happening to them?"

Lazar told him. The roving bands of Jews who had escaped to the hills fared badly. It was a question of survival. "You can't be noble when it is a matter of survival." Lazar avoided Joshua's eyes.

"Go on," Joshua said, sensing something wrong.

"The partisans won't risk the Ghetto or the Auschwitz railways. But there are a few men already organizing a stand before every Jew in Warsaw is murdered.''

"Mordechai Anilewicz," Joshua said. "I've heard."

"And a few others," Maresh added. "Itzhak Zuckerman. Szymon Gotesman."

"And you!" Joshua said in alarm, understanding suddenly. "You two are going in yourselves! But you'll never get out."

"We'll get out," Maresh said. "Lazar looks and talks as Polish as I do, and I've been in and out a lot." The Polish underground got them in easily enough. Finding the papers to get them out was often a problem. Up to now they had been lucky.

"Listen, Josh," Lazar said. "There's no choice. The ones left inside have plenty of spirit. What they need is something to fight with and someone to lead the fighter groups."

"But what good will it do?" Joshua protested. "There's no way in the world you can keep the Ghetto from falling once the Germans decide to level it!"

"Agreed." Lazar nodded. "But we can get a few more people out. And we can fight! It's worth the risk." He looked at Maresh, then at Joshua. "Isn't it?" It was a serious question. He waited for an answer.

Joshua regarded both men more intently. There was something very wrong, a pervasive sense of doubt he had never known before in either of them. He was beginning to see it more and more in men who had witnessed brutality and cruelty even beyond the cruelty of war. It was seeing the depths to which humanity could sink that made them wonder if they should risk their own lives to save others'—or even to fight the Germans.

"You sound as if you want to be convinced. Why?"

Lazar and Maresh were tense, their heads down.

Joshua's mind reversed to that moment when he'd first sensed something amiss. "Tell me about the partisans—the ones who have to survive."

Lazar's shoulders dropped. His voice was low. "They're wild, like savages." His blue eyes met Joshua's, pleading, excusing. "They can't help it, Josh. They have to steal every scrap they eat. They dress in rags, pieces of moldy blanket, German uniforms they steal from the dead—some from the men they kill themselves." He stopped pleading. He just talked. "Last month eighteen of them gang-raped one of the women—I don't know why. One of our own women, a partisan, a Jewish woman! We tried to stop it, Maresh and I. But the ones who weren't doing it held us back, as if they were used to it. When it was over, the woman didn't seem to care either. She stuffed a rag into her underwear, picked up her rifle, and walked on.'' He shook his head. ''I couldn't believe it. They *know* what's happening to girls in the camps—and they're doing it too.''

''But there's worse,'' Maresh said, as if Lazar had opened up a dam of images for him. ''Something I can't understand. I'll never understand it.'' He took a deep breath. ''There's a small camp, not a death camp, an officers' rest camp where they keep the pretty young Jewish girls. It wasn't too hard for us to pick off the guards—there weren't many. It's right near a town, and they never expected us to get so close. We opened the building where the girls were locked up.'' He looked at Joshua, perplexed. ''They were all naked, just sitting on their beds. It was warm there, but there wasn't a stitch of clothing in the place.

''They were all tattooed, here.'' His hand crossed his massive chest. ''In German. It said 'Field Whore.' We told them to hurry, to get out before a German patrol came by, to come with us. We took off our jackets so they'd have something to wear. They were so young, some younger than my own daughters.'' He shook his head as Lazar had done.

''They wouldn't come with us, Josh. They wanted to stay where they were. They said the Germans would know the partisans killed the guards, not them. They said it was warm there, they had food to eat, they would have a better chance to survive where they were than with us.'' His face was a study in bewilderment, begging for an explanation. ''I couldn't blame them. The woman who'd been raped was with us. When the girls told us to get out and leave them where they were, that woman laughed. I never heard a woman laugh like that. It was terrible.''

The three men were silent for a time. When he spoke, Lazar's face was rigid. ''Ari said it once, at Giora, remember Joshua? We're not saints, we're not noble. We're just like them—animals, just like them.''

''No!'' Maresh hit the table with his fist. ''We're *not* like them! In the whole history of the world there hasn't been anyone like them. I don't know who your Ari is, Lazar, but he's wrong.

I don't understand any of it, but I know he's wrong. Nobody has ever done what they're doing. Never!''

Lazar put his hand on Joshua's. "But are they still worth fighting for, Josh, our people in the Ghetto?" He did not sound as sure as Maresh. "Are *we*—if we have it in us to be like that too?"

Joshua gripped the hand. All his life he had believed that human nature could be molded into goodness or its opposite. All his life he had believed in the justice of a good cause. But if he convinced these men, he would be risking two lives that were dear to him to try saving a few he would never know. And was he right? If a man like Lazar Kramer could doubt his whole life, was Joshua right?

"I can't answer for you," he said after he had thought a long time. "I can only tell you what I believe for myself. Yes, they're still worth fighting for, because civilization is worth the fight, and men are the vessels of civilization. The partisans who rape, the girls who preferred to stay where they were, even the millions who go meekly to their own destruction—that's what happens without civilization. When you see what happens to ordinary people without it . . ." He sat back in his chair. "Even if people have been brutalized too horribly to be worth saving, we have to save *it*." He looked at each of them. "For its own sake, if not our own, we have to save it. That's how I feel."

Maresh nodded, breathing deeply. "I knew you'd be able to tell us. Lazar, I always told you Joshua explains things."

Lazar's face looked less rigid. "Things get out of focus unless you see both sides, like the Rabbi. I guess we can't let Josh's civilization go down the drain because its only keepers have been driven mad. But I sometimes wish we could teach the animals to play music and read books. Our accomplishments would be safer with them."

"Does that mean you're going into the Ghetto?" Joshua asked.

Lazar nodded. "I'd have gone anyway—but I wouldn't have known why."

The three men sat drinking the tepid ale the English favored. Soon they talked of home and friends, wives and children. It might have been any other city in any other year; but it was London, it was almost 1943—and then it was time for them to leave.

"Hey, rabbi!" One of the men at the bar spotted Joshua's insignia as the three crowded toward the door. "How about a blessing for *our* New Year?"

Joshua smiled. "Okay. I'll give you one you may not understand, but it can't fail."

The group within hearing distance of him fell quiet, waiting. Joshua's eyes traveled over their faces, and he said something in an unfamiliar language. Then he smiled again. "That'll get you through—I guarantee it."

The men relaxed, loud and happy once more, calling out good-byes as the three friends left the pub. Outside they looked at one another. Joshua put his arms around them, repeating what he had said in the pub. Then he said, "Take care of each other," turned, and walked rapidly away from them into the damp, cold new year, shrugging into his greatcoat, his eyes blurred with tears, afraid he would never see either of them again. Only a miracle could get them out of the Warsaw Ghetto. Like most people, Joshua only relied on miracles; he didn't believe in them.

"That was Hebrew, what he said, wasn't it?" Maresh wanted to know after Joshua was out of sight.

"No, it was Arabic—I think it's an ancient Egyptian blessing." Lazar thought for a moment, trying to get it exactly right. Then he said, "May God be between you and harm in all the lonely places you must walk."

22

WARSAW
MAY 1943

Maresh stood with a group of men just outside the wall that separated the Ghetto from the rest of Warsaw. His hands were knotted inside the pockets of his shabby jacket, and he felt cold, although Maresh was seldom aware of the weather, except for his crops, no matter what the season.

Acrid smoke hung over the Ghetto and—no respecter of walls—

for blocks around it. Maresh was glad of that; it covered the strong smell of the cheese he had hung around his waist and his knees under the baggy clothes. The cheese and one small loaf of bread was all he had been able to bring with him this time. It wasn't much—but then, there was no way of knowing how many of them were left in there. They were fewer each time he went in.

A roar of laughter from the men around him shook his attention away from where he was going, and he laughed along with them. The one thing he mustn't do was seem different from the rest of them until he found a chance to get into one of the sewer entrances.

"I'd like more of it myself, wouldn't you?" The man next to him poked Maresh's arm suggestively.

"Don't think I ever had any," Maresh mumbled.

"You don't know what you're missing—it's some of the juiciest. Hey!" the man called to the others. "Here's a fellow never had any Jewish cunt."

They laughed again. One of them stepped closer to Maresh. "Listen," he said. "You wouldn't believe how tight mine was. But she was hot! She was hot like a nice roast goose. She fought a little, but I could tell she wanted it. And when I got it in her, she wiggled like an eel on a line—my line." They all laughed again. "She was so tight and she wiggled so much I didn't have to move my ass hardly at all before I came like a rocket."

"A virgin?" One of the men, as big and blond as Maresh, wet his lips.

"How do I know? But she had a tiny little twat, like a pink clam with fuzz on it when they held her legs open for me. I was the first one, and nobody saw any blood until the fourth or fifth."

Maresh felt his pants begin to bulge in spite of himself. It had been a long time since he'd had a woman. "Where did you find her?"

The man, smaller and not as fair as the lip-wetter, hooked his thumbs into his belt. "We went inside before they built that." He jerked his head in the direction of the wall. "Looked in the windows until we saw one we wanted. She had tits like big snowballs! We got in the pantry window after we saw her old man—must've been her father—go out the front. A Friday night it was, you know, when all the men go and do their praying instead of like decent Christians on a Sunday. She was lighting her candles when we jumped her. She got a few more candles that night than she bargained for.''

Maresh kept his lips in a lubricious grin, but the erection their talk had pumped up was gone. He could think of nothing but Manya Fursten on Rivington Street, lighting her candles on a Friday night long ago when his Anna was in labor and he came bursting into their apartment for help. Sarah, standing there with her, had looked up in alarm, but Manya, her eyes covered with one hand while the other held the match, murmured her prayer to complete the ritual before she turned to him.

"Please, Missus," he begged. "It's Anna's time—the baby comes the wrong way. Please!''

"Oh, but she can't go out now, it's Shabbas," Sarah began. She was only a child then, twelve or thirteen, but already a beautiful girl.

"Sha!" the mother commanded, and then to Maresh, in Polish. "The pains come closer together?''

"Yes, Missus, please," Maresh panted, frightened out of his wits. His Anna was all he had left of the old country, and if this baby was a boy, after two girls . . .

"All right, I'm coming," Manya said. She spoke a few words to Sarah in Yiddish while she collected some things from the big wooden sideboard where they had been standing. Maresh never knew what she said, but Sarah nodded, looking at her mother as though she were seeing her for the first time, putting on her coat while Manya hurried out with Maresh.

She was to hurry many times after that night, for other babies, newborn or ailing, for Maresh himself the winter he had pleurisy. He never understood why Manya, whose strict religious observance was the talk of the neighborhood, would put her piety aside to go to the aid of anyone who needed her. She went once on their holiest day of the year to do what she called a *mitzvah*— a good deed, Joshua told him later. "If enough people do enough of them, it balances the scales for those who don't do any.''

Well, she did enough! His meat she wouldn't buy—it was *trayf*, she said, unclean. And he had to take down the crucifix and the picture of the Holy Mother before she could cross the threshold of his home. But she never refused her help. For that he honored her as he would his own mother.

He respected Arnold, even if he couldn't really talk to him. He worshiped Joshua, whose lessons had helped to change Maresh's life. He would have killed anyone who put a hand on Sarah—like this dirty bastard here. And he had come to love Lazar almost as much as Joshua. Lazar, who was inside the Ghetto waiting for food right now.

He still grinned, but anger burned in his throat as this turd of a man who had raped a young girl like Sarah on a Friday night like that one. And yet his prick had started to swell, listening. Maresh gave his head a mental shake. He couldn't understand these things. They were beyond a plain, simple man. Yet even a simple man looked for an answer. Joshua always answered even his most perplexing questions, better than the priest did. He wondered what Joshua would say to this one! He was afraid he would never find out. Joshua was somewhere with the American forces; there had been no messages from him in months, until today. And who knew how long it had taken the message to get to him—or if Josh was still alive.

The men began to talk about German plans to wipe out the last resistance in the Ghetto that night. Maresh listened carefully. It was no surprise. It would be no surprise to the ones inside. The Germans had only waited so long to take some of them alive for sport, but now they were beginning to feel foolish: a handful of Jewish sheep making an uprising!

"I saw the tanks," the turd said. "It's tonight for sure."

"About time too," Maresh forced himself to say. "Where?"

"On the other side."

"You think we could get a look?" the lip-wetter said.

Maresh held his breath. If only they'd clear out, he'd have his chance to get into a sewer and follow the conduit to the alleyway near Lazar's hiding place. He relaxed when they began to move off, following along with them until he was able to slip away in the descending dusk and retrace his steps. He waited awhile longer until he was sure that no one lurked in the shadows. Then he turned into an alley, lifted a heavy plate from its resting place, and disappeared into the sewer, hardly noticing the stench that came up to claim him. He was used to it by now.

Mechanically he transferred the food packets from waist and

knees to around his neck before he made off into the rank waters of the sewer. He moved quickly, sliding and cursing, sometimes in a half-crouch, sometimes creeping. But there was a faint smile on his lips. He had resolved the problem in his mind: he could laugh with the others about other Jews. Jews were Jews, after all. But the ones he loved, they were *his* Jews, and he was ready to die for them tonight—with them, if he had to. He had no intention of leaving Lazar inside to die when the Germans came in. He would never be able to look Joshua in the face if he did that.

Jesus, how he loved that man! Lazar too, but not as much as Joshua. There was nobody on earth or in heaven above like Joshua. And Joshua had told him to take care of Lazar. . . .

"So where is he tonight?" one of the men said, drawing a grubby sleeve across his forehead before proceeding with his work.

"God knows," Lazar answered. "Probably waiting for a chance to get in. He hasn't failed us yet."

He went on carefully filling bottles with kerosene and passing them to his neighbor, a round little man with sad eyes, who stuffed the bottles with rags. "Look how nice and plump our Mendele keeps on the delicacies Maresh brings."

The third man, much younger than his companions, stacked the bottles in a crate against the bunker wall. "Plump! My uncle was twice this size before the war," he said, wrapping another bottle in rags. "Aunt Yetta will faint when she sees him so thin."

There was a silence. They all had the strange habit of talking about people they knew were dead—had seen shot down or deported to be gassed—as if they were still alive, as if some minor domestic chore or social function had kept those people from joining this bottle party in a filthy coal cellar.

It was years since there had been coal in this cellar. Who had coal to burn in the Ghetto—or anywhere else in Warsaw, for that matter? Who—except the Germans? The cellar door had been obstructed by old furniture, boxes of half-broken crockery and worn clothing, baby carriages, sleds—the kind of debris people once kept in sculleries and cellars before the wall was built and every stick a family possessed became precious again for use or barter. It was then that the man called Mendele had uncovered the coal-shed door—and when Lazar came, he decided it would make a good hiding place for those who were determined to resist to the last, the ones who knew what "resettlement in the East" meant and who were determined to let everyone in the Ghetto know it and to fight to the end rather than surrender, like so many sheep.

Lazar sighed now. Most of them *had* surrendered like sheep, all the same. What had happened to the blood of warriors that once flowed in Jewish veins? The ancient Israelites were fighters when they had to be, farmers when there was peace. Sometimes he despaired, when he was far from the fountain of hope that Palestine was for him, that all the centuries of persecution had bled them dry of any spirit or goal save to survive by blending into their adoptive countries if they could; by living quietly by whatever trade their masters permitted them and clinging to the study of their accursed law to perpetuate a purely religious legend rather than their pride as a nation.

Then he shook his head. No, it wasn't too late. Get their own land back for them, and there would be no more sheep. There *had* to be an Israel after this. The world would have to accept that there was going to be an Israel, even if he himself would not be there to see it. Joshua would see it. Joshua must get through the war and see it. *She* would see it—he could not chance thinking too often of her, it would break him. His own children would see it.

He didn't mind dying. He had been brought up by men who were prepared to die to get what they wanted. There *would* be a Jewish homeland as long as there were men like Joshua and women like Rachel and . . . His mind veered away again from thoughts of Sarah, the only creature on earth who made leaving it a horror of the heart.

He glanced at the fifth member of the group, a woman with features that might have come from a Greek carving or an Egyptian frieze. The planes and angles were sharp in her hungry face; there were dark circles under her enormous, tilted eyes, like pools of dry ink that reflected no light. She could not have been older than his Sarah—his heart tightened again in his chest—but her black hair was marbled with gray, and her skin was pale from years of malnutrition and weeks of hiding in this dark, stuffy hole, where only a small grate at the top of the coal chute gave them ventilation.

She rarely spoke, this woman. No one knew where she came from on the night she joined them with two pistols and a butcher knife. Nobody asked. Her dirty dress was still streaked with the dried blood that had glistened on it when they lit their lantern in this cellar that night. She was cleaning her guns and theirs in silence, as she did each night before they went out to kill Germans.

"So where is he?" the first man said again, dragging the last can of kerosene from the wall.

"Patience, Avram," Lazar said. "He'll be here if he's still alive." He grinned. "You remind me of my brother-in-law, an impatient Avram, although he calls himself Arnold."

Avram looked up from the can he was opening. "I thought you had only one brother-in-law, Joshua the rabbi."

"Well, I also have Arnold the merchant—except sometimes he forgets he's a Jew."

"Hah!" Uncle Mendele snorted. "When trouble comes, everybody remembers who's a Jew."

His nephew looked up, his eyes ablaze. "Someday they'll remember who's a Jew for other reasons. Just you wait . . ." His voice tapered off. There was very little time for them to wait.

Lazar glanced at the woman again, but her face was impassive. No hysterics from her. "Listen, all of you. There won't be much time when Maresh gets here. I want to send him right back out before it's too late . . ."

"Send him out?" Avram objected fiercely. "Send out a Polish jackal? If you send anyone out, send a Jew, save a Jew. There are few enough of us left!"

The others stopped their work, except for the woman. They looked angrily at Lazar, a leader of the Ghetto uprising and a hero to them since its start. It was the first time they had questioned one of his decisions.

"I know how you feel. But even if Maresh weren't a special Pole, a friend from years back, he *is* a Pole and the only one of us with half a chance to survive, to get out of Poland, to tell our friends, our people, what happened here, to make sure the world knows."

"May God damn the world," the nephew whispered. "A lot the world cares."

"It will!" Lazar's body was too tall for him to stand upright when he got up to face them. His flaxen hair was black with coal dust, and his blue eyes were red from smoke. "But someone has to tell them what it was like in here. Someone—preferably not a Jew—has to make sure they all know—our enemies, our friends, our people—that at the end we found our heritage and fought like Israelites!"

His voice had become intense, as compelling in this filthy hole as it had been in bare lecture halls and sumptuous private salons throughout the world.

"Do you realize what it will mean to our beaten people that at last"—his fist hit his thigh for emphasis—"at last we stood on our hind legs and said 'No!' and fought like our ancestors?"

They were quiet, their hostility fading, another kind of anger replacing it.

Lazar went on quietly. "If you have any messages you want Maresh to take out, write them now. This is his last trip—we all know that."

"What messages?" Avram demanded. "To whom? My family's all gone."

"Write to any Jew in the world," Lazar said shortly. "They are your family now. That's all there is and all we need."

For the first time the woman raised her head and looked at him. One eyebrow rose cynically. Then she returned to the one submachine gun, paying no attention as Mendele and his nephew began to write on the precious paper Lazar gave them before he sat down to write himself. Avram shrugged and went on filling bottles.

In the momentary hush a shuffling sound was heard from the other side of the cellar wall separating them from a small, inner court where the sewer opening was. They picked up whatever weapons they had. When the right signal came, they dropped them and began removing the carefully fitted bricks from the alley wall one by one, until the hole was big enough for Maresh's enormous shoulders. They pulled him through without talking. The bricks were replaced before anyone spoke.

"Phew—you stink!" the nephew said.

"No worse than this place." Maresh grinned. He removed his

jacket quickly and passed them the food packets. He dropped his
trousers and untaped rubber-wrapped bullets from his thighs.
That done, he pulled up his pants, buckled his belt, and clasped
Lazar in a bear hug.

"You all right? I have a message from him!" He took another
wrapped envelope taped to his side and handed it to Lazar. Both
of them stooped like cavemen while Mendele held the lantern and
Lazar read as if he were drinking nectar. He looked around the
expectant circle, smiling, holding Joshua's message.

"He's got them! At least six boats and more to come. I told
you, I told you! As soon as the war is over—maybe even before
then if I know my friends—they'll start taking Jews to Palestine,
no matter what the British shits have to say about it." He clasped
Maresh again, and they sat down while Lazar ate with the others.
They all looked at Maresh expectantly.

The big man looked forlorn. "No schnapps. I couldn't get
any, not with all the money Joshua sends me. Water's the best I
could do. I'm sorry." He looked ashamed of himself.

"Never mind," Avram said gruffly. "Water's good enough.
Hand it over."

The simple meal finished, Lazar turned to Maresh. "All right—
what?"

Maresh swallowed hard. "Tonight."

"Where?"

"Near. Two squares over. Tanks—at least a dozen in that
place alone, it looked like."

Lazar patted his arm. "All right. Maresh, you have to get out
now, before it's too late."

Maresh looked at him, then shook his head violently. "You
crazy, Lazar? I'm not leaving you in here to die alone."

"I'm not alone," Lazar said.

"You know what I mean! What would I tell Josh? What would
I say to Sarah and your kids?"

Lazar reached for the notes three of them had written. "Here's
what you'll say." And as the big man shook his head stubbornly:
"Listen, Maresh, Josh is going to need you. They're all going to
need you. He wants you to come out—and there are some things
I've written here he has to know."

"Then come with me," Maresh said. He looked around at the
others. "All of you. I can get you through the sewer and out at

the other end, one at a time. Come with me!'' He turned back to Lazar.

"Even if we got out of the Ghetto, we'd never make it out of Poland.''

"Why not? You all speak Polish! *You* even look Polish.''

"I could look like Pope Pius himself and so could they, but without papers we'd never make it. You know that—we all know it. So don't argue, Maresh, there isn't time. Take these letters and get out, get out of the country. Get to Palestine—you know the routes. After the war, find Joshua. Fight, Maresh. Fight for us.''

Maresh looked blank, his mind strangled by another problem for which he could find no solution. "Joshua,'' he said. "Joshua wants me to leave you and go out?''

Lazar nodded. "He says so—in the letter. It's in Hebrew, or I'd let you read it for yourself.''

Maresh slumped where he sat, his eyes filling with tears as he looked at his friend. "If Joshua says so . . .''

"Come on, then, while there's time.''

They all stood, even the woman, half-hidden in the shadows cast by the lantern.

"You know, Lazar, Joshua once told me his name in Hebrew is Yeshua.''

"Yes,'' Lazar said. "Why do you remember that now?''

"Well, he told me that Yeshua was Jesus's name in Hebrew too.''

Lazar was puzzled but patient, while the others stood transfixed at the strange conversation and the sight of the big Pole, tears running down his cheeks.

"Then maybe,'' Maresh said hesitantly, "if they have the same name, it's okay to love a man as much as God?''

Lazar took his hand. "They say that every soul is a candle of the Lord, Maresh, so I think it's okay.'' He put the letters into Maresh's hand. "Go now—and get these to Joshua.''

Maresh stuffed the letters into the rubber pouch and taped it back to his side. He embraced Lazar, then turned to the others, touching each of them in turn in a kind of dumb farewell before he took away the bricks and went through the wall. They replaced the bricks, blotting him out.

"Poor bastard,'' Avram said. Then he picked up a gun. "Come

on, let's have a look before we take this stuff out. If we can see where they are, we can kill more of the devils before they kill us."

"You go ahead," Lazar said. "I'll finish the rest of these bottles."

"I'll load the guns," the woman said, taking the packet of bullets Maresh had brought in.

The three men went carefully up the wooden steps to the inside door of the coal cellar and cautiously raised it. They disappeared into the scullery of the house they were under, closing the door silently behind them.

Lazar and the woman worked without speaking, the clink of bottles and the soft sound of each bullet clicking into place the only noises in the bunker. From outside an occasional gunshot or the rumble of a heavy vehicle was borne to them on the smoke-filled air.

When the woman had finished, she stacked the guns on a piece of canvas and started folding the leftover rags they had used to stuff the bottles, gathering the empty kerosene cans, picking up the wrappings of the pathetic meal Maresh had brought. Lazar watched her until, aware of his sympathetic attention, she stopped, shrugged her thin shoulders, and went back to her place near the guns.

"The last place you leave is home," she said. Her voice was husky, rusted from disuse. She had been silent for so many days—he couldn't remember how many. "Even a hole like this."

"It's not a hole," Lazar said, his eyes remote. "It's a lovely, sunny room in a small house near a lake—a clean house. There's a soft rug on the floor, and a little spring breeze is making the curtains at the window dance—such white, clean curtains! The air is filled with the smell of spring flowers and lake water, and there are two people in the room who are just content to be there with each other."

"No," the woman said. "It's a fine, clear winter night. The moon is shining on the snow and beyond the mountains—so big and mighty and protecting. There are so many stars, so many! The air is very cold and very dry, like fine champagne, and every breath is intoxicating, every touch is warm even through the fine wool and velvet cape I'm wearing. Our breath comes in clouds that touch in the cold air, like kisses, like promises of more kisses to come . . ."

They looked at each other, not seeing each other; seeing another man, another woman. The air in the bunker was heavy with filth, hunger, and death, but for him it was a gentle spring in Palestine and for her a winter like champagne. For him the dark eyes that looked at him from her sooty face were Sarah's eyes; for her his mouth was a mouth she longed to touch again with her own. It was the lantern playing tricks on their starved imaginations. It was the nearness of death that made them yearn for the fullest expression of life.

They moved nearer to each other until they stood together. Her arms went around him, her eyes closed. He held her with love and regret when he kissed her welcoming mouth. They lay down together on the dirty stones that were a soft rug, that were a velvet cape. The reek of their bodies when they joined was the perfume of snow and spring flowers.

She whispered his name when he moved inside her. "Oh, David, yes, my darling, only you, oh, David, yes." He answered the thrust of her body with his own and whispered against her mouth, "I know, my Sarah, I know, my beautiful love."

They mingled in a last desperate tribute to their loves and to the last they would ever feel or touch or taste of life, and there was no way of knowing whether there were two souls blending in that moment when they both spun into space—or four.

They lay together in silence when it was over, afraid that the slightest movement, the smallest sound, would raise a cloud of black dust to blight their single yet separate visions.

The door from the scullery opened, and steps started descending the stairs. They drew apart hastily in the shadows, arranging their clothing, as Avram came down the stairs with Mendele and the nephew close behind.

Avram handed his gun to Mendele and bent to the heavy case of bottles with the nephew. "Come on," he said. "It'll be too dark in half an hour to count how many we kill."

"How many tanks?" Lazar asked.

"Enough," Avram said. "It's hopeless. We haven't got a chance."

"So what else is new?" Mendele said. "Come on, Nephew, help me shlepp this up the stairs."

"Get my machine gun," the boy said to his uncle.

They all stopped for a moment and looked around the place that had harbored them for their last days.

"The last place that you leave is home," Lazar said, his eyes on the woman, hers meeting his.

"Sure," Avram said. "We could stay in here and be burned alive like the rest of our kind, but in our own private oven if you want to be exclusive. Personally I prefer to die in the street."

"Shut up, Avram," the nephew said. "Move your ass."

The two labored up the stairs with the heavy case. Mendele went next with two revolvers and the submachine gun. The woman followed, carrying a gun and her knife, with Lazar behind her. They went through the house to the front door and out into the street.

As they came to the smoke-filled avenue leading to the German attack point, Lazar reflected that he didn't even know her name, and never would.

He reached for her hand, and they went down the avenue together.

23

SANDS POINT
JULY 1943

Arnold sat alone in front of the fire as he had done every evening for a week. He could hear the children's voices from upstairs. Rebekah cried softly from time to time; Seth talked about his father, little-boy-brave and angry. Julie listened, trying to comfort them both. She had loved her tall, blond uncle Lazar almost as much as her aunt Sarah.

Sarah was upstairs in the room she always used at Sands Point, and at last she let Naomi sit with her. If only Sarah would talk!

Or cry! But she had been silent, even with her own children, since news of Lazar's death had come a week ago.

Arnold held the letter, written in Joshua's spiked script. It was short, it was anguished, it was final. Lazar was dead. The war had come to claim this family as it had claimed so many others.

Arnold's hand brushed his eyes. Lazar was a good man. A crazy kind of man who chose to go blundering around in a desert instead of using that fine mind of his for better things. Arnold could almost see his long, lazy body, always out of place in a formally furnished room; could hear his voice, with its slight appealing accent that made people give him such enormous sums of money. He remembered Lazar's blue eyes, sharp, penetrating, always on Sarah with the kind of love Arnold had never been able to show.

Arnold flinched. He could only hope Sarah had forgiven him for the stupid things his temper had driven him to say a few months ago. Maresh had already deserted him—and now Einhorn was going to war too.

"Einhorn!" Arnold had blustered to Sarah in this very room. "Frightened of his shadow, only happy making fragrances and chemicals. I could have kept him out, he's needed more here, doing an important job. What business has such a person in a war? He couldn't fire a gun if his life depended on it!"

"He'll fire a gun at Nazis," Sarah answered grimly. "He's a Jew. His life does depend on it."

"You believe all that propaganda? They used it in the first war too—posters with Germans bayoneting Belgian babies! No country would do what they say the Germans are doing." He had ignored Sarah's ominous silence. "It was bad enough losing Maresh—and he didn't even join *our* army."

"You know he's with the Polish underground," Sarah replied tightly.

"Much good may it do him and them—a big, blond peasant like Maresh."

Naomi tried to stop him from saying any more. "From what I hear about the Warsaw Ghetto, that big, blond peasant is just what they need." She was sitting on the couch next to Sarah.

"More propaganda."

"Goddamn it, Arnold," Sarah said, getting up from the sofa. "Will you *shut up*? Lazar's with him. They'll both die in the

Ghetto because of what you call propaganda.'' She paced, her face white, her dark eyes glinting with anger and fear. ''You're entitled to your opinions, but do me a favor and keep them to yourself when I'm around.'' She ran her fingers through her cropped hair, a nervous gesture she had, and went back to Naomi, taking a cigarette from the coffee table as she sat down, lighting it, inhaling deeply.

Arnold leaned forward now, his head in his hands. He knew it was more than propaganda, the whole world knew by now. He'd have given a lot if he'd never said it. And Sarah had decided to move to Palestine with her children because that was what Lazar would have done. He knew she would go; there was no stopping Shai once she made up her mind. Then how would he ever make amends? What demon of bitterness made him bait her like that—this sister he loved so much? It was the same demon that made him speak sharply to his vice presidents, that made him impatient with his little girl. It was Naomi, and the fact that he still loved her, still wanted her, still resented his brother—and feared daily for Joshua's life, thought of him every time he looked at Naomi. Having a mistress was not the comfort that it should have been.

Images of Annalise came to him. She was still the same quiet, undemanding person who had joined the company as a junior chemist years ago, before Julie was born. She was an executive at Duchess now—and not because she slept with Arnold. She had earned her title well before he went to her that first time, needing what she gave him because he didn't have to share it with someone else. She had lost her entire family in Europe. The occasional company of a man who cared for her was all she wanted. They were extremely discreet. Arnold didn't think Naomi would accept a mistress if she found out; there was no reason for him to have one, for one thing. Only suspicion.

Naomi had never refused him, not once in their fifteen years of marriage. She had never said no to him—but there are unspoken refusals that are worse; there are withholdings that are worse than withdrawals. She had withheld from him the part of herself he needed most. They still slept together when desire for her over-came him. But it was not love, not love at all. Not from her. And he kept his feelings hidden; he couldn't let her see that it was still love from him.

With Annalise he had, if not love, then loving; if not a

reciprocal passion, then at least a pleasure mutually shared. Her apartment was small—he would have preferred a larger one for her, but she refused it—and cozy, simply furnished and cluttered with chemistry books and journals. She knew how to maneuver him to the bedroom without embarrassing Arnold. And she let him know she liked it when he made love to her.

Afterward they would talk about the one thing that interested both of them most: Duchess. He would leave her feeling relaxed and satisfied. Annalise gave him peace without suspicion. But it was not enough.

He looked at Joshua's letter again, ashamed of the turn his thoughts had taken. His brother might be dead or dying. There was an ache in his throat of fear and regret, an ache of loss for Lazar—and for so much more. Had he been too quick to judge Naomi? Should he have tried to understand? Life was so short and death so final.

He sat on alone, staring at the fire, hoping Sarah had forgiven him, hoping his brother was safe, wanting to talk to his wife.

Sarah sat on the edge of the bed, hugging herself, her eyes closed.

"Stay in the world," she whispered softly. "Please stay, darling, stay just a little longer."

Naomi held her, trying to comfort when there was no way to comfort, loving, protecting, helpless.

"I just wish I could touch him once more," Sarah said. "Hold him once more, only for a minute. I hope it didn't hurt him at the end. I hope he had someone with him when he died—a friend, a woman maybe. Lazar loved women. I hope he didn't die alone." Her face was wet, although she made no sound of crying. "You know, Naomi, I always wondered if it could have stayed as good as it was between us. Maybe some things are too good to last. I never wanted the mellowness of age and the comfort of companionship—not after what I had with him. But he was too young to die." She shook her head, protesting. "He had too many songs unsung inside of him. He was always having to run around after money, but he was really a writer, a poet—he really was." She looked at Naomi, her face ravaged by a week of unbearable sorrow, by months of unbearable suspense.

"Oh, Sarah, no. There were no songs left unsung in Lazar.

That's what people felt about him, that's why they followed him the way they did, trying to be like him."

"I loved him so much. That's such a stupid way to say what I feel, but I don't know any other words for it. I knew we belonged together the first time I looked at him—and he knew it too. He was a part of myself I'd been looking for, and now I've lost it." She stared at Naomi like a frightened child.

"I know," Naomi whispered, rocking her, relieved that Shai was crying openly at last, breaking her dangerous silence.

"That's what you think Joshua is for you," Sarah said.

Naomi tensed.

"No, don't be surprised. I've always known about you two. But he isn't right for you. Loving a man like Joshua is like walking in a mist; when you're in the heart of it, it's gone." She took Naomi's face in her hands. "Listen to me, I have to tell you this. You'll never understand him, and you can't love a man you can't understand. You can want him, but you can't love him. If he's still alive, go to bed with him. That's as close to him as anyone can get—and it's what you want. But it's Arnold you belong with. It always has been."

"Yes," Naomi said, only agreeing to quiet Sarah. "But lie down now and rest. You haven't slept in days. The children are going to need you."

Sarah lowered her body slowly, as if every bone in it ached. "I'm right about Joshua, you know. Lazar says so too, and he knows Josh better than anyone." She spoke as if Lazar were still alive.

"Yes," Naomi said again. "I know. We'll talk more later. Sleep now."

"I shouldn't have cut my hair," Sarah murmured exhaustedly. "He liked it long." She reached to the night table for the last note Lazar had written, a message she would share with no one yet. "I'll never let it grow again," Sarah whispered.

Naomi put out the light and sat in the darkness, heartsick over Lazar, anxious about Sarah and the children, worried about Joshua. Of course, Sarah was right about Joshua—she would never understand him; she had realized that the day Josh went off to England and the war almost three years ago. But that didn't mean she couldn't love him, that she could want only him.

And Sarah was wrong about Arnold. He and Naomi went on together, but there was a wall between them Naomi hadn't been able to breach. If they really belonged together, as Sarah and Lazar did, she would have reached him. She would not have been afraid to try.

Arnold had changed so much since the day Joshua left. He was short-tempered and difficult, even with Julie. He was critical of everyone around him—except Naomi. Yet it was impossible for her to talk openly to a man who treated her with extreme consideration in public and distancing politeness in private—except in bed. He came to her very seldom, but when he did, he was passionately demanding, even vaguely exciting. He never asked anymore if she loved him. He never said he loved her. He seemed to be there against his will—and whether she wanted him or not.

She shook herself slightly. This was no time to ponder her relationship, intimate and otherwise, with Arnold. There were the children to be cared for and Sarah to be helped now that the numbness had given way to searing pain. And she had work to do with the pitifully few refugee children being brought into the country for adoption. It was the most important job she had to do, had ever had, aside from raising her own little girl.

Naomi left the room quietly, intending to go to the playroom, but she went down the graceful staircase instead and into the drawing room. The heavy carpet muffled her steps, and she watched Arnold from the door.

He was sitting as he had been for most of the past week, somber, unapproachable. He was there when he was needed, but he never went to people impulsively. Suddenly she knew it was because he was unsure of his welcome. Her eyes filled with tears at the thought.

He was holding Joshua's letter. Strange, how he kept it with him the way Sarah kept the little note from Lazar. Joshua's letter—so brief, so heartbreaking, telling of the death of a man Joshua loved like a brother. No, Naomi knew, more than his own brother, the way his own brother wanted to be loved.

All at once it didn't matter to Naomi that she and Arnold should never have married, that they had grown so far apart. She wasn't looking at her husband. There was a lonely man sitting in that chair. Arnold had become so cold and hard in the last few years because he was lonely, and it was horrible to be lonely in the midst of life.

Without stopping to think how he would react, Naomi went to the big chair and curled up in Arnold's lap, her arms tight around him, her face buried in his shoulder, crying in love and loss and pity for them both, for Lazar, for Sarah. He held her until she stopped. Then he dried her face gently with his breast-pocket handkerchief. His handkerchiefs always smelled of attars from the lab. It was comforting, familiar.

"Help me," Naomi said. "I need you."

He nodded, unable to speak. She held him close for another minute, then they both got out of the chair and went toward the stairs.

It was the first break in the wall he'd built the day Joshua went away. Naomi had a chance to get back something of what they had once had, and she was going to take it, as much for Julie's sake as her own. Julie must not suffer because Arnold was embittered. Something had convinced Arnold, that day, that his suspicions about Joshua were justified; Naomi would never let that happen again. She reached for his hand, and they went up the stairs to the children.

If there was still a song unsung in her, it was not Arnold's doing but her own, and she was damned if either of them would suffer for it anymore.

24

GERMANY
APRIL 1945

The trees looked like tortured hands, charred and twisted, begging for an end to it. There were seven Allied armies spread over Germany, pushing east to finish the war; the Russians were driving westward, and the paraphernalia of death was everywhere, brilliantly conceived instruments for ripping flesh, smashing bones, combing out entrails. The targets on both sides were men in similar uniforms with buttons, tabs, and insignia to tell them who they were and a special code for walking, talking, saluting—as alike as the trees that fringed the route near Weimar.

The trees were ushering the men to a place where killing was of a brilliant simplicity, without salutes or insignia, requiring only gas and fire. It was simple, so diabolically simple that only a highly advanced civilization could have conceived and executed it.

On this early April day the armored spearhead of General Patton's Third Army rolled out of Weimar like iron roaches, secure behind their bristling cannon-feelers.

Joshua walked in the lee of a tank, shaking his head in disbelief.

"What's the matter, Padre?" one of the tank crew, perched on its iron shoulder, called down to him. "Can't you believe it's springtime in jolly Germany?"

Joshua looked up. "I can't believe that men like Liszt and Goethe came out of this place."

"If we find them, they'll be sorry." The slim man smiled dangerously. "The only good Kraut is a dead Kraut."

"Damn right," a companion too far over for Joshua to see, agreed.

"Hey, Padre," the first man said. "Are you supposed to be here?"

"No, but I'd like a ride."

The man laughed. "Always good to have a chaplain aboard, especially a maverick. Get to the rear, and I'll give you a hand up." Strong young arms reached down to haul Joshua over the stern of the slowly moving tank.

"Hey!" the second soldier said when he saw the insignia. "He's a rabbi!"

"So what? You can bury all kinds, right?"

Joshua nodded. He had performed all the rituals of death, holding hands that clawed for life, whatever its religious denomination. It was his apparent reason for being here; his further purpose was to advance the Zionist cause when the war was over, by getting as many Jews as he could to Palestine—if there were any left alive. Lately something else was driving him, something so impossible that he tried not to think of it. . . .

"But maybe he shouldn't go in there with us," the other man, much younger, persisted. "Not the first time."

The older man looked at Joshua more carefully. "Oh," he said. "Yeah. You sure you want to go in there with us, Rabbi? We heard some pretty awful stuff about these places."

"I'm sure," Joshua said.

The men lapsed into silence, leaving him apart. They had treated Jews with a peculiar kind of embarrassment, added to whatever other feelings they had about them, since the Russians had liberated the notorious Auschwitz extermination camp in Poland. The place just up the road would be the Americans' first look at the unbelievable.

Ironically it was near the famous Goethe oak, where the poet had gone to invite inspiration. But now another muse prevailed.

The place was Buchenwald.

Joshua felt the tank rumble underneath him, a shuddering mass of metal. Ever since Auschwitz was liberated, he had been trying to reason for himself. But it was known that anyone at Auschwitz who could walk had been sent westward by the Germans to camps inside Germany before the Russians came. The living were dangerous evidence, like the ovens and gas chambers the Germans tried to blow up. But only the strong would have survived a forced march such as that.

Lazar was a strong man.

Joshua swallowed hard, forcing himself to remember that Lazar was reliably reported dead in the Warsaw Ghetto by the same Polish agent who had reported Maresh's death two months later. He had believed it—believed and written to Sarah to tell her so. Yet how could anyone be sure in the rubble and confusion of Warsaw?

Again and again Joshua had used his lines of communication with both the Jewish and Polish undergrounds to be certain—and always with the same reply. But that was never enough to cancel out another fact for him: More than fifty thousand Jews were in Warsaw when the Ghetto finally fell—and only twenty-four thousand of these were accounted for as killed in the final uprising or at Treblinka II. The Germans usually spared anyone strong enough, to work them to death at the labor division of the Auschwitz camp.

And Lazar was a strong man.

He had only been inside the Ghetto for a few months before it fell, not enough to sap the vigor in his big, lazy body. If he had survived Auschwitz and been sent on that forced march west . . .

Impossible. Joshua knew it was impossible. He had forced himself to believe that Lazar was dead—until the moment he crossed into Germany.

Then something pulled at him, something said Lazar was alive in spite of Joshua's monumental crime in persuading him to go back into Poland. Lazar was alive and somewhere nearby—or why should Joshua be with the army that took Weimar, with Buchenwald just down the road? Why was Joshua here and not somewhere in Italy or France? It could be true. He had seen stranger things in this war.

But he had never believed in miracles before. He had not believed in sin either, or in a never ending battle between God and Satan, only in the eventual predominance of the intellect which sparked the universe and had to be, if not divine, then at least benign.

But here in Germany a malignant intelligence had been at work for years, and the sight of it destroyed him. He believed in nothing now except his own sin in speaking his thoughts to a man who would be influenced by what he said. If Joshua lived through the war—and he hoped he would not—he knew he would never damn another soul with the power of his own beliefs.

The tank halted. There was an eerie silence. Ahead of them was an entrance gate with two mottos written in wrought iron above it.

"What's it say?" the young soldier asked.

Joshua translated. " 'Right or Wrong—My Country' is the first one."

"Hey, didn't an American say that?"

"And the other one?"

" 'To Each His Own,' " Joshua said.

"What the hell did they mean by that?" the older man wondered laconically.

"Nothing's moving," his friend said nervously. "Why did we stop?"

"Captain's just checking it out. Grab my rifle so I can take a look with the field glasses." He raised them to his eyes. "Oh, Jesus," he whispered. "Jesus God Almighty."

"What is it?" the boy demanded, holding his gun at the ready.

The other man's mouth began to tremble. "It's men. I think they're alive. Oh, Jesus Christ."

Joshua never remembered sliding down from the tank, hitting the churned-up earth, and running toward the gate. He never remembered the sunken eyes that watched him while he tore it open, only the shame he felt for his health, his full belly, his life.

He remembered the voices of the tank crew calling him back and his own voice calling, "Lazar, *Lazar,*" over and over. He remembered the stench and the tortured hands that plucked at him, pleading like the trees along the road, a forest of supplicating hands, so many, so many.

He remembered a trembling, tall body lying just inside the camp, an arm that raised feebly when he called again, and how he stopped and stood over it.

It was as tall as Lazar, but there was no hair, no flesh to tell him how it had been cloaked in life. It was not trembling. The movement was its blanket of swarming lice.

"Lazar," he said. "Lazar?" he asked.

Eyes fluttered open, blue eyes like Lazar's but pale. Wouldn't eyes grow pale in such a place as this?

He dropped to his knees, sobbing. Sobbing, he took the body in his arms. He thought he heard it say "for me" before its final breath, and then he heard nothing but his own convulsive crying until a warm hand on his shoulder dragged him back to life.

"Put him down, Rabbi," a strong voice said through a handkerchief. "He's dead." A pause. "Put him down—there must be typhus here."

"Typhus?" Joshua shouted at him. "Look around you, man. There's worse than typhus here. There's no name for what's here. Leave me alone with him." He held the body close to his chest, rocking it. "Lazar," he said, "don't ever forgive me for this."

"Christ, did you *know* him?" the voice asked in muffled horror.

"He answered when I called his name."

"Rabbi, lots of men have the same name—anyone would have answered you. They tell us there are twenty thousand here. Now put him down. If anyone needs you, it's the ones who are still alive.''

Joshua put down the filthy bundle, not as heavy as a baby. Had it been Lazar? He would carry the pathetic weight of it with him for the rest of his life, because it could have been Lazar.

This could be his friend, lying dead on such indifferent earth after such unspeakable suffering. How many friends are there who know your mind, spark your soul, accept your failings, grant you an open ticket on the way through life, a place to go when there is no other place? How many friends like this do you find between the beginning and the end of you?

The others no longer mattered to him. His imbecile illusions had not sent the others here. He had not loved the others like Lazar, and they had not suffered by loving him.

He was deloused and sent back to a field hospital and eventually from there to England, where he refused to eat or drink or officiate at the services he was there to perform.

He was terrified of the future. The future was written in the past. The crime was too enormous to be understood, but eventually it would be accepted; that was the evil. Once the world accepted a slaughter of this magnitude, it could accept a bigger one. After a while no infamy would be too great. After the planned murder of fourteen million people, it would be easy to murder twenty million, fifty million, the whole insane species, dreadful and befouled as it was by millennia of crimes against itself.

Finally he began to function again. But for him the war in Europe still went on inside the gates of Buchenwald. He was locked inside those gates along with love and tenderness and all the fearsome passions that might bind him to anyone—or worse, bind anyone to him.

He had only an obsession to keep him alive. He would do what Lazar would have done; he had no right to do anything else. *For me*, the voice had whispered.

All right, then, for you, Joshua swore, for my dearest friend, for you.

25

SANDS POINT
DECEMBER 1945

Naomi checked to see that her gifts for the family were in her suitcase before she closed it and snapped the locks shut. Everyone was at the Domain in California to celebrate this first peacetime New Year in four long years—everyone but Lazar and Joshua. And no one knew where Joshua was.

Naomi's parents, Martin and Leah, still ran the Domain. Her brothers, Simon and David, had gone out the week before with their wives and children. Sarah had brought Seth and Rebekah from the kibbutz Yad Mordechai in Palestine—she called it Israel—and had left for the West Coast with Arnold and Julie three days ago.

Only Naomi refused to leave until adoptive parents arrived from Phoenix to take two of her silent little orphans to a new home. No one had even suggested that she leave the final details to one of the committeewomen; they knew she considered the children she placed her personal responsibility, up to adoption. She was glad she had stayed; she thought the children and their new parents had a chance for happiness. After years of working with orphans of the Nazi terror, Naomi knew that a chance was all anyone could hope for.

She was almost ready to buzz the chauffeur to come for her bags when the telephone rang. The house staff had already left on vacation, and she answered it herself.

"I'm trying to find Mrs. Kramer," a man's voice said. "I thought she might be at this number."

"She was, but she left . . ." Naomi stopped, her heart banging against her chest. "Joshua?" she whispered. "Is that you?"

She thought she might be mistaken. It sounded like an old man's voice, and Joshua was only forty-two.

"Who is this?"

"Naomi," she managed to say. "It's Naomi." She waited a moment. "Where are you?"

"At Fort Dix. I just finished and I—I wanted to see Sarah—someone . . ."

"Joshua," Naomi said firmly. "Write down this address." She gave it. "Call a taxi and come right here. I'll be waiting for you. All right?"

"Yes," he said, as if he welcomed direction, as if he could not have directed himself. "I'll come."

She replaced the phone and sat for a while, her heart still pounding. He sounded mortally tired and terribly lost, the way her own little Julie sounded sometimes. She was sure he was close to collapse, that he needed rest before he could go anywhere—to California or to Palestine.

She picked up the house phone and buzzed the chauffeur's quarters, telling him her plans had changed, he could leave on his vacation now. She called the caretaker's cottage and asked him to leave the gates open until a taxi she was expecting had come and gone.

Then she sent a telegram to the Domain, telling the family she would be a day or two late because of the adoption proceeding. Her voice would have given her away if she had telephoned them. Joshua was home at last, home safe. It was selfish of her to keep the news from them, but there was Arnold to consider. Things had leveled out to a workable arrangement for them; they expected less of each other and gave more. But it would be too much to ask Arnold to believe that Joshua was at Sands Point, alone with Naomi, simply because he hadn't the strength to go anywhere else. It was the truth, but Arnold would never believe it.

She went down to the study to light a fire and sat on the small sofa, watching the flames. The lamps glowed softly in the winter dusk. It was still difficult for her to breathe.

How desperately sad he sounded. She hoped he wasn't sick. What was he doing in America? Rachel and his son had been in Palestine throughout the war. Maybe he had to return to the States for official discharge from the army: that was it. Dix was a discharge center. Maybe they'd given him several days' leave for the holiday. But he'd said he had "finished."

Five years since she had seen him. And so much had happened to all of them. Lazar was gone. Sarah and the children lived in Palestine on a kibbutz named for the Ghetto hero, Mordechai Anilewicz. They ignored the dangerous anti-British feeling in the Holy Land that was driving the Yishuv into opposing camps. They ignored the even greater danger if Israel were to be granted statehood over violent Arab opposition. That was where Lazar would have gone, Sarah said. She had offered to sell Arnold her shares of Duchess, but Arnold refused. He still hoped his sister would take up her active partnership once the situation in Palestine was settled. In the meantime she had given almost every cent she possessed to Israel—and Sarah was a wealthy woman. Duchess had prospered during the war and was still expanding, with Arnold acquiring subsidiaries whenever he could.

And Arnold had not tried to dissuade Sarah. That was partly because of Lazar's death and the "workable arrangement" he and Naomi had extended to most other people as well. He was still an abrasive personality, still a perfectionist with his business associates and his daughter. But he was less cold, less withdrawn, easier to approach.

Naomi had never been able to speak to him about Joshua. She was grateful enough that she could speak to him about Julie— shy, frightened, trying-to-please-her-father Julie. She was grateful they had achieved an unspoken, affectionate understanding.

And that understanding must not be threatened now that Joshua was back. Naomi went to get a brandy from the bar, taking out a second glass for Joshua. He sounded as if he would need one. She walked to the window with her glass, watching the drive for headlights, even though it was far too soon for Joshua to arrive. The thumping in her breast had subsided, but she was nervous. In a little while she would be face to face—alone—with the man who had been a secret, intimate part of her life for years, a man who must have changed radically, a man she had never understood but still loved.

She went back to the couch and sat looking at the fire, remembering, until she heard his taxi pull up to the door and stop.

26

He leaned against the door as if he hadn't the strength to stand alone, his face shadowed by the visor of his cap. She could see the hollows under his cheeks.

"Come in, Joshua," she said. "Come inside and rest."

He followed her into the lighted study, carrying a small canvas bag, still wearing his heavy overcoat. He looked at the beautiful, warm, book-lined room as if he had forgotten such things existed.

"Put the bag down and give me your coat," she said, feeling again that he had no will to act on his own. She took the coat and propelled him gently to the couch in front of the fireplace. When he sank into the plump cushions, she took his hat from his head and put it with the coat on a bar chair. She poured two large brandies and gave him one. Then she sat beside him, holding her glass, waiting.

He took a deep swallow of brandy. She could see how gaunt he was, not only his face but his tall body. He had always been slender, but now he was emaciated. The olive-drab jacket and khaki shirt he wore were inches too big around the neck. His hair was almost all white.

He sat for some time with his head back, first with his eyes closed, then looking at the fire while he sipped the brandy. Finally he turned to her, and she saw his eyes clearly for the first time.

"Oh, Joshua," she said, stricken by those eyes. She moved close enough to put an arm around his shoulders, taking his hand in hers, trying to ease the desolation in him that no words could either express or acknowledge. "Oh, Joshua," she whispered again. She stroked his hair, murmuring softly as she did to her child when she was hurt, as she did to her orphans, saying,

"You're here with me now, it's all right now, all that is over," saying anything to give him comfort.

After a time he finished his brandy and she got him another. He spoke for the first time. "Thank you," was all he said.

"Are you hungry?"

He shook his head.

"Then you must sleep," she said, holding out her hand.

He took it and followed her up to Sarah's room, carrying the glass of brandy. She took it from him and turned back the covers of the bed while he undressed. When he was in bed, she covered him. "Now go to sleep, Josh." She kissed his forehead. "It's all right, just go to sleep."

He was sleeping when she turned the lamp off and went downstairs to check the fire, lock the door, and put the lights out. She went back to her own bedroom to undress. She got into bed and lay thinking, feeling so many kinds of love.

She had seen that same desolation in the eyes of children but never with the bitterness, never to the depths she had just seen in his, as though he wandered, lost, on some dead star from which he could never escape, where warmth could never reach him. He was in torment, and she had to help him. She would have tried to help even if she didn't love him as she did.

He slept until noon the next day. She was sitting near the window in Sarah's room when he awakened, visibly confused, trying to remember where he was and how he had come there. His eyes were still great caverns of despair, but he looked less ravaged by exhaustion.

"Naomi," he said, years of memory in his voice.

She smiled. "Would you like some coffee?"

"Yes—but I'd like a bath even more."

She pointed to the bathroom door. "You'll find everything you need—and a big terrycloth robe too." It had been Lazar's, but she didn't want to tell him that. "Do you want your bag?"

"Yes, it has some clean clothes."

"I'll leave it near the bathroom door."

She brought the bag up and then went back downstairs to fix coffee, juice, sweet rolls. She carried the tray up, put it on the foot of the bed, and sat waiting for him to come out. When he did, he looked even more pale after the shave. He got back into bed and took the tray on his lap, pouring coffee from the thermos carafe.

"This is unbelievable," he said.

"I was just thinking the same thing."

"Why are you here alone? Where is everybody?"

She told him.

"How are Sarah and the children?"

"Fine—but Sarah can't sit still. Before it was vitality and high spirits; now it's nerves, as if she were running some kind of race with herself. She needs you. You'll come to California to see the family before you go home, won't you?" She waited for his assent. "It'll do you good to see Sarah."

"It won't bring *him* back," he said, putting an arm over his eyes. "Or any of them."

"No, but you were always Sarah's rock."

He shook his head, his arm still covering his face. "I'm nobody's rock anymore. I can barely keep myself together."

She crossed the room and sat on the bed near him. "Then we'll have to help you for a change."

"Nobody can help me." He took her hand. "But I'm glad you were here."

"We'll go to Los Angeles as soon as you're rested." She put the tray on a table and came back to sit near him. "I didn't tell them you were back. I sent a wire last night saying I'd be delayed, but I didn't tell them you were here."

He looked at her, understanding. "We'll tell them I got back today."

"Stay with me and rest today, Josh. We can tell them you got back tomorrow. We haven't been able to talk to each other alone for years. Stay with me." She meant so much more than she said. It was in her voice.

"I'm not the same person I was, Naomi," he told her, hearing all the things she could not say.

"Nor I."

He made no answer, looking past her at the large room.

"What are you thinking?"

"How different this room is from our room in Palestine." He was reminding her—and himself—of Rachel.

"When will you go back?"

"As soon as I can. There's going to be trouble before there's an Israel. I'll be needed." He raised a cynical eyebrow. "Lazar isn't here to get his Jews a homeland, so I have to do it for him."

She had never heard him speak like this. "Aren't they your Jews too?"

He reached for the brandy, still sitting on the night table from the night before, and drank it down. "They're everybody's now," he said bitterly. "The Chosen. Well, let the bastard choose another lot next time."

She watched him apprehensively, not knowing what to say.

"You think I've lost my mind," he said. "But you're wrong. I've finally found it. It started when Lazar and Maresh went into the Warsaw Ghetto because of something I believed, the wonderful pair of fools. Two puny heroes—the beautiful poet, the beautiful peasant. Two pathetic Lears, thinking, 'We will do such things . . . they shall be the terrors of the earth. . . .' They thought they were the unquenchable human spirit conquering the terrors of the earth! But the joke is that the human spirit created the terrors in the first place."

He smiled bleakly, lowering his voice. "There's a legend that when God looked at His creation and saw what man had done to it, He blew Himself into a trillion pieces. Man's job is to find those pieces, generation by generation, and put God back together again with bits and pieces and fragments of good." He looked at her, mocking himself. "I used to believe rot like that. I used to think the creation was a symbol for thought, civilization. I used to think God was just another word for good." He looked away, his face shattered. "But not after what I saw and smelled and touched. A man would have to be mad to suppose there was any good." His voice sank even lower. "Jesus," he moaned. "I can't get it out of my mind. It will never go away." His hands hid his face. "It is . . . unspeakable."

"Joshua," she pleaded. "Don't. You have to stop."

The sound of her voice lapped against his private hell like cool water, and he looked up at her. For a moment it seemed he might come out of his nightmare, but then he shook his head. "I can't stop. It's part of me, in my pores, in my lungs, in the sockets of my eyes." Those eyes were wet. "How could people do such things? Why did people let them do it? We tried, we could have ransomed them, some of them, we had the money—but somebody stopped it. *Why?* And so they perished, not only Lazar's

Jews but fourteen million people. Do you know how long it would take to count fourteen million people? Poles, Slavs, Gypsies. People. Little girls like yours, little boys like mine.'' He grasped her hands. ''I *can't* stop thinking about it. The only oblivion I'll ever find is death, and I can't let Lazar down by taking it before it comes to me. I love his stupid valor as much as I loved him. I have to do what he would have done. I can't do it for all of them, so I have to do it for the Jews. And they're human too. And human nature is—unspeakable.''

She was afraid for him. She had never seen a man in so much pain. She had no answers for him. How could she? She knew nothing of what he had seen. All she had to offer was love. ''I love you so much,'' she said. ''Is there no way I can help you?''

He looked at her with empty eyes. ''There's no way anyone can help me.''

She put her arms around him, knowing it was true. She drew his head to her shoulder, her lips against his hair, her body curved around his, sheltering, protecting. She had dreamed a thousand times of being close to him, but never like this, with no desire but to help him, to make him forget his misery for even one moment.

This was not the erotic fancy she had created for herself over the years. This was love, pity, care, and compassion she could express in no other way than to offer him physical sanctuary, a cradle to rest in, arms to hold him. She had neither the experience nor the philosophy to give him any other kind of help.

He held her lightly, gently, still separate in himself, immune to such a little thing as physical comfort; could a man find comfort drinking tea while the planets collided?

Then he kissed her, with a sigh of relief—or was it resignation? He kissed her mouth, her eyes, her hair. ''So soft,'' he whispered. ''So soft and clean and sweet.''

His hands took off the robe she wore and caressed her body. His lips touched her breasts. She lay down beside him to warm him, surprised that he was taut and velvety against her, but not in her, that he was warm with a wetness that came from her.

He rose into her body like a drowning man rising for breath. Did he not love Rachel, then? Yes, he loved her, her devotion, her strength, her nurturing—of the soil, of his son, of himself. But Rachel was reality, and there, under his body, now joined with his body, was a dream, the best of all his dreamings, a souvenir of youth untouched by fear and pain and horror. Here was the grail, the fount, the magic spring that every man searched his whole life for and knew he would never find to keep.

For her the years of reverie had come to life at last. The girl's idyls of pure passion and the woman's sublime abandon. The welcoming of a knight so sorely tried and most embattled, come home to feast upon his lady, his woman, his first and most enduring love. She gave all she was to him, all the light and magic and unsung song she had. If that meant she must share with him every horror he had known to help him bear it, she was ready to share it. She could not say it—she could only show it, be it, do it. The girl she had been could never have done it. The woman she had become did.

They went back together, back to the time before life lost its fine, sweet novelty, back to the age of discovery, to the first time they looked at each other with a longing to join, to be one, to be taken up and folded in without thought, design, or reason, without care, reproof, or responsibility. Memory, strayed and life-demolished; memory, battered and grown old before its time; memory came back and lived again.

Book
Four

27

GIORA
FEBRUARY 1946

"I should be used to this," Sarah told Rachel, mopping her eyes with one of Lazar's handkerchiefs. "There are reunions every day, but it makes me feel so good I could burst."

"Oh, Mom," Seth protested, eyeing his mother anxiously. "You're always ready to burst over something." He hated to see his mother cry.

"Heartless child." Sarah smiled, kissing him. "Stop scolding your poor old mother and go play with your friends."

Reassured, the boy moved away to join the other youngsters he knew at Giora.

"Can you believe he's almost fifteen?" Sarah said to Rachel. "Can you believe any of this?" Her eyes took in the crowd of noisy people in the watchtower enclosure at Giora.

Across from the two women Joshua was in earnest conversation with old friends and new companions. Reuven was there, a sturdy, weathered oak of a man. Isaac Levy had returned from his post at a children's camp in Aglasterhausen near Heidelburg, thin and quick as always, with a wider border of white edging his beard. Ari and some of his lieutenants were there too, the "general" still speaking in explosive bursts, his troops still ragged and bulky and quiet but younger than they used to be. The older men were still trickling back from Europe.

Rachel's son, Benjamin, was in training already. Eventually he would be inducted into the Haganah, as were all boys at sixteen.

"Our children play strange games," Rachel said.

Sarah agreed. "We'll have to fight if we become a state. It's as well to be prepared." She looked more closely at Rachel. "It's not any better, is it?"

Rachel shook her head. "I don't think it will change."

Sarah put an arm around her. "Some men need more time than others."

Watching Joshua, Rachel didn't think it was a question of time. She should have known; looking back, Rachel realized she should have known. How could a man who built his life on belief in human intellect witness infamies so intelligently planned and still keep his faith in humanity?

He lived, he planned for the fight that would come when the United Nations gave them a state and the Arabs came to stamp it out. But he had removed his emotions to a realm apart; or, she had begun to fear, he had abandoned them altogether.

At first she had done that herself. They all had, in a self-protective narcosis, a crushingly hated, monstrously hounded people. On the day he came back to Giora, her eyes had depths like his own. Her work-strong hands had traced his face as if to learn what new being stood behind the hollow cheeks, the rigid mouth, the white hair.

But she hadn't asked how it was with him. She knew. All he had seen she knew from the refugees they were smuggling into Palestine, and it was almost the same with her.

The world was reeling at the magnitude of it, withdrawing from truths too terrible to contemplate. In later years an attempt would be made to understand how such madness could infect one of the most highly civilized nations on earth—and if *they* could do such things, came the question no one dared ask, couldn't we?

Joshua had dared to ask and dared to face his answer: It was a universal aptitude for evil that would ultimately prevail. That was all he said to her. For the moment there was another war to win, a country to be secured. What did it matter how it was with him? With any of them?

Rachel thought at first that they would find the way back together from this anesthesia, that soon they would hold on to each other and cry and then go on together. She was desperate for more children—she was almost thirty-five. So many had been lost, the most giving thing she could do was to have more children, to defy grotesque death with life. And Benjamin needed a family. He needed brothers and sisters as much as he needed his father. Ben Horowitz had been more a father to him throughout the war than Joshua.

For weeks after Joshua came back they sated themselves in

each other, trying to forget in wordless, soundless passions that blotted out all thought, all emotion, leaving only their senses to wander night after night on the lonely plains of Eros. They themselves never met. It was a colossal feast of the senses they shared, but soon she began to fear its emptiness. It was an escape, not a fulfillment, to mate like that, each of them in a separate universe of unremembering.

She had no need to ask if he loved her still. That was not what made her feel so lonely with him. It was the way he loved her. He had always been a sensual man, but now he used his sensuality like a drug, to blot out all that rankled in his soul. If he could not share his bitterness with her, neither could he share his passion. He took it and he gave it, but he did not share it.

It would have been better, she had come to believe, if he had only held her hand. It would have meant more. And yet she was as hungry as he for the nights they shared. At first.

And then one night, in a fever of lust to absorb his body so totally that she might at last break through to him, she kissed him as if she were dying. "Don't pull away tonight," she murmured, breathless, clasping; and again, when he moved frantically away toward what she knew was his solitary oblivion, "Stay, stay inside me. I want a baby, I want a child."

He stopped as if she had stabbed him, and she whimpered, her inflamed senses hungry for repletion, her heart more hungry still for *him*, not just his body but himself.

He lifted himself and lay beside her while the pulsing in her slowed and stopped and night noises crowded into their silence.

"Why?" she demanded sadly. "You must tell me."

"I won't bring another child into being."

"A child of ours? A Jewish child?"

"Rachel, for God's sake, what difference does that make? We're preparing for a war right now. We'll kill, we'll destroy. And the child will grow up to kill and destroy. You have Benjamin. Be content with only one eleven-year-old who must fire his gun first or be shot himself."

She had been speechless at that. Still she thought he would change with time. She watched him working in the fields and orchards as he had done since his return, his body filling out, his strength returning. She watched him with Benjamin, her little companion through long years of war and worry. He loved his son, she was sure—but he made an effort not to love him too much.

And he had not changed. Even Sarah and her children made no difference to him, except to remind him of Lazar, it seemed, to bestir him to the job he had said he was determined to do—for Lazar. No one alive seemed worth striving for, to him.

That was what he couldn't see—that he was doing a job out of love itself, because there was so much love in him. That was what made her go on loving this effigy of Joshua. It was ironic that his obsession with Lazar was the kind of idolatry he had always rejected, as he now rejected the risk of feeling anything too much.

Soon she gave up trying to persuade him. She loved him, but even if he chose to deny her himself, he had no right to deny her a child. She didn't care that it might be only blind nature seeking to replace what had been lost—there was always an explosive birth rate after a war; Rachel had always lived close to nature. She was a part of it, and if she wanted an affirmation of life in this most primal way, he had no right to deny it to her.

Now, still watching him, she said to Sarah, "I'd rather anything than this. I'd rather he gave some love away because he had too much to give than nothing at all." Words unspoken—"even to her, to Naomi"—hovered between the two women.

Sarah held her closer. There was no way to refute what Rachel said. Sarah had always been a celebrant of life. It was her nature. Her sorrows were as boisterous as her joys, her lamentations as free as her laughter. As soon cap a volcano as isolate Sarah from life, whatever it brought.

She had wondered about the real nature of the change in Joshua as soon as he got off the train with Naomi, last Christmas in California. Naomi was different; that it was a sexual change Sarah, with her unfailing intuition about men and women, soon detected. She was grateful that Arnold didn't sense it, that to him Naomi was more genuinely loving—because she was more genuinely understanding—than ever.

But Joshua was a man Sarah no longer knew. There was no hint of love about him. An hour's escape was all Joshua would ever seek or share with a woman now. Such empty minglings were neither love nor adultery, Sarah knew.

It was fortunate, she had thought then as she was thinking

now, that he and Naomi would see very little of each other, or the fact that sex was only an escape for him would become as apparent to Naomi as it was to Rachel. And as unacceptable, for vastly different reasons. Naomi would feel ashamed, without love to justify her passion. Rachel felt lonely.

A shout roused them. One of the girls standing near Seth and Benjamin turned for a second before she ran to meet the dusty truck just rolling into the gate, her face radiant. "It's Abba," she told them. "It's my father!"

"Did you see that child's face light up?" Sarah was crying again. "Who is it?"

"It's Natan!" Rachel said. "It's our Minotaur. I have to tell Aviva . . ." She stopped and looked again at the crowded truck. And Ben's with him, dear Dandy Ben." She started toward the truck, looking back with the kind of smile Sarah hadn't seen on her face in years. "He's home!"

She ran to the truck with the others, Aviva forgotten. Sarah watched her go, hoping that Ben's return would jolt her brother out of his wretched isolation. They were such old friends—and Ben had always been there during the years Joshua was away, when Rachel and little Benjamin needed someone.

Suddenly she pressed Lazar's handkerchief to her mouth, feeling there was an inevitability about Ben and Rachel, hoping that it wouldn't happen, knowing she would not blame Rachel if it did.

28

TEL AVIV
SEPTEMBER 1946

Haganah headquarters in Tel Aviv was on Hayarkon Street in a stucco building they called the red house.

"That's because it's pink," Isaac remarked to Joshua as they approached the building slowly, two friends out for a stroll. "The British are of a literal turn of mind—they'll only search red houses."

Joshua frowned, not hearing. "Where in hell are they?"

Isaac shook his head. "You know they aren't coming."

Joshua fell silent again. A number of men were drifting past them and into the house at discreet intervals. But Natan and Dandy Ben were not among them.

"Come on, Josh, it's time to go in."

"Damn them," Joshua swore softly, half in anger, half in regret. "After all these years together." They turned into the walk that led to the house. "Natan was always a hothead. But Ben! To join the Irgun! Hell, we'll probably end up working together if things keep up as they are—but as an army, not as terrorists."

He was right. What had seemed impossible a few years ago had come to pass on a limited basis, although Menachem Begin's irgun Z'vai Le'umi and Avraham Stern's Lech'i, better known as the Stern Gang, had been totally unacceptable to the Haganah and the Yishuv throughout the war. There were German panzer divisions all over North Africa, and Britain had given the Haganah "unofficial" status as an army, along with "unofficial" weapons. And when Germany was beaten from the continent after El Alamein, there was still the evil ex-Grand Mufti, Haj-Amin al Husseini. An open Nazi sympathizer, he sat plotting in his lair, threatening British army security, infiltrating British intelligence. Haganah men were used for counterintelligence, but once the Germans were beaten, their army was no longer "unofficial." It was once more illegal.

They "cooperated" with the British army by searching for Irgun men and Irgun documents. The British could not read or speak Hebrew, and the Haganah could. But somehow most of the men held for interrogation slipped away; the most incriminating documents were destroyed. The Haganah might not agree with the Irgun, but Jews were not to be turned over to anyone for hanging, imprisonment, or deportation to Eritrea, where there had been camps for dissidents for many years.

Even so, "the Aunt"—one of the code names for the Haganah (another was Hashura, "the Lion")—might have remained loyal had Britain's post-war policy not changed so radically.

The hundred thousand survivors of the Holocaust, Foreign Minister Ernest Bevin declared, had come through the war. True, they had suffered, but they had come through. There was no longer any need for a Jewish homeland. Hitler was dead and the Nazi horror with him; the refugees had only to go back to their homes.

"Their *homes*!" Natan roared. "They *have* no homes. Or does Bevin intend to build them little farms in the country near Auschwitz and Buchenwald and Belsen? There's plenty of bone meal around for fertilizer."

"They'll come around," the others told him, trying to believe it themselves. "They'll work out a compromise. What use would it be to fight the British?"

"To get them out of here!" Natan argued. "They used us when it was convenient, and as soon as they're secure, they take our weapons from us—and our homeland. *We* are not secure. Those poor, miserable bastards in the DP camps in Europe aren't secure. There was a pogrom in Poland two months ago. Without a state no Jew in the world is secure. And Bevin wants them to go back to their homes!"

The uproar at that suggestion was colossal—from the Haganah, the Yishuv, and the Jewish Agency in America, and from President Truman. Equally colossal was the warning from the Arabs should Britain give in and allow enough Jews in to produce a Jewish majority in Palestine.

The Nazi persecutions in Europe, the Arabs said, were not their fault. Jews were "people of the book" and had never been persecuted in Arab countries—except by crusading Europeans. If the Americans were so anxious to give the refugees a home, let them open America; it was big enough to absorb them, and Palestine was not. Why should the Arabs be penalized—who were not guilty of any part in the Holocaust, either directly or indirectly? They referred obliquely to the failure of the Allies to stop the exterminations once they had incontrovertible evidence of them, or to bomb the rail lines to the crematoria at Auschwitz as the Jews had begged them to do, or to ransom the Jews Eichmann had offered to swap, or to let in the few hundred who had tried to find haven with them before the mass murders even began.

Even Ben Horowitz had lost his temper in a dispute with Joshua over the Irgun's intention to drive out the British. "Are you going to say Britain is right?" he demanded, his lips white with anger. "Are you going to see both sides again? Or maybe all three? You're good at that."

But there was only one point of view for Joshua now. Along with the Yishuv he abhorred violence. But along with the Yishuv he knew the Irgun was right. If the British would not let the refugees in, the British would have to go. And they could be pushed out only by desperate tactics. The day was coming when "the Aunt" might have to coordinate activities with the Irgun. At least, unlike some, the Irgun's policy was to force the British out, not merely kill them.

They would crack British morale to the point of withdrawal by warnings of bombs that sometimes exploded and sometimes did not; by kidnapping army officers when any Jew was threatened with hanging; by rescuing men from the British concentration camp in Eritrea.

They had a chance, doing it that way, Joshua knew. The British must either live up to their promises or get out. Given enough provocation, they would get out rather than persecute an entire people. They were an honorable enemy.

An "honorable enemy"—Joshua pushed the thought out of his head. He and Isaac crowded into a room in the red house where some fifty men were sitting.

Ari was there but not in charge. He shook his bristly head slowly after Joshua's eyes made a sweep of the room, looking for two familiar faces he knew he wouldn't find. Ari had watched for Ben and Natan too, hoping they would change their minds about joining the Irgun Z'vai Le'umi. There were still other ways. Jewish leaders like Weizmann and those in the Jewish Agency could deal on a diplomatic level. And if Weizmann resigned or was forced out for failure to stop Jewish rebellion, Ben-Gurion would make sure "the Aunt" fulfilled her two main functions: smuggling in refugees and acquiring arms. They were talking about partition as a solution if everything else failed.

The partition of Palestine was better than being stateless—but Begin was against partition. He felt the Jews should occupy both sides of the Jordan, that the boundaries of the state should be Biblical. It was their land. It was written in the Scriptures that it was their land.

The man who stood now to address the meeting was skinny and rumpled, with overlong dark hair. He was dressed as casu-

ally as most Palestinians, in work pants and a faded shirt unbut-
toned to his pale, hairless chest on this warm September day. His
thick glasses slid down his perspiring nose, and he pushed them
up persistently, doggedly, as if he knew that someday they would
stay where they belonged.

"A *yeshiva bocher*," Ari murmured to Isaac. "Why do they
send us seminary scholars? Two days in the field, and he'd be
dead."

Isaac only had time to grin before the seminary scholar began
to speak. His voice was as big as his body was small. He spoke
in Greek-accented English, heavily laced with Americanisms.

"I have news from the Old Man," he said, referring to
Ben-Gurion. "They've raised the money in America—enough to
start, anyway—but we have to find the weapons to buy with it.
We picked up some from the North African campaign, even
some from the British Tommies here, but that's peanuts. We
have to pick up plenty more in Czecho, Hungary, especially
America." He pushed his glasses up. "Now that the Japs have
surrendered, the War Assets Administration will be selling off
leftover stuff."

"To us?" one of the men snorted.

The speaker smiled. "They don't have to know it's us, do
they?" He paused to let that sink in.

"How do we get guns and machinery past the Brits?" one of
the men said. "They won't allow us explosives for construction,
much less guns!"

"The same way I did. The big stuff we dismantle and ship
piece by piece. Can they tell the whole picture from one piece of
the puzzle? The small stuff we ship in hidden with other goods.
Do they have X-ray eyes? When everything's here, we use some
half-dead engineers the Germans overlooked that we just smuggled in from Cyprus; they'll put the pieces together, show us how
they work." He stopped again, looking gratified. "What you
people have to do is raise and train an army—fast."

"An army?" Ari protested. "All we have is two thousand men
in the Palmach and a few thousand reservists! If the British won't
permit immigration, where are we going to find a Jewish army?"

The speaker sighed, removed his glasses, and wiped them on
his shirttail. "First you conscript anything old enough to shoot,

male and female. Then you wait until we smuggle in more
men.''

"Who? Those poor, starved bastards from the camps?"

"They make the best fighters," the thin little man said sharply. "Once you've been inside one of those, you aren't afraid to
fight for your life if there's a chance to keep it. You can take my
word."

His eyes, curiously large behind his thick glasses, looked
steadily at Ari, who nodded shortly and sat down. The room was
very quiet for a few seconds. The camps. Here they were, alive,
and so many were dead in the camps.

"Aside from that," the deep voice continued, no longer re-
sentful, "we're going into the chaplaincy records from the war.
We'll contact every American Jew who fought, see if they want
to visit Palestine. The Brits can't keep American tourists out."

No one asked how the Jewish Agency would get into the army
chaplains' records. They had learned a lot about infiltration from
British intelligence during the war.

"Then, there are mercenaries. Some men just like wars. We'll
get you the men, and we'll get you the weapons. All we need is
money and people who can track down the merchandise and buy
it. People who don't look like arms buyers—people like me."

The men laughed while Ari and Isaac turned to Joshua. His
face was impassive. Anyone with an American background and,
even better, an American passport would be invaluable in the
game of mass deception that was about to begin. It seemed
inevitable that Joshua would have to return to the States.

The speaker continued. "Anyone you know who might be the
kind of man we need, send him here one week from today, same
time. The next thing: We need a communications system to link
the settlements to headquarters and each other, to warn about
British search parties—or Arab raiders. We have a man working
on it. We have a transmitter that looks just like a table radio—the
only difference is the crystal." The man smiled, gratified again.
"Little things like that the customs inspectors can't be expected
to know. Expect a lot of radios." He leaned against the table.
"There isn't much more I can tell you. The main thing was to let
you know the Old Man raised the money, at least enough to start.
When we need more"—he took a deep breath—"we'll get more."

By now there wasn't a man in the room who doubted that the hungry-looking speaker and his friends would raise more money.

One of the men raised a hand. "Did the Old Man find out why in hell the Limeys have taken such a sudden liking to the wogs after all the help we gave them in the war?"

"Oil," the speaker said. "The Arabs have it—we don't."

"What did you think it was, dummy?" a very dark man asked. "Anti-Semitism? That's all there is out here is Semites. I look like a wog myself."

"The dummy was Abraham the Patriarch," Ari said. "All those years in the desert and he squats on the only piece of sand that has no oil under it. You." He pointed at the very dark man through the laughter of some of the men and the disapproval of others. "I can use a man who looks like an Arab. You know where to find me if you're interested in taking chances."

There was a hum of conversation when the meeting was over. Ari shook hands with Isaac and Joshua as men trickled toward the door in twos and threes.

"I'll miss them," Ari began with no preamble. "Natan can kill a man quietly with his fist—even if he does talk with the jawbone of an ass. As for the Dandy, we'll have to find another English-looking Jew to infiltrate British H.Q." He grunted. "Damn fools. You, Rabbi." He peered at Joshua from under heavy brows. "You'll go back where you came from—again. Probably just as well. You aren't a born killer like some of us." He left them in his usual abrupt way. After a few minutes Joshua and Isaac went out into the sun-flooded street.

The Doctor reached up to rest a sympathetic hand on Joshua's shoulder. "It's a damned shame. All you ever wanted since I met you was to stay in Palestine."

Joshua only looked bleak, a look his friends had come to know well.

"Let it go, my friend," Isaac said softly. "There has to be an end to mourning." Then his kindly face hardened slightly. "If not for your own sake, then for your family's. Sometimes I think you forget you have a wife and child here."

Did Isaac think he was unfaithful to Rachel? He hadn't been—he would never be unfaithful to Rachel. He treasured Rachel for what she was, and he had taken nothing from her in those few days with Naomi. What threat can once-upon-a-time be to now—

and-for-the-rest-of-our-lives? Long ago he had learned from Lazar that sexual adventures were fleeting pleasures, warm like wine, like sunflowers golden in a field. Rachel had grown up knowing that. What Rachel could not accept was his own insufferable disillusion.

If he were guilty of any infidelity, it was to Arnold. He was taking something from his brother that Arnold needed to possess solely for himself. Sexual fidelity was still basic to Arnold's world.

And yet Joshua had no intention of denying himself for Arnold's sake if Naomi still wanted him to satisfy a part of her nature that Arnold couldn't reach. Naomi was the only dream he had that wasn't linked to a nightmare. This very country that he had sworn to defend—and everyone in it—was eternally tied to his personal hell.

There was nothing he would not do to secure a Jewish state for Lazar's sake. And there was nothing he would refrain from doing to find a moment's release from the memory of that fragile bundle near a barbed-wire fence.

"Rachel wants another child," he said suddenly.

Isaac smiled. "Of course she does. Doesn't everybody?" He filled his pipe as they walked, talking into Joshua's silence, not noticing it. "There's not a woman in Palestine who doesn't want to replace a part of what was lost."

"Then there'll be a lot of old souls dragged into the world against their will."

Isaac was surprised. "Where did you hear that expression?"

"I grew up on it. I'm an old soul myself, replacing other unfortunates who perished long ago in other flames."

They had stopped under a tree, and Joshua's face was patterned with the shadows of its leaves. He looked perplexed, the way he used to look, the Doctor remembered, when he had first come to Palestine, madly in love with a girl and a dream, having to choose between them. The leafy shadows obscured the white hair that was such a startling contrast to his still-young, very handsome face, and Isaac shook himself mentally to remember Joshua was a man, not a boy, and that this man carried a burden foisted on him, all unknowing, by ignorant parents with emotional needs of their own. Obviously Joshua held himself accountable to every Jew who died in violence, and Lazar was their symbol.

The Doctor's face was a study in understanding and compassion. "It's only a figure of speech, Joshua, a comforting fancy. An old soul carries too great a burden. Be a young soul. Don't do what anyone expects of you. Do what you want."

Joshua started walking again, unhearing. "I'm not about to produce another heir to human history. He'd be a martyr or a murderer. That's the way of the world. But Rachel . . . Rachel wants a child."

Isaac puffed his pipe silently for a time. "Go to America, Josh. Sometimes problems solve themselves if you leave them alone for a while. You can work it out with her when you come back to stay. Staying here is what you've always wanted."

Joshua heard his own voice telling Naomi so many years ago that Palestine was his life, that she mustn't ask him to give up the most important part of himself.

He shook his head. "Oscar Wilde said life has only two tragedies: One is not getting what you want. The other is getting it."

"He was a cynic," Isaac said. "You're a fighter, a gun-running rabbi. Come on, I'll buy you the lousiest cup of coffee in the Middle East."

Walking beside his friend in the warm sun of the place that was his life, Joshua reflected that he had already known both of life's tragedies once and would certainly know them again.

29

GIORA
SEPTEMBER 1946

Rachel put away her ledgers when Ben knocked. They had agreed at supper to take one of their long, quiet walks around Giora. She snapped out the light and went out to him, giving him the slight nod that was all she could manage when things were going badly. He understood her moods. "Although," he once said, "you have only two I've ever noticed, good and not so good."

She linked her arm through his, and they walked, not talking, just breathing the fresh night air. The moonlight played on their faces—hers strained, his thoughtful—and on the high fence, the watchtower, the dim lights in some windows. They headed toward the citrus grove, keeping clear of the barbed wire that had been set up around it. Absurd, to string ugly wire around a grove of orange trees! But it was Ari's rule.

"It might give you an extra second, and that's all you need to prime a rifle," he'd told them.

She shivered slightly.

"What is it?" Ben said.

"I was thinking how much I hate the barbed wire. But you know Ari." She glanced at him. "Why aren't you in Tel Aviv, you and Natan, with the others?"

"Things to do," he answered briefly. He rarely referred to his activities, but he seemed especially reluctant to talk about them tonight. "I'll be leaving soon for a long stretch."

"Benjamin will miss you," she said, her eyes steadily on the orange trees ahead of them.

"He has Joshua. He's too happy to miss anyone."

"I'm not so sure," Rachel said.

He waited.

"You've seen how he is," Rachel said quickly, not wanting to involve Ben but having to talk about Joshua. "Ever since he came home." She sighed. "He only had one dream all his life; now it's a compulsion. It shuts out everything else, including me, including Benjamin." Years ago she'd realized Joshua had left Naomi more because she didn't fit into his life than because he loved one woman more than the other. But he had crossed the line of ambition, into obsession.

Ben lit a cigarette as they reached the end of the grove and turned back. "Give him time, Rachel. He's seen some things it takes a while getting over."

She shook her head. "We've all seen things we'll never get over. The difference between him and us is that he doesn't want to, he wants to hang on to it. I love him, Ben, but he won't let me in to help him. The worst of it is, he won't let Benjamin in either. Benjamin will have to grow up before he understands why—and even then it will hurt him just as much as it does now."

Her voice was shaking, and he took her arm. "Let's go back. You need a brandy." He spoke softly to her as they walked. "War changes everything. And when a man has one behind him and another ahead, it's even worse."

"It didn't change you," Rachel said.

He looked at her in the moonlight. "Oh, yes, it did. It killed my sacred honor. It took away all the standards I was raised to consider before taking what I wanted." He turned his head away from her. "I've joined the Irgun."

She caught her breath. The Irgun was underground. It had one immediate goal: to get the British out of Palestine. The Irgun wasn't interested in restraint. But Joshua and his friends were against extreme measures. Between them they had held others back, even the frustrated, temperamental Natan. It was hard to imagine Ben, even-tempered, gentlemanly Dandy Ben, harming anyone except in actual self-defense.

They reached the little shack Ben used at Giora and went inside. Ben took a brandy bottle and two thick tumblers from a shelf.

"Does Joshua know?" Rachel asked, taking the glass he handed her.

"He knows now that Natan and I didn't show up." He shrugged. "He's with Ari and the Haganah. I'm not. They want to do it their way—we want to do it ours. It's stupid, we're on opposing teams fighting for the same goal."

Rachel leaned against the wooden wall of the shack. "What's happened to all of us? I used to be so sure of some things—and now the surest things have changed. I don't know what to do."

"Can I help?" He patted her back, as he had done often in the past when Joshua was away and she and little Bejamin were alone.

But this time she was not insulated from Ben's touch by the feelings that bound her to Joshua. This time the kindness made her ache, because the bonds between her husband and herself were gone, maybe for good.

"Rachel, you're tired. Do you want to go back?"

Oh, yes, she wanted to go back. She wanted her Joshua back, with his deep voice and his sweet smile. She wanted her life back, the way it had been. Her throat ached with wanting. She leaned against the rough wall and cried, her shoulders shaking.

"Rachel? Oh, God, Rachel, please." She was not a woman who cried. He turned her to him and put his hands on her shoulders. "What is it? Tell me, I'll help. I'll do anything. But I can't stand to see you suffer like this. Rachel, my darling, tell me."

She saw his face through mists and memories. She was so utterly alone, and now there was this face, familiar, older, dearer for all the years of friendship, carefully guarded, even though she was his darling. "Just hold me, Ben, just love me. I can stand anything if there's somebody who loves me."

His hands were gentle on her face. "I love you, you know. I do. So much. For so long. Don't cry, my Rachel. I'll always love you."

She moved into the circle of his arms, put her own around his neck, and kissed him. She felt him tremble, and that moved her more than anything, that he loved her enough to tremble like a boy but had never kissed her in all these years. He hadn't lost his sacred honor, it was the most wonderful thing about him. It was not in her to toy with feelings that were so deep, so warm. But she wanted that warmth. She loved him for giving it to her so openly, without demanding that she love him equally.

But his desolation was very real to her, as real as her own, the desolation of loving someone who loved someone else or who was too locked away in himself to want any love at all. Why did it take so many years of living to know what someone else was feeling? Why was that so hard to learn when it was what mattered most between people?

She held him closer and kissed him again, pulling him down with her to the mattress on the floor of the tiny shack. It seemed they had been making love together all their lives, so tenderly, so gently, and so well. This was not the husband of her body and the darling of her heart. This was a friend who loved her. In her isolation from Joshua she needed someone who was there with her in the act of love, not lost in his own remote oblivion.

A flood of comfort filled her body, and she kept him close to her.

"Rachel . . ."

She hushed him. There was nothing to be said until they thought it through, and right now she simply did not want to think. She reached for him, kissing him deeply. This time it was she who trembled at the waves of love he let loose over her across a broken dam of years.

30

NEW YORK
DECEMBER 1946

Naomi used the key he had given her to let herself into the hotel room. Joshua was late again. It was a long drive back to Sands Point, and she had to be there by five, when Julie came home from her piano lesson.

She undressed to save time, reached for Joshua's robe, and wrapped it around herself, laughing at her reflection in the long mirror on the bathroom door. Yards of garnet silk splashed over her hands and around her feet onto the floor. She had bought it for him, but the color became her. Baby blue was beginning to seem insipid. This color was better for a scarlet woman. She got into the bed and lay there, waiting. The sheets were cold. Her smile faded.

It was ridiculous to think that way—a scarlet woman was the kind of thing her father would say. This wasn't casual. It was a love affair. They had been in love for nearly twenty years, and they needed each other. Marriage was impossible because of the children, because of his work. But to deny themselves what little they could have would be a stupid waste, no matter what she had been taught.

She knew her parents would have been shocked and humiliated if they knew; and Arnold . . . it was better not to think about Arnold. She moved restlessly. She simply did not have this kind of love for Arnold, even though she loved him as much as she could. There was just something missing, a luster, a glow. Why be ashamed of having found it with the man she should have married in the first place, no matter what her parents had thought at the time. Shame was a matter Joshua never pondered, she was sure.

Anticipation rippled through her. There were even times when she was as sensual as he. Startling, the sensations, the lusts he aroused in her to explore physical passion in ways she would have been mortified to do with Arnold.

Yet it was not only for sex that she was here. Sometimes she hoped there wouldn't be any sex, that they would just sit together quietly and talk about the things he had locked away inside him ever since that anguished outburst on his first day home from the war. But he seemed to want that deep physical contact with her, as if it gave him a kind of comfort mere talking never could. Under his expert hands she was always aroused enough to enjoy it, even at times to crave it. What she craved more was that he trust her enough, love her enough to tell her about himself.

She looked around the room. It was small and very clean, with striped wallpaper, a chenille bedspread, and a writing table near the window, facing on an inside court. She always pulled down the shade the moment she arrived. An office building backed into the hotel. It wasn't sordid, but it was not the sort of room she had imagined for herself and Joshua.

They met so seldom and never, of course, in public. He had come back in October, and he traveled most of the time, looking for sources of arms and ammunition. He had refused Arnold's invitation to stay with them at Sands Point or use the Fifth Avenue apartment. He said it was because this hotel on East 60th Street was where many Haganah men stayed, but Naomi knew it was impossible for Joshua to live under his brother's roof now.

The journey to California last Christmas was very different from the way things were now. They had sat together, not talking much of the time, watching a country unpocked by bombs move past the window of the train's drawing room like a peaceful movie on a screen. Even when they made love, it was in silence, as if he must have quiet after the screaming pandemonium of war. There had been more love than affair in the Pullman bedroom, idyllic days that surpassed her most exquisite dreams of love with him.

This time he had come back changed in a way that escaped her understanding. He was more remote with everyone, including her. She was sure the real Joshua was still somewhere in him, the young man with the vibrant voice and compelling eyes who would have magnetized people even if he were not so beautiful, so brilliant, so perfect.

She knew she could not bring Joshua back again from behind the stern, unsmiling man he had become—except in bed. There he was not remote. There the idealistic passions of the boy emerged in the demanding eroticism of the man. But was that the only way she could reach him?

The sound of Joshua's key in the door made her sit up, flushing with excitement. She could always sense his mood the moment the door opened, and today he was pleased. She knew what he wanted to hear.

"What did you find?" she asked eagerly while he turned to lock the door.

"Rifles, medium machine guns, all kinds of diabolic toys." He turned back to her. "And you. I'm always astonished to find you." He slid out of his overcoat and came to the bed, reaching for her. His face was cold, but his mouth was warm, and there was that scent about him that was uniquely his. She breathed him in deeply. "I would know you anywhere," she whispered, "even in the darkest dark."

He laughed softly. "Madame, you excite me." He was unbuttoning his shirt, undressing. He turned back the covers and saw the robe. "Oh, no, you mustn't hide in that."

The thought of the undressing, the slow opening to his eyes, his hands, his mouth, made her warm and wet before he touched her. She was ready to be engulfed in that lusty silence he wanted when they made love.

When she opened her eyes again, he was watching her intently.

"What do you see when you look at me like that?"

"Many things," he said, stroking her hair. "I see the day we all went rowing in the park, when I first realized you were a woman, not a girl. I think of the times in your father's house when I talked about politics and dreamed about you. I think of family Sundays when you were just a little girl. You had a smile that lit up the world, my mother used to say. You still do."

She kissed him, with vague disappointment. "Do you see nothing of now?"

He closed his eyes, shaking his head. "You're the one person in all the world who makes me forget about now. Make me forget about now,'' he whispered, holding her close. ''Naomi, make me stop thinking of anything but the way life used to be.''

The small cloud of disappointment scudded away. She helped him forget about now.

The sun was starting downward when she finished dressing. It would be an early winter dark. She came out of the bathroom, her face alight with love and contentment. ''I must run. Julie will be home at five.''

He was completely dressed, smoking a cigarette and looking through some papers on the desk. ''I'm coming to dinner tomorrow,'' he said, dropping the papers and going to her. ''But I'm free tomorrow morning. Can you come?''

She was alarmed, even though she knew she must inevitably confront her husband and her lover together. But she could never behave naturally if she had been to bed with Joshua that very morning. How could he?

''No,'' she lied. ''Tomorrow's Friday, and Julie has something on at school.''

''I'm sorry,'' he said, his arms around her. ''We'll have to wait for a week or two, then. I'm going to California.'' Some of the biggest arms manufacturers in America were on the West Coast.

She was tempted to agree to come when he kissed her, but the thought was too uncomfortable. She said good-bye and ran down two flights of stairs rather than lose time waiting for the elevator. She went swiftly through the lobby without looking at the manager or the bellboy and hurried to the garage where she always parked her car. By the time she crossed the bridge and was well on the way to Sands Point, she was calmer.

It was perfectly natural for Arnold's brother to come to dinner— he was hardly a stranger, after all, and that was how she must act. Damn it, most of life was acting, anyway. People acted one way in business, another with friends, still another with children or strangers, husbands or lovers. Tomorrow night Naomi would act like the wife and mother she was.

She thought of asking Julie to spend the whole evening with them, then shook her head. Even though Julie's presence would make it easier to sit there with the two brothers, Naomi's apprehension and the reason for it were her own business, no one else's, least of all Julie's.

She smiled, thinking of her daughter. Julie only seemed to have the same gentle, obliging nature people liked so much in Naomi. Behind the quiet demeanor people mistook for feminine acquiescence, Julie had a will of iron—a phrase Naomi's mother used with dark disapproval.

"What's wrong with her having her own ideas?"

"What does a child know?" was the eternal answer.

A lot, in Naomi's opinion. Her own mind, if she had a chance to discover it—if not, she would always be a child. Arnold had already decided that his daughter would be just like her aunt Sarah. He had never accepted Sarah's decision to live in Palestine, and his dream was to have Julie take her place at Duchess someday. It was beginning to worry Naomi.

Sarah was certainly the most capable, lovable woman in the world, but mainly because she was so very much Sarah. Naomi wanted that for Julie. She had never had it for herself, not even now. She had always done what would make her parents proud and happy, and after them, her husband. And now her lover. But that was different, Joshua was different. Only Sarah knew how Naomi felt about Josh—but Sarah had once said that feeling was not love. If what she felt—had always felt—for Joshua was not love, what was?

The sound of another car startled her, and she found herself sitting in the drive in front of the house, where one part of her mind had led her automatically, like a homing pigeon. Julie was getting out of the car that had chauffeured her home.

"What were you thinking about, Mother?" No eleven-year-old in Julie's class would use "Mommy," although "Daddy" was still acceptable.

"About love, darling," Naomi said, getting out of the car and putting an arm around her daughter. "About how much I love you."

Julie snuggled closer as they walked to the house. No matter what Arnold wanted for this child, Naomi was determined that Julie would have what she wanted for herself.

31

Julie listened intently to everything Uncle Josh said about the family in Palestine. She was used to grown-ups, but he seemed more grown-up than anyone else, even her father. Maybe that was because he had been in the war. It had turned his hair white. It had killed Uncle Lazar.

Julie remembered Uncle Lazar from when she was very little, but she had no memory of meeting Uncle Josh before last year, when her mother brought him out to California, looking so sick she wanted to comfort him all the time. He looked strong now, not at all as if he wanted comforting. He was tall and very good looking, like the hero in the novel she was reading, a book Daddy thought was too "risqué" for her, whatever that meant. Her mother let her read anything she wanted to read.

"Now it's your turn," her uncle was saying while dessert was served, sharp cheddar cheese with crispy red apples. "Tell me about school." Everyone asked about school, but Uncle Josh must really want to know. He never just talked. Neither did Daddy. They were really a lot alike.

"I have to take civics and geography—but that's not what I like. I like English and history and French." Julie waited to see what he'd think of that. Daddy thought she spent too much time on those subjects. "Impractical," he called them, "useless in business." Her uncle looked as if he were still considering it. "What does Benjamin like best?" she asked finally.

Arnold's eyes met Naomi's, and then he looked at Joshua with a warning glare. Arnold had listened to his brother often enough at the office to know what Benjamin had to learn in Palestine. It wasn't anything he wanted Julie to hear.

Joshua resumed peeling his apple in one long, red ribbon with his graceful hands. "He likes math and chemistry—and and tinkering with machinery. He wants to be an engineer."

"If I were a boy, I'd want to be a pilot," Julie said.

"Rebekah's a pilot," Naomi said. "She really is."

"With my crazy sister for a mother, anything's possible." Arnold was openly annoyed. "Buying Rebekah that Tinkertoy!"

Julie and Naomi exchanged a little smile. Arnold loved his sister more than anyone in the world after his wife and daughter, but he was always pretending to disapprove of her. That was Arnold's way. Since Mother had explained that, Julie didn't mind so much when Daddy criticized her.

After dinner, when Julie had gone upstairs, Arnold closed the door to the study. A fragrant fruitwood fire hissed and sputtered in the fireplace. He took a small cup of black coffee from Naomi. "I can't understand why you have to travel around over Christmas and New Year's. Can't they let you fly home?"

"No," Joshua said, nodding at Naomi to put sugar in his coffee. "It costs too much—in time more than money. If we don't get to the available supplies, someone else will." The Jewish Agency was having problems, not in finding the machinery they needed to make their own weapons but in exporting it. It was legal to buy any kind of machinery, but State Department permission a required to export it—and the State Department was not about to cross Britain by giving permission for shipments of machine tools to Palestine. Joshua had to use devious methods, set up dummy companies to export "farm machinery" and "sewing machines" to other ports.

He looked up, realizing his brother was talking to him. "I'm sorry, what did you say?"

"I asked how things are going," Arnold said. "Are you all right, Josh?" He was a little anxious. His brother's apparent calm made him uncomfortable, like a tight lid over a bubbling vat of oil at the factory. Joshua had never been boisterous, but he had always been enthusiastic about whatever he was doing, full of vitality.

"I'm all right, but things are lousy. We've managed to scrape together only five thousand rifles, a few hundred machine guns, and not enough ammunition to hold off the Arabs for two days."

"Maybe you won't have to fight them," Naomi said. She didn't want to think of him in another war.

"After we get rid of the British, we'll have to fight them." Joshua was positive. "They don't want us there, and it's the only place our people can go. But even if we get the guns, we need an army to shoot them. Britain has just rejected another appeal from Truman to let in those hundred thousand refugees. That rescinds the Balfour Declaration—which was why Britain was awarded the Mandate in the first place."

"How can they get away with it, after all that's happened?" Arnold demanded. "It's breach of contract."

"How could all that's happened happen?" Joshua had that bleak look they all knew so well, the same look Naomi had seen in this room a year ago. "They'll kill us all if they can—but not without a fight this time."

Arnold leaned forward. "Josh, it's a hopeless fight. Why not take the family and come home?"

Joshua looked at his brother with open contempt. "There are thousands waiting to come home, Arnold. Haven't you heard what I said?"

"Oh, for God's sake," Arnold said hotly. "You haven't changed a bit." Joshua always made him feel personally responsible for whatever was wrong with the world.

"Nor you," Joshua observed coldly. "Except to get rich."

"And that's what you want, my money!"

Joshua nodded. He was always calm when Arnold was angry, infuriating his brother even more. "And you have to give it to us, because we're fighting your fight."

There was never any answer to that. Arnold sat back in his chair, still fuming. It was always the same between them, this familiar antagonism. And yet—Anold's eyes went back to his brother's face—this was not the same. Their ideas had been different, but Joshua had only gone his own way; he had never criticized, never goaded his brother before. Arnold glanced at Naomi. She was pale with shock.

"Josh," he said quietly, "what is it? There's something else bothering you, I know there is. Tell us." His voice was gentle, persuasive.

Joshua's head dropped wearily into his hands. "It's Rachel," he said, the coldness gone from his voice. "I had a letter today."

"What about Rachel?"

Naomi waited, not really wanting to hear him talk about Rachel, ever, but having to know.

"She's pregnant," Joshua said.

Arnold looked frankly puzzled. "Is there something wrong? Is it dangerous for her to have a child?"

"Christ Almighty!" Joshua shot out of his chair and began to pace nervously. Naomi watched him, feeling betrayed, envious, knowing she was wrong. He had every right to go to bed with Rachel; she went to bed with Arnold. They were equally guilty— or equally innocent. But she had not been thinking about any of this tonight; she had been able to keep their intimacy out of this house. He had seemed so different, anyway, until now. She watched him pacing, in that nervous way he had.

"Dangerous?" he said finally, anger pushing him. "Palestine is a garrison state, for God's sake! Don't you ever hear what I say?"

"Then bring Rachel here," Arnold said.

Joshua shook his head, furious. "Don't you understand? She wouldn't come, not now, when they need everyone they can get. She wouldn't come—but even if she did, who in his right mind would bring a child into this world? No matter where it was born? She knew I didn't want another child. She knew it!"

Naomi wanted to ask him why not, she wanted to tell him how much she longed for more children herself—he should have known that. She wanted to defend Rachel, brave enough to have stayed out there and defiant enough to have another baby all alone, no matter what he said. He had no right to say it.

"She didn't conceive by herself." Her voice was very hard. "It's as much your child as hers, isn't it?"

Joshua's head turned sharply toward her. His eyes narrowed with anger, then suddenly they widened, as if another thought had struck him. He had stopped his pacing.

"Let's stop this," Arnold said. "A baby's not something to argue about." He went to his wife, and his tone softened. "It upsets Naomi to hear you talk that way. Do you know what we'd give to have another child?"

Joshua nodded, looking at her white, tense face, so unlike the face he had seen yesterday. "I'm sorry. Forgive me, both of you."

"It's all right, Josh," Naomi said. "I'm sorry too. I must be very tired. I'll say good night now—and good luck on your trip.''

Arnold opened the study door for her, and she touched his cheek as she went out. ''I know you can do something to help.''

She went upstairs quickly in a jumble of suffocating emotions. He was still as troubled as the first night he came home from the war, and she was worried about him. But she was angry too at his attitude toward Rachel, a woman she had never met. He had no right to refuse her another child; no man had that right. A few minutes ago she had resented Rachel. That seemed so childish now. Now she wanted to help her. Maybe Sarah could tell her how.

But who could tell her what to do for this troubled man she loved so much and understood so little? She had supposed she knew exactly what she meant to him and even what Rachel meant to him. Now she was not so sure.

32

GIORA
MAY 1947

Sarah wrapped the tiny boy in a soft cotton blanket while Isaac Levy finished caring for Rachel. ''Is she all right?''

''Fine. You're a real Amazon, Rachel, but I'm damned if I know why you wouldn't let anyone but Sarah help. She's one hell of a woman, but she's a lousy midwife.'' He smiled fondly at both women and went out, carrying a bucket and a bundle of bloody sheets.

Sarah handed the baby to Rachel and sat down near the bed.

''Did I say anything?'' Rachel asked.

Sarah shook her head, and then the room was quiet while Rachel inspected her son, his fingers, his toes, his ears. Then she studied his face.

''He looks like me,'' Rachel said. ''What do you think?''

"I think it doesn't matter a damn who his father is, if that's what you mean. We decided that months ago."

"Except that one father wants him and the other doesn't."

"Rachel, shut up about the two fathers, will you? I'm no good at moral issues, and you're worse. You loved one man as much as the other for those few hours. It would never have happened if Joshua weren't . . . the way he is."

"He's still that way, and I still love him, so that's no excuse."

Sarah got up and went to the window, rumpling her short, gray-streaked hair. Her tall figure had slimmed and hardened with all the outdoor work she did at Yad Mordechai, but she was still a strikingly voluptuous woman, even in khaki pants. A white cotton shirt set off the tan she had never allowed herself when she worked for Duchess. Now her home was here.

"Lazar never believed in excuses," she said. "And I agree with him. Lazar believed in life, that's all, life. And you're holding it." Her eyes were wet. "Now rest, darling. I'm going to tell Benjamin and my kids about Buster, here. What will you name him?"

"Eleazar—if it's all right with you."

Sarah nodded, smiling at her sister-in-law. "You're a lovely person, Rachel. I'm going to cry if I don't get out of here, and you know how the kids hate that. Now go to sleep. I'll be back later."

The baby mewed, and Rachel held him to her breast, but he waved his tiny hands, refusing it.

"You're stubborn, just like your father," she said. But who was his father?

Ben had listened quietly at first when she told him months before, that one night was all there could ever be for them.

"I can't use the way you feel about me, Ben. It isn't fair, not when it's Josh I really want."

"Rachel, do you think I care whether we love each other equally?"

"I won't use you for sex and comfort, Ben. No, don't look that way. I know that's not what it was last night, but that's what it might become. Listen to me. There are things between Joshua and me that will keep us together as long as we live. It's always that way when two people have loved each other in the same way at the same time."

"He might as well be dead now," Ben said.

"But he isn't. He's wounded, Ben, but he's not dead yet. He's terribly sad and he's angry, but he didn't go away like that, it's not his nature."

"You still think there's going to be some miracle?" Ben lost his temper. "You still think there'll be a bolt of lightning and Josh will be the way he was?" He shook his head. "I never knew a man I admired more, except Lazar. If I had to lose you, at least it was to someone like him. Joshua's not an ordinary man . . ." He stopped, his anger and his admiration mixed, canceling each other out. "I'm arguing for him now," he said, giving in. "But I'll always be here for you, Rachel, no matter what happens."

He had gone away almost immediately, his shoulders broad and square under a well-cut safari jacket, his blond hair glinting in the sun, ageless, the way some people are. He had spent the war in counterintelligence for the British, and he was going to use what he had learned against them now, in the Irgun.

He came back months later, when she was visibly pregnant, demanding to talk to her alone. "I heard about you from one of the Haganah men. Why in hell didn't you get word to me? Isaac knows how."

"But why, Ben?"

"Why? This changes everything. I couldn't stay away once I knew." His hands gripped her shoulders. "Marry me, Rachel. You know he'll never accept this child. Even if he did, he wouldn't be more of a father to it than he's been to Benjamin, and God knows that was little enough."

"He was fighting a war, Ben! He still is."

"Forget about him. What about us? What about our child?"

"Ben please. I can't be sure this baby's yours."

He moved back from her as if she had slapped him, and she sat down, feeling weak. Could a man understand that the nature of sex could change enough to be heartbreaking without stopping altogether—that you always hoped it would change back to the way it used to be?

"What kind of man is he, using you like that?"

"I wanted him—and you know what kind of man he is. He'd accept the baby even if he were sure it wasn't his. It's why I still

love him. It's why you and I had to stop. I wanted him, I still do.
It wasn't fair to you.''

"Fair? Is it fair that I've always loved you—and no one else?''
It was a reference to Joshua's love for another woman. She let it
pass. "Is it fair that I'll never marry anyone else, that I'll never
have a child I can call my own?''

"I never asked that of you, Ben.''

He sat down near her then, his temper fading into resignation.
"No, you didn't. I just wanted to give you everything.'' He took
her hand. "Don't be upset, darling, I'll stop. But you can't
change how I feel. I still love you—and as far as I'm concerned,
that baby is mine.'' He put their hands for an instant on her
swollen body. Then he got up to go, kissing her cheek as he had
always done.

"Be careful, Ben, please.''

He nodded. "When will you know?''

She knew what he meant. "Probably as soon as the baby's
born.''

"Will you tell me if it's mine?'' His back was toward her. "I
won't make a fuss, Rachel, I promise. I just want to know.''

She was afraid she might relent completely at the sight of his
broad back and the way his hair curled, defenseless as a child's,
at the nape of his neck. What was this mixture of trust, respect,
and caring she had for him if not love? If she had never known
Joshua, it would have been love enough for her. Maybe she
loved them both—the way Josh loved two women.

Ben was waiting for an answer.

"Yes, Ben, I'll tell you.''

She hadn't seen him since. She looked down when the baby
cried. "Well, whose are you, then?'' she asked, starting to feed
him. His eyes were closed. Were they blue? Even so, some
babies' eyes were blue at first. Not young Benjamin's, though.
His were as black as Joshua's from the moment he opened them.

"You're bald as an egg too,'' she said to her new son,
laughing softly at the sheer bliss of nursing him. Would he have
hair when Joshua saw him? She thought she knew Joshua very
well, but how would he feel if he found a blond, blue-eyed
infant, very obviously not his? He would not react in any classic
jealous-husband fashion, she knew. It hurt to think that he would
accept her infidelity because he had refused her a child. That was

the kind of man he was; there were times when she wished he were more conventional, less fair, that he cared more about home and family than he did.

But he cared for nothing but his work now and for no one but Lazar.

"I think 'Lazar' is too heavy for you to carry until you grow into it," she said to the baby. "We'll call you Elea."

When would Joshua be back? Certainly not before the newly formed United Nations committee had recommended the partition of Palestine—they must, she thought, they *must*—and the General Assembly had voted on it. The Jewish Agency would bring every pressure to bear for the recommendation and the vote. Things were changing again in Palestine because of that.

The Haganah would accept partition; the Irgun would not. The settlers were loyal to both sides, for the most part. They hated terrorism, but they understood the anger that fed it every time they, their homes, their trucks, were seized and searched for hidden arms to which they felt they had a right; every time they thought about those survivors of the Holocaust who were still barred from Palestine. If partition was granted, they would all be fighting the Arabs, not each other or the British.

And where was Ben? Ben was not the kind of man to condone any kind of killing, yet he would kill to force the British out. The Irgun's rule was to take no life unless it was strictly necessary; it was the Haganah's rule as well. They differed about what constituted necessity.

The baby was asleep. Rachel closed her eyes. For these few hours she would think about nothing but the joy of holding her infant son.

In America all eyes followed a ship called the *President Warfield*—she would become *The Exodus*—carrying forty-five hundred refugees. She had been boarded by the British, and her passengers were returned to the French port they came from. But the refugees, most of them survivors of the camps, refused the French offer of homes and jobs and the privileges of citizenship.

"They don't want to live in France," Joshua said to Arnold. "They want to live in Palestine. After what they've been through, surely they have that right."

Arnold agreed. "But those fanatics in Palestine are turning sympathy away from the Jews."

"We don't need sympathy. We want a country of our own."

"You'll need sympathy to get it, whether you want it or not."

When the refugees were returned to Germany in August, sympathy went to the Jews. There was a wave of anger from people all over the world who had no idea of the political implications of Britain's travail in Palestine. They knew only that it was cruel to send victims of German atrocities back to the scene of the crime.

"Isn't it just as cruel for the Irgun to kill British soldiers?" Arnold said. "They don't make policy, but they have to carry it out."

"That's what the Germans said," Joshua replied curtly. "I don't want to hear about it. In a fight like this I can only see one side—ours. I stopped looking at anything but our side long ago. Don't talk about it."

And Arnold stopped talking, more worried about his brother than ever. He saw him very little; most of the time Joshua was traveling, looking for money, looking for guns, looking for ways to get the guns past the British and into Palestine.

For the first time in his life Arnold felt his brother needed him. It was never an open appeal, but Joshua called him at Duchess almost every day—to talk about a book, about the weather, about anything at all, as if he had to hear Arnold's voice. It was impossible not to be there when his brother needed him, even if his behavior was so erratic. Beyond telling Arnold that Rachel had given birth to a boy, Joshua never spoke about his second son.

At the end of August the UN Special Committee on Palestine recommended that Britain surrender her mandate and Palestine be partitioned. On November 29, 1947, the UN General Assembly voted in favor of that recommendation.

33

NEW YORK
DECEMBER 1947

The celebrations in New York were longer than those in Palestine—
they were all beginning to call it Israel now—where Arab opposition mounted like a fever every day. Naomi was not surprised
that Joshua took the news with more worry than elation: they had
a state, but could they keep it?

"Will you be going back soon?" she asked him one day in yet
another room at the same hotel. They had been together no more
than a half-dozen times in the past year, and she was beginning
to hate this hotel.

"Yes, next week."

She was somehow relieved to hear it. "For how long?"

"I don't know. We need a plan for what's coming after the
British pull out. We'll need guns to implement the plan." His
hand went to her breasts. "Don't talk about that here."

She sat up, holding the sheet against her body. "There's
something I have to talk about. I've been feeling this is wrong,
Josh, for a long time." She waited, wondering what he would
say.

"Since you heard that Rachel was pregnant, I know."

Her blue eyes turned on him. "Then you knew! You felt the
same way!"

"Not at all the same way. I'm not a hypocrite, Naomi. I don't
think it's sinful to make love when Rachel's pregnant and perfectly acceptable when she isn't."

"Is that what I am?" Naomi breathed. "A hypocrite?"

He pulled her down to lie beside him. "No, darling, just
naive. Did I need you less because of the baby? Or you me?"

"Would you have needed me if Rachel were here?"

His face changed. "I'm not going to speculate. My wife isn't
here."

"My husband is." She had not meant to say it.

"I'm aware of that."

They were both angry now.

"We're a fine pair of lovers," she said. "You're guilty about my husband, and I'm guilty about your wife."

He shook her slightly. "Do you really wish this had never happened, that we weren't here together? Well, I don't. You're all I have left." He kissed her as if it were the first time. But how could she be all he had left? He loved Rachel, she knew it; he loved his sons. Would he still feel like this about her when he had seen his baby? Fear of losing him swept over her. No, she couldn't wish this had never happened to them, she was glad they were here together like this. She let him pull her closer.

When she left him, she was still uneasy about their relationship but not sure exactly why. That was something she would have to think through while he was away.

Arnold took his brother to La Guardia Airport for the twenty-hour trip to Tel Aviv.

"I can't count how many planes I've put you on," he said while the chauffeur maneuvered the Rolls. There was no reply. Arnold expected none.

There had been times when he was glad to see his brother go. Joshua was the family's hero, and he was its banker; that kept them apart. The warrior king and the worker. Once he had resented that, just as once he had envied Joshua his self-assurance, his charm—and Naomi. He envied him nothing now—except, in a distant kind of way, his second son. His Julie was more to him than ten children, but he would have liked a son.

Joshua would be seeing Elea for the first time. Surely he had abandoned his irrational objections to this baby by now. He didn't talk much about his family. It was hard to tell what he thought about anything but politics.

The car swung onto the departure ramp. Joshua never let Arnold wait in the terminal, but Arnold got out of the car when it stopped and opened the trunk.

"Here." Arnold handed his brother a package. "Gifts for Rachel and all the children. Let me know whatever they need. If you don't, Sarah will."

Joshua nodded briefly, shook his brother's hand, and picked

up his suitcase. "Thanks, Arnold, for everything." He vanished into the crowded terminal, and Arnold got back into the car, glad he would soon be home.

Usually Arnold used his travel time to sort out business projects. It was amazing how quickly markets were returning to order after the war. Business was a lot more stable than politics. Business was only about money; politics involved power and lip service to the concerns of many people, even though its ultimate goal was riches too.

Arnold was still expanding Duchess, still collecting companies that produced pharmaceuticals—and baby foods. People would always need medicine, and the first wave of post-war babies had already arrived. In fifteen years, after Arnold had fed them, the girls would be buying his cosmetics.

Tonight, though, he was counting wealth of a different kind. His place in the business and social hierarchy, his beautiful home, his daughter. And his wife, most of all his wife. He always saved the best for last. She was beautiful as ever; more so, with a new kind of ripeness.

She had very definite ideas about a lot of things now, including Julie, but assurance made her a more exciting woman. There was something about her that aroused him more than ever, even though she was still sexually passive. He could sense something in her reminiscent of that unforgettable week when Julie was conceived. It excited him so much that sometimes he wanted to take her to bed without waiting until night and bedtime and make all kinds of passionate love to her in ways he knew from that one affair with Annalise but had never attempted with his wife. Yet, he would not risk offending her—and it was not something a man could do after twenty years of marriage.

He was embarrassed to find himself fully aroused just thinking of how he would touch her tonight. Suddenly he wondered if Joshua was thinking the same thoughts about Rachel. But his brother's sex life was none of his business. He turned his thoughts back to Duchess.

Joshua had spotted two Haganah men on the plane, but he had no desire to talk, and he managed to sit with strangers.

He always forgot New York the moment he started back to Palestine, where he belonged, where it was almost unbearable for him to be now that everything there trapped him in the past, linked him mercilessly to what he must not forget, even if he could.

And now a son, named after Lazar. But was the child his?

The ruthlessness of Naomi's remark that night—"She didn't conceive by herself. It's as much your child as hers"—had pushed a button somewhere inside him, had made him remember that he had not once lost control in bed with Rachel, had made him wonder why Rachel had cried the night before he left, Rachel who never cried. But that night she had clung to him like a child, telling him she loved him. They had never needed words to tell each other that. It was in their eyes, a simple touch of their hands, the hours they spent living together, not only the hours they spent making love.

Or had she been asking him to tell her he loved her still? He tried, God, how he tried to tell her. But he could not get over the fear of feeling anything, lest he feel too much. The only emotion familiar—and safe—to him now was fury, and he could barely control it lately. He could not blame Rachel for wanting reassurance from such a man as he was.

And he hadn't given her that reassurance. Had she found it with Ben? He was the only man she would turn to, he was sure of that. Was it Ben's son or his? Would Rachel tell him, or—he couldn't stand it, he couldn't—would she leave him for Ben? In such a marriage as theirs, more apart than together, it wouldn't take much for her to leave. But he couldn't contemplate life without Rachel. She was part of everything he had built for himself.

And part of the now he could only forget with Naomi. Even Naomi was less willing to dwell in a never-never land with him. She was no longer a hopeless romantic but a woman with insight who was beginning to question what he knew would not bear questioning.

"A fine pair of lovers," she had said, guilty not over their own spouses but over each other's.

No matter what Rachel wanted, she had a right to it. It was her body, after all. And he remembered it, and her, with a different jealousy from what he had felt in the early years of Naomi's marriage to Arnold. That had been a melancholy yearning; this was a piercing pain.

He had no right to either feeling. He had no right to any feelings at all. He put his head back on the seat and settled himself for the long trip. He hoped Isaac had received his message. Nothing was certain, the way things were out there now. . . .

34

GIORA
DECEMBER 1947

Isaac was waiting for her when she came out of the dairy wearing a milk-splattered apron under a heavy sweater and carrying Elea in a basket.

"He's outgrowing this one too." The Doctor smiled, putting out a finger for the baby to grab. "High time his father saw him."

Rachel looked up quickly. "Have you heard anything?"

"He's on his way—just got it on the radio from Ari. He asked us to tell you and Benjamin he'll be here in three days, four at the most."

She closed her eyes. "Thank heaven," she whispered. "I hope he's better."

"Doesn't he write?"

"Of course, but I can't really tell from letters."

Isaac looked grim. "What does he say about Elea?"

Rachel sighed. "The right things, but his heart isn't in it. He just didn't want another baby." She turned away. "I must go in and feed him. Let me know if you hear anything more."

Isaac helped her carry the basket to the door of her room. Once inside, she undressed the baby, removed enough of her clothing to expose her breast, and sat down to nurse him.

"Maybe when he sees you," she said to Elea. He was a jolly baby, not serious the way Benjamin had always been. He had her eyes, not Joshua's, and the fine fuzz that covered his lovely little head was dark brown. Sometimes when she turned him over in his bath, she thought he was far broader in build than Benjamin had been; she and Joshua were both taller than average, but not broad. And sometimes there was an expression on his face . . . but there was no real resemblance to anyone. As soon as Joshua was back, she would forget the whole thing.

Ben had seen the baby once. Only once.

It had been so quiet that night, an ominous quiet. The British were there in name only now; they would neither protect nor punish anyone. The Arabs were there with the clear intent to kill every Jew they could.

She had been inside her room when voices split the dark outside. She turned out the light and took a repeater rifle from under the bed. Benjamin slept in the children's house; Elea didn't stir in his wooden cradle, a gift from Sarah. She pushed aside the curtain and looked out the window, waiting. She could almost hear the collective sigh of relief when the watchtower sentry shouted, *"Ha'kol b'seder"*—"It's okay"—and lights blinked on again.

She heard steps approaching and Isaac's voice, angrier than it had ever been.

"You bloody damned fool, coming in like that. You could have been shot. If that sentry knew you were Irgun, he might have winged you anyway."

"I had to see Rachel," Ben's voice said, tight and sullen. She could see two dim outlines outside her window.

"I would have brought her, idiot!"

"Too dangerous now for her to go any distance from Giora," Ben said impatiently. "I want to see her alone, Isaac."

"Madman. Well, go ahead, you're both over twenty-one. I'll wait for you at the end of the walk."

Isaac's steps retreated, and Rachel opened the door. Ben shut it quietly while she lit the lamp. She gasped at the sight of him. His face, his clothes, his hair were covered with mud. He carried a machine gun. There was a pistol in his hip holster and belts of cartridges over his torso.

"I should have changed, but I had no time. Don't look at me like that, Rachel." He smiled, Ben's sweet smile. "I'm only a terrorist, not a devil."

246 *Leona Blair*

She went to him then. ''Are you all right? You look so thin. Do you want a drink? Wine's all I have here.''

''Where is he?'' Ben said.

She took his hand and led him to the cradle. She brought the lamp so that he could see the sleeping baby. Elea's little face was almost hidden. He slept on his stomach with his head jammed against the side of the cradle, padded for his protection with old blankets.

After many minutes Ben looked up. ''If I take off this jacket and wash my hands, can I hold him?''

She nodded, putting a basin of water on the bureau for him. She picked up the baby and waited until he had dried his face and arms, then handed the child to him. He cradled the infant against his face, and she looked away. The moment was too intimate for anyone to see, even her.

He would ask her, she knew he would ask her. What good would it be to tell him the truth, that she honestly didn't know? It would only trouble his mind, and from the look of him he was already living on his nerves. How long would he last, living as he did on the edge of disaster every minute? Better to tell him he was holding Joshua's son and put an end to it.

''Rachel, he's marvelous.''

His voice was full of wonder, as if he had seen something of unutterable splendor. How could she take it away from him, a man who had nothing in his life but guns and blood and killing— and his love for her?

It's not my fault, she shouted at him in her head. *You could have married, you could have married any woman you wanted, as dear and good and sweet as you are. Why do you have to love me?*

''Is he mine?''

Mine. The way people said that word. Why did it mean so much to possess a thing, a person, a piece of land? The world was choking on its possessions.

Leave me alone, she almost told him. *Leave me alone with this infant who is not yours, not Joshua's, not even mine as much as he is Lazar's.*

''You promised, Rachel. I'll never bother you. I swear it. I just have to know.''

She put a hand over her eyes. ''Yes, Ben, he's yours.'' What else could she give him, this dearest friend, but a little speck of joy? He would keep his vow. An honorable man, their Dandy Ben.

"I knew it," he said when she turned back to him. He had the baby against his cheek again. "I'm glad you named him after Lazar." He bent and put Elea back in his cradle, on his stomach, not too close to the padded side, as if he knew Elea would squirm there soon enough. He took a gold chain from around his neck, with a Hebrew *chai* on it, the sign for "life."

"Keep this for me until I get back. When he's thirteen, I'll give it to him myself."

He was buttoning his jacket, strapping on the holster, picking up the cartridge belts. He took the glass of wine she gave him and drank it down.

"If you need me, tell Isaac. And be careful. From now on it'll be more dangerous than ever." He kissed her cheek, holding her away from the dirty jacket. "I have to go now." He went to the door. "Thank you, Rachel," he whispered over his shoulder. "Thank you for my son. I love you." Then he was gone.

She stood there for a long time before she replaced the lamp on the bureau, turned it out, and lay down on the bed, holding the chain and the *chai* he had given her.

Now she put the baby back into his cradle and looked at herself in the mirror. She had to do something about her hair. She wanted to look pretty for him. But only Joshua could do something about the worried look in her eyes.

35

TEL AVIV
DECEMBER 1947

Ari led the way to a battered old Austin parked near the airport.
"You don't look very rabbinical," he said, talking around a big
cigar. "Where's the hat, the curls, the beard?"

"Black is pious enough for America," Joshua said. He tossed
the jacket of his worsted suit into the back seat with his raincoat
and baggage. The sun was burning hot, the breeze cool. It was a
typical Mediterranean December day.

"Well?" Joshua demanded when they were rolling.

"As usual. The British hate us. We hate the British. The
Arabs hate everybody. It's Eden all over again."

"And the Irgun?"

"What can I tell you? Sometimes we're with them, sometimes
we're not. Blowing up hotels isn't our line of work." He shrugged.
"If the Irgun were French, they'd be called the Resistance. In
Yugoslavia they'd be Partisans. Nobody knows what to make of
a fighting Jew. They're supposed to live quietly and die without a
fuss."

"Do we have a chance against the Arabs when the British pull
out?" Joshua asked.

"I'll tell you in May." Ari pressed on the car's horn, and it
squawked like a soprano past her prime as they shot across a
blind intersection. He grinned. "If we live that long."

They parked the car a few blocks from Hayarkon Street and
walked toward the red house. Joshua refused one of Ari's cigars.

"You're the one who should hand them out," Ari said. "That's
some baby you've got."

Joshua looked at him, curious to hear more.

"We were out that way when he was about six weeks old," Ari
continued in his pungent sentences. "Had a little celebration
for your wife. Your sister was there too from Yad Mordechai.

Fine figure of a woman. Your big boy's almost as tall as you. Can sneak around in the dark like a cat, they tell me, the way Wingate taught us. They'll be glad you're home for Christmas.''

Joshua smiled. "Hanukkah."

Ari shrugged. "In this country what difference does it make? We have three sabbaths: Moslems close on Friday, Jews on Saturday, Christians on Sunday. Easter. Passover. It's all mixed up. Christmas brings the most tourists, though. You explain it to me, Rabbi. Some Jew is born in a stable, and for two thousand years the whole world makes a *bris*. But where is it written in the New Testament about his circumcision?"

Joshua laughed outright this time. "I don't think it is. I didn't know you pondered matters of religion, Ari."

They turned off the street into the red house, always the first stop for Haganah men returning from abroad. There were men working in most of the rooms on the ground floor, poring over papers, maps, assembly instructions for the machinery being smuggled to them. If a British patrol came by, Bibles replaced the documents, and the men chanted in Hebrew.

Ari and Joshua went up the stairs to the radio room, where the consumptive-looking Greek—his name was Andrea—who had led the meeting many months ago waved a hand and went on deciphering a radio message that had just come in. A licensed amateur radio operator in New York transmitted in Dutch call letters and was answered from Tel Aviv in Greek. It confused the American authorities, who cooperated with British policy, no matter how popular partition was in the United States or how apparent the need for the Jews to defend themselves.

Andrea, still bone-thin but with a tan that made him look healthier, pounded on the table when he finished deciphering the message. "The bastards!" he yelled. "They've slammed the door on us."

Ari and Joshua waited until he calmed down. A few men came to the doorway from adjacent rooms.

"An embargo," Andrea finally managed to say. "The United States put an embargo on all arms sales to the Middle East. Can you believe that? One week after partition!"

"That means the Arabs as well as us," one of the men said.

"The Arabs have all the equipment they need already," Joshua told him. "And no British army watching to see that they can't get more."

"To hell with them all, the whores," Ari said. "We'll make it on our own."

Andrea nodded without conviction and sat down at the table again. "Whatever else they are, the Brits are good soldiers, and they trained that Arab legion sitting across the Jordan."

"Camel shit," Ari said. "They trained us too. The Arabs are only men, Andrea. The only difference between them and us is that they have five countries. We've got one." He glanced at Joshua. He would have to go back sooner than planned. If the embargo had happened two days earlier, he could not have come at all.

Andrea nodded again. "Sit down. We have a lot to talk about."

It was dark by the time the meeting ended. Ari handed Joshua the keys to the Austin.

"Take it, you won't be away that long. But don't go across country alone at night."

"No, I'll stay with my sister and go home tomorrow."

They set an hour for their next meeting, and Joshua pulled away, leaving the chunky man standing on the quiet street. He drove through Tel Aviv and headed south on the coast road toward Ashkelon. Yad Mordechai was beyond Ashkelon, right near the Gaza Strip. It would certainly be one of the first Egyptian targets.

Suddenly realization hit him: The road he was on was a Jewish road in a Jewish state. Something he had longed for since early childhood was a reality. He had never thought to see it in his lifetime, only to work toward it. If only Lazar . . . but Lazar had always been sure it would happen.

He was too tired to do more than eat a light meal with Sarah and his niece and nephew before he fell into bed. Sarah woke him at daybreak.

"You look crummy," she said when he had washed and shaved and was drinking strong tea with her. "Anything wrong?"

"No, we just have a hell of a job in front of us."

"We always have had, one way or another."

"I think you and the kids should get out of here. You know this place will be hit first."

Sarah poured more tea. "If you can convince my kids, you can convince me," she said. But he knew Seth and Rebekah would never leave this place. Most of the settlers here were from Poland, some of them escapees from the Warsaw Ghetto. It was a link to Lazar for them.

"Then promise me you'll get out before the Gyppos get to you, Shai."

She promised. He asked for more tea, but she shook her head. "Sooner or later you have to go home. There's no use pretending with me, Joshua. I'm your sister, remember? I know all about you."

He turned away from her. "Sarah, don't meddle."

"What am I supposed to do, sit and watch you ruin everything?"

"If that's what I'm doing, yes." He got up from the table. "It's my life."

"Not anymore, it isn't," she said, one of her terrible tempers rising. "There's Rachel and Benjamin and the baby. He's here whether you want him or not."

His hands were clenched. "Did Rachel tell you that?"

"She didn't have to tell me, the way you are."

"How am I?" he said, trying to control his voice.

"Dammit," Sarah shouted, flushing with rage. "When did we ever fight before?" She lowered her voice. "I don't know what happened over there, Josh, but no matter what it was, you're alive. Live, you damned fool!" She leaned across the table and took his hands in hers. "You can't bring Lazar back this way. You can't bring any of them back."

He almost told her then. She was the one person he could have told, because she never judged. But she was Lazar's wife. He pulled his hands away, still in control of himself. "I have to go."

"Then go!" She was angry again. "But don't punish Rachel for having your son!"

"Suppose he isn't my son?" Finally he had said that much.

"What if he isn't? You're the last man in the world to demand fidelity of a woman." She stopped. She had answered him out of her anger, not because of what she knew. She didn't want to say too much.

He had no way of knowing whether she meant Naomi or the

casual affairs of his past. There wasn't much Sarah didn't catch. Either way . . . "You're right," he said softly.

"And you're out of your mind to say such a thing." Sarah's anger had vanished too. "Damn." She sat down and lit a cigarette. "Arguments are a pain in the ass." She looked up at him, the little sister he loved so much.

He sat down and put an arm around her. "Okay, Shai, no more arguments."

She put her head on his shoulder, and they sat together the way they used to do long ago. "I must go," he said finally.

She walked to the Austin with him. "I'll see you on Saturday—the three of us will drive over to spend the weekend." She bent and looked at him through the open window of the car. "You all right?"

"I'm fine," he said, smiling at her.

"You have a gun?"

He opened the glove compartment to show it to her.

"Put it on the seat and point it at anyone who tries to stop you."

"Suppose it's a Jew?"

"You can't tell a Jew from an Arab without a program," she said. "Just don't take chances."

He could see her waving in the rearview mirror as the car bumped down the road. Telling his sister about his suspicion had made it seem ridiculous. He put the car in top gear and headed north to Haifa; from there he would cross the Galilee to Lake Kinneret and travel south to Giora. The most direct route would have been a northeasterly one in graduated steps: east to Hebron, north to Jerusalem, east to Jericho, north along the Jordan. But that area was teeming with hostile Arabs and inquisitive British. The roundabout way was safer—and he wanted to see this new state of Israel on the way home to Giora. Their own tiny two-room cottage at Giora was almost finished by now. He was anxious to see that too.

Book
Five

36

NEW YORK
SEPTEMBER 1950

Julie smiled brightly and followed her father through the Long
Island plant, hoping she wouldn't disappoint him again. This
time she would really concentrate on everything he told her about
the new equipment, the new methods of layer-blending perfumes,
and the economics of it all. This time she wouldn't start dreaming about the romantic history of her father's business: the first
great lady to perfume her gloves with castoreum; how the Sun
King loved fragrance so much that he went to his flowered
pavillion for deep breathing between encounters with his minis-
ters or his mistresses; how Mme. de Pompadour wore a different
perfume each day and used beauty patches all over her body so
King Louis XV could hunt for them with great delight in bed.

Julie blushed. She was doing it again. She listened to her
father.

"There!" he said proudly. "Impressive, aren't they?"

"Oh, yes," Julie breathed, looking up at the line of stainless
steel vats looming over her head like monsters. "But how do you
clean them?"

Arnold pointed. "That hydraulic jack raises a man high enough
to scrub them with a long-handled brush."

When she was a child, the plant had frightened her, with its
antiseptic atmosphere, its bubbling tubes and huge machines.
Now, at fifteen, the impossibility of mastering the intricacies of
cosmetic and perfume manufacture frightened her more than the
machinery. Her head began to ache while she groped for an
intelligent question to ask. "How much do they hold?" was all
she could think of.

"Ten thousand gallons. We can really mass produce our best-
selling items in these."

"And the more you can make in one run," Julie added,

repeating what she had heard him say so many times, "the less it costs and the higher the profit margin."

Arnold smiled his approval. "Absolutely right." He put an arm around his daughter. "We'll make a businesswoman of you yet, just like your aunt Sarah."

Julie covered her familiar hollow feeling with another bright smile. She knew she could never run her father's gigantic empire, not even a tiny corner of it. Even worse, she knew she didn't want to. In the first place she wasn't a bit like her aunt. Sarah was a fantastic woman who had helped her kibbutz hold off the Egyptian army for six vital days during Israel's War of Independence. Her cousins Seth and Rebekah had helped their mother—and Julie wasn't a bit like them either. They preferred to stay and rebuild Yad Mordechai from its ruins when the war was over, rather than enjoy life here in the United States. They were always doing spectacular things. Julie knew she would never do anything spectacular.

She was a dreamer. Her father said so often enough. She loved books and music, poetry and plays, movies above all—anything that touched her imagination and set it in flight. Her father had no patience with dreamers, and his approval was the one thing Julie craved. She knew she had her mother's. She hoped her mother would get here soon. Naomi always managed to quell Arnold's expectations about Julie's future at Duchess.

They walked on through the plant, where department supervisors in gray smocks presided. Women in pink smocks made sure that the jars of delicious-smelling creams were properly capped, and packers in green smocks ranged the jars in neat cartons marked with the Duchess coronet, ready for shipment.

"You know," Arnold said when they were in the corridor separating the building's two wings, "Shai was your age when we made our first batch of face cream from your grandmother's recipe." He shook his head. "It's hard to believe it was so long ago."

"Is she coming soon?" Aunt Sarah was Julie's favorite woman, after her mother. Even having to live up to her, a hopeless task, would never change the love Julie had for Sarah, the loneliness she shared with her for that lost, blond uncle who had seemed like a prince out of the tales he used to tell her when she was little.

Arnold shrugged. "I keep telling her we have problems to talk over. And she keeps telling me she's too busy to get away. Busy—on a farm!" He opened a safety door, and they went along the bare, gleaming corridor.

"What problems, Daddy? You said last night cosmetics are booming, even without all those other things the company owns."

"Subsidiaries," he corrected her. "Use the business term. Our chief problem is competition. We have to keep ahead of the others. We got way out front with our own perfume, but you can't rest on one gamble that paid off. Now Arden has opened a men's salon. I think it will fail, but we should have thought of it at least. Sarah's good at new ideas." His expression changed to annoyance. "And Revlon comes out of nowhere and plasters the country with this 'Where's the Fire?' gimmick. It's cheap, sensational advertising, but it's profitable—and we have nothing to match it."

He pushed open another pair of doors and strode ahead of Julie into the perfume division of Duchess. There was still only one fragrance made here, and it was still a best seller. Since the war, it was advertised as an American fragrance and accepted as such. But the war was over now. A lot of new money was out there to be spent, and Arnold was certain that things would follow the old pattern: anything French—wine, couture, fragrance, or love—was believed to be superior. Duchess needed another fragrance, bottled in France.

The scent of Duchess was heavy in the air, but it was comforting to Julie. It reminded her of her mother, who had worn it exclusively since Julie was born.

"I wish Einhorn would get on with the new perfume," Arnold fretted. "The man's so stubborn. He likes to play around with 'flavors' for our household products. The man who created Duchess fussing around with toothpaste and room spray! What a waste!"

Julie looked around for Otto Einhorn, that funny, messy man her father allowed to break so many rules. She still called him Uncle Otto because he liked it. Einhorn had no family of his own. He couldn't, people said, since he was wounded in the war. That had puzzled Julie until her mother explained it to her. At first Julie was embarrassed whenever she was around Uncle Otto, but now she was just sad for him. She thought his injury was more of a waste than flavoring toothpaste, and realized she had just said it out loud to her father.

Arnold was shocked. "A young girl shouldn't even know about such things, much less have opinions about them. Who told you?"

"Mother," Julie said, furious with herself. Now he was angry, and the whole evening would be spoiled.

Arnold made a small sound in his throat, but he never criticized anything Naomi said or did. He would make his disapproval known by oblique remarks to his wife, and Naomi would wait until he had made enough of them to ease his annoyance before she swept his objections away with some gentle comment. It was a way her mother had that Julie longed to imitate but never could. She was always nervous when her father got angry; her mother never was.

She watched him sniff nervously at the testing sticks for attars and fragrances he always carried in his breast pocket. Aunt Sarah said you could always tell Arnold's mood by his testing sticks.

"If he sniffs more than two, watch out!"

He was sniffing four now as he led the way to a long line of rooms for the large staff of blenders Duchess employed to create the right scents for cosmetics, lotions, deodorants, shampoos, household sprays, furniture polish, detergents. The list was endless.

The perfume wing had stores of every kind of fragrance in the world. Flowers—jasmine, rose, orange, violet, geranium. Herbs—lavender, peppermint, patchouli. Spices—clove, cinnamon, nutmeg. Sandalwood from the East Indies. Grasses, roots, and mosses, lemon, orris, oak.

And there were the animal essences used to "fix" the fragrances once they were blended. Musk from the Asian deer that were lured to clearings by hunters' flutes and killed for their precious musk sacs as soon as they appeared. Ambergris, by-product of a disease of the sperm whale, horrid to smell in its natural mass yet precious in tiny, refined quantities to highlight a perfume or make it linger on the skin. Civet from deer, the best fixative for floral scents.

There were thousands of vials of natural and synthetic essences. From these a blender would select a few: heavy scents for base notes, gradually lighter ones for middle and top notes, and a fixative. The blender would go into a tightly sealed booth, from which all air and odor had been pumped out before clean, odorless air filled it, and in that room "compose" a fragrance.

It had always been amazing to Arnold. "They can recognize so many scents. I'm always trying, but I can only spot one once in a while. It's like having perfect pitch."

Einhorn, Julie knew, could tell you not only what a natural scent was and where it came from, but with floral absolutes he knew at what altitude the flowers had been grown. He was the finest "nose" in the industry and the most eccentric.

He came out of this glass-enclosed office now, his mop of gray hair untidy and wild, his white smock rumpled and stained with smears of oil.

He embraced Julie, smelling strongly of cloves. "How is my little princess? Arnold, she is more like her mother every day. Only your eyes she has, green like a mountain lake." He beamed at both of them. "Soon she gets married, and we have a grandbaby."

Julie blushed, even while she laughed, but Arnold didn't find it funny. "Otto, she's only fifteen, still a child."

"Yes, yes. But such a child. The young men must be clustering around her already."

Julie and her father exchanged glances. Julie didn't like boys of her age. She was much happier with books than with the prep-school brothers of her schoolmates. It seemed to Arnold that she should go to a party now and then, learn to mix with people. A businesswoman couldn't be shy.

He watched her laughing with Otto. No, she was no longer a child. She was taller than her mother, but she had Naomi's delicate coloring, the same wide eyes, well-turned little nose, and full mouth. Her figure was less round than Naomi's at her age—his eyes remarked this only briefly—but she had the same flair for choosing clothes and colors that became her most.

If Naomi's color as a girl had been blue, Julie's was pale green. Her taffeta dress, bought during their last shopping trip to Paris, was snug to the waist, then billowed out over wide petticoats. Julie looked beautiful in that dress. High heels made her taller than she was—and, *yes*, he repeated to himself with a sense of surprise and dismay, *she is no longer a child*. Perhaps it was just as well that she didn't like to date young boys.

"Come, Julie, let him go back to work," he said abruptly. "Anything new, Otto?"

Einhorn shook his head, still beaming despite Arnold's obvious impatience with him. "A fragrance is like a symphony—or a poem. The mind must open its doors and drift here and there to pick harmonies out of infinite possibilities. Patience, my dear Arnold."

Julie kissed him and left with her father. "What a sweet man he is."

"He'd be a lot sweeter if he'd make me a new perfume." Arnold opened the doors to his office. "Symphonies!"

Naomi was sitting in his desk chair looking out at the smooth lawn that surrounded Duchess Long Island. "You're early," he said, smiling when she turned the chair and got up.

She kissed him and turned to Julie. "How did you like it, darling?"

"It's wonderful!" Julie said, hoping her father wouldn't remember her knowledge of Otto Einhorn's misfortune.

"She's beginning to take a real interest in things," Arnold said with satisfaction. He looked at a few papers on his desk, then up at his wife and daughter. He cleared his throat. "You both look so beautiful," he said. Naomi wore a suit of navy tissue faille with a froth of white lace at the neck and cuffs and a small hat that curved over the crown of her head, sweeping her hair smooth. Sometimes he couldn't believe in his own good luck when he looked at them.

"Well, so do you," Naomi said. "It's an occasion, after all. Our nephew's starting school here, and Julie's turned fifteen. It'll be a beautiful evening."

"If Benjamin doesn't turn up in shorts and a bush shirt," Julie said.

Naomi laughed at the expression on Arnold's face. "Arnold, Julie's only teasing. Benjamin's not a savage."

Arnold looked doubtful. "They're all savages out there."

"I'd love to go back with him at Christmas vacation," Julie said wistfully.

"Well, you can't. That's like taking a vacation in a war zone. Only nuts like my sister live in such a place with children."

"Uncle Josh isn't a nut, and he lives there with Aunt Rachel and Benjamin and Elea."

Arnold was busy with his papers. "Ask your mother if she would have stayed in such a place when you were only a baby like Elea, with a house like ours to come to."

Naomi shook her head. "No, Julie, I'd have come to America. But I'm not Sarah or Rachel . . ." Her sentence hung unfinished in Arnold's ears.

"And I'm not Joshua," he finished for her, but calmly. He had made his private peace with that fact several years ago, and he was convinced that nothing could ever unsettle him again. "We'd better leave—we'll be late for Benjamin's plane."

Julie followed her parents out to the car, wondering how much taller Benjamin had grown. He had come to America with his father a few times since the war ended and always stayed with them. He had taken special courses to make up for the education he had missed during the Israeli War of Independence. He hadn't missed much—Benjamin was a genius. He would do well at prep school and at Harvard, but it was easy for him. He was brilliant— just like his father, Aunt Sarah said.

He looked a lot like his father used to in old pictures Julie had seen of him, but he was open and frank, far less reserved than Uncle Josh. Julie had never met her aunt Rachel and her baby cousin Elea—none of them had—but she knew all about them from the stories she had heard all her life.

They were different. Benjamin wasn't like American boys his age. Nobody ever called him Ben or Benjy. He was too serious to have a nickname. He was strong, vital, and determined too. His father was silent, driven, and withdrawn, totally preoccupied with money. He made frequent visits to America, but they hardly saw him. He was always traveling on some business and for fund raising.

"Our fathers have one thing in common," Julie had said to Benjamin the previous summer. "Money."

Benjamin agreed. "But it's about the only thing."

No one talked about it, but Julie knew Arnold was paying for Benjamin's education. It was generous, but Julie thought her father had some other motive. And of course he loved Benjamin. Everybody did. Julie had a little more than a crush on her cousin. She thought she might marry him. That would please her father— if Benjamin would agree to stay in the States and go into Duchess. Then he'd have Fursten children to leave his empire to.

One thing Julie was certain about: When Uncle Josh came, her father welcomed him, but her mother was really happy to see him. As she grew older, Julie was aware that her parents were still doing things together in bed—and the thought occurred to her most often when Uncle Josh was in this country. She had no idea why that was so, but she had sensed it too often for it to be only a coincidence, and it always disturbed her.

It was hard to imagine her parents together any other time. Did they see each other completely naked, her beautiful mother and her handsome, frightening father? Julie knew all about sex and babies, but all the books in the world couldn't make her feel what it was like. Benjamin knew, though. Daddy said everybody in Palestine was a free-thinker, and he meant sex, not politics.

She got into the silver-gray Rolls with her parents and tried to stop thinking about sex. The car bowled silently down the drive, through the wrought-iron gates discreetly marked "Duchess Limited Long Island," and took the road to the airport. Benjamin was coming, and it was always good to see Benjamin.

37

GIORA
SEPTEMBER 1950

Rachel came into the same living room of their tiny cottage. "I always hate it when Benjamin leaves," she said.

Joshua looked up from some lists he was compiling. "You have Elea," he said.

"I also have you."

"How about a visit to Sarah?" he suggested.

Rachel sat down in an armchair and gazed at him. "Do you think I'd go to Yad Mordechai while you're here?" She shook her head. "I spent five long years without you during the war. I spend months without you as it is. I just miss my little buddy, that's all."

Joshua got up from the desk, his head almost grazing the ceiling. "You know I have to go."

"Of course," she said equably. "But when you're here, I'm here, and that's that."

He sat on the arm of her chair and took her hand. "You never complain about anything," he said.

"You're not around to hear me." She looked up at him, laughing.

It was good to hear Rachel laugh. She had changed since the War of Independence two years ago. Hard work and danger had traced more lines around her eyes than should have been there at thirty-nine. There was an endurance about her that had nothing left in it of youth. She was fuller of body and sturdier of spirit than he. He wondered sometimes if that was despite his emptiness or because of it. Or had she simply been born to fewer illusions, to suffer less the losing of them?

He kissed her and went back to his desk.

"What are you working on?" she asked.

"The usual. More trips, more meetings in fancy parlors to convince people that we've only won the first battle. I have to shame them into giving more than they want to."

"It won't kill them," Rachel observed, picking up a book. Psychology, he saw.

Joshua returned to his papers, but he could not concentrate. The ticking of the clock on the sideboard disturbed him. It did feel strange without Benjamin. It was no easy matter being father to a genius—maybe that was why Rachel was reading psychology books—although Benjamin seemed unaware that he was extraordinarily brilliant. He soaked up knowledge like a sponge from the truckloads of books Sarah had always sent to Giora for him. Now Arnold and Naomi sent them for all the children.

"My two aren't like Benjamin," Sarah always said. "Life will be easier for them than for him. They're like me. I don't think Papa had any idea you were a gifted child, Josh. They didn't know about such things in those days."

"Don't ever let Arnold hear you say that," Joshua told her.

"Oh, he's gifted too, but in only one way. He hasn't any— well, emotional circuits in his crackerjack mind, only business. He was never carried away by music or poetry or anything as intangible as an idea. I don't think he ever let himself be carried away by anything.''

Except his wife, Joshua knew. But Arnold had never been able to show it to her, never been able to let the spark escape that would have welded them together. Joshua's own erotic interludes with his brother's wife were an escape for him and a release for Naomi, whenever they could see each other. That was so rarely that there was no time for talk, no time to define the nature of their relationship. Joshua preferred it that way, and now, apparently, so did she. It somehow kept their intimacy in a world apart from reality, no threat to him or anyone else. It surprised him that he even thought of Naomi when he was home in Israel. He didn't want that part of his life to overlap this one. That way they were all safe.

Only his own covert rage was a threat. Sometimes it surfaced the sharp, wounding tip of the iceberg, and he couldn't help what he said, wanting to hurt as much as he had been hurt. It was there with the wealthy men his brother knew, with Arnold himself.

But for the most part he managed to keep his anger under control, along with his melancholy. He must not compound his felonies by inflicting them on his wife and child—children, he corrected himself.

He was virtually certain that Elea was Ben Horowitz's son, but he had never said so to anyone but Sarah, that one time. His certainty was built on fragments, things Rachel had said or done, more than on the happy baby who was the image of his mother. Only Elea's smile, sometimes, was Ben's.

Joshua looked over at his wife's dark hair, still untouched by gray under the reading lamp.

Fragments . . .

Rachel's tears the night before he left for America, before she knew she was pregnant. The tears had not been for the child.

Rachel's face the day he came back to see Lazar's namesake for the first time. Tentative, slightly anxious. That could have been because of Joshua—''the way you are,'' Sarah had said. But Rachel had given him the baby as if she defied him not to take the child and accept him as his own. Joshua had never been afraid of losing any woman until that moment. He would have accepted Elea under any circumstances rather than risk life without Elea's mother.

Rachel when Yad Mordechai had fallen after holding off the Egyptian army for six critical days, and they were sick with worry for Sarah and the children. They had all been in the communal hall when the message came through: Sarah was safe; Seth and Rebekah had filtered north to Gvar Am to fight on. Old Reuven's eyes were clouded when he told them the rest of the message.

"Ben Horowitz was at Yad Mordechai. He's dead."

Aviva's voice had protested for all of them. "Oh, no, not our Ben, not our Dandy with his sweet smile."

Rachel had disappeared without a word from the anxious circle and come back with the sleepy baby, raining tears on his little head while they sat in rage and sorrow, mourning Ben. It was for something more than comfort that she held the baby—she could have held Joshua.

But there had been no time then to unravel personal problems. A group led by Moshe Dayan was holding back Syrian tanks nearby, with two French cannon so old they called them "Napoleonchiks." They were all fighting for their lives.

It was only after the cease-fire that he had time to think. By then it was too late to talk.

Fragments, like bits of cloth tied together to make a rag doll, a doll that took the form of Ben, alive and loving, loving Rachel.

He pushed away the chill the image brought. He must not, could not be jealous. Conventional morality had no place in his life. How could a man who posed as a rabbi in order to buy munitions be moral? How could a man who sent his dearest friend to death and betrayed his own brother be moral?

There was a noise in the doorway, and he looked up to see Elea, flushed with sleep and clutching a teddy bear.

"What is it, darling?" Rachel said calmly, putting down her book and getting up to go to him. But the baby ran across the room to Joshua, who picked him up.

"Boom," Elea said, clutching Joshua and his bear, his sturdy little body trembling. There had been savage bombardments at Giora during the war, and the children, even in their underground shelters, had heard the noise and been terrified.

But why had the child come to him? Probably because he was tall and serious like his big brother, Benjamin, who had assumed a father's role from the minute Elea was born.

No, the child was calling him Abba—Father.

Joshua held him, talking softly, stroking Eleazar's back. A tremendous surge of love for the little boy rose in him. He thought that he would die of grief when harm came to this innocent, as come it must to everyone who lived.

Oh, God, he thought, *oh, God, I can't feel this again or I know I'll crawl into a cave somewhere and end it before I do what I swore to do.*

With a desperate effort of will he pushed the feeling from him, raised his head, and looked at Rachel.

"Take him."

Disappointment flickered over her face for a second. Then she came and took the baby from him without a word. He heard her footsteps taking Elea into the bedroom while he sat, shaking, at his desk.

By the time she came back, his face was calm. He returned to his papers, she to her book. The clock ticked steadily in the room.

38

SANDS POINT
AUGUST 1953

Julie let the horse amble through the woods. The reins were slack, so Tarquin could duck his beautiful head and munch whatever took his fancy in the underbrush. She had been out riding for two hours, and it was almost time to go back to the house for her sitting. The thought excited her. It always did.

It should have been boring, sitting for a formal portrait in the fluffy gown her father had chosen, rather than in her riding clothes and astride Tarquin, the way she wanted to be painted. But nothing was boring when the painter was a man like Paul O'Connor.

At first she had thought he was the homeliest man she had ever seen. The men she knew best—her father, her uncle, her cousins

Seth and Benjamin—were very handsome. O'Connor was almost ugly. He had a wide mouth, smallish blue eyes keen as blades, and hair cut very close to his head, like a soldier's. He even wore old army fatigues, and he was more often rude than not. There was nothing romantic about O'Connor.

But she always hoped he would throw down the brushes and sweep her off her feet the way the painter did in the Duchess portrait. It still hung over the fireplace in the big living room at Sands Point. It had been more than a pretty picture to her for a long time.

She had no idea what it was that made her want him to do that—she was more or less in love with Benjamin. And O'Connor had a very low opinion of sheltered young girls with millionaire fathers, probably because Arnold had insisted that he paint the portrait here, in a guest house on the estate, and had offered O'Connor more money than he had the willpower to refuse.

"I will not allow my daughter to go to a studio alone with a man," Arnold announced. "You say you can't work with a third person around. So it's either Sands Point or another artist—and I'll pay you four times your fee."

O'Connor had asked for even more, and Arnold agreed without batting an eye. Arnold liked O'Connor's work—he had done Naomi's portrait two years ago—and Arnold was used to having what he liked.

So a room in one of the cottages had been chosen for its light and set up as a studio. Once a week for the last two months the Rolls had picked O'Connor up and deposited him, cursing and grumbling all the way, at the cottage. Julie was accustomed to his language. She supposed all artists spoke as pungently as he did. And soon she couldn't imagine why he had ever seemed homely.

"Come on, Tarquin," she said softly to the horse as she took up the reins. His ears told her he had heard, and she patted his gleaming coat. "You're the most magnificent creature on four legs. You feel like a gallop, don't you, boy? As soon as we get clear of the trees, we'll fly. It's still cool enough."

She inched the reins forward, and Tarquin trotted effortlessly through the woods, twigs popping under his hooves, a rich smell of loam and moss and curried animal rising to Julie's nostrils. It was exciting to both of them, the girl and the stallion, to trot like that through the trees, holding back, getting ready, knowing that as soon as they reached the meadow all the power in the stallion would explode, carrying the girl along with it.

"Steady, Tarquin, not yet," she whispered. "Hold back just a little longer, not yet, don't let go yet." She closed her eyes, waiting for the heat of the sun to tell her when they cleared the trees. Yes, there it was, warm and intoxicating, and "Yes," she said to him, "now!" The reins slackened even more, and the bay stallion shot into a gallop, his mighty power surging while Julie clasped her knees around him harder and gave him his head.

She was breathless with delight when Tarquin slowed himself to a dignified canter, then to a trot as they reached the stable paddock. Julie slid down from the saddle and ran to throw her arms around the horse's neck.

"You're wonderful," she said. Then she moved to stroke his muzzle. "There's not another one like you in the world. Here." She gave him sugar from the pouch at her belt, and he munched placidly. "I'll see you again this afternoon, when the sun's going down."

She waved to the groom when he took the horse and got into her MG. She wouldn't be eighteen until next month, and she drove it only on the grounds. She zipped up the road to the guest cottage, let herself in, and glanced at the clock. Almost eleven. She had time for a shower.

By the time O'Connor arrived, she was in the white silk organza gown, sitting in her chair on the slightly raised platform O'Connor had ordered built.

He was more grumpy than usual. "On time, for a change," he muttered, rolling up his sleeves. He would never wear anything so pretentious as a smock. He wore his khaki pants and a white shirt, open at the neck. He had a way of standing with his hips thrust forward that fascinated Julie. Movie stars stood that way. So did models. It was a sexy way to stand.

He picked up the brushes he always cleaned thoroughly before he left each time and turned to look at her. Or her outline—he never really saw *her*, Julie thought. He nodded briefly, as though satisfied with the angle, then started fussing with his paints.

"We'll be finished today," he said. "And a good thing too. This taxi service is a pain in the ass. Whatever else I have to do I can finish in New York—I won't need you." He laughed. "Your father can sleep soundly in his bed. Your maidenhead is still intact.''

Julie flushed.

"Holy shit, don't go all blotchy on me," he said. "I'm trying to get your skin just right. You have beautiful flesh, like your mother.''

She tried to relax, and the blush faded slowly.

"What's the matter with that dress?" he asked suddenly. "It's all bunched up around your waist.''

"I couldn't manage to hook the sash," Julie said in a small voice.

"Well, stand up, then, and I'll hook it for you. It looks like a potato sack.'' He came to the platform, turned her, and began hooking the wide, crushed-velvet cummerbund that molded the dress to her waist. He turned her back and adjusted the off-the-shoulder bodice. It was the first time he had ever touched her, and she felt the blush again, spreading from her cheeks down her neck and over her breasts, demurely covered but very clearly outlined.

He smiled at her; it was almost a nasty smile. "So that's how it is," he said softly. "Another eager virgin." His hands slid down over her breasts. "And all real too. I wondered.''

She was sure he would kiss her, but he didn't. He sat her in the chair again and knelt beside it. He watched her face while his hand went under the dress and up her thighs, pushing them apart and touching her, there. Very slowly, he touched her, at first, watching her while he did it until she closed her eyes, half-ashamed, half-eager for him to go on.

It was the same feeling she had when Tarquin moved under her in a trot before his power swelled and he hurled them both into a rocking gallop. She was almost out of the forest now, and in a second she would feel the sun on her face and tell him.

"Now," she whispered, "yes, now." She felt her body moving.

It was over, all too soon.

He walked back to the easel, still smiling. "Well, now, that will settle you down. Let's get to work.''

At the end of the session she watched while he cleaned and packed his painting gear and then called the chauffeur on the cottage telephone. He picked up the canvas carefully and bowed to her, a mocking little bow.

"Adieu, fair firecracker. If you're wondering why I didn't go ahead and screw you properly, it's because I find virgins very dull in bed." He laughed. "Also because your father would cut my dick off if he ever found out. My advice to you, though, is to marry young or join a bordello."

She watched him go and walked back to the house, glad her parents were both in the city. If just that had been so blissful, what must the rest be? She wanted to think about it. Why had she wanted O'Connor to touch her when the attempts of all the other young men she knew had been revolting to her? Benjamin had never tried, but she knew she would like it with Benjamin.

All she had read, then, about the "chemistry" between men and women must be true. It was far more fascinating than lab chemistry at school.

Her chemistry tutor would be coming after lunch, a pudgy science major from Yale. He would have no idea that she was different in any way. Her father wouldn't dream that she had done such a thing, much less liked it and wanted to do it again. But her mother . . .

She had never noticed any chemistry between her parents. They must have had it once.

Suddenly she wondered if her mother had found O'Connor as attractive as she did. But her mother was not the kind of woman to sleep with strange men. Her mother would never be unfaithful to a husband who loved her so much.

39

SANDS POINT
SEPTEMBER 1953

Arnold left his place at the end of the beautifully decorated table and came to sit near Naomi. Their guests were dancing, but there were two places at the table in the country club that had obviously not been occupied at all.

"I hope they get here before dinner is served," Arnold said, watching the entrance to the ballroom.

Naomi hid her own impatience. "The plane was late. They'll be here soon." She looked at the dancers. "She looks beautiful, doesn't she?"

Arnold agreed, watching his daughter. "Too bad there aren't more young people to celebrate her eighteenth birthday. We've got a few of our friends—and Otto." Arnold didn't believe in mixing business with pleasure. Naomi's brothers and their families weren't invited to social occasions outside their home. Otto, as always, was the exception. He had finally produced an exquisite, lilting fragrance they called Princess. It was an instant success, and Otto was more indulged than ever as a result, although he never asked indulgences.

Julie had gone to dance with him. He always said she was his inspiration for Princess.

"I suppose we're partly to blame for it," Naomi said, "but Julie's more comfortable with adults."

Otto's voice corrected her as he sat down at the table. "At the moment, not."

"Who did you leave her with?" Arnold demanded, turning to look.

"I don't know him—he cut me out," Otto said, sipping champagne. "An attractive specimen, no?"

The man dancing with Julie was more than attractive, Naomi thought. He was older than her daughter, well into his twenties. He moved and talked with an assurance no college boy would have. He was fairly tall, above Arnold's height, and he was elegantly tailored. Arnold was asking again who he was.

"I don't know, dear. But he must be all right if he's here as someone's guest."

Otto chuckled. "Every man to him is the Duke of Mantua, trying to seduce his Gilda. Come, Rigoletto, relax—or sing us an aria."

"Don't talk nonsense, Otto. I just don't like her dancing with any old Tom, Dick, and Harry." Arnold scowled when Julie smiled up at her partner.

"Maybe his name is Max," Otto teased.

"There they are!" Naomi stood up, elegant in champagne chiffon, her short hair making her look younger than ever.

Benjamin and Joshua were coming into the ballroom, both of them in evening clothes. She had never seen Joshua dressed like that before, and she loved the way his body looked in the black tuxedo. He was the best-looking man she had ever seen—and how much Benjamin resembled him. Except for Joshua's white hair—and the beard. He had grown a beard, short, distinguished. It outlined his beautiful mouth. What would the beard feel like when she kissed that mouth?

"With that beard he looks more like a rabbi than ever," Arnold whispered. "I just hope he doesn't start fund raising here at the club."

They waited for the newcomers. Naomi said nothing. She hadn't seen him for several months, and it was hard to watch him without running to him, hard to greet him with a chaste, sisterly kiss when she wanted him to take her in his arms and hold her. She was forty-four, yet every time she saw this man—and especially after a long separation—she felt the way she had when she was nineteen: breathless, in haste to be near him, watch his face, listen to his voice.

No one could have guessed that from the way she kissed him and his son, talking animatedly to both of them while they said hello to Otto and the others, who knew Joshua's demands upon their money well enough.

"Does she know?" Benjamin asked. "Did you tell Julie, Aunt Naomi?"

Naomi was always faintly annoyed when he called her "Aunt"— he was so manly, he made her feel older.

"No, I didn't tell her. Just stand there, you two. You're taller than anyone else in the room. She'll look this way in a minute."

"Not the way she's looking at that fellow," Benjamin said. "Who is he?"

"That's what I'd like to know," Arnold said.

The dance ended, but the band slid into another song, "As Time Goes By." Julie stayed with her partner.

"I think we'd better sit down," Joshua said. "I'm glad to see her looking so happy."

"I'd still like to know who that fellow is," Benjamin said. He was very protective of his cousin, just as he was of his mother and his little brother. Benjamin, Sarah always said, was a born protector and his mother's best buddy. He'd go through Harvard in three years, then enter the Massachusetts Institute of Technology. Julie would start her freshman year at Smith this month.

"What difference does that make if Julie likes him?" Joshua asked his son.

"It makes a lot of difference." Arnold bristled.

"How's everyone at home?" Naomi asked. No matter how things had improved between the brothers, Joshua always had an abrasive effect on Arnold. But it was not because of her. She was certain Arnold suspected nothing; she was determined he never would.

Then Julie was there, surprised and delighted to see her uncle and Benjamin. The other man stood nearby until Julie introduced him to her family. His name was Parker Mitchell, and he was there as a guest of the Bradens.

He was definitely attractive and looked at least ten years older than Julie, with dark, heavy brows and the kind of hairline that would begin to recede when he was about thirty, without ruining his good looks. That was because he had enough charm for three men, Naomi thought. Not the same kind of natural magnetism Joshua had but a more specific kind, directed almost uniquely toward women. He said something in a low voice to Julie, then smiled at all of them and left.

"I don't like him," Benjamin announced.

"Then you don't have to dance with him," Julie told him. "Gosh, it's good to see you." It was too bad if Benjamin didn't like Parker Mitchell. Looking at her disapproving father, Julie didn't care whether or not anyone liked Parker. He was the first interesting man she'd met since O'Connor, and she felt more than a desire to have him touch her. She hadn't seen O'Connor again, but she was going to see Parker, she knew that.

By the end of the evening they had arranged a dinner date. It was an evening that changed a lot of things for Julie. She had always had a crush on Benjamin, even supposed she would marry him someday. Now he was just a cousin, and dancing with him was the same as dancing with her uncle or her father.

It was something very different to dance with Parker Mitchell, and not all of it was sexual attraction; she knew that now, thanks to those few minutes with O'Connor. There was a lot of that— but there was something more too.

"This has been the happiest night of my life," Julie told her parents when they were home again and going up the curving staircase. "I'm so happy I could burst!"

"You sound just like your aunt Sarah," Arnold said, beaming at her.

"I know just what she means by that now," Julie said. She kissed her parents. "Thank you for everything, and the two surprises from Israel. Aren't they gorgeous, the two of them?" She whirled along the upstairs balcony to her room and disappeared.

Arnold and Naomi looked at each other. "I'm going to find out about that man," Arnold said, opening the door to the sitting room that separated their two bedrooms. "She's all upset about him."

"She's not upset, Arnold. She's happy and young and maybe a little in love. What's wrong with that?"

"Julie can never be 'a little in love.' She's just like me." His look had changed from one of concern for his daughter to something else. "She's like me," he said again. "She'll fall in love just once, and she'll give everything she has." He put his arm around his wife and kissed her. Year in, year out it was always the same, his love for her, his desire for her. Maybe it was because, even loving him as she did—and he was sure of that now—she had never returned his passion. "Let me stay with you tonight," he said.

"Of course."

She always said "Of course." And he would go to her and find her loving, receptive—and cool. A delight to hold, to touch, to kiss—but cool, too passive for him to dare anything beyond the simple love he had made to her on their wedding night. Whatever he had learned from Annalise would certainly offend Naomi.

Annalise liked sex. Their physical relationship had changed over the years when she was his mistress. At first she had been subtle; then she was explicit in showing him where and how he could give her the most pleasure, and her pleasure was contagious; it heightened his. After a while he had been able to let her touch him in ways he would never even expect Naomi to know. Annalise had liked things no man would do with his wife.

Sometimes Annalise had waited for him on the bed, her nipples rouged, her thighs spread wide, naked except for a black garter belt and lacy black stockings that drew him like a magnet to the oiled and perfumed place between her legs. He did any-thing she wanted of him on those nights, not caring about the shame that would claim him afterward.

He had been ashamed because he never loved that woman. He loved Naomi.

He undressed in his room, giving Naomi time to do the same, but he wanted to undress her himself. When he went to her, he was decorously clad in pajamas, and he turned out the light as usual before he took off the pajamas and got into bed.

Touching her, he was amazed to find her naked—she always wore a gown. Once in a while she let him take it off. The surprise of it excited him. So did the way she kissed him.

His mouth went to her breasts, his hand slid down below her waist. She pushed it lower, showed him where, told him urgent-ly, "Yes, faster, don't stop," reached a climax in a flood of wordless little sounds, pulled him to her, and closed around him, warm and wild and pulsing, until he finished, shocked, elated, spent.

They were both exhausted, and she seemed to be asleep when he moved to her side. He closed his eyes, his thoughts racing. Why? Why tonight? The champagne? But she had drunk cham-pagne before.

And why tonight, of all nights? Had she been too sexually aroused to keep from showing him what she wanted? How could she have known what she wanted, unless she had learned it from someone else, the same way he had?

Joshua? He was fifty, withdrawn, and given to unexpected tempers, a man with an extraordinary wife, by all reports, and two wonderful sons, but driven by some devil to care only for his work. Joshua had no time for furtive love affairs. No, not Joshua. If seeing him again had so aroused Naomi, why had his other visits made no difference? No, it couldn't be Joshua. Arnold knew his brother.

And he knew his own wife. There was no one else. There hadn't been anyone else all those years ago, just before Julie. He had always known there was more in Naomi than modesty or inhibition would allow her to show. It only surfaced once in a great while. He fell asleep, hoping it would happen again.

Naomi lay beside him, keeping her breathing even until she

was sure he was asleep. She was as astonished as he must be. She always found it nice and comforting to go to bed with Arnold. He was gentle, sweet, and loving in bed—in a way, exactly as she was herself.

But there was more to her, a side of her Joshua had awakened and even sometimes aroused to equal his own. She always pretended it did—she felt she had failed him when it did not. Seeing him tonight, she wanted him. In bed with Arnold, she wanted more than comfort, she wanted satisfaction. Now that she knew what that meant, it was hard to remain totally immune to her husband's caresses, discreet as they were, and hard to stay unsatisfied once she was aroused. How could her body refuse to sing now that it had learned the song?

What troubled her, what she knew would trouble Arnold, was where she had learned it. He would never ask, but he would surely wonder.

She would have to blame it on the champagne and the party and wait to see what happened the next time. In a way it *was* the party. Her little girl was no longer little. Julie was clearly ready to fall in love, probably had already. Life was drifting by, and Naomi, deep inside herself where she really lived, was not anyone's aunt, anyone's mother, anyone's wife. Although she was all those things as well. She was Naomi, still in love with a man who, her instinct told her, would never let her know him. She had never dared to ask him why they were together—for her it was certainly not only for sex. And she was beginning to think that for him it was for nothing else. Once it had been more; but he was not the same man he had been, and she was losing hope that he was ever coming back.

Suddenly she was feeling very lonely. She was glad Arnold was near her tonight.

Across the U-shaped balcony Julie sat looking out at the beautiful night, wide awake. Love at first sight was not something you only read about in books. It must happen, or it wouldn't have been written about in the first place.

Parker Mitchell. There was something overwhelmingly appealing about him, something behind his manner—"smooth as silk," the girls would call him—and something other than his sex appeal.

"Marry young," O'Connor had advised her, "or join a bordello."

But in three weeks school would start, and what chance would she have to get him to marry her? A man like Parker didn't come up to Northampton on weekends to take little girls out on decorous dates and then sign them in at midnight! Anyway, she knew she would hate school.

Well, a lot could happen in three weeks. Look at what had happened in just one evening! And she knew she could count on her mother to help, no matter what her father said.

The rest depended on Parker.

40

"He's a mongrel," Arnold said to his wife and daughter two weeks later. It was Sunday morning, and they were at breakfast in the small dining room overlooking the flagstone terrace and the lawn that sloped down to the water. Julie and Naomi were in batiste morning gowns and Arnold in a light, brocaded silk robe that would have eclipsed a lesser personality.

It was Indian summer, and bright sunlight sparkled through the mullioned Tudor windows onto a silver fruit bowl filled with grapes, mangoes, and avocados; on Baccarat crystal and crisp Porthault linen. The butler was arranging a series of covered silver dishes on the sideboard. Coffee steamed from a Georgian silver pot. A smaller urn held the fragrant spiced tea that Arnold now had blended to his taste. He nodded to the butler for another cup, then dismissed him.

"What do you mean by that?" Naomi asked.

"Parker Mitchell. I found out all about him," Arnold said. "His mother was a Boston WASP, and his father was a Jewish playboy."

Julie laughed. "Daddy, what difference does it make who his parents are?"

"Were," Arnold said, taking a brioche and some imported strawberry preserves. "They were killed in an accident when he was fifteen."

"That's one of the saddest things I've ever heard," Naomi said. "Who took care of him?"

"Boarding schools. The WASPs didn't want him because of the Jewish blood, and his father was an orphan—but you can bet his family wouldn't have taken him either."

"That's rotten," Julie said softly to her father. "I don't see how you can talk about it as if it were the weather."

Arnold sipped his tea. "Because it doesn't seem to have cramped his style. He had a good education, courtesy of the Boston branch. He's a dilettante stockbroker, and he has a small annuity from his mother. But all he's after is women—wealthy women."

Julie blushed.

"Arnold, please," Naomi said. "I don't think this is necessary."

Arnold dropped his dry, cynical air. "Julie's been seeing too much of him. I think she ought to know what he's really after—her money."

"What makes you so sure he's after me—or my money? If you want to know, I'm after him, so you can stop spying, because I don't care what you think! He hasn't called me for three days, anyway. That ought to make you happy." She threw her napkin down and went to the door. "I'm going riding," she said over her shoulder, adding, "Mother," in a clear affront to Arnold.

He sat, leaning his head on his hand. "What are we going to do?" he asked Naomi, looking hurt and worried.

"Stop talking like that, for one thing."

"All right, I made a bad mistake." He sighed. "She's never spoken to me like that before. But I had to do something, Naomi. The man's notorious around New York. He's had more mistresses than I can count, most of them older women, all of them rich. He tried to marry a lot of the younger girls, but their families always put a stop to it. What are we going to do?"

Naomi leaned across the table and put her hand on his. "Julie's not a fool, Arnold. If she loves him, there must be a good reason."

"How would she judge? She's only eighteen."

"I was hardly more when we were married. Yes, I know, that was different—but only because we were less sophisticated than Julie is. She was born to a way of life we had to grow into. Her picture's been in *Vogue* since she was three. She's traveled all over the world with us, and she's at ease with people who'd have frightened us to death. How can you say she knows her mind any less than we did?"

"I still say he's not good enough for her. I don't trust him."

"You don't even know him," Naomi said reasonably. "Anyway, he hasn't called her lately. Maybe we're worrying about nothing."

"I think we have a lot to worry about."

"I'll talk to her when she comes back—or when she's cooled off. And you . . ."

"I won't say another word," he anticipated. "I don't want to lose her." He looked frightened. "She always used to listen to me. She never spoke to me that way before."

They heard Julie running down the stairs and watched her cross the terrace, dressed in riding breeches, and streak off toward the stables in the MG.

The room was very quiet once the roar of the motor died in the distance.

Julie let Tarquin race almost as soon as she left the paddock. She was furious with her father—and furious with Parker for rushing her after her birthday party and then dropping out of sight. She had never had such a wonderful time in her life. He liked all the things she did—plays and movies, little bars with dreamy piano music, great jazz at The Embers, wandering through museums and making up silly stories about the Greek statues at the Metropolitan or the cavemen at the Natural History.

He had never spoken about his family or that awful childhood. She understood better what his hidden appeal for her was: loneliness. A different kind from hers, uninterested as she had always been in the things her schoolmates liked: dates and clothes and more dates—but loneliness all the same.

She knew he didn't have much money, but he made no attempt to hide his comparative poverty, even though it made him uncomfortable. She wanted to tell him that she didn't care which of

them had money, but she had never dared. It might have embarrassed him.

How could her father be so unfair to Parker, so uncaring of her
own feelings? What if he did run after women? They ran after
him. She had seen it whenever they met friends of his in a
restaurant or at the theater. Women ignored their dates, even
their husbands, when Parker was around.

With her he was only affectionate; he'd never even kissed her!

She pulled Tarquin up, and her eyes filled with tears. Maybe
he did want her only for her money, but then she shook her head.
She could change that later. The important thing was to make
him want her enough to marry her.

Parker threw the Sports section of *The New York Times* aside
and went to the kitchen for another cup of coffee. It was a
beautiful day, the park would be lovely. His eyes went to the
telephone; he wanted to call Julie, but he had to wait a few more
days or all the time and effort he had put into making her fall in
love with him would be wasted.

Well, not wasted, because she was so adorable. But there was
a lot at stake, and he had to be careful. He was twenty-six,
and he thought it was high time he did what he had always
planned to do: marry a very wealthy woman. Now that he had a
chance at a rich, beautiful girl, he wasn't going to make any
mistakes.

He lit a cigarette and picked up the phone. There was a click
and an answer three rings after he dialed.

"Good morning, beautiful," he said, his voice silky and intimate. "I hope I didn't wake you."

The woman on the other end of the line laughed softly. "It's
after one, and I'm still in bed. Awful, isn't it?"

"I think it's delightful. Shall I join you?"

The woman laughed again. "Parker! I have to give the poor
thing a rest once in a while."

"How about lunch? Shall I pick you up in an hour?"

"Make it an hour and a half. And meet me at Rumpelmayer's.
The doorman here is getting very interested, and I don't want any
trouble with Richard."

Parker whistled as he dressed—Brooks Brothers gray flannel
slacks and blazer, button-down Oxford shirt, polished, hand-

sewn mocassins. He didn't want any trouble with Norma's husband either on the rare occasions when Richard was in New York.

He'd been filling Norma Mason's lonely hours for months now, and he was no nearer getting her to divorce Richard and marry him. She was generous about money, and she was certainly generous in bed, but the affair was going nowhere. And now there was Julie.

He stopped whistling, and his face was thoughtful as he started walking west across Central Park toward the restaurant.

Julie was gold to Parker, not only as fortune but as symbol. She was smooth and shiny. Her skin was like the satin sheets he was sure she slept on, her hair a honey-colored richness. Her clothes were soft, imported silk and leather. Her makeup, when she wore any, was discreet. Her nails were short and buffed. She had his mother's elegance, and he wanted that in a woman. Above all, she had money and no brothers to stand in his way at Duchess.

In the short time he had known her, he had strained his limited budget at first. But then he had begun to avoid fashionable places and expensive theater tickets in favor of simpler pleasures. He bought her unpretentious little gifts: a small Bisque shepherdess, a thin Mexican bangle bracelet he found in the Village. He took her to quiet, offbeat restaurants and for long walks around the city.

He was charmed by her. And then he became aware of an underlying sensuality in her that first intrigued, then aroused him. It was nothing overt, but all the more powerful because she was unaware of it. He knew women, and he suspected that she was sensual as well as virginal. If he could get her to bed, she would surely marry him, no matter what her parents said. He could make sex an addiction for her—and girls like Julie married their first sex partners.

So he was gentle with her, very attentive and openly admiring, but from a distance. He knew he must make her believe that he wanted her, not for sex, above all not for money, but for herself. It came as a great surprise to him to discover that he really did. He hadn't seen her for three days now, and he missed her. He would have to go to Northampton to see her when she left.

The women he knew seemed slick and predictable; as for the

girls, chastity was a commodity to them, something they were brought up to use as barter for marriage to the highest bidder.

He wondered if he could keep from calling Julie for four more days. Maybe a silence that long would be too much for her pride. Maybe he would call her tonight—if he got Norma out of his bed and back home early enough. He would persuade the woman he was going to meet that a matinee would be more exciting and less dangerous—thank heaven for the nosy doorman—than an evening performance.

Julie ran to her mother's room the minute she hung up the phone. Naomi was writing to Sarah. She smiled when she saw Julie's face.

"Don't tell me, let me guess. That was Parker."

"We're having dinner tomorrow night. I knew he'd call, I knew it."

"Did he say why he hadn't?" Naomi was interested but not disapproving.

"He said he could tell me a lot of lies, but he wanted to tell me the truth tomorrow night." Julie sat down on a big satin pouf. "I wonder what it is. I don't care, though," she added. "I'm in love with him." She looked at her mother.

"I know, darling."

"What do you think?"

"It's what you think that matters," Naomi said.

"Daddy would be furious if he heard you say that."

Naomi got up and went to the bay window, cushioned and curtained in white silk and embroidered lawn. "What if Daddy's not being difficult, Julie? What if he's really, truly sure you'd be making a mistake if you married Parker?"

"He hasn't even asked me yet," Julie said.

"But you know he will."

Julie looked determined. In her determined moods she resembled Arnold more than she knew. "If he does, I'll marry him."

"You haven't known him very long," Naomi cautioned.

"I don't think you have to know a man long to know him well. Aunt Shai loved Lazar the minute she looked at him and still does."

"Sarah is different from most women," Naomi said. "Thank God," she added.

"You always said everyone's different from everyone else," Julie reminded her.

"I still think so, but we have some things in common. Mistakes, for instance. Everyone makes them."

Julie studied the heart-shaped diamond ring Arnold had given her when she was sixteen and the malachite Sarah had sent with Uncle Josh for this year's birthday. "You didn't," she said to her mother.

Naomi almost told her then—she seemed to be asking. But this was no time to burden Julie with her own problems and certainly no time to influence her one way or the other. She had tried to develop Julie's character so she could make her own choices. It was why she hadn't interfered more forcefully with Arnold's plans for Julie. If Naomi had succeeded with her daughter, Julie would decide for herself whether or not she wanted to go into Duchess.

She walked over to Julie. "I knew Daddy from the time we were born. We grew up together."

Julie laughed, looking up at her mother. "You were lucky. I didn't grow up with anyone like Daddy. For a while I thought I wanted to marry Benjamin—or Seth, when I was really little. But that was before I met Parker. Now I know there are different kinds of love, and only one you marry for."

"Is it the kind of love that makes a good marriage?" Naomi was asking herself that question too.

Julie shook her head. "It isn't only that, even though I—well, I do feel that for him. I just understand him, I know how he feels. I'm sure of it. And I think he knows about me in the same way. He wants the money—oh, yes, Daddy's right about that—but he wants me too, even if he doesn't know it yet."

Naomi took her daughter's hands and pulled her up. She put her arms around Julie. "All right, darling. I just don't want you to get hurt, and neither does your father. Be sure about what you want before you marry Parker. Be sure it isn't just 'chemistry.' There's only one way to do that, and even then, it takes a long time before you're sure."

Her mother's meaning was unmistakable, but it didn't embarrass Julie, even if it surprised her a little. "I'm sure of that already," she said, thinking of O'Connor. But if she had any plans about making certain, she didn't elaborate, and Naomi didn't ask.

Julie kissed her before she left the room. "I'll probably stay at the apartment tomorrow night, but I'll call you as soon as I'm safe and sound. Without that apartment I'd be geographically undesirable."

"Call no matter how late you get there."

"No matter how late," Julie promised. She left in a whirl of happy anticipation.

Naomi sat down at the desk and looked, without seeing, at what she had been writing to Sarah. She had not seen Joshua since the night of Julie's birthday party, but he was expected back in New York with Benjamin in a few days. There would be no chance to see him until Benjamin and Julie left for school in another week.

You didn't make a mistake, Julie had said. Oh, but she had. There was more to marriage than sex, but it ought to be there. There was more to living than passion, but how terrible to miss it entirely. She was not deeply erotic by nature, but because of Joshua she had known some moments of passion.

And, lately, because of Arnold too. Blaming her behavior that night on champagne had been well enough, but having discovered what pleased her, Arnold wanted to please her more. She neither could nor would refuse him. It was incredible that the first sexual satisfaction she had known with her husband should be after twenty-five years of marriage, when she was middle-aged. But it changed nothing. She had, after all, made a mistake.

She didn't even know Parker Mitchell. She could only hope that Julie's instincts were better than her own had been, that her only child would not be hurt. She had done all she knew how to prevent it.

She sat down to write it all to Sarah. She had an idea what Sarah would say: "If you live, you get hurt. The only way to avoid it is to die, like my Lazar, and that's a pretty radical cure."

41

Parker didn't even know how much he missed her until she walked into the restaurant. He had forgotten how lovely she was.

"These are for you," he said when they had been seated at a quiet table in the corner. He gave her a bunch of violets in an old-fashioned silver holder.

"Oh, Parker, it's beautiful—and the flowers too."

"The holder was my mother's. She carried it at her debut."

"What was her name?" Julie was more touched by this than anything he might have given her.

"Paige Parker—before it was Mitchell. She was very beautiful—like you." He stopped and signaled the waiter. They ordered drinks, and then he said, "You should always wear that color. With skin like porcelain and hair like honey, I don't know which part of you I want to touch first."

The waiter brought the drinks, and she took a good taste of hers, acting as though she always drank, as though she weren't underage. "But you never—touch me. For days you haven't even called me."

He lit a cigarette, avoiding her eyes. "Not because I didn't want to."

She waited, saying nothing, expecting more.

"Damn it, Julie," he said finally, "you know how things are. You know how I feel about you, but there isn't a chance in the world I can marry you. Not for a long time. Not until I have something to offer." He hadn't meant things to happen so quickly, but at least he had mentioned marriage. He wanted her reaction.

"You're talking about money," Julie said. She didn't say money didn't matter. She knew all too well that it did.

"Yes, of course, money," he answered abruptly. "I've never

had a lot of it, but I never cared much. Now I do. There's not enough for someone like you—or your father.''

"You don't know how much money is enough for me—and my father has nothing to do with us.''

"He'd think that's why I married you," Parker said, bitter because it was true at the start, was still partly true. He looked at her as guilelessly as he could. "Wouldn't you?''

She nodded, and his heart sank. Then she said, "At first I did. But not now.''

He reached for her hand. "Why not now?''

"Because it isn't true anymore.''

He held her hand, astonished by her perception. Then he kissed it. It gave him time to think. He was confused. A strategic success had become an emotional reality. The money was no longer all he wanted. "No, it isn't true anymore," he whispered. Absurdly he meant it. He was as much in love with her as he could be with a woman. He wanted her almost as much as the money.

"What are we going to do?" he wondered aloud, shifting the decision to her. "He'll never believe me.''

"We're going to your apartment. He'll have no choice.''

He hadn't intended the suggestion to come from her. He hadn't expected that she would be so forthright—or that she would want to go, knowing he had really been after her fortune.

"Julie, it's not the right way for us to start out. It's no way to get your father's approval.''

"It's the only way." She looked at him in that direct way she had. They needed Arnold for different reasons, but they both needed him.

They got up to go, dinner forgotten. When she was finally in his black-brown-white-checked bedroom, where so many women had been, she looked out of place. Her hands removed her jewelry. She was smiling, but her eyes were not.

He went to put his arms around her. "Julie, let me take you home. You don't have to . . .''

"I want to," she said against his cheek. "I just don't know how.''

He took off his jacket, but he didn't undress, feeling strangely shy. He unzipped the silk dress, and she stepped out of it. She wore a pale-green satin chemise trimmed with Alençon lace. He moved the straps and felt her tense, although she didn't move away. Her modesty touched him as much as it excited him.

He turned her around to face him and kissed her tenderly until the tenseness disappeared. Then he took her to the bed and removed the wisp of underclothing while he stroked her back. He held her against him, breathing in the fragrance of her hair. His hand came from her back to her round breasts, caressed the nipples, and moved to her thighs. She sighed with pleasure when he touched her. She was silky soft and moist, and he could have taken her then, but he waited. He wanted to tie her to him with sex as well as love. Men might be driven by sex; women were bound by a man who gave them the right kind.

He waited until she breathed in short gasps and her body trembled. When he slid into her, she met him with her hips, and when he moved inside her, she matched his rhythm. Her mouth against his was as open as her body was, her thighs held him with unexpected strength. He knew she was a virgin, even without the traditional barrier, but she was as sensual as his intuition had told him she would be.

It overwhelmed him that she gave love with such abandon. And he was triumphant that his taking of it would commit her irrevocably to marrying him.

And then his senses took over, and he forgot she was Julie and he was Parker.

What he did not feel afterward was that vague repugnance that always flickered after orgasm, never dominant, hardly equal to the pleasure he had known, but always there for a split second. He felt nothing of that. It had been sublimely sensual, but it was something so much more. He was unaware that he trusted her implicitly, that he wanted her adoration, apart from her money. He needed money far less than he needed her.

"Stay here tonight," he pleaded. "Can you?"

"Yes." She kissed him. "But I have to call Mother to say I'm safe."

"Do you want to go to the apartment to do that?"

"No, it's all right. Mother would never call to check up on me once she knows I'm safe. Am I?"

"No," he said.

It was almost two before she remembered to call her mother, and she was right. Naomi didn't phone the apartment back to check up on her.

Arnold did.

"She isn't there," he said, bursting into Naomi's room. "I called the apartment, and the maid said Julie wasn't there. It's almost two! She's spending the night with that money-grubbing son of a bitch."

"Arnold, there's nothing you can do about it."

"Do you think I'm going to let my Julie marry a rotten bastard like that?"

"Maybe she won't want to marry him now."

He looked at her, shocked, then comprehending. "You mean she might get him out of her system! God, I hope so. But how can you be so calm when you know she's—in bed with him. The thought of it disgusts me."

She got up and put on her robe. "Arnold, it had to happen sometime. Married or not, you wouldn't have liked the idea. She's still a little girl to you, not a woman with a life of her own." She held out her hand. "Come on, let's go down and have a brandy. You look like you need one."

He followed her downstairs, still mystified by the calm way she was taking it. The way Naomi had always been about sex—until recently—he had expected some kind of moral indignation. He had no idea she was as anxious as he that she might have let Julie make a terrible mistake. Going to bed with a man was what she should have done before marriage. But Julie was her daughter, not herself.

"Shall I say anything to her tomorrow?" Arnold opened the door to the study.

"God, no! She'd be very angry."

He took the glass of brandy she gave him. "But she was *lying* to you just now on the phone!"

"No, she just said she was safe, not where she was."

"Safe? What if she gets pregnant?"

"She won't if she doesn't want to." She saw his question before he asked it. "I had her fitted with a diaphragm last year."

He sat down. "I don't understand you anymore," he said, his voice very hoarse. "Did you want her to do a thing like this?"

"I wanted her to have a choice. I didn't want her to marry the first man she thought she loved. I wanted to give her enough time to be sure it wasn't just sex." She watched him, trying to choose her words. "She's not like me, Arnold. She feels . . . she isn't cool the way I am." She had never realized it would be so hard to say.

"But you're not, not really. It's the way you were brought up." He was embarrassed, thinking about the way she was now, the small demands, few but very clear and insistent, that she made in bed, the way she touched him now.

She took a deep breath. "That's why I brought her up differently."

He said nothing for a while, drinking the brandy, thinking. "And you can let her be used by a man you don't even know without batting an eyelash?"

"When it's that strong, you can't stop it. And Julie's not a fool. She knows he wanted the money at first—but now he wants her." She looked pale and nervous. "I'm so afraid we'll lose her if we do anything to break this up. Arnold, I couldn't stand that."

"Neither could I." He was quiet again, trying to fathom all of it. It was a shock to him that his gentle, pliable daughter had a will as strong as his own.

"Arnold," Naomi said hesitantly, careful with her words again. "We didn't have it, that side of love. Don't take it away from her."

He stood up then, Julie forgotten. "Don't say 'we,' Naomi. I've always had it for you. My God, I still want you every time I think about you." His eyes were cloudy with anger and an old, old rebuke. His hand hammered his chest, and his voice shook. "*I* love *you*, damn you, I *love* you. But every time I touched you, I knew you didn't want me."

Her hands held the brandy glass tightly. "I didn't mean to hurt you, Arnold. It's just the way I am."

"Like hell it is! You wanted my brother that way. From the day we were married, you wanted him. Do you think I'm blind?"

The brandy glass slipped out of her shaking hands, making a little thump the carpet. "All these years you thought that and you never said anything?"

"I was afraid I'd lose you, that's why. But I never really had you. You never loved me. I don't know why you married me, except to tear my heart out."

She thought she would never breathe again, but he was still talking fiercely. "And when you got over him because he loves nothing but his precious Israel, there wasn't much left for me."

She sat down suddenly, covered her face, and cried as she hadn't cried since the night Joshua left her to go to Palestine. She cried because Arnold loved her too much to suspect that the desire had become the act, because he had borne the hurt in silence rather than risk losing her, and that was more love than anyone deserved.

He was right too, about Joshua's loving nothing but Israel.

He was only wrong about one thing. She wasn't over Joshua, much as she wanted to be. But after tonight how could she possibly go on with him?

Arnold watched her, torn between fury and relief that he had told her at last. He had never heard her cry like this, not even in all those years before Julie had been born, as if there were nothing in the world that could ease the pain.

It was hopeless for him; she hadn't torn his heart out, she'd only shattered it, and what was left still loved her as much as ever, maybe more. He had just lost Julie to another man; he didn't want to lose Naomi too.

He went to her finally and lifted her, still sobbing, to hold her against him.

"Never mind, darling, I didn't mean all that. I'm worried about Julie. Don't cry like that, I can't bear it."

He talked until she stopped, her head against his shoulder, her arms around him. "I do love you," she whispered. "I do." She leaned against him as if she would collapse without him.

"I know," he said. It was not the love he wanted, but it was better than nothing.

They started up the stairs. A shudder shook her once, and he held her closer. At the top of the stairs they both looked at Julie's empty room, then at each other.

"Arnold, please—I don't want to lose her."

"Don't worry, I won't make any trouble if he's what she wants. I'll just keep an eye on him." He was used to controlling his feelings to keep what he loved.

He tucked Naomi into bed, kissed her, and went back to his own room. He had a lot to think about. If he could get Julie off to school, it would give him time. She might change her mind now that she was—satisfied. He grimaced at the idea and pushed away the thought of her coupling with a man like Parker Mitchell.

Another coupling replaced that image. His brother and his wife. *When it's that strong, you can't stop it.* Had it ever been too strong for them to stop? She might have tried to fight it, but not Joshua, not the way he was now, caring for nothing but his crusade. Yet Naomi had called herself "cool." If it had ever happened at all, when had it happened?

He put the light out and with it everything that had happened tonight. Neither he nor Naomi would mention it, that was the way of their marriage. Their life together would go on as always. Julie would go away to school, and then they would decide.

But in late November, Julie came home from college for the Thanksgiving holiday and told them she was pregnant. She looked too happy for him to do anything but accept the inevitable. There was nothing to decide except for wedding arrangements. By then Arnold had met Parker Mitchell a few times and confirmed his low opinion of the man.

"I think you'd better elope," Arnold said, trying to look at Parker and failing, as usual. He looked at Julie instead, avoiding the idea of her pregnancy.

"Because of the baby," Julie agreed.

Naomi broke in. "We'll let everyone know as soon as you're married. That way no one's feelings will be hurt. We might have a big reception right here at home during the Christmas holidays."

Arnold agreed. He was too well known to let his only daughter marry without some kind of party. It was bad enough that the child would be "premature." His grandchild.

"Is that all right with you?" Julie asked Parker.

A look of disgust crossed Arnold's face. "I think anything we want will be all right with him," he said pointedly.

Parker colored. He was under no illusions about Arnold's opinion of him. He thought Naomi liked him, though. "Whatever Julie wants," he said, emphasizing her name. The only way to control Arnold was through Julie.

Naomi put a restraining hand on Arnold's shoulder. It wasn't going to be easy. "I think you'd better get on with this elopement."

They were gone in the MG before there was any real trouble. Naomi liked Parker, but Arnold didn't have to know. "Try not to judge him until you know him better," she said when they were alone in the too-quiet house.

"I'll have to work with the bastard when he comes into Duchess," Arnold said. "Judging him is easy compared to that."

"Have you ever mentioned Duchess to him?"

"I was hoping I wouldn't have to. But he doesn't make enough to feed Julie's horse, let alone give her what she's used to."

Naomi took his hand. "It'll work out, Arnold, if you take it easy with him. He does have pride."

His voice was tired. "I don't give a tinker's curse about his pride. He's not screwing me out of what I worked so hard for without paying for it. It's enough he's screwing my daughter."

He had never used rough expressions before. It surprised her, but it made him less disciplined, not so astringent. There wasn't much they hadn't said to each other now—only one thing, and that she had sworn he would never know.

"I'd better start composing a telegram," she said. "Maybe Sarah will come over for the party!"

"I hope she does," Arnold said. "I'd like to hear what she thinks of our son-in-law. Nobody can fool that woman."

Naomi glanced at him, but there was no hidden meaning in what he said. And he was right. There was very little Sarah didn't know about the people who interested her.

42

YAD MORDECHAI
DECEMBER 1953

"I think you two should come with me," Sarah said, watching Elea run toward the fields. She laughed. "Look at him, he can't get to his damned rocks fast enough. Maybe today he'll find a fossil." She turned back to Rachel. "I really think you should come. It'll be a good way to celebrate the new year."

"I don't know. It's a long trip, and I've never been out of Israel in my life. What would I do at a swanky party?"

"Astonish everyone with your wit and beauty, what else? We'll go to that shop in Tel Aviv and get us a couple of Paris imports. There's nothing like a smashing outfit to give you confidence. When I was Arnold's entire sales department, I spent every cent I had on one scrumptious dress and coat. Made me feel as confident and swanky as I turned out to be." She smiled at her sister-in-law.

Rachel smiled back. "That would surprise them—the pioneer woman in a Paris gown. They probably expect me to come in overalls."

"More likely girt about the paps with cloth of gold—King Solomon's mines and so forth. Well, what about it?"

"I'd have to think it over," Rachel began, but the sound of a pneumatic drill cut her off. There was always the sound of building at Yad Mordechai. Only the overturned water tower remained from the original village, a reminder of the battle for independence that had taken Ben's life and so many more. Since 1949 the kibbutz had been rebuilding from scratch, gradually abandoning the austere concrete buildings, punctured by bullet holes, for tiny family cottages of two rooms each.

They were building a museum dedicated to the Warsaw Ghetto, and their library was going to be impressive. Yad Mordechai was much larger too. It incorporated villages deserted by the

Arabs when the tide of war changed in 1948. The camps in the Gaza Strip, still housing Arab refugees after five years, were visible from the settlers' rooftops.

"It's still the same old story," Sarah used to say. "I think of the Warsaw Ghetto, and I know we have a right to be here. I look at those camps, and I know they have rights too. Why don't the Arab nations take them in? They have more room than we do in this pint-sized Eden."

But after a while the settlers stopped talking about it and simply went about the business of building a kibbutz and living in it. Roses flourished at Yad Mordechai—there could be a big export market for fresh-cut flowers shipped to Europe by air. They would produce honey too, as well as citrus and dairy products.

The drilling stopped.

"Have you thought it over?" Sarah said.

"It's expensive."

"Come on, Rachel. Money's not the problem. It's meeting Naomi, isn't it?"

"Yes. Suppose you had to meet a woman Lazar loved before he loved you—while he loved you. How would you feel?"

"Before doesn't count," Sarah said.

"Well, then, while," Rachel persisted.

"Not applicable. He was over her when he married you. And then—he changed. I don't have to tell you how much he changed. Love, as you well know, is far from the central issue in my brother's life—not this brother, anyway." She ruffled her short hair. "It's funny, you know. Josh was always the romantic one; but it's Arnold who's the constant lover."

"Naomi's lucky to know a thing like that."

"How can she know if the damned fool doesn't tell her? He treats her like a Dresden doll. He ought to whomp her ass and drag her into bed! That's what she thinks she wants—just like in the movies."

Rachel frowned. "From his pictures he doesn't look that sort of man."

"That's the trouble—he isn't. But neither is she, really. Naomi was pining after a Sheik of Araby character, the kind of thing that ends with waves beating on a shore. Joshua seemed to be that."

Sarah was careful to use the past tense. She was never sure that affair had gone beyond a few days on a train at the end of the war.

"Joshua *is* that—without waves," Rachel said.

Sarah stood up. "Don't reveal the secrets of the bedchamber, or I will too."

"Oh, Sarah, is there someone?"

"There have been several someones, but it's no good. I keep looking for him, you know what I mean? Every once in a while there's something about a man that's almost Lazar, so I let him get closer. But it's always just one thing about him, not everything, and that makes me miss him even more." She peered into the distance, hiding her face from Rachel. "Where is that child of yours? You're going to lose him to a dinosaur if you're not careful. There's something odd about a little boy who likes to dig up antiquities the way Elea does. You should ask Isaac for a pill."

Rachel put an arm around Sarah, letting her chatter. Sometimes she thought it would be better for Sarah to leave Israel now that the children were grown—Seth was twenty-one, Rebekah twenty-two. The sense of loss would never lessen while she lived here in a monument to the men who had died with Lazar. Maybe Arnold could persuade her—or Naomi, Sarah's oldest friend.

Suddenly curiosity overwhelmed her reluctance. Who was this woman who had captivated two brothers and Sarah—even Benjamin, who placed his affections so carefully. He talked a lot about his aunt since he started school in America. She wasn't just pretty, Benjamin never noticed things like that. She must be more, a lot more.

"All right," Rachel said. "We'll come with you."

Sarah hugged her. "I'm so glad."

"You'll probably be the only one who is."

"You mean Josh? Well, to hell with him if he doesn't like it!"

"Shai!"

"I mean it. He can't ruin your life along with his."

"Something else ruined his life. He's not to blame."

Sarah's temper cooled. "I guess you're right. But the war ended eight years ago. It's time he forgot it, whatever it was." She hesitated. "How is he with Elea?"

"Reserved, the way he is with Benjamin, but more so. And Elea adores him."

"Damnation," Sarah said softly. "Has he ever said anything?"

"No, but I'm sure he thinks Elea's not his."

"You know, Rachel, it might be a good idea to tell him."

"How can I tell him what I don't know myself?"

"Bullshit!" Sarah was angry again. "It's only in the movies that women get pregnant in one shot. I'm sure you and Joshua weren't exactly strangers when he came back."

"Not at all—if you mean sex."

"Why should he have any suspicion at all, damn it! Except to get himself off the hook because he's against reproduction. Oh, Christ," she said, annoyed with herself. "Here we are chewing it all over again, and I swore I wouldn't. Forget it. Let's go rescue Elea from his old bones. We'll drive into Tel Aviv and see about some clothes. Then you can't change your mind."

43

NEW YORK
DECEMBER 1953

Joshua hung their coats in a closet near the door. "It's pretty dreary, isn't it? I never notice where I am unless I'm with you. Then everything suffers by comparison."

Naomi crossed the room and sat on the frayed sofa. They had not been alone together for months, but he didn't touch her, and she was glad of that.

"Would you like some tea—or a drink?"

"Tea, please." She watched him start to fix tea in the tiny Pullman kitchen of his residential hotel in Greenwich Village. She couldn't see his beard or the lines chiseled into his face. Except for his hair he might have been the same young man who walked out of her life so long ago. But by now she had given up trying to find that man again.

"Why do people always try to change each other?" she said. "Time does it anyway."

"Whom did you want to change?"

"You, once." She was glad he wasn't looking at her. "I wanted to change you back to the way you were."

He did turn to look at her then. "If anyone could, it's you. There are moments when you do."

She was still enchanted by his face. But she said it anyway. "I can't do that anymore."

"Why?" He was very still.

"Because of Arnold. He doesn't know about—this. But he's known since the beginning how I felt about you—he told me so." She shook her head. "I know it won't make any sense to you, but it was different when I could pretend I hadn't hurt him because he didn't know. I can't pretend that anymore."

His face was impassive. He leaned against the wall of the wretched little kitchen looking like a prophet or a Greek statue, looking like anything but a gun-running rabbi. Or a lover.

"It makes no sense at all," he agreed. "But it's up to you. It always has been."

"Not always."

"Yes, always," he insisted. "You made your choice. I made mine. That's still the way it has to be." His voice dropped. "But I need you. When I'm with you, I can forget about all the insanity out there. When we're together, it seems right to love life, even if we have to leave it at the end. Don't say good-bye before the end, Naomi. Please don't."

It seemed a rather empty gesture to deny one man for what the other need never know. The trouble was that she loved them both, and one of them suffered because of that. "I can't stay trapped like this, between the two of you. I never understood how you could."

"Don't try to understand me. Just stay with me. He'll never know, I swear it."

"And Rachel?"

"Rachel has always known."

"Oh, God." She turned her head away. "What did she say?"

"We've never discussed it. She understands."

She was amazed. "You can't know that if you've never even talked about it!"

"I know my wife," Joshua said. "She was raised in a different world from yours, with different values. For her a marriage doesn't stand or fall on fidelity."

"Not for me either, until now."

"Whose fidelity, yours or Arnold's?"

"Mine, now—and I suppose because of that, his too. Wouldn't you care if Rachel . . .?"

His face changed. "I can't have one set of rules for myself and another for her." His eyes dropped. "I'm not sure Elea's my son."

"Oh, Joshua, no!" How could a woman married to him want another man? "Was it because of us?"

He shook his head.

"Because she was alone so much?"

"I was in Israel at the time. But I didn't want another child." He looked at her, questions in his eyes. "Or maybe someone loved her in another way, and she needed his way then. It doesn't matter. She belongs to no one but herself."

But Naomi knew it mattered to him. Except for the night he had told them about Rachel's pregnancy, Naomi had never thought of Rachel as a person, only as Joshua's wife. But from all she'd heard about Rachel, she did belong to herself. Naomi didn't. She belonged to a lot of people. Including this man, who doubted his own fatherhood.

"Is that why you were so angry with her when you heard about the baby?"

"Of course not. I thought he was mine, and I still didn't want him." He was trying to keep his temper. "This isn't a world for innocents, Naomi. It's a cruel and terrible place. What little there is in it of beauty or love is just another one of nature's monstrous little tricks, a way to hide the brutal truth from us. It's only with you that I forget the truth." He hadn't moved, but he seemed to be reaching for her. "You're all I have that isn't tied to fear and sorrow and implacable death. I need you just as much—more— than he does."

She should have been glad to know that, but for some reason she was angry. "What does that mean? That I go to the highest needer? I don't want to be needed. I want to be . . . known. For myself. I wanted to know you, but you never let me near you, not really." She had never really let Arnold near her either—it made her feel shallow, unfair. She spoke more calmly. "I exist, Joshua, apart from anyone's dreams, even my own. What am I supposed to do with all the hours when I'm not somebody's fantasy?"

"What do you want to do?"

"I don't know," she told him honestly. "Stop pretending to be something I'm not, I guess. I'm not so sweet and good and charming—and I'm not particularly passionate either, except once in a while, with you. Did you know that?"

He shook his head.

"Oh, Josh." Her blue eyes were puzzled. "How little we really know each other." She got up. "It's late. I have to go."

He watched her go to the closet for her coat. She looked elegant, as always. Except in bed. There she looked rumpled and young. That was only another illusion. He knew he had been watching her grow up since that night he came home from the war.

"Will you come back?"

Her voice was muffled by the closet. She thought if he touched her now she would stay. He knew that, but he was not the sort of man to use it. That only made her love him more.

"I still love you. I'd divorce Arnold and marry you if you wanted me to. But I can't live my life two ways, even if you can. I have to do what I have to do."

She put on the coat, glanced at him for a second, then went out, closing the door softly behind her.

He stayed where he was. A trace of her perfume lingered in the lonely little room. She hadn't said no—he was sure she would come back. She was the only comfort he had. There was a softness about her, a calmness that was as soothing as honey. The only peace he knew was with her, in her. But she was right, he had never let her near him. He didn't let anyone near him. He had been too badly battered by his own loves to handle anyone else's.

The water boiled out of the kettle with a savage hiss. He took it off the burner and turned out the flame.

So Arnold knew, had always known—and had said nothing. He hadn't thought Arnold capable of such iron control. It occurred to him that he knew very little about his brother. Their present relationship was cordial, even friendly. Only Joshua's temper threatened it—and Arnold now accepted that with surprising equanimity.

His brother's wife . . . He remembered how it felt the first time he knew she was his brother's wife. She had grown up enough to give in to the feeling that once pulled them together—and enough to resist it for some belated moral principle.

Principles were a luxury enjoyed by few. If he had any left, he could not do his work. What life would perish at the point of a gun he put into some unknown soldier's hand? What flesh would be savaged by a grenade he bought? How many lives would be canceled because of him? Yet it must be done, and if he had no scruples about this, he had none for anything else.

He sighed deeply. He had a meeting this very night with Arnold and some of the wealthy men Arnold knew. He would have liked to cancel it. He had never wanted Arnold's wealth or his position or his life. Only his wife when he was young and—for different reasons—now. But Arnold's money was essential, and Joshua would go to the meeting to get it, keeping the same distance between Arnold and himself that he kept with everyone. There were times, though, when he had to see his brother or talk to him. Arnold had a kind of steadfastness that acted as an anchor when things got very rough. You always knew he'd be there.

Joshua poured some brandy into a glass and looked through the mail he had tossed on the desk. There was a letter from Rachel that he read—and read again.

She was coming to Julie's wedding party with Sarah and Elea. The letter left no room for discussion—Rachel was like that when she made up her mind.

And so they would meet, the two women in his life. He had a feeling the meeting would change things for all of them. He sat sipping the brandy and wondering how. One thing: It would either bring Naomi back to him or separate them forever.

Finally he put it aside and went to the six o'clock meeting at Arnold's Fifth Avenue apartment. Tonight he was more impatient than ever with the need to explain to these barbered, manicured, polished tycoons that every inch of ground in Israel was in constant jeopardy and every soul in the tiny country on constant alert. Tonight he was insulting in his refusal to accept what these men offered. He demanded more.

"The Arabs outnumber us by forty to one—you gentlemen are good at figures. The Syrians can blast the Galilee from the Golan Heights whenever they want to. There are Jordanian troops flanking our sector of Jerusalem. And our immigration is dropping, not only because Soviet bloc countries have cut off exit visas to Jews; even the people who can stand the living conditions we have to offer them are not all Einsteins! We have to teach Yemenites from the Stone Age how to produce, how to assimilate, how to fight. We have to teach every immigrant how to speak Hebrew. That takes money! And you give me excuses!"

He faced the well-tailored businessmen sitting in a luxurious room, drinking twenty-year-old whiskey. He looked around the room pointedly.

"This is a far cry from some isolated settlement in Israel open to a surprise attack at any time. They need more than your feeble excuses to defend themselves."

"We've already given millions," one of the men objected. "Why do you insist that we're responsible for every Jew in the world?"

"Only the living," Joshua said contemptuously. "We can take care of the dead."

"I think you fellows are making a mistake by talking so much about all of that. The world wants to forget it."

"Indeed," Joshua said, packing more derision into those two syllables than Arnold had ever heard. "What precisely does the world object to?"

Arnold moved uncomfortably. "To your—your rubbing everyone's nose in it. Let it be, let it rest!"

Joshua looked at his brother, then at the circle of faces in the room, his expression rigid, unforgiving.

"Do you think this fight is over?" His voice was loud, incredulous. "There is massive border infiltration by Arabs—and terrorist attacks on settlements well inside our boundaries." His hand came down hard on the polished mahogany table. "It isn't over. It is *not over*! Do you think for a moment that any Jew is safe in his bed because they've bulldozed all the corpses into holes and covered them over and the grass grows sweetly now at Auschwitz above such obscene fertilizer? My God, how can anyone let that rest?"

Arnold drew back. The other men were quiet.

"Remember too," Joshua went on, "the ones who did it were human, like you, like me. If you want to forget the victims, take pity on the perpetrators, the other side of our natures, the dark side. There will be more killings, you know."

The men looked at one another. "What in hell are you talking about?" one of them said.

After a second Joshua's voice resumed its usual tone. "Money. That's something we all understand. I need money to buy guns. I'm demanding that you give me more than you want to give. It's as simple as that." He was direct, urbane, darkly charming.

"Well, if you put it that way . . ." The men took out their checkbooks, laughing uncertainly at first. They refused Arnold's offer of another round of drinks; they had things to do—parties, theater tickets, bridge games.

"I'll say one thing for you, Rabbi," one of the men said on his way out. "You never stop."

For a second it was Isaac's voice he heard, that first night he saw Giora, Isaac talking to Lazar: *You never let us forget, do you?* And Lazar answering, *Neither do they.*

The man was looking at him.

" 'He who keepeth Israel,' " Joshua said sardonically, " 'neither slumbers nor sleeps.' "

He closed the door and went back to Arnold. He was mixing two more drinks, obviously furious but trying to control himself.

"I don't think any of them will ever come back."

"They will," Joshua assured him. "Guilt brings a heavy ransom. I should know."

The bubble of anger burst. "What are you?" Arnold demanded. "Some kind of messiah that you have to suffer for all of humanity?"

"Suffer?" Joshua looked haggard. "No, I'd bring them back if I could." Then he was mocking himself again. "But you see, my powers as a savior, unlike those of our hallowed ancestor of Nazareth—who, incidentally, did not see fit to appear in the camps—are limited to the Jews in Israel. And I will save as many of them as I can. Now, how much will you give me?"

"Whatever you want," Arnold said hoarsely. Joshua terrified him when he spoke like that. And he felt pity for his brother as well as fear. He wanted to go home to Naomi and Julie. He wanted to be sure they were safe. He even wanted to comfort this

anguished man who had what Arnold wanted most in the world
and was fool enough—thank heaven—to care only for something
else.

Joshua drank his brandy. "I have news for you," he said. He
spoke normally, the specter that had possessed him gone again.
"Rachel and Elea are coming to Julie's party."

"I'm glad of that," Arnold managed finally. "You've been
married for twenty years, and I've never met your wife. She must
be quite a woman, with a son like Benjamin."

Joshua said nothing.

"How is Benjamin?" Arnold had to fill the yawning silence.

"Doing very well. Someday he'll be stealing atomic secrets."
He spoke lightly. It was hard to tell what he meant when he said
things like that.

"I suppose he'll be getting married soon."

Joshua smiled. "No. Benjamin thinks marriage is obsolete. So
does Rebekah. She's been living with the same man for five
years, but she won't marry him."

"She will if there's a child," Arnold said, studying his glass.

"Is Julie pregnant?"

Arnold nodded. "That was why they eloped. I'd like to kill
the son of a bitch. Instead I have to give a big reception because
he seduced my daughter."

"Maybe it was mutual. No, don't be angry. Julie is too
strong-willed to be seduced. And they both look too happy for it
not to be mutual—both the marriage and the baby."

"Don't tell me he's in love with her!" Arnold said. *Tell me if
Naomi is still in love with you,* he went on in his head.

"Love is a thing I know nothing about," Joshua answered.
"But he's as devoted to her as she is to him, in my opinion."

If you know nothing about love, he shouted to himself, *how did
you take hers away from me?* "He's devoted only to her money,"
Arnold insisted.

"As I am to yours." Joshua rose. "That doesn't mean I don't
care about you." He began the nervous pacing that had replaced
his former calm.

Arnold watched him, touched and confused by this unexpected
declaration of affection. He knew nothing about love, but he
"cared about" Arnold. It was a welter of conflicting emotions.

Arnold hated disorder too much to dwell on it. He cleared his throat.

"Naomi says I have to give him a chance at Duchess."

"She's right." Joshua's face was hidden in the shadows of the room.

"It isn't easy. She's my child."

"They both are, Julie and The Duchess. And you've always wanted a son."

"Not like him! Like—well, for a while I thought she might marry Benjamin."

Joshua stopped his pacing. "Yes," he said softly. "You would have wanted that. But you've had everything else you ever wanted."

"So have you," Arnold said, leaving the lie still there between them.

Joshua seemed not to have heard him. "I must go, I have a meeting."

"And it's time I went home."

They turned out the lights, got their coats, and left the apartment.

"Can I drop you?" Arnold asked in the elevator.

"No, it's just a few blocks away. I'll call you in a day or so." Joshua left him abruptly.

They set off in opposite directions. It was the way they had always gone, Arnold knew, but this was different. He stepped into the waiting Rolls.

Something about Arnold—not anything he did, but something he was—tormented his brother as much as his brother's very being tormented him. Yet they "cared about" each other, two men who shared a bond no other men in the world shared with them: brotherhood.

The realization made Arnold want to cry for all the lost years gone and to come, because, however much they might care, they would never really know each other.

44

SANDS POINT
DECEMBER 1953

There had never been a party like this at Sands Point. The many dinner parties over the years had been only superficially social—the guests were people important to Duchess. Julie had few friends, and Naomi's life centered on her daughter, not on the few charities she helped or on the country club. Arnold detested any publicity about his private life.

"I'm not going to use my family to sell anything," he said in an obvious slur on one of his more flamboyant competitors, whose parties were well documented in the press.

Even tonight many of the guests were connected with Duchess in one way or another. But tonight there were young people too, most of them Parker's friends. The house was banked with Julie's favorite yellow roses and feathery ferns. Music from the dining room, cleared for dancing, rippled through the spacious rooms on either side of the entrance hall. All the double doors of carved oak had been opened, and by nine o'clock the house was aglow with happy, handsomely dressed people, laughing, talking, dancing.

Naomi wondered why this little family had lived such a splendid isolation. There should have been more parties like this, more family gatherings. This was the first time so many family members were under her roof together: her brothers and their wives—she hardly saw them because Arnold preferred to keep his distance from men who worked for him; Sarah, who came and went and hardly changed at all; Naomi's parents, round, brown, and sure that Los Angeles was the only place for Julie and Parker to live; Joshua, with Benjamin and Elea—and Rachel.

Naomi had been apprehensive almost to the point of illness until Rachel finally arrived with Sarah and Elea. The unexpected news that Rachel was coming left her no time to prepare to meet her sister-in-law, or to take stock of what was happening to her life. Waiting for that meeting while she was coping with the details of Julie's marriage, her clothes, her party—the loss of her, the *loss* of her!—had been infinitely more painful than the meeting itself.

Her intimacy with Joshua was over, but it didn't matter when things happened, only that they had, and that, except for a heartbreaking scene with Arnold, she might have gone to bed with Rachel's husband after more than a year's separation from him. Most important, she still wanted him. Surely his wife would sense that.

When two women finally met, the feeling that obscured everything else for Naomi was the most unexpected one: liking. Rachel was not conventionally pretty; but she had the kind of face you remembered. She was magnificently dressed, but she gave Sarah credit for that. And she was marvelously entertaining, without trying to be, because her life had been a vast adventure, compared to Naomi's and Julie's.

"They make me feel so useless, Sarah and Rachel," Naomi said after that meeting. It was during the drive back to Sands Point from the New York apartment where Sarah was staying with Joshua and his family. "Like some kind of decoration."

"That's ridiculous," Arnold declared. "Everyone's not cut out to hoe and plow and milk cows."

"What about all the work you did during the war, Mother? And all the work you do now?"

Parker patted Naomi's gloved hand. "You're a lot more than a decoration. I don't know what any of us would do without you." He was sincere, and he said it in spite of the way Arnold scowled whenever Parker spoke as a member of the family. Parker genuinely liked his mother-in-law. She was a lovely-looking woman, but that wasn't all. Naomi hadn't a shred of meanness in her, and that was more than Parker could say about most people. Neither did Julie, even though she knew what she wanted and would do anything to get it—the way she had him.

"That's sweet, Parker. Thanks." Naomi smiled.

Arnold was quiet, wishing he had said that. He eyed his son-in-law with cold disapproval.

"He's absolutely right," Julie said, "not sweet. My husband is many things, but sweet isn't one of them."

How proudly Julie said "my husband," Naomi thought while the car rolled along. Thank heaven Julie was happy—it was what Naomi had always wanted. Naomi had private doubts about the future fidelity of a man as attractive to women as Parker Mitchell was, and how Julie would react to that troubled her. How would any woman react if she loved a man?

She was sure of one thing after meeting Rachel and spending an evening with her and Joshua: Rachel knew only that Naomi and Joshua had been in love as youngsters. Rachel had no idea there had been any more to it than that. Joshua was only dodging the truth by pretending his wife "knew" and "understood" something he had never discussed with her. She had never believed Joshua capable of such dishonesty—that was the only word Naomi could think of. And yet—she blushed in the dark of the car—hadn't she been dishonest to pretend Arnold knew nothing all these years?

It wasn't simple dishonesty. It was self-preservation not to look at certain things. The truth about yourself was sometimes too hard to live with—or made it harder to do what you wanted to do.

"I'm mad about that little boy," Julie said, breaking into Naomi's thoughts. "I love to hear him talk about his 'digs.' He'd dig up Central Park if they'd let him. We're going to take him to the museum to see the dinosaurs."

Arnold smiled. "He's not as serious as Benjamin was. And he looks just like his mother."

Now, while the music played and people laughed, Naomi watched Elea's mother. In a Grès gown of pale apricot chiffon Rachel looked like a woman who had never hoed a field or milked a cow. She was standing with Joshua, listening with him to their small son's remarks as if Elea were Ben-Gurion himself.

They were man and wife; they shared things that no two other people could ever share, not even if they were to divorce and remarry. And they shared their sons. Naomi definitely put aside Joshua's suspicions about Elea. Another varnishing of the truth. She would not have blamed Rachel—she was hardly in a position to blame anyone—but Rachel loved her husband. It was in the way she looked at him, the way she looked when she was near him. She was not remote, not in some terrible distress, as he was. She was simply more suited to him than any woman Naomi had ever met—including herself.

But people don't always love where it's suitable. And there was no doubt in Naomi's mind or body that she still loved a man she couldn't have.

Hardest of all to resist was his need for her. Why was need more absorbing, more compelling than love? Love was constant, as Arnold was constant. Need was as vagrant as the wind, and as exciting. The two rarely seemed to go together.

Her eyes looked for Julie in the beautiful rooms. She could only hope that Julie was loved more than she was needed. She found her daughter finally, standing between Parker and Sarah, looking very lovely, very young, and very vulnerable.

Parker laughed with this tall, striking woman he couldn't think of as an aunt. Her short, shaggy dark hair was streaked with gray, and she had a way of rumpling it when she spoke, a welcome change from the dyed, teased, and lacquered hair styles of most women her age. She had a strong, voluptuous body covered with black matte jersey and a single spray of diamonds. Her skin was golden tan, like Rachel's, and her eyes sparkled with fun. It was hard to believe she was forty-three years old.

"Enough of this nonsense," Sarah said. "When's the baby due?"

"Did Daddy tell you?" Julie asked, surprised.

"Don't be a goose. Your father is an old-fashioned man! Nobody had to tell me. You just look like a woman with a delicious secret. Everybody knows about this"—she patted Parker's arm—"so it must be that. When's it due?"

"In six months," Parker said, delighted with her.

"And you're joining Duchess?"

Parker nodded.

"Think that's a good idea?" Sarah was more intent than she appeared.

"*He* does, so I have to give it a try." Parker rarely called Arnold by his name.

"After the honeymoon, I suppose. Where are you going?"

Julie shrugged. "We haven't had a chance to think."

"Well, I have. Why don't you take the *Ballade* and cruise around the Mediterranean?"

"What's the *Ballade?*" Parker asked.

"She's a yacht, a beautiful one." Sarah laughed. "We said she was a yacht to get her past the Brits and into Haifa, but she made a marvelous gunboat. She got a little beat up during the war, but she's been fixed now, had a face lift and lost tons of cannon, so she's a yacht again. You could pick her up in any Mediterranean port."

"Aunt Shai, you're an angel. I've always wanted to cruise around the Mediterranean with a man like Parker."

Sarah smiled. "I can see why. Now go away and let me get acquainted with my nephew. I see Benjamin looking for you."

She turned to Parker when Julie was out of earshot. "Well, then, what manner of man are you?" she asked, watching him carefully.

"I'm damned if I know," Parker said. "Not the kind *he* thinks, anyway." He glanced across the room at Arnold.

"Okay, so you're not a fortune hunter and a big mistake for Julie," Sarah said. "But it doesn't seem such a good idea to waste your time trying to change his mind about you. He guards Duchess the way he does his daughter—better, obviously." She smiled briefly. "He won't give you the freedom to accomplish anything on your own."

Parker's mouth set stubbornly. "I wouldn't bet on that." He wasn't going to lose the chance of a lifetime no matter what Arnold did. "Anyway, it'll take me years to learn all *he* knows." He looked at Sarah. "I do love her, no matter what he tells you."

She studied him, her dark eyes appraising him. "I believe you really do." Her mood changed, and she took his hand. "Welcome to this peculiar little family, Parker. You're the best-looking thing I've seen in a long time—it's going to be a magnificent infant. Now, how about waltzing your Aunt Sarah around the floor?"

He relaxed and followed her toward the dancers, waving at Julie on the way. Whenever Julie was in sight, his spirits rose, and he was sure everything would smooth out, that he would do wonderful things at Duchess. He needed her reflected image of

himself. It was a comforting fantasy he'd had since his parents
were killed: He was some kind of enchanted prince, denied his
birthright, alienated from both tribes as he had been.

He had a family now—and a rather extraordinary one, to judge
from the Israeli branch. It felt warm, welcoming, secure to have
a family—even if one member of it was Arnold Fursten. And the
key to all this, to everything, was Julie. She had already defied
her father for his sake once: He was sure she always would.

Arnold watched Sarah and Parker, then lost them among the
dancers. He wondered what his sister would have to say about
Parker. Every day he resolved to keep his distaste for his son-in-
law hidden, at least from Julie: And every day he broke his
resolution. There was something about the man that set his teeth
on edge. He sighed.

"Sighing?" Rachel's voice said. "At such a happy time?"

Arnold was glad to talk to someone and especially to Rachel.
He was drawn to her as he was to few people. She seemed so
steady, so ready to accept life as it was instead of as it might
have been. He wished he could do that. She knew about Joshua's
work—she was even proud of it. She had no idea that Arnold had
been at some pains to keep his brother's activities secret from the
press. It was hardly a conventional profession.

"I guess I don't like change," he said after a moment.

"Ah, yes," she agreed. "I know what you mean."

He sighed again. "I just hope she'll be happy."

Rachel thought about that. "I don't think I know anyone who
is," she said. "Oh, once in a while, perhaps, but it's the
exception, not the rule."

"For you too?"

She laughed. "I know, we're supposed to be drunk on milk
and honey and dancing the hora all day. Well, it isn't like that. It
never was." She paused. "I don't mean to be—sarcastic, is it?
But happiness is a thing that comes to very few." He liked the
sound of her voice. She had almost the same accent Lazar had
had. "Even your Constitution doesn't guarantee it, you know,
only the pursuit of it. And even then it only comes from what
you accomplish for yourself."

"I understand that. I feel the same way about my business.

But Joshua should be happy—his dream came true. Israel is a state.''

Her dark eyes regarded him thoughtfully. "It cost too much. His illusions died while his dream was coming true. My husband is a man who cannot live without illusions.''

"To hell with illusions! He has you—and his sons.'' Arnold had never had this kind of conversation before. He could talk to this woman—his brother's wife—as he could not talk to his brother, as he had never been able to talk to his own wife.

Rachel shook her head. "He's removed from us—from joy, I think, since the war. He takes no pleasure that he raises more money for Israel and buys more munitions with it than anyone else. He's as remote from the two boys as he is from me. It's as if,'' she went on, after a moment's reflection, "he can't trust himself to love anyone again. But he wants to. He goes through life with his head in the clouds and his feet in quicksand.''

"What do you mean by that?''

"Reality keeps pulling him back down to earth—reality and the inevitability of his own ultimate eclipse. But at least''—Rachel smiled slightly—"he saw the stars once. They're as much a part of reality as the quicksand, aren't they?''

Philosophy was beyond Arnold, but he watched his brother across the room where he was talking to Naomi and Sarah. He was moved by a new compassion for this man. With Rachel there jealousy didn't distort his view. He forgot Joshua's white hair, the lines in his face. He saw the big brother who had helped him grow up, when their own father was such a stranger to this big, new country that he might still have been back in Russia. He remembered Joshua bringing him books, taking him to the library on damp winter days, when the smell of musty book bindings mingled with the smell of wet, woolen mittens and snow-crusted rubber galoshes. He remembered reading about the history of America as hungrily as Joshua studied the history of Zionism, then trudging home, his hand in Joshua's so he wouldn't slip in the snow, to tell it all to Sarah, stuck in the house helping Mama. And the way all three of them talked and laughed and planned their secret futures.

How far they had all come! How much they had won—and lost! He sighed, and Rachel, watching him, watching Joshua with

Naomi, was not crushed at the sight of the woman her husband loved differently from the way he loved her. It was a fact of life, no more, no less, and there wasn't a thing anyone could do about the facts of life but accept them—as Arnold obviously never had. For herself, if Rachel regretted anything, it was Joshua's self-disgust—overly indulgent of him, she thought—at using the rabbinate to cover his munitions dealings. If he cared very little for what he called superstitious religious observance, it still went against his grain, he said, to use it for a cover. It was sad, she thought, that he had also to bear the guilt of loving his own brother's wife.

Would she have been so understanding, so accepting of that if there hadn't been Ben? The greatest saints had always been the greatest sinners, after all.

Glancing at Arnold again, Rachel was convinced that much as he might suspect the whole truth about those two, he didn't know it for a certainty, probably because he didn't want to know it. From Joshua, she knew, he never would. Nor would she, unless she asked, and she had no need to ask.

"Confession might be good for the soul," Joshua said once, pointedly, she thought. "But only for the soul who tells. It can destroy the soul who listens. That's the thing the Catholic Church understands: Keep your guilts for the impersonal ear of the confessional instead of unloading them on your friends and family." Tell me nothing, he seemed to be warning her; ask me nothing.

As for Naomi, Rachel knew what Sarah had been talking about all these years. Naomi never made an issue of her looks, her wealth, or anything else that might make another woman ill at ease or even jealous. Benjamin had called his aunt "a good egg," and Rachel thought she was exactly that, good-hearted, good-natured, *good*. Whether she would ever tell her husband what he didn't want to know was something Rachel couldn't predict on such short acquaintance. She had a feeling, though, that some day Naomi would.

Arnold felt her eyes on him and looked back at her. So many things had to be left unsaid. And yet, he thought, she understood. He felt better than he had in many years. He wanted to speak to his brother, who was now standing alone while Naomi and Sarah walked toward the door.

"We can't leave him all alone like that," Arnold said huskily. "Not at a party."

"No," Rachel agreed. "We can't leave him alone."

They went to join Joshua together.

Sarah smiled at Naomi and put an arm around her waist as they walked through the drawing room. "Another wedding," she said. "Remember yours? Remember mine? How shocked you were that Lazar and I hadn't waited! But how calmly you take it that Julie didn't either."

"I've grown up," Naomi said. "Or something."

"I'll bet on 'something.' Nobody ever really grows up. But you have a very decorative son-in-law, which is more than I can say for myself."

"What's Rebekah's young man like?"

"Oh, large and fierce and as dedicated as she is. Looks like somebody's idea of an Israeli, the way Joshua did. Lazar was too blond."

"Lord, what a pair of men they were," Naomi said. "Right out of the movies."

Sarah nodded, preferring to ignore Naomi's use of the past tense for both men. She knew why Naomi used it. "This is a remarkably handsome family," was all she said. She looked through the open doors to the next room, where Arnold and Rachel were talking to Joshua.

"She's not what I expected," Naomi said, following Sarah's eyes.

"She *is* kind of special."

"Lazar said that about her once, remember?"

The two women were quiet, absorbed in memory. When the orchestra began a new song, they were still thinking of the two men who had changed their lives, one vanished, although he was there in this house; one lost in eternity, if such a thing existed.

It was an old song, played in waltz time, and it said something different to everyone there over forty.

"*Are you lonesome tonight?*" the song asked a lot of smiling people who were. "*Do you miss me tonight? Are you sorry we drifted apart?*"

"We can't stand here and cry over an old song," Naomi whispered to Sarah.

"Who says we can't? And who says it's the song?"

"What will people say?" Naomi said, not caring.

"To hell with them. You look like you need a good cry as much as I do."

"Okay," Naomi said, touching her wet cheek to Sarah's. "To hell with them."

The two of them stood together while the dancers whirled and talked and laughed.

"Is your heart filled with pain?" the song asked. *"Shall I come back again? Tell me, dear, are you lonesome tonight?"*

45

MONTE CARLO
JANUARY 1954

Julie and Parker lingered on the deck of the *Ballade* in Monte Carlo harbor. They had just spent an evening at the casino after a day driving in the hills behind the French littoral. It had been an unusually balmy day, the last one of their honeymoon, and the patches of golden mimosa on the Maritime Alps were magnificent.

Tomorrow they would leave from the Nice airport for New York, via Paris.

"I wish it could go on forever," Julie said.

Parker held her against him. "It's been the happiest time of my life, but I have to get to work."

Julie wished her father could hear him. Arnold was convinced that, given the chance, Parker would have spent the rest of his life gadding about the world in pursuit of nothing but pleasure. She was sure her father would make Parker pay for this marriage, even though she was as much to blame as her husband for the pregnancy that had precipitated it. He wouldn't believe that she would have married this man sooner or later, pregnant or not. But she could only see trouble ahead for them now.

"Parker, don't you think it might be better for all of us if you weren't with Duchess?"

He shook his head. He wasn't about to work his ass off someplace else when he could start at the top with his father-in-law. And they'd think he was Fursten's spy, anyhow, no matter where he might go because of Julie's connections; this industry guarded its secrets like the military.

"That would mean coming between you and your father," was his short reply to Julie. "There's a key to managing everyone. All I have to do is find his."

She let it drop. He had never been angry with her, and she didn't want him to be, ever. "I'm glad you found mine," she said, moving against him. She was sure of this, at least.

"You're a wicked woman, aren't you? And pregnant to boot." He kissed her.

Her eyes closed, and a little smile curved her mouth. "It's a beautiful night, and I want you. Right here. Right now."

His hands slid under her cape to touch her bare skin in the low-cut gown she wore. "What about the crew?"

"Aunt Sarah's trained them," she whispered against his mouth. "They never come up on deck unless we ring. And there's the playpen." Her head moved slightly toward the louvered enclosure on the deck. There was a large, round mattress inside covered with velvety towels for nude sunbathing. Her hands opened his shirt, and she kissed his chest, her tongue flickering. "Come on," she said.

They walked into the enclosure, and she unzipped the gown and let it slide to the floor. She stood there naked except for the short cape, her tummy just a little round. "The air's wonderful," she said, stretching her body lazily. "Lie down."

She opened his clothes and lay on top of him, her lithe, tanned body moving along the length of his, stroking him, kissing him. She knew when to touch him lightly, when to tease, when to linger.

Then she straddled him, her body tilted back, her eyes closed, her hands holding his as she moved. He was newly excited by the wanton pleasure she showed, but suddenly he felt that she was possessing him, moving with such sure sensuality that it was she who commanded, he who obeyed. It gave her a mastery over him that he could not accept from Arnold Fursten's daughter if he had to accept it from Arnold Fursten as well.

Abruptly he grasped her and pulled her down to him, rolling over so their positions were reversed and he was above her. Her eyes were still closed in a fever of passion, but now it was he who controlled her.

As, he was sure, he would eventually control her father.

But the fact was that he never felt other than a schoolboy with Arnold Fursten. If there was a key to the man, he never found it.

Arnold thought he kept his antipathy hidden, even at Duchess. He thought no one on the outside knew. The Parker Mitchells had everything they wanted—but Duchess paid the bills, not Parker. His enormous salary was paid into a trust fund for the baby's benefit. His cash supply was doled out as pocket money, through Julie. Credit cards in profusion paid for everything else; cars, houses, planes—they were all at his disposal, along with a huge executive office at Duchess, furnished by Arnold in pricelessly austere Louis XVI, with Oriental carpets on the floor and a vice presidency to top it off.

His position in the company had all the trappings of power but none of its force. And the rest of the industry, adept at reading signs within its inner circle, soon sensed it.

"He's like a snake," Parker raged to Julie one day in June. "There's nothing I can put my finger on, but it's obvious to everyone that he thinks I'm some kind of halfwit. He gives me nothing of importance to do. I might just as well sit in that museum of an office and play with paper clips."

Julie could only listen and sympathize from behind her huge belly. Parker had refused to let her talk to her father, much to her relief; it would humiliate him more, he said, to have his wife beg for him. Privately he was convinced that once the baby came, Arnold's attitude would change, and he wouldn't need Julie to help him on his way.

For the most part he controlled himself when he was with Julie, but he was edgy. The doctor had said no sex for the last few weeks, and he needed more than what she did to satisfy him. He needed the sense of power he missed in substitute sex. What he needed most was some way to prove himself—and he had always proven himself most spectacularly with women.

But an affair was something he couldn't dare. He loved her too much, so he waited for his child to be born, hoping for a son to inherit Duchess. He knew that he himself never would.

Waiting with his in-laws in the Fifth Avenue hospital when Julie started labor, Parker had a horrible sensation of impending loss. The last time he had been in a hospital was on the night his parents died.

The labor dragged on, and they waited in the quiet, air-conditioned room that was too impersonal to absorb the anxieties and resentments that bounced off the gleaming floors and the pale green walls to make the waiting even harder.

"This is taking too long," Arnold said, fiddling with his tester sticks. "Why don't they tell us what's happening?"

Naomi sat near him, worried about Julie and concerned about Arnold and Parker. The war between the two men was getting worse, but she had decided to say nothing about it. Like Parker, she hoped that the baby's birth would make things better.

She got up and crossed the small private waiting room. "Parker, you mustn't tear yourself up like this. We knew it would be long—first babies always are." She put an arm across his shoulder. "Why not go downstairs for some coffee?"

He shook his head, but his hand closed over hers. "Thanks, Naomi, but I can't leave. It's hospitals—I hate them."

"I know, dear, but this isn't an accident. Women have babies every day, and Julie's a healthy woman."

"She's not all that strong," he said in a strained voice.

It deepened her affection for him. She had no illusions about her son-in-law, but she was sure the man loved her daughter, and that was all she cared about.

"I'm frightened myself," she confessed.

Minutes later the door opened, and the obstetrician told them Julie and a baby girl were both fine. They would have to wait a while to see Julie, but the baby would soon be in the nursery. The doctor congratulated them and excused himself to check on his patient.

"I'm so happy for Julie," Naomi said. "She wanted a daughter."

"So did I," Parker told them. "But it's too frightening, all that waiting. One's enough.'' A smile changed his face. "I'm a father,'' he said.

Arnold watched him, resenting him bitterly for his joy. What right had a man like Parker to Arnold's daughter—to his grand-daughter? He realized all at once that he had a grandchild. The reality was far more overwhelming than the expectation. "I want to see the baby,'' he said.

Minutes later they watched through the glass while the nurse wheeled over a tiny red infant, mewing in its bassinet.

"She looks like Julie did,'' Naomi said. "What are you going to name her?'' She had never been able to find out—Julie and Parker were superstitious about it, they'd said.

"Paige Parker Mitchell,'' Parker told them proudly, "after my mother.''

Arnold felt something for this baby that was different from the love he felt for Julie. Julie was an extension of himself; he had to worry that she might not be perfect. He could demand less of Paige and enjoy more of her. He stopped puzzling over his emotions. He was glad she was a girl. He knew all about little girls now, and he could spoil this one to his heart's content.

As for the baby's father, he liked Parker less than ever. Parker had offered some of his own ideas lately, with as much assurance as if he had been in the business for years, not months. He was shrewd, Arnold had to admit, and he learned fast. But he was the sort of man who had to be watched, or he'd end up taking over. He turned his attention back to his granddaughter.

In the months following the baby's birth it became obvious to Parker that the hoped-for transformation in Arnold's attitude had not taken place. Arnold was, if anything, more rigorous in his refusal to trust his son-in-law. He was subtle about it, giving Parker more projects to handle; but none of them could get underway without his personal approval. Even Naomi's brothers had more responsibility than that.

Parker was once more outside the pale, as he had been through-out his youth. Then he had belonged to two tribes but was not a part of either. Now he was titular vice-president of a gigantic corporation but had absolutely no hand in running it.

Still he refused to leave the company, no matter what the cost to his pride. He was good at this business, and he knew it. He soon convinced himself that he had given up a chance at recognition in another company because he hadn't wanted to come between Julie and her father. It was for Julie's sake, all of it.

That gave him all the justification he needed to make up for his professional castration in any way he chose. And he chose women: He had always had great success with women.

Letting him do it was Julie's way of making a lot of things up to him. She *had* seduced him. It was *her* father who was doing this to him.

And he loved her. Even with his women, Parker could never resist the voluptuary in his wife's polished, fragrant body. Julie was a pagan packaged in filigree. Their physical relationship kept them together, no matter how many affairs he had.

Above all, the possession of Fursten's daughter against Fursten's will was the only triumph he had over the man.

Naomi watched it with the sinking feeling that she had brought Julie up to have not what Julie wanted, but what Naomi wanted. And all she could do about that now was to make things as pleasant as she could between Arnold and Parker and be there if Julie needed her.

Once she thought it would be better to stop pretending that everything was wonderful, but she knew what a shock that would be to all of them, including herself. She had been pretending that everything was wonderful all her life.

Book
Six

46

GIORA
MAY 1960

Elea walked slowly, keeping several hundred yards away from the shores of Galilee—he called it Kinneret. His head was down, and his eyes swept the ground carefully for any little mound or ridge that might be a pillow of earth over ancient history. It was silly to look—he knew every inch of land within a five-mile radius of Giora—but it was a habit.

Archaeology had always fascinated him, even before he knew the name for the science of exploring the earth's past. You never knew when you'd stumble on some secret of the long-ago. The kibbutzniks of Beit Alpha had been digging in their fields when they found a sixth-century synagogue in 1928. And the wondrous discovery of the Dead Sea Scrolls in 1946 had been an accident. It was an exciting science and, in this ancient land, almost a national hobby. Just as soldiering was a national necessity and a strong link between all citizens.

Sometimes the two sciences went together: The operations commander of the Israel Defense Forces in 1949, Yigael Yadin, was a graduate student of archaeology who used his knowledge of his country's terrain to move troops with lethal effect. Moshe Dayan was absorbed in archaeology. Both men were Elea's heroes, but he dreamed more of making a big find himself someday than he did of battles. He and his girl friend, Miri, wanted to study archaeology together at Hebrew University. Either that or he would go to an American prep school in October and then on to Harvard when he was eighteen, just like his brother.

It was a big decision to make: Hebrew University or Harvard. America was tempting, but he'd be so far from everything he knew. Israel was where he wanted to live, but on the other hand he didn't particularly care for soldiering, and it was part of life here. *Ain brera,* people said—there was no choice.

He looked across the lake toward the heights of Golan in Syria. They were a constant threat, demilitarized or not, to settlers from Lake Kinneret north to the Lebanese border. There would be a real war with the Syrians someday, not just retaliatory raids against terrorists; everyone knew that. Miri's father, Natan the Minotaur, wanted to start it before the Arabs did. Ari, the perpetual soldier who roved the desert like a Bedouin, predicted war every time he passed through Giora. Isaac Levy, the doctor who had delivered Elea and his brother, Benjamin, and Miri, the last of Natan's five daughters, agreed. So did Benjamin and Abba—and they were in the best position to know.

Benjamin was in intelligence, although Elea didn't know whether it was Mossad or Shin Bet or another branch. As for Abba, nobody really knew what Joshua did since he stopped chasing around the world about five years ago. He still left the country once in a while, but most of the time he was in Israel, somewhere to the south in the Wilderness of Zin, a place few people had seen.

His father. A man everybody admired, Elea most of all. Once it had seemed to Elea that his brother, Benjamin, was more his father than Joshua. But since Abba had come home to live, it was Joshua whom Elea wanted to emulate, and that was hard to do because his father was a hard man to know. And different. Each time Joshua came out of the desert, he had changed again.

He and Benjamin looked a lot alike, except for Abba's silver beard, which made him look like a Greek philosopher, and his hair, but there was a big difference. You could tell how Benjamin felt about you. Joshua wasn't that concerned with people, only with his work, whatever that was, and Elea respected that. It was the way his generation wanted to be—far better than being all emotional, like his cousin Seth and his aunt Sarah. Elea and Rachel were somewhere in the middle.

When he was little, feelings had come easily to Elea, but he was learning to control them. Israelis had to be brave, strong, courageous. They were in constant danger, and there might be things to do in the future that didn't allow for sentiment. But they were never afraid.

"Zombies," Aunt Sarah called them. "This country is breeding a generation of emotional zombies! They think it's weak to feel anything. Seth is the only boy I know who'll say he's in love. I haven't known a thing about Rebekah since she was thirteen.''

Love, Elea believed, was a dangerous thing. People got through life a lot better without it, and not only men like Joshua either. His cousin Rebekah had two children by the man she'd been with for twelve years, but she wasn't in love, and she wouldn't get married. Benjamin slept around wherever he wanted; secret agents couldn't get involved with love either. Elea and Miri had decided they would sleep together when they were sixteen and get married after their two-year military service . . . unless he deferred his service by going away to Harvard.

They both became members of GADNA when they started high school. It was a paramilitary organization dedicated to physical fitness and useful skills such as signals and marksmanship. There were long hikes in the broiling summer desert, Spartan tests of strength and endurance to prepare them for whatever hardships the future might hold.

" 'Those who do not remember the past will be condemned to repeat it,' " was their favorite quotation. None of them intended to relive the Jewish past.

Elea went ten yards inland before continuing his walk. The old days. Abba and his friends were walking textbooks of their country's recent history. They were part of the old days and part of the new. Just listening to them, young people learned the truth about life, not a bunch of pretty fables about honor and decency. They got the straight story from old guys like Ari, even if he got worked up and flew off the handle all the time.

The Sinai campaign a few years back, for example. It didn't happen the way they told it in the newspapers. Elea knew all about it from Ari's explosions, even though he'd been only nine at the time.

"Whores!" Ari said. "*Kurvehs*, the lot of us! A plan, a choreography you wouldn't believe. We pretended to attack the Suez Canal when we really want to open the Tiran Strait and clean out Gaza. France and Britain come onstage to 'stop' us, when what they want is to secure Suez. In the wings Nasser has egg on his Russian MiGs, while Eisenhower gets a wild hair up his ass and aborts the operation because the Soviets object! *Object!* While they're slaughtering Hungarians, yet! Why not fight for what we really want instead of doing a song and dance like that?''

Joshua and Benjamin always insisted that Israel had to cooperate. Israel needed French hardware as much now as she needed it in 1956, so they had to make a deal.

"Never mind your deals," Ari told them. "I'm not a dealer, I'm a soldier. This country is still at war and will be until we have borders that make sense. Make a deal on *that!*"

But the Sinai campaign did bring 125,000 new immigrants in two years, and what Israel needed as much as guns was settlers. Ari knew that, no matter how much he might want to play a dirty game by honorable rules. No one in his right mind would come to Israel if everything that went on behind diplomatic doors was known.

Elea liked Ari. He was sturdy and barrel-chested and fierce, even though he was near sixty, as old as Joshua. Ari was a brilliant eccentric in Israel's citizen army. He once led an independent brigade; he was still an active volunteer. Men like Ari had built this country. And the men like Joshua. They were a far cry from the immigrants who had come in after World War II.

Elea's father and his friends had nothing in common with survivors of the Holocaust, but—and this was what puzzled Elea—they had sympathy for them. The young people didn't. Among themselves they called the survivors ''soaps,'' a grisly reminder of how the Germans rendered human fat into soap in the camps. Those Jews had let themselves be herded off to death like cattle. But the new Israelis wouldn't die without a monumental struggle. They were brave, courageous—and they were ashamed of the six million who had perished without a fight—except for a few like Uncle Lazar and Mordechai Anilewicz.

There was a statue of Anilewicz at Yad Mordechai. It loomed larger than life, but it represented the kind of men Natan, Ari, and the Doctor were.

And Joshua, most of all, because he never lost control, never let emotions interfere.

Elea turned back toward Giora. There was another name to add to that list: Ben Horowitz. He pulled the *chai* out from under his shirt. This was Ben's, and his mother had given it to Elea when he was thirteen. The *chai* on its gold chain had been around his neck ever since.

All the old friends talked about Ben a lot—almost as much as about Lazar. They called Ben "the Dandy" and remembered his exploits inside British headquarters under the Mandate. They even talked about his adventures with Natan when the two of them joined the Irgun. The differences between the Irgun and the Haganah were virtually ended now. There wasn't even a Palmach anymore. There was just Zahal—the army.

He put the *chai* away as he approached Giora. His ears, trained to interpret sound, missed the buzz of tractors, the voices of people working in the fields and orchards. They had stopped early today to get ready for a big party: Giora had been founded fifty years ago today, and people were coming from all over to celebrate.

In the spring afternoon the sunflowers rustled their applause of this golden anniversary, the air was sweet and the sky was blue over Kinneret. To Elea this was the most beautiful place in the most beautiful country in the world. Suddenly he wanted to see Miri, to tell her he had decided not to go to America.

He quickened his pace and ran toward Giora at an easy trot, passing the main gate, the watchtower, the new dairies that were his mother's pride and responsibility.

A feeling that something had happened pushed him to go faster. He got to the communal hall and made his way inside to find the community standing in silence, watching Joshua, dusty from the road, while he finished saying something. A moment passed while they absorbed it, and then they burst into a loud sound that was not a cheer. It sounded like anger to Elea. Yet they were cheering.

He slipped through the crowd to his father and tapped Joshua's arm. "What is it, Abba? What happened?"

"They got him," Joshua said, almost crying. Elea had never seen his father like this. It was more than embarrassing, it was frightening. Who could make his father care enough to cry?

"Who?"

"Eichmann," Joshua said. "They got Adolf Eichmann. He's here in Israel, and he's going to be tried. By us. By Jews."

One of the chief organizers of Adolf Hitler's "final solution."

A pioneer in mass extermination. An enthusiastic user of Zyklon B, a gas that killed in only ten to thirty minutes. The Israelis had hunted him since 1945.

"Was Benjamin in on it?" Maybe that was why his father was acting like this.

"I don't know. That isn't important. The important thing is that we got him, after all these years."

"I don't think it's something to celebrate," Elea said.

The people near them were suddenly very quiet, intent on him. His father's dark eyes examined him.

"Why not?"

"We'll have to hear all about it again. We've heard enough. Nobody's interested but the 'soaps' anyway."

His head snapped back when Joshua hit him. He was breathless. His father had never hit him, never hit anyone.

"Don't you ever call them that," Joshua said fiercely. "Don't you dare, you rotten little bastard."

Rachel's voice stopped him from hitting Elea again. His hand dropped, but his eyes were still angry; then the fury faded, and he looked more like himself again.

"I'm sorry, Elea, for what I called you, not for anything else. You have no right to say a filthy thing like that unless you know what you're talking about, how it happened." He took a deep, uneven breath. "You'll learn now. It's a sad thing that you'll have to learn it from Adolf Eichmann."

The man and the boy looked at each other in silence. Then there was a horn blast outside, and in a minute Sarah ran in, her expression one of grim exhilaration.

"Did you hear it?" she called as she came through the crowd to them. "Was it Benjamin?" She stopped near them. "What is it? Is everything all right?"

"Yes," Joshua said. "A little misunderstanding, that's all."

Elea nodded. It had been a long time since he had cried, and he was afraid he would if he tried to speak. More than humiliated by the slap, he was infuriated that his father could care that much—but not for his family. How could he love people who died before Elea was born more than his own son?

He took his father's outstretched hand as if the argument were over and everything were all right again. But everything was changed. He knew his father had never cared about him at all—only about *them*. His father wasn't unemotional—he was simply indifferent.

As for trying to please Joshua, Elea had just forfeited his chance of that forever.

He would go away to school in America in the autumn. *Ain brera*—there was no choice.

47

SANDS POINT
DECEMBER 1964

"He's here!" Paige shouted from her lookout post at the bay window of Naomi's bedroom. "Elea's home!" She streaked through the room toward the stairs while Julie and Naomi smiled at each other.

"Shall we give her a few minutes alone with her idol before we go down?" Naomi said

"She'll just send us back up if we don't," Julie agreed. "It's funny—I used to wait for Benjamin like that, didn't I?"

"More patiently, maybe. Once upon a time I thought you might even marry him."

"Would you have let me go off to the wilds of Israel?" Julie smiled.

"Oh, yes," Naomi said emphatically. "I've never believed in telling other people what's best for them—not even children. Especially not children."

Julie studied her mother. "You sound as if someone told you—and it wasn't best."

"Everyone told me," Naomi said.

"Were they wrong?" Julie was hesitant. She had never questioned her parents' apparently stable marriage, but eleven years of her own had taught her things were often not as they seemed.

Naomi looked away. "I believed everything they told me, that's what was wrong. Whether or not they actually were wrong—well, you can't live two lives, so I don't think you ever know.

And there's no point wondering at my time of life.'' Her blue eyes searched Julie's face, almost saying that there was still time for Julie to wonder; there was a vastness between twenty-nine and fifty-five.

Julie stood up, slim and casual in cashmere and tweed. "I'll go and fix my face. Parker and Daddy will be home soon."

Naomi watched her go off to her old bedroom across the balcony. Julie still wore very little makeup, and her cropped hair needed no attention beyond a brush. She left because she didn't want to talk about Parker.

Naomi sat down at her dressing table. Parker was a problem, even though he worked harder than anyone at Duchess. But no matter how profitable and innovative his ideas, Arnold didn't trust him. The fact that Parker was notoriously unfaithful to his wife didn't help.

Most of the time Naomi just listened to Arnold. It was better for him to blow off steam in private. But lately she objected to the things his remarks revealed.

"I told you he was no good from the beginning," he had said only last night.

"You act like there's some merit in being right about such a thing," Naomi protested.

He stopped his fuming at that. After a minute he said, "He doesn't love her; he never did."

"For some people, Arnold, love and sex are two different things. We both know that."

He turned away. "Don't say that. Don't say that to me."

"I'm sorry—but your constant criticism makes me angry, and it hurts to see Julie hurt, whether you're right about him or not."

And she didn't think he was right. She was sure Parker loved his wife, faithful to her or not. Why Julie tolerated his infidelity had been a mystery, until she heard her daughter say, "He does a lot of things to get back at Daddy."

By inference those things had nothing to do with Julie. But they did! They hurt her.

In a way Julie was right; it was an easy way for Parker to provoke Arnold, to pay him back for his patronizing attitude. How to convince Julie that a reason was not an excuse? How to tell her only child that no one had the right to use her like this? And how to make Arnold see the connection between Parker's vindictive behavior and his own? Never having examined his own motives, Arnold didn't analyze anyone else's. He couldn't see that Parker needed the approval he worked so hard for—and needed it from Arnold because the younger man was as much bereft of a father as Arnold was of a son.

Parker was a natural in the cosmetics industry, but neither that nor the stimulus he gave Arnold to try new things was enough. Arnold treated him with subtle contempt, until Parker behaved contemptibly, as was expected of him. People usually did what was expected of them, not what they wanted to do.

Naomi looked at herself in the glass. Was that why she had ended the affair with Joshua—because it was what was expected of her once she knew Arnold had been hurt? The love she felt for Joshua had softened with age, along with everything else: her body, her energy, her longing to be with him. But it wasn't gone. There was still that familiar little leap inside and she was nineteen again whenever she heard his voice, on the few occasions when he came to America, or, as now, his son's voice.

She could hear Elea downstairs now, home from school for Christmas vacation, trying to quiet Paige. Paige was irresistible, as Sarah had been. She had Julie's green eyes and Parker's dark hair, but her nature, loving and tempestuous, was Sarah's.

Julie interrupted the reverie. "Wake up, Mother. Time to go down to Number Two Boy." For Julie, Benjamin was Number One, still a boy at twenty-nine.

"Go ahead, darling. I'll be right down. I hope Parker and your father get home on time—Elea's always ravenous."

Maybe the two men would be on good terms tonight. She was weary of smoothing over arguments, and it would be a pity to spoil Elea's first night home.

But this wasn't Elea's home. Giora was, a place Naomi had never seen. They all traveled a lot more since Julie's marriage, but Arnold refused to go to Israel.

"It's too dangerous," he always said. "And the food's terrible— gamy meat and unpasteurized milk."

But of course it wasn't the diet. Time hadn't done enough to ease the tension Arnold had always felt in his brother's presence, as if his own accomplishments were a puny display compared to Joshua's. He worried about his brother, but he was jealous of him still. The habit was impossible to outgrow, just as impossible as his love for Joshua.

Naomi knew he still had reason to be jealous. Her excitement was over and the fever to possess Joshua, but not her love for him. Naomi looked at herself in the glass again. She was beginning to feel that the inside of her went with the outside now. There was no way to look eighteen again—or thirty, or forty; it was easier not to try. And it was easier to live without stifled longings or guilty fulfillments, easier not to pretend that sex was all she had wanted with Joshua simply because it was all he wanted with her.

She opened a drawer and took out Rachel's letters. They had been coming regularly since it was decided that Elea would stay at Sands Point while he prepared for Harvard. She reread the first one, received four years ago.

"He will seem moody and unapproachable," Rachel had written. "Our children grow up rather abruptly here with no time to learn compassion. They're afraid to risk getting too close to anyone. A siege mentality transforms people—but I know you understand that."

She meant Joshua as well as her son. And *was* Elea his son? For a long time after they parted, Naomi had missed Joshua too much to remember what he'd said about Elea that day. For a time she thought he might have been seeking justification for his own infidelity; but Joshua was not a man who justified his actions. As a young man he had done what he believed in; now he did what he thought had to be done. There was a great disparity between the two.

She had seen Joshua with Elea. He was not fatherly. He probably believed Elea was not his. It must have mattered more to him than he knew.

Naomi riffled the letters, remembering Rachel's growing pleasure as America changed her younger son. A lot of it was Paige's doing. Young as she was, she nurtured him; some souls are born with that gift. Naomi had had a share in it too. She thought the change had really started when she found her nephew in the den late one night, right where his father sat so many years ago.

The boy had rekindled the dying fire and was staring at it, looking young and lonely.

"What is it, Elea?" Naomi came to sit near him on the couch.

He knew how much they all loved him, but he might still be homesick.

He didn't answer for a while, but he didn't withdraw from any intimacy as he usually did. Finally he pointed to a newspaper that headlined Adolf Eichmann's hanging.

"It's him," Elea said.

The gathering of evidence and the trial itself had mesmerized the world for two years. That innocuous-looking man had somehow crystallized the horror of the Holocaust as nothing else, not even those terrible films, had done. He humanized bestiality by putting a harmless-looking mask on it. He made people suspect their own potential for infamy—and fear their own helpless surrender to it on such a scale as little Adolf Eichmann had executed it.

She waited for Elea to speak.

"My father told me I'd learn how it happened from that man—and I did."

"Surely you knew before, Elea!"

"Yes, but I hated them—the Jews, I mean, for letting it happen. I thought there must have been a way to fight." He shook his head. "I still think they they should have fought, but I understand why they waited so long that they couldn't. They didn't believe any of it until it was too late. Nobody did. Who could believe a thing like—him? Thousands of 'things' like him?" He was intent on the fire. "I wish I could tell my father I understand now."

"Why can't you tell him?"

"It wouldn't make any difference. My father doesn't care about me. He never did."

"Oh, darling, he only seems that way because of all that happened to him." Elea couldn't know what Joshua suspected!

"No, he's got too many other people to worry about who deserve him. He hasn't got time for me."

She wanted to put her arms around him. It was unutterably sad to hear him so resigned. She took his hand.

"Once when I was little, my brothers and I told my mother she must love one of us most, she couldn't love all of us the same. My mother lit a candle. 'That's like love,' she said. Then she made each of us light a candle from hers. They all glowed the same, and hers was just as bright. You can light a thousand candles, Elea, and still light a thousand more.''

Elea left his hand in hers for a while. ''Thanks, Aunt Naomi. But he's my father, and he never even let me near the flame.''

''Maybe he's afraid,'' Naomi said, suddenly remembering Joshua's refusal to share anything with her but their past, to share their present only in a silence that virtually canceled it.

''Afraid of what?''

''I don't know—but when you start crying, sometimes you can't stop—if that makes any sense.''

Elea said nothing, but before he went up to bed, he bent and kissed her for the first time since he'd come to live in this house. She thought he started to change that night, that he grew less afraid to be himself. And Rachel's letters, when he went home for the summer, told her she was right.

The letters had established a strange friendship between two women who had met only once but knew so much about each other through Sarah. Naomi had no women friends but Sarah and, lately, Julie. Her life was still focused on her family, as it had always been. But Rachel was a friend. They both loved the same man and the same boy.

And Rachel knew it, Naomi was aware of that now. It should have pushed them apart, by all the standards of love and jealousy Naomi had been taught. Instead it drew them together. Totally different as the two women were, they liked each other. It was one of the mysteries of Naomi's middle age until she stopped seeing Rachel as an extension of Joshua and thought of her as a woman and a friend. Rachel lived with a man who was afraid to love anyone. It must be a very lonely life. As lonely, Naomi knew, as the hours she had spent making love with Joshua.

Love didn't start and end in bed. That was only one place for it to live.

She put the letters away and went downstairs to the children, still hoping Arnold and Parker had managed to get through the day without another bitter argument.

48

Parker Mitchell turned his back on his father-in-law and pretended to study the New York skyline, but he was watching, reflected in the enormous wall of plate glass, the figure bent over a huge desk in the executive office of Duchess Limited. He loathed Arnold Fursten and everything about him: his gray-blond hair so neatly combed, his manicured fingers folded tightly together on the edge of the desk as he read, his hand-tailored gray suit and his gray-green eyes, cold as agate behind round, gold-rimmed glasses.

Parker let his eyes rove over the city, with its lights blazing in the early winter dusk. Parker knew his project on a new line of men's toiletries was a winner. The old man knew it too by now, damn him—but he'd let Parker sweat out an answer with no indication of his reaction to it, no clue as to his final decision. Just a silent reading followed by a pronouncement. He liked to remind Parker of his absolute authority in ways like that.

An autocratic son of a bitch, Parker thought, as if *he* had been born to society, instead of Parker. But the old man played his part well for an upstart, you had to give him that. Arnold wallowed in luxury, but the right kind. Following Julie's example, Arnold and Naomi traveled a lot more now, and Arnold had homes in the south of France, London, Barbados—each of them richly appointed—as well as the establishments in New York. He spent time in each place, but largely to oversee his business affiliates.

It was odd, Parker thought, that he had no property in Israel and would never go there—and odd to how he shunned publicity about himself and that Don Quixote brother of his.

There were Bentleys and Jaguars and Rolls-Royces in his garages, never a Mazeratti or a Porsche. His yacht and his plane were not ostentatiously large and not vulgarly baptized with the name of his wife or his company. The only initials that appeared on his apparel were his own, though there was no way of mistaking whatever belonged to Arnold Fursten—things or people.

He steered his ever-expanding empire with skill and foresight, although the cosmetics branch was his favorite, as it was Parker's, and he put all his creative effort into it, letting the subsidiaries run themselves once he had acquired and organized them. To his family he was a benevolent dictator. The only one who had any influence on him was Naomi, yet she rarely exercised it.

Parker sometimes wondered about his mother-in-law. She could have wound her husband around her finger, but she behaved as if she owed him something. Only twice in these last eleven years had she given Parker any help: first when he and Julie married, and a few years ago, when she gave her approval to a sexier kind of ad campaign for two new perfumes.

"Advertise a Duchess perfume with a naked woman?" Arnold had objected. "*Vogue* won't print it."

"They'll print it," Naomi assured him. "It's Duchess, and it's art. Sarah wanted to use that painting for Duchess years ago, but we decided the world wasn't ready for it yet."

Arnold simmered down. "And now you think it is." The opinions of his wife and his sister carried a lot of weight.

"Yes, I do. It's going to be the sexy Sixties. Parker's idea isn't cheap or vulgar, it's what the public wants, and the only way to sell anything is to give the public what it wants."

Arnold took her advice, but he was surprised at it. "I never thought you were so . . ." He looked for the right word.

"Calculating?" she filled in for him while Parker watched, fascinated.

"No, of course not. Call it realistic."

"Call it what you like," Naomi said crisply. Then she took his hand affectionately and smiled at Parker. "He still thinks I'm the same girl he married."

She was right, Parker thought. It was obvious from the way Arnold treated her, talked to her, that she hadn't changed at all in his eyes. It was a surprising streak of sentimentality in such a cold-hearted bastard as Arnold.

Both the brothers were cold, but on the few occasions Parker had met Joshua, he was relieved to see he kept his ice water in his veins instead of drenching everyone around him with it.

Parker's field of vision shortened again from the city's mosaic of light and stone to a reflection in the heavy, tinted glass. His dark hair was graying at the temples, but at thirty-seven he was very attractive to women from fifteen to fifty. Over the bridge of his straight nose his heavy brows almost met. He never allowed his barber to trim them—he thought they gave him character. He had fine, even teeth, white against a complexion bronzed by tennis and surfing in summer and skiing in winter.

Parker didn't patronize his father-in-law's conservative tailors in Savile Row and Jermyn Street, but his six feet were handsomely dressed. He was still slim enough to dress in the vanguard of French fashion, although he avoided some of its more foppish tendencies. His shirts were silk, his ties and shoes handmade.

And he deserved it. He was damned good at his job. He knew he was selling not only status but mystique, and he had the style and the training to do it well. Yet his father-in-law persisted in treating him like an occasionally inspired playboy who had to be led and, more often, curbed. Their arguments were frequent and heated; but each time Parker "resigned," Fursten contrived a "reconciliation": more shares in Duchess, another Matisse. These were the only things Parker owned in his own right.

He searched out the reflection of Arnold's figure in the glass again. Arnold turned a page and went on reading while Parker raged inwardly, waiting.

Fursten cleared his throat, and Parker turned.

"It will do," Arnold said. No enthusiasm, no encouragement. Just "It will do."

Parker walked across the thickly carpeted office to the desk, smiling as if he'd been mightily praised.

"Glad you like it," he said, reaching for the presentation folder.

His father-in-law's hand flicked him back. "I'll like it when it shows a profit. As usual, you want to go overboard on advertising."

Parker straightened and took back his outstretched hand. "It's the only way to get a new line off the ground. You've said so yourself often enough." *Naturally the others were your babies,* he thought. *Gladiator is all mine.*

"Look," he went on, opening the folder. "We can keep the packaging at fifteen percent instead of twenty or more. Plain black linen looks good. Plain glass, not etched crystal. This new bottle design—here's the sketch—is dynamite; it'll make up for the plain glass. We can even monogram it, here on the metal disc."

He took another sheet from the folder. "Raw materials are fairly low, less than eight percent. Would have been lower, but petitgrain citrus just went up again. We can't change administrative costs and taxes, but there's no royalty to pay on a designer name. Our research has been minimal—that Einhorn is a genius. I asked him for a cross between tobacco and leather, and he came up with Gladiator in two months flat! And there's no need for extensive quality control."

Arnold looked up sharply. "This is a quality house. I won't let that bitch corner the quality image." He never referred to his latest rival, a fantastically successful woman, in any other way.

"Of course not. But we've already tested and established the quality. Otto only took a tested experimental formula and added another 'base note'—hyssop, I think. Anyway, it's good."

Arnold nodded tentatively.

Parker continued. "We could cut the special department store staff, but I don't think we should. Those girls can be a terrific boost for a new line. And I don't think we have to cut them. You add up all the cuts I've just been talking about, and there's enough to throw forty percent into the advertising, not the usual twenty-five or thirty."

Arnold leafed through the pages again. He looked up. "You know what the mortality rate is on new products."

"Granted—but it took Princess cosmetics only one year to cover cost, not two or three, precisely because of the ad campaign. It has to be big and it has to be classy. We're not selling eggs, we're selling fantasies."

"At a retail that has to be near twenty dollars for a four-ounce cologne and fifteen for the after shave," Fursten said, "these are expensive fantasies, not to mention the soap, the body lotion, and the moisturizer—for men!"

Parker shrugged. "Men's cosmetics are definitely 'in,' and they won't buy them for less, we know that. Half the job of convincing them they're buying magic is to price it sky-high and give the product an image they can hang on to.''

"Why a name like Gladiator? I built a fortune on a rank and royalty image. Why change now?''

"Because times change,'' Parker said, trying not to sound impatient. Hadn't Arnold himself dropped the Aurora line for that very reason, when Duchess went public? "Royalty's fine for a standard market, but it's too conventional for this one. We need something that will appeal to men and women of all ages and persuasions. You know the statistics on homosexuality as well as I do—and that's my Gladiator. He's all things to all beholders.'' Parker laughed. "Hell, he even has a net and a mace for the sadomasochist crowd.''

"I find that more than distasteful,'' Arnold said stiffly.

"The profits won't be distasteful. I think you'll be pleasantly surprised.''

"Do you?''

"Yes, I do.'' Despite himself Parker's voice took on enthusiasm. "Every woman who buys Duchess or Princess for herself will buy Gladiator for her husband or son or boyfriend—aside from the men who'll buy it for themselves. And the way I've planned the introductory campaign . . .''

"It's the selling that counts,'' Arnold said flatly, corking Parker's bubbling spirits.

Parker sat down in the chair opposite Arnold. "I think I've shown I can sell in the last eleven years.'' His voice had an edge.

"You were selling to women buyers, not to men.''

Parker flushed. "Not always. A lot of perfume buyers are men. Some of my biggest accounts are with men. What's that got to do with it?''

"Your methods of selling are sometimes too gallant.''

Parker's voice was smooth again. "What do you mean by that?''

"I disapprove of buying business with sex and champagne parties, the way you do it,'' Arnold said.

"They expect it! Do you think Richards and West and all of them in the cosmetics division don't do it? Even Naomi's brothers?''

"In my day it wasn't done.''

Parker said nothing. He'd had enough without risking another sermon on how the old man had made it to the top of the industry. He knew it all by heart: the hard work and the slow crawl out of Rivington Street, the struggles and the bitter infighting. There were easier ways of making it.

"Things have changed somewhat since then," Parker said finally. "You objected to Duchess of Alba and Duchess of York, and they were both tremendously successful, even if they were my ideas."

There was no way Arnold could deny it. It had been Parker's idea to expand operations, even before the Princess cosmetics line to go with the perfume, to include Duchess of Alba perfume for sophisticated women who fancied themselves as seductive as Goya's Naked Maja, and Duchess of York for the horsey, tweedy set, who liked to be associated with the lady who brought the celebration of Christmas with trees and gifts to England from her native Germany. His advertising ideas were imaginative, using the portraits and short histories of the two duchesses. His packaging was expensive: Daum crystal *flacons* and fine fabric coffers. But the higher the cost, the higher the sales.

The two men looked at each other, the cord of dislike taut between them. Arnold broke the silence with one of his unpredictable reactions.

"All right," he said. "Go ahead with it. Just as you set it up. But only if you take full responsibility right down the line."

Parker was too startled to do more than pick up the folder before his father-in-law spoke again.

"But I mean *all* the responsibility. If it's a flop, it's your flop."

Parker flushed. "It won't be a flop."

Arnold stood. Privately he thought it would be a tremendous success—and so much work for Parker that it would keep him out of other women's beds. He would have given him a sure loser to spare his Julie after what Naomi had said last night. That was the point of the whole thing. "We'd better leave now," was all he said. "Elea's home."

Parker got his coat, and the two men left the building together, the picture of family unity, Parker told himself. He was almost ready to explode with this long-awaited chance, but he wasn't about to let anyone know that but Julie.

He would be coming home late for the next six months, but

not because he was screwing. He'd be working. If Gladiator went
over, he'd be able to write his own ticket. The sense of power
that gave him was more satisfying than putting his hands under a
silken rump and slipping into a new snatch just so Arnold would
hear about it, as he invariably did. This was success he wouldn't
have to hide from Julie, the kind Arnold couldn't hide from
anyone.

49

ISRAEL
JULY 1965

Joshua piloted the jeep skillfully along the road leading out of
Jerusalem, not really hearing the chatter of his friends. Heat
unfurled from the secret, sandy earth around them, and Joshua
welcomed it. In the last ten years he had spent a lot of time in the
Negev, that womb of silence of which the Judean hills were but a
faint suggestion. The savage wilderness asked nothing of men
and gave them nothing; it took—endlessly it took what was
sacrificed to it. There a man could hide anything—or let the
heavens witness his confession.

Joshua had come to love the desert; he could be himself there.
But it was harder for him to replace his mask each time he left it.
The sands eroded stronger stuff than rock. They eroded Joshua's
capacity to sequester his emotions. Each time he left it, it took
more discipline to deny his feelings as he must. Long ago he had
decided it was the only way for him to keep going.

Deliberately he turned his thoughts to more important matters.
The old dream of irrigating the Negev was coming true. There
would be real settlements, not just outposts at the desert's threshold. There would be green fields, homes, roads. The heart of the
desert would stay as inviolate as his own, but now water would
flow to it from the Sea of Galilee. The pipeline traveled west
from the sea, under the Emek Yizre'el, and through the southern
hills of the Carmel range to disperse its bounty in the northern

Negev, as far south as Beersheba. The work had gone on without a stop. Syrian bulldozers trying to divert the headwaters of the Jordan, which fed into the Sea of Galilee, had been stopped first by Israeli artillery. When the Syrians tried that tactic again, the air force had dispatched them.

Some of the planes they flew were still French, some even left from the Sinai campaign. But since 1957 Israel had been producing Fouga Magister jet trainers under license from the French and sending young pilots to France for training. Joshua saw signs of a serious change in French policy, though; it had been coming ever since de Gaulle took office in 1958. In Joshua's opinion things were getting worse. The Israeli government's decision to diversify its sources of munitions was a wise one.

He felt the hot sun on his face and arms, relishing it. Summer was the best time for him. It was May—Israeli summer—when he had first come to Palestine and met the men riding with him now. Lazar's time was summer too.

Isaac Levy, sitting next to him, raised an eyebrow. "For a minute there I thought you were going to smile."

From the back seat Natan hooted. "Him, smile? The great stone face never smiles."

"Personally," Ari put in, "I'm used to the Rabbi like this. If he smiled, I'd look around for a burning bush. When a man buys munitions from the Germans on Monday, the French on Tuesday, and somebody else on Wednesday, it's better he has a poker face."

Joshua did more directing than dealing now, but he never described his work in detail. "The Tuesday market is making peculiar noises," he said. They needed arms, as always. Israel was not secure.

"What's the matter with the French? They don't want us to try out their new weapons for them anymore? They don't like our nuclear reactor seven years after they helped us build it?"

Ari scratched his chin. "Natan, I keep telling you. They're all whores. So are we. If we don't make love with the French, we'll make love with the Germans."

Natan heaved a great sigh. "Did you think you'd see the day we'd buy guns from Germany?"

Isaac shrugged. "You buy from any source you can."

"But Germany? The psychologists say Eichmann was some

kind of purge for us and for them, but I don't buy that." Natan was angry. "I wouldn't trust any son of a bitch German. To me a German's a goddamn Nazi until he proves he ain't!"

"And even then!" Ari said. "But the reparations came in handy."

Natan's face darkened even more. "I never thought we should take any goddamn German money."

"It wasn't German money," Joshua said. "It was stolen Jewish money."

Isaac intervened. "Let's not get started on that again. This is a family reunion, not a parliamentary debate."

The men relaxed into friendly silence, contemplating the evening with pleasure. They'd held a summer picnic for themselves and their families for the past five years. They saw one another all the time—in tiny Israel you bumped into everyone you knew—but their "reunion" was important to them in a different way, more important as they grew older.

They were all gray now—except for Natan, who was bald—and their ranks had grown. Isaac and Ari were bachelors, but Natan and Aviva had five daughters. Sarah was a grandmother five times over: Rebekah had three—"How can I be a grandmother when I'm not a mother-in-law?" Sarah always demanded of her daughter—and Seth had two. With any luck Benjamin would make it to Giora tonight from wherever he was. And the men in the jeep were on their way from a meeting in Jerusalem—still ringed about with Jordanian guns—to the dig at Masada where Elea was working again this summer. From there they would drive back to Giora.

Their route was a wide detour westward, around that great bulge into Judean land that had been seized in 1948, along with East Jerusalem, by Jordan. The annexation of both areas had been formally recognized by only two nations, Britain and Pakistan; yet it was impossible for Israelis to travel freely in them.

The jeep swung over a crest in the Judean hills, and they saw it in the distance, the awesome sight that was Masada. It loomed, thirteen hundred feet high, brooding and majestic over the western shores of the Dead Sea. From the jeep they were still too far away to make out the workers excavating at the summit, patiently dislodging potsherds and relics two thousand years old. The great tower of earth looked as somber and desolate as it had been in the

first century, when nine hundred Jews withdrew to the fortress at
the top and held off the Roman Tenth Legion for two long years.

Only when the Romans built a ramp to the summit did Masada
fall. But it was an empty conquest: Only two women and three
children were alive. On orders from their chief, Eleazar Ben
Yair, the Zealots of Masada had killed their families and themselves rather than surrender alive.

Since 1963 young people had come from all over Israel and the
world to work on the Masada dig under the direction of Professor
Yigael Yadin. It would take several years to uncover, but its
treasures were astonishing in more ways than one. The hot, dry
sand had preserved more than sandals, braided hair, needles,
combs, and clay jars. For the Israelis pride and identity lived in
these dusty ruins. They were discovering a history that included
more than the recent humiliating past. After two thousand years
of exile and slavery they were discovering themselves.

"Whenever I see it," Natan said, "I get a feeling."

"What kind of feeling?" Ari sounded skeptical.

"That we have nothing to be afraid of. If the Zealots could do
it, so can we. I've always been afraid, somewhere deep in my
bones. I look at Masada, and I'm not."

Ari shook his head. "I'd have liked it better if Ben Yair's men
had won without knocking themselves off. It's bad strategy to
paint yourself into a corner—or up a mountain."

Joshua pulled the car to a stop outside the dig. "Or into a
ghetto. Well, we *are* in a corner, on the lip of the sea. But
anyone who pushes us off the edge this time goes down with
us." He opened the door and got out of the car. "It's after three.
Elea should be here any minute."

There was a shout from the dig, and Elea ran toward them. He
was not quite as tall as Joshua, but he was broad-shouldered,
bronzed, and as graceful as a dancer. His dark hair, wet from the
hose, glistened in the sun.

At the sight of him Joshua felt something rise inside him like a
flame. He was such a beautiful boy! So like Rachel. In the same
way Rachel was not conventionally pretty, Elea was not handsome. They were both simply beautiful.

Elea was eighteen, Benjamin past thirty, Joshua himself sixty-
two. *My life,* he wondered, as he wondered often in the desert,

what has become of my life? Elea was running toward him, but he might have been running away, taking years and decades with him. *My love*, Joshua thought in anguish, controlling his face, *what has become of all my love?*

"That kid," Ari, "is built like a gladiator. Your brother should have used him in the ads. I could make one hell of a soldier out of him."

Elea reached the car. "Hi, Dad," he said. "Where do you want me?" He got into the back of the car. "Hi, everyone. What's new?"

"You used to call your father Abba," Natan said.

"I got out of that habit in the States." Elea smiled. "Does anyone know if Miri got a package from New York? We're waiting for some records."

"The package is there, but no Beatles tonight," Natan implored. "Under the stars in Israel it doesn't seem to go somehow."

"Did you ever see the Hasidim dance?" Ari reminded him. "They say it's a godlike rapture, but if you ask me, they look like Elvis Presley in a smock. Now tell us, Elea, what have you found this week?"

The boy's enthusiasm, his real knowledge of archaeology fascinated all of them. But a stranger, Isaac Levy reflected, would never have known which of them was his father. Listening to the boy, Isaac smiled and patted Joshua.

"What's that for?" Joshua asked, under the voices of the three in the back seat.

"He reminds me so much of you when you first came out here. He draws people to him like a magnet."

Joshua negotiated a crossroad carefully before he answered. "I thing Benjamin's more like me."

"Now, maybe. But Benjamin was born serious. No, this one is you, when you were young and full of dreams. He brings it all back."

Joshua said nothing.

"Don't resent him too much for making you remember," Isaac said.

"That's ridiculous. No armchair analysis on me, please. I'm not ready to be uncovered layer by layer, like Masada, or peeled like an onion either."

"You're right," Isaac said, noticing Joshua's rigid jaw. "Peeling onions makes you cry." He turned to the conversation in the back seat. Joshua was in a strange mood; he was better left in peace.

Joshua headed back to Giora on the same roundabout route, skirting Arab territory. Had he ever been like Elea? Not at eighteen, certainly. He had been a rabbinical student then, still unwilling to hurt his father by rebelling. Elea had been born free; Joshua had first known freedom at twenty-five. In one year he had discovered freedom; discovered love and lost it; discovered Palestine and loved it; found his future and denied it. Rachel, swift-moving yet quiet, with her dark hair in braids. Was it a young man like Elea she had waited years for, until he knew he loved her too? And when that young man was destroyed, had she loved Ben? It was Joshua's doing, she was not to blame. But had she loved Ben?

He pushed it all away. There were larger problems to ponder than his ties to Rachel, to the boys, to Naomi. He was responsible to one man: Lazar; and to one reality: Israel. Joshua's covenant was not with God—that would have been easy—but with a man he had carried in his arms for twenty years. Lazar would have loved what was happening in Israel. He would have listened grimly to the Eichmann trial and been grateful that it healed the country instead of destroying it. He would have cheered when the Sinai campaign created an atmosphere of security which brought them so many immigrants. He would have written pages about Masada and smiled sardonically when German reparations helped them build a country for the Jews.

If Lazar hadn't gone, Naomi would never have happened. Once again it was Joshua's doing, Naomi was not to blame. Night after silent night in the desert he thought about her too, why it was that the physical cradle of her body had given him more comfort than anything else, enough to make him forget Rachel and his brother. That was the point: to make him forget. She had no connection to his real life, and that too was the point: He could only escape from himself with someone who was not a reminder of his pain, as Rachel was and these men and Benjamin. And Elea, Lazar's namesake, most of all. Whose child was he?

"There's Mom," Elea said suddenly. "She looks beautiful."

She did, perched on the gate in a white dress tinted orange by the sunset. Her dark hair was tied back, spilling over one shoulder. From the road Joshua couldn't see the streaks of gray, he couldn't see the lines. She looked as young as on the first day he had come here with Natan and Isaac and Ben. Ben and Rachel. Had they?

"I'll get out and walk up the road with her," Elea said.

"No, I will," Joshua told the boy. Whose child was he? Oh, Rachel, did you love him? "Isaac, will you take the jeep up?"

He stopped the car and got out without a backward glance, walked to Rachel, and swung her down from the gate and into his arms before she could say a word to any of the others. Isaac slid over to the wheel, and the jeep rolled ahead, leaving a trail of summer dust behind them and Joshua holding Rachel as if he hadn't seen her for a long, long time.

Elea turned from watching them. "What's all that about?"

"Love," Isaac told him.

But his father was the least romantic man Elea knew, and his mother a practical woman. This was not their way of caring for each other. Something else was troubling his father. "I don't know about that," Elea said.

"You'll learn," Isaac assured him, concealing his private concern for the cracks in Joshua's armor.

"Just don't practice on my Miri," Natan warned while Elea flushed hotly under his tan and Ari laughed aloud. The jeep rumbled up to Giora, leaving Joshua and Rachel at the gate.

"What is it?" she asked, close against him. He was shaking.

"Nothing. Everything."

"Tell me." Her hands stroked his back, his head.

"No. Some things are impossible to tell." He was on the brink of it, but silence was a habit with him. Better not tell what she need not hear—it might make her ask what she must not tell. But there was one thing he had to say.

"I love you, Rachel." It was wrenched from depths he had closed and locked twenty years ago.

"My darling, yes, I know." But she didn't know, not really. Love is never known until it is said.

"Rachel, I can't feel all that again. I'll fall apart if I do." His body shook.

She steadied him against her. He seemed ready to break now. "Then don't. It's all right, don't."

The trembling stopped. "Oh, God, Rachel, help me, please help me."

"Always," she promised, frightened for him. The youth he had hidden away in the darkness of the man was still there, mourning, demanding to be heard. She would wait, and when the time came, she would listen.

He had been such a shining youth—he deserved to have someone listen to him.

50

NEW YORK
FEBRUARY 1967

The plane began its approach to the airport, and Sarah forgot she was tired from the flight. It was always a thrill to see the lights of New York when she came back, but this time was different. For the first time since 1945 she was coming back to stay.

Her daughter thought she was mad. "You can't live that kind of life anymore," Rebekah kept saying. "How are you going to wear crazy clothes and makeup to impress people after living a real life here?"

"I don't need crazy clothes and makeup. It's America I miss. That's real life too."

"They have assassinations and race riots. I'll be worried to death for you."

"And we have bombings and terrorist raids." Sarah laughed at her. She hugged Rebekah. "I won't worry about you if you won't worry about me."

Sarah took out a compact while the plane descended and considered powdering her nose. There was no way they wouldn't both worry; they loved each other. But she hadn't really known either of her children since she had brought them to Israel. The country had taken them over completely, young as they were at the time, while she was still rooted in another life. She and Lazar had only lived together for any length of time in America, and her roots were in her life with him. All the ones that mattered, anyway.

Seth understood, but her son had always been the more sensitive of the two, and even he was only Israeli-sensitive, not sensitive as others were. Any Israeli of thirty-five had fought in two wars and any number of skirmishes with Arab infiltrators, had lost someone to war, and had lived on constant alert for the next attack. They were bound to be immune to the problems that preoccupied citizens of more secure countries.

Sarah put away the compact, her nose unpowdered, and leaned back in her seat. If she were perfectly honest, the person she would miss most was Rachel. Hardly a month had passed in twenty years without her seeing Rachel. They had shared so many things, a lot of them unspoken—and they had Joshua to worry about again.

If it had happened years ago, this breakdown of his carefully constructed wall, his old self would have been there to take over. But there might be very little left of that man now; if Joshua had become a part of his wall, he might crumble with it.

The plane bumped gently and set down on the runway. Home again. In the general stir of the bustle of people about to be liberated from an unnatural machine, Sarah thought of those who would be waiting for her here.

Arnold, certainly, eager to have her back. Maybe Parker too, but not so eager; Sarah might go back to Duchess, and Parker would be understandably nervous about any threat to his foothold in the company. Sarah decided to take a very close look at that situation before she made any decisions.

Naomi—that was always a delight, even though Sarah fumed sometimes when a wistful phrase in one of Naomi's letters showed she still thought of Joshua as the love of her life. But Naomi was doing what she had always done—making life confortable for the people she loved, one way or another. Naomi tended them all: Arnold, Julie, their granddaughter, Rachel's two boys, even Seth and Rebekah, far away in Israel. Naomi smoothed things over; Sarah blasted them into the open.

What a damned shame her screwball brother never let Naomi

visit Israel, Sarah reflected. She could never imagine anyone
telling *her* what to do, now or ever. She had shared her life
willingly, but blending was easy with Lazar, very easy. Doing it
now would be virtually impossible. She could never be carried
away by a man again. Any woman past fifty knows too much to
be carried away.

As Julie had been. To judge from Naomi's anxious letters,
Julie had cause to regret it. Parker adored Julie, Naomi wrote,
"but he's still chasing women, or letting them catch him. I don't
know why Julie puts up with it, but how can I interfere?"

"How can you not?" Sarah had written back. "They're inter-
fering with you by making life unpleasant."

Lately Naomi sounded if she might explode, as if her perpetual
patience were wearing thin at last. High time too. In Sarah's
opinion that whole family would be better hearing the truth about
one another instead of using civilized manners to cover ruined
hopes. Sarah wanted to be there when it happened.

The motors stopped, and Sarah put on her coat. It was her
usual cashmere wrap coat, and the hat was her usual felt slouch.
Her family spotted her as soon as she left the plane. Sarah had a
style of her own that had nothing to do with fashion.

And then she was with them, feeling as if years hadn't passed
since they'd all been together, as if she knew Paige as well as she
knew Elea. Sarah today was the same as Sarah five years ago;
she was always herself.

"Come on, all of you," she said. "Take me home. The old
lady's tired. She needs a bath and a drink and a month to
recover."

But her high energy came back in a week, and she moved from
Sands Point to the New York apartment. She spent two months just
reveling in the electric atmosphere of the city in winter. It had
changed a lot; it was dirty, dangerous, and shabby, but it still had
its own special intoxication for her.

Arnold wanted her back at Duchess. She still owned half of it.
In a company of that size there would have been room for talent
anyway. But it was obvious that she might easily become involved in the power play between Arnold and Parker. Arnold
knew Parker was worried, but he wanted him worried, not resting

on his laurels. Gladiator had been an astonishing success, and the hard work that went into it kept Parker away from the fleshpots—although apparently there had been rumors of late.

They fought each other for every inch of authority, not only over the men's toiletries division of Duchess but over Paige and Julie and now over Sarah. If she went back to Duchess, Arnold would score it as a victory and Parker as a defeat. Julie would be used to redress the balance, probably in the usual way. The only one exempt from the rivalry was Naomi, ahd she was weary of its tensions.

"I don't know how you can sit there pouring oil on the waters all the time," Sarah said one day over lunch at "21." "Always anticipating a row, changing the subject, watching Julie pretend there's nothing wrong. How do you do it?"

"I don't know anymore. I thought somebody had to," Naomi said with a wry smile.

"Baloney," Sarah said. "Let them all have it out. It would clear the air." She leaned across the table and took Naomi's hand, suddenly contrite. "I shouldn't judge you, honey. Most people can't put their cards on the table."

"Sometimes we do," Naomi said.

"You and Arnold?" Sarah was openly skeptical.

Naomi nodded. "He's always known about Joshua."

"*What* does he know?"

Naomi blushed. "That I was in love with him."

"Are you still?" Sarah ventured, leaving the rest of the relationship a secret if Naomi wanted it that way.

There were some things Naomi couldn't say, not even to Sarah. "I don't know, Shai. I don't think much about love these days. I see what it does to people."

"For instance?"

"Julie. I swear she helps Parker punish Arnold by letting his affairs go on. She's as much a part of the plot as he is. He'd never do it without some crazy kind of consent from her."

Sarah nodded. "It takes two to tango."

"And me. I've lived a half-life because I couldn't go with Joshua, and I couldn't let him go. I didn't care who suffered for it—and I know Arnold did; maybe Rachel too."

Sarah looked dubious. "It still takes two. Maybe they all

wanted to suffer a little for something, and you were helping them out.''

Naomi frowned. "I'll have to think that one over." After a moment she added, "It'll probably be a lot more helpful than thinking about love. I think I've outgrown it.''

Sarah nodded. "So have I, for different reasons. But at least I knew it when I had it, and that's more than I can say for you. You should have forgotten Josh long ago.''

"Don't people tell you the same about Lazar?''

"Sure, but it's hard to forget someone who never grew old or crotchety or boring—or agonized, like Joshua. I never had the time to get enough of Lazar, much less see his warts. Nobody can compete with him because he's forever new to me.''

"What happened to Josh, Sarah?''

"I don't know—something he couldn't take and can't talk about.''

"He went away to war—and just never came back.''

Sarah patted Naomi's hand. "I expect you thought you could bring him back.''

"I tried.''

Sarah signaled for the check. "So did we, but it wasn't any use at all.''

"How is he now?''

Sarah reached for her handbag. "He's all right when there's a crisis—and out there, there usually is. But Rachel says he's more shaky every time he comes out of the desert. Maybe it's not a good idea to confront yourself alone.''

"Maybe it's better not to know yourself at all.''

Sarah signed the check. "Most people don't have a choice. They trip over themselves sooner or later. Arnold's the only man I know who's coasted this far through life without inspecting his own merchandise. Maybe Parker too. They make quite a pair when they aren't fighting.''

The two women got up to leave. "That's what's so stupid,'' Naomi said. "They're a lot alike.''

"Well, I'm about to beard both the lions in their den. They've got a new idea, something hot, I'm sure, because they're both in a flap about it. Where are you going?''

"To pick up Paige. She wants to shop for Elea's birthday present. We only have two months left.''

They parted, two women in their late fifties. They were nice-looking, but that wasn't much to get excited over on a lovely April day in New York, Sarah thought. So Naomi went on mothering and Sarah kept on working—except she wasn't sure she wanted to get into a war over it.

Minutes later she was in Arnold's office, talking to Parker while Arnold and Ellis Trent finished some business. As usual they were waiting for Einhorn.

"What's all the excitement about?" Sarah asked Parker.

"Sorry, I can't tell you until everyone's here."

"I'll bet it's a new 'personal deodorant' spray for men," Sarah said.

"No, but I had that idea; it's a natural." Parker frowned. "But he won't approve it."

"Why not? He markets one for women, and the poor dears buy it by the gross."

"But he sells it through a pharmaceutical branch. This one would be part of Gladiator."

"Dear me." Sarah smiled. "Are gladiators all that dainty? What were you going to call it?"

"I thought of 'Below the Belt,' " Parker said, perfectly serious.

Incredible, Sarah thought, *he has absolutely no sense of humor, just like Arnold.* "How about 'Cocksure'?" she said, exploding in mirth.

After a second Parker laughed too, drawing a cutting look from Arnold just as Einhorn walked in and sat down, looking more like a mad scientist than ever.

"Sorry, Arnold," Sarah said, restraining herself with difficulty. "I just love a good joke."

"Well, what we're here to talk about is no joke," Arnold said. "There's a potential fortune in it."

"I'm ready," Sarah said.

"It's a new makeup that lasts for days. Won't wash off or rub off. Needs a special lotion to remove it. A woman can make up once a week, and that's it! She can sleep in it too. She can splash plain water on it. Think of the time she'd save. We want to do the whole makeup: foundation, rouge, eye shadow, lipstick. No mascara—too near the eyes for safe removal."

"It sounds wonderful," Sarah said, completely serious now. "If it's safe."

"That's what we have to determine," Ellis Trent said. He was still as spare and dapper in his sixties as Sarah had always remembered him. Ellis Trent was the consummate aristocrat—he would look smashing riding to hounds—with or without clothes. And he flirted with panache. But he wasn't Sarah's type; too effete. "Although I think we're being a little too careful this time."

"Not so," Einhorn warned. "There are allergies. Also who knows what are the long-term effects?"

Parker crossed one long leg over the other. "If we do the usual tests . . ." he started.

"We'll do more than the usual," Arnold said shortly. "I remember what happened with Pale Hands. That was already on the market. I don't want this released until we're absolutely sure."

"What the hell," Parker said. "If it doesn't work out, we can write it off."

"That's my opinion too," Ellis Trent agreed. "It would take years for the FDA to prove it unsafe—the burden of proof is on them. By that time you'd have made your profit on the shelf goods."

"Listen," Arnold commanded. "I don't want to recall anything with a Duchess label on it, and that's final."

"But you have to write off the research anyway. What's a few million more or less?"

"Mitchell's right," Ellis said.

"We'll wait!" Arnold repeated angrily.

"Then what are we here for?" Sarah asked.

"To choose a name." Arnold subsided. "To decide on the first press release so we'll have everything ready if we decide to roll. This is strictly secret; we don't want anything to get out until we're ready. Now, are there any suggestions?"

There was a thinking silence.

"Idée Fixe," Parker said.

"That's terrific." Sarah smiled.

"Except that it's not an idea that's 'fixed,' " Arnold objected. "It's a thing, a makeup."

There was another pause before Parker spoke again. "Fait Accompli," he said.

Sarah held her tongue. There was no use threatening a brilliant suggestion by praising Parker again.

"I like that," Trent said. "But don't take any notice of me, I'm just a dusty old lawyer."

To Sarah his high opinion of himself was always most apparent when he called himself a dusty old lawyer.

"I like it too," Otto said emphatically. "An accomplished fact—for five days at least after the woman applies it."

They all looked to Arnold.

"Yes, that's good. The ads will explain it to anyone who doesn't understand French."

Sarah laughed. "Anyone who doesn't understand French won't be able to afford it!"

They discussed advertising strategy—that was important. Any claims on the label itself had to be demonstrably true; in the ads a manufacturer could promise women anything and usually did, by powerful suggestion, without using specific terms the government could question. They formulated a lead line for a press release. All of them were excited about the possibilities before the meeting ended.

Sarah shook Parker's hand. "Congratulations, you're very clever."

"Don't tell *him* that," Parker said. "But thanks. Excuse me, Sarah. I want a word with Ellis before he leaves."

Sarah felt her old enthusiasm taking over while she listened to Arnold and Otto talk about testing. It was exhilarating to be in on the ground floor of a product that could revolutionize cosmetics. It would be wonderful to shape the marketing plans, start an ad campaign rolling. Her impulse was to tell Arnold then and there that she was coming back, but she turned to look at Parker, talking to Ellis Trent. No, it would be better to wait just a little while longer, until she was sure he wouldn't take it the wrong way.

Her face sobered. There was trouble at home in Israel too. Russia was pouring arms and "instructors" into Egypt, looking for a stronghold on the Middle East, as she had always done. Nasser was as clear about his intentions regarding the Jews as Hitler had been: "We shall not enter Palestine with its soil covered in sand," he asserted. "We shall enter it with its soul saturated in blood."

With Nasser's blessing the Palestine Liberation Organization terrorized from Sinai and the Gaza Strip, right near Yad Mordechai. On the other side of Israel, El Fatah struck from Syria's "demilitarized" zone, joined lately by regular Syrian troops, ambushing and killing.

When the war came—nobody said "if" anymore—they would be in mortal danger, all of them: Seth, Rebekah, the children, Joshua, Rachel, and Benjamin.

Sarah only seemed to be listening to Arnold and Otto now. What she was debating was how she could possibly get excited about fooling women into painting their faces while the fate of Lazar's country and Lazar's children hung in the balance.

51

Parker dropped his coat on a chair in the entry hall of his apartment and went right to the study, taking his briefcase with him. He fixed a drink quickly at a small, portable bar, the case still under his arm; then he carried the glass to his carved mahogany desk. It was the only thing of value his father had left him. It had moved around with him for years until it, and he, had found a permanent home with Julie in this duplex apartment on upper Fifth Avenue.

Julie and Paige smiled at him from a frame on the desk, but he hardly saw them. Sipping his drink, he went through the notes he had made, then lit a cigarette and glanced at the telephone, waiting for it to ring.

He leaned back in the soft leather chair and looked around the room, basking in its luxury. A fire crackled between the brass fire dogs he and Julie had found in Singapore, casting shadows on an Oriental carpet they'd brought back from their last trip to Iran.

The shelves were filled with books—a whole section devoted

to the history of perfume. It was a subject that had fascinated him ever since he joined Duchess. It had the romance that other businesses lacked, a mystery all its own that made people buy it no matter what the cost. It dated back to the beginnings of recorded history, when it was part of religious rites.

There were all kinds of scents. Sex-stimulating, like musk and costusroot and ambrette seed; narcotic, like some flowers and balsams; refreshing green resins from the sap and leaves of camphor, pine, and mint. Parker knew he could never create a fragrance—he wasn't a "nose"—but he wanted to travel the world buying some of the raw materials.

The chance of that was slight with Arnold Fursten in command of Duchess. So was making money on his own, or having a share in Duchess. He had some stock, doled out by the old man from time to time, a few paintings Arnold had given him to settle some towering arguments, but that was all. The rest was Julie's in trust for Paige. Parker had a salary now, but it didn't approach their living expenses. He was still being supported by Julie—literally. And now there was Sarah to take more opportunities from him. No matter how much he liked the woman, she was a threat.

He put his feet up on the desk. He had a chance to make a killing. All he needed was enough money to buy a lot of Duchess shares, someone to front for him, and a little luck.

Any blocks of stock over ten thousand shares would be recorded—and the whole scheme depended on Arnold's ingorance of it; that was why he needed a front.

If things went as he planned, the stock would shoot up in several days and could be sold at a profit; that was why he needed a little luck.

The money was another story. He would be a lot richer and no one any wiser—or poorer. The advance publicity over the new makeup could only help sales once it was on the market.

The telephone rang. It was Ellis Trent.

"I think we see eye to eye on a lot of things," Parker said after the usual preliminaries. "Try this on for size. Do you remember what happened a few years ago when word of a new cosmetic leaked?"

Ellis laughed, naming a large cosmetics company. "The stuff that was made of horse serum—supposed to turn prunes into plums for eight hours. They had it on the market for a year before the competition caught up.''

"And the stock went up sixty-six percent," Parker said, underlining it.

"I see," Trent returned.

Parker waited.

"I see a few problems too," Trent said.

"Anything you can't get around?"

There was a pause. "You could use a foreign co..npany to buy the stock—that way your name won't appear as purchaser of a large block of shares. It's not worth it unless you buy a lot, because you won't have a year for the stock to rise. He'll be angry enough to deny the whole thing as soon as he hears the news leaked. He might scrap it altogether."

"If it's an inside rumor instead of a press release, it could take a few days for him to hear it. That's all we need. Besides, he'd never scrap it. It's going to make too much money." Parker was smiling. They understood each other. "What's the other problem?"

"Money," Ellis said.

"I'll take care of my share of it," Parker assured him. "The shares are selling at twenty-eight. Let's say the foreign company buys one hundred thousand shares on margin—all we need is fifty percent of the total." He laughed. "I'm assuming you won't charge me any legal fees for setting up the company."

"My dear fellow," Trent said. "Of course not."

"How long will it take you to set it up?"

"I have one, actually, floating around Lichtenstein."

"Perfect. When would you need the money?"

"The weekend before the rumors begin, say one week from Saturday."

"You'll have it," Parker said. "The timing's good. He'll be in Barbados on vacation. It gives us five market days for the stock to jump. Even if it only jumps ten points, that's a tidy profit on a quick turnover."

"Very neat," Ellis agreed.

Parker took his feet off the desk. "Shall we put something on paper about who controls the foreign company?" He didn't trust Ellis Trent.

"Why don't we share it—behind the fellow in Lichtenstein, of course.''

Parker smiled again. It was exactly what he wanted. If they were both in it, he could be sure of Ellis. He didn't mind Ellis making a profit too.

"Perfect," he said. "Talk to you during the week."

He put the receiver down, more excited than he had been in a long time. He went to get himself another drink. At least he would have a nest egg of his own, something that Arnold didn't control. He went back to the desk and opened the top drawer, where Julie kept her check books. All he had to do was transfer money from her account to his; she kept a large balance, but he would have to make up the margin requirement by selling some of her short-term paper and replacing it as soon as he took his profit.

Julie's signature was easy to duplicate. He had been doing it for years when he wrote the monthly checks. It was clear, round, like a schoolgirl's. She would never know, and if she did, she would never do anything about it.

He went upstairs almost floating. He undressed quickly and stepped into his shower, turning on all the wall jets so the hot water could massage his body, relaxing his muscles.

Then he toweled himself dry, splashed on a cologne he liked better than Gladiator, and walked naked into the beige and white bedroom. The covers of the huge, canopied bed were already turned down. Two exquisite Chinese butterfly lamps glowed on either side of the bed. A silk robe was on the linen-covered wing chair near his side; one of Julie's gossamer silk nightgowns was on the companion chaise longue opposite. Near the window, draped in beige brocade over sheer lawn curtains, was Julie's small rosewood Louis XV desk, its marquetry a masterpiece of perfection. On the other side of the room there was a pair of small beige velvet sofas on either side of a low-burning fire deep inside a beige marble surround. The carpet was beige velvet, and the many vases set on the end tables and the mantel were filled with the only spots of color in the room: anthurium in every shade from satiny scarlet to paler tints of coral, salmon, and white. They were the only cut flowers Julie liked, because they lasted so long.

He felt like shouting. For once he was going to screw Arnold Fursten, and women had nothing to do with it. The faint twinge of guilt he felt when he thought about his many affairs was easily quelled. A man needed to prove he was his own master *somehow!* But he didn't need an affair now, not with something like this in the oven.

The sense of power was making him horny, but he could get all the sex he needed from his wife. He looked down, smiling. He had a huge erection, and Julie would be home any minute. He lay down on the bed, lit a cigarette, and started thinking about making love to her. It would be better than any sex they'd ever had together, better than Gladiator, better than anything.

Except taking Arnold Fursten for a million-dollar ride.

52

ISRAEL
MAY 1967

"Hey, listen to this!" the radio operator yelled. "Begin wants the Defense Ministry to go to Ben-Gurion!"

Ari looked up from his gritty lunch. "Terrific. What else?"

"Isn't that enough?" Natan said. "They're blood enemies from way back."

The boy squatted near the field radio, listening. "He says if not Ben-Gurion, then Dayan."

Ari and Natan exchanged satisfied glances. Either the old lion or the young one was acceptable to the nation. In the undertow pulling them inexorably into war, they looked to the leader of the 1948 war or the leader of the Sinai campaign. Aside from an army of 50,000 men, they had 250,000 reservists. Since the mobilization men and women were moving up to the borders, digging in, getting ready to defend their settlements one by one if they had to.

"What I want to know is why we're waiting," Natan said. "Our only hope is to get the jump on them, and we ought to be in the front lines."

"Relax, hothead," Ari said. "In a country this size everybody's in the front lines. We're within belching distance of the enemy right now. You're not even supposed to be here." He looked up at the Golan Heights, rising seventeen hundred feet in some places of the northern Galilee, rocky cliffs bristling with heavy artillery that had been dug in for years, raining shells on the settlers of the Chula Valley. To the south, facing Giora, the emplacements were lighter. Isaac was down there, but Natan had come north with Ari, whose experience was too valuable for the army to refuse, no matter what his age.

Natan spat. "I'm too old for the regular army, too old for the reserve—but I'm still young enough to piss across the middle of this country that I built! That's gratitude for you!"

"God of our fathers," Ari intoned, lighting a cigar. "Send Joshua to quiet him. I can't."

For Joshua the time bomb ticking inside him for more than twenty years picked up its rhythm as the threat of war grew. Before mobilization he was at Dimona in the Negev. The huge reactor there was guarded by a double ring of American Hawk missiles Joshua had helped to procure. His headquarters was a mass of data on available weapons—and their crucial replacement parts—from every known supplier in the world. It was connected to army intelligence; even though Israel was manufacturing some of its armaments, she relied for the most part on provision from other countries, who sold or did not sell according to the prevailing political winds. There had been times when it was politic to sell indirectly, as the United States had done through Germany, of all countries—until they were discovered.

And Joshua was one of the desert's own—stark, silent, undisguised by the cosmetics of illusion. He could trust himself only here and with Rachel. Neither the place nor the woman demanded anything from him. They took him as he was.

Benjamin had reservations about his father, but he was too preoccupied now to ponder them. The younger man drifted in and out of the intelligence center at Dimona, first to build a dummy of the huge defense complex at Um Catef in the Sinai, for Israeli troops to train on until they could take the real fortress in the dark if they had to. The details of the fortress had been duplicated exactly from aerial photographs.

Lately it was a different kind of aerial intelligence that Benjamin collated.

"We know what time the Gyppos fly their morning patrols," he told his father. "We know when they come down for a coffee break, when the gun crews at the air strips eat lunch, when everyone on the field takes a shit!" He smiled confidently. "We'll be able to get the drop on them, you'll see."

And Joshua had asked Natan's question. "When?"

"When it's time," Benjamin assured his father. He looked more closely at Joshua, noticing that his face had aged enough to go with hair turned white twenty years ago. "You okay?"

Joshua nodded.

"Listen," Benjamin said, not convinced. "We can go home for a day. We'll requisition a jeep."

A visit home would do Joshua good. He had been less morose since the tension over a real war had begun to build. Once, his father would have been the last man to see the threat of war as a way to forget whatever haunted him. Benjamin had been almost six when his father went away to Europe, and he remembered a very different man, quiet but loving, gentle but happy, a man totally opposed to violence. Now, embittered, he dealt in the instruments of violence, a thing repugnant to him still. Love and happiness were not his preoccupations.

Sometimes Benjamin was angry for his mother's sake. How could his father keep a wall between himself and Rachel like that—never mind the way he was with Elea? Yet Rachel was always there for him, and Benjamin finally accepted that she wanted to be; his mother had nothing of the martyr in her. They must have loved each other very much once for her to live on just the memory of it. Benjamin had never been in love like that. He had no such memories, and beyond today, he had no future plans. Intelligence work was an all-consuming passion; there was no time left for love. But Benjamin had always been that way. Joshua had not.

They didn't get home until the third week in May, when Giora was most beautiful. There was a soft haze over the Sea of Galilee, and the trees and fields were fresh and green after the harsh, glaring heat of the Negev.

They were all there, Joshua's special friends, but it was Ari who hugged Joshua first, covering his feelings at the sight of Joshua's face, burned so brown from the sun, and his hair, turned so white.

"Rabbi, you've turned into a desert rat! The first time I saw you with Lazar, it was like David and Jonathan, so gorgeous you were." He took Joshua by the shoulders, his bullet head with its shock of iron-gray hair wagging left to right. "Ah Josh, why did you have to go and get old on me?"

Father and son went to see Rachel, and Ari looked at Isaac and Natan. "I haven't seen him for a while. He looks like hell on a stick."

"He's all right," Isaac said. "He's got a strong constitution."

"I have the strong constitution," Natan said. "He's only got something inside his head that keeps him alive."

They sat on the grass waiting until Joshua and his son came back from the little office in the dairy where Rachel was. Natan was beside himself.

"What do you think, Josh? Shouldn't we attack now?"

"Not yet," Joshua told his burly friend. "We've been warned by France and the United States not to strike first."

"Those whores again?" Ari said. "Do you think they'll keep their promises to help if we do wait and get caught with our asses in a sling?"

"You know it's our only chance," Natan argued. "We have the weapons this time. We don't need them."

"That depends on how long the war lasts."

"We can't win a war that lasts more than four days," Benjamin put in.

"I'll write you an order for a four-day war," Ari said. "You've got to be joking, kid." It was hard for him to remember that Benjamin was thirty-two.

"No, we can't hold out in a war of attrition. So first our planes will knock out the Egyptian Air Force on the ground, then they'll be free to help us take the Sinai, but this time from the north, where they don't expect us. Next the air fields in Syria and Iraq. Finally the Golan." He smiled at them. "Simple," he said.

Ari shook his head, openly skeptical. "Tell me how we're going to get up those cliffs." The Golan Heights were steep and rocky.

Benjamin smiled. "I can't tell you everything. It won't be any fun if there are no surprises."

Rachel's voice called from the little office in the dairy. "Benjamin, telephone for you."

He got up easily, unfolding his tall body from where he sat cross-legged in the circle of his father's friends, most of whom had been there the night he was born.

"Something's up," Ari said, watching him walk away.

The men waited, not talking, anxious to know what had happened but reluctant to hear it tonight, when they were all together once more. Who knew when they'd meet again? They waited until Rachel and Benjamin came out of the office.

"We've mobilized," Benjamin called to them. "I'll tell the others, then we'll have to go."

For Joshua the time bomb started ticking faster. There was a bustle in the buildings of Giora while the men collected their field equipment and said their brief good-byes. Every reservist in the settlement was prepared for duty at prearranged rendezvous points. Most of these men would move to the northern Galilee to take positions facing Syria. Isaac and the older men would stay at Giora. Joshua and Benjamin would go first to Dimona for instructions, then wherever they were sent.

Joshua felt Rachel near him, and he turned to put his arms around her. "It might still be all right. Mobilization isn't war. But be careful." He held her close, talking softly against her cheek. "Rachel, if anything happens to me, call Arnold. He'll know what to do for you and the boys."

"But we're all right here, Josh. The boys are grown-up now, and this is home for us." Rachel didn't bother to deny that something might happen to any of them. It was one of the reasons he loved her: She was a woman who never pretended.

"But if we lose . . ."

"We won't lose," Rachel said. "We can't afford to."

He looked down at her. "Elea," he said.

"Yes?"

"Don't let him come back if there's a war. Cable Sarah to keep him there."

"No one could keep Elea away!"

"Naomi could. Promise me you'll ask them to try."

Benjamin's jeep squealed to a halt beside them. "Come on, Dad, we're wasting time. Be careful, Mom."

"Promise me," Joshua said.

She nodded. He kissed her, and she watched him get into the jeep and join the crowd of men who were leaving Giora on foot or in the vehicles requisitioned by the military for emergency transport.

She could still feel the warmth of them—her husband and her son—on her skin. Finally it was quiet again, and she went back to the little office to cable Sarah as soon as she could get a line.

53

NEW YORK
MAY 1967

It was one of the warm days of May, when at last the trees bud valiantly in Manhattan against carbon-monoxide odds. Naomi and Julie window-shopped along Fifth Avenue on their way to Duchess, admiring some of the new fashions. Skirts were short this year, but mother and daughter had always preferred Chanel to any other designer, and Chanel, like all great houses, was always classic, never trendy.

Naomi was too nervous to be interested in fashions. Since she and Arnold had come back from Barbados last night, she had been wondering whether she should warn Julie that a big storm was brewing between Parker and his father-in-law, far more serious than anything that had happened in the past.

Arnold's rage was apoplectic when his bankers and lawyers in Zurich discovered who was behind that large purchase of stock the day before the news leak. Naomi was afraid this argument between Parker and Arnold would be their last.

"I can't believe he would do a thing like this," Arnold had shouted, his gray eyes cold as steel. "Trent is a slimy bastard, always was; but this son of a bitch is married to my daughter! He's supposed to be a member of my family."

He had dismissed Ellis Trent with a short cable. But Parker could not be dismissed so easily. The thought was in both their minds all the way back to New York: If Parker went, Julie might go with him.

Listening to Julie, Naomi almost decided to tell her before they went upstairs to meet Sarah, Parker, and Arnold. But there was a chance that Sarah had succeeded in calming Arnold; Naomi had stopped trying to do that on the plane. And she was disgusted with Parker herself.

The doorman smiled at them when he opened the bronze doors of Duchess, and they waited for Arnold's private elevator on the ground floor. Julie was excited about the evening: an opening night, then supper at Sardi's.

"I'm glad Daddy bought a piece of a Broadway show," Julie said. "It might take his mind off the great traitor hunt."

"Only if it's a hit," Naomi said doubtfully, walking into the elevator and using a special key for the top-floor stop. "And maybe even that won't be enough."

Julie sighed. "I wish he'd forget about it. He denied the rumor and stopped work on that makeup. It's all over, and there's nothing more he can do."

Naomi shook her head, defending him. "Your father won't accept disloyalty from someone he trusts." She realized that the statement could apply to Julie and Parker as well. How much could Julie need Parker, to go on accepting disloyalty such as he had shown throughout their marriage?

"Maybe Aunt Sarah will calm him down," Julie said briskly, echoing her mother's thoughts and changing the subject, as always. "Do you think she's going to stay?"

The elevator doors opened. "I don't know, darling. Things in Israel are getting worse." Here as well as there, she added privately, wondering why there were no angry voices coming from Arnold's office.

Arnold heard the elevator. He wanted Naomi and Julie to be here for this as well as Sarah. He wanted his daughter's reaction to her husband's treachery. Julie would finally realize her father had been right all these years and would leave Parker. He wasn't worth her little finger.

Arnold saw Naomi's anxious face. He knew she was frantic about the danger of an open breach between Julie and her parents, but Arnold had choked back legitimate wrath too many times in his life to avoid losing people who didn't care about him anyway.

His parents didn't care. They had always favored his brother even when Joshua turned his back on them, totally unconcerned about them no matter how old and frail they were before they passed away. How many times had he listened to them talk with pride about their faraway idol while Arnold sat there choking back what he wanted to shout at the top of his lungs: "But what about me? Why don't you say you're proud of *me?* Because he's tall and heroic and builds countries? Why is that so important when I do everything for you and he does nothing?"

And there was Lazar, who used Arnold's property to hide his guns. He'd have helped Lazar had he asked, even though the risk to Duchess was very great. But no, Lazar preferred to go behind his back, knowing Arnold needed the other conspirators too, his own sister and that poor bastard, Maresh, stolen from Arnold by Joshua—always Joshua—to fight in Poland. Even Otto Einhorn, whom Arnold treated like a brother, was always on their side. His own well-paid lawyer of close to twenty years, Ellis Trent . . . people he trusted, who knew he needed them; people he loved, who knew he would sit there and take it and take it and *take it,* because he didn't dare lose them.

And Naomi, most of all Naomi. Years of knowing—and not saying—that she was in love with Joshua, years of feeling cold inside until he went to some other woman for a little warmth. He would never have done that for its own sake, the way some men—like Parker—did. It made no difference that he had finally told Naomi what he knew; the hurt had been too deep. It had left ugly scars since that night so many years ago, before Julie married Parker.

Parker. He looked at his son-in-law, young and smug, sure he had pulled it off, sure he had screwed Arnold as easily as he screwed all his women. This time Arnold was not going to choke on his rage. He didn't have to. He had nothing to lose but Parker. Julie would realize she was better off without a husband like him.

Arnold waited until the greetings were over and then, ignoring a last, cautionary look from Naomi, he told them what Parker had done, relishing every word of the filthy story. His eyes never left Parker's face until he had finished. Then he looked from Sarah to Julie.

"Can you believe he'd do a thing like that to me?"

Sarah was near the display case that held part of Arnold's priceless collection of perfume bottles. Her arms were folded, and her face was closed.

Parker sat in a Louis XVI chair in his usual posture, one ankle crossed over his knee. He seemed unperturbed by the tirade, intent on his Gucci shoes, but Naomi had seen him like that before. It was only a momentary calm.

"Oh, for God's sake, Parker!" Julie sank into a small sofa near Sarah. "Why?"

Parker lit a cigarette before he answered. "To make some money," he said. "Of my own." He looked at Julie. "After so many years with this company I thought it was high time I did."

"You had no right!" Arnold's fist pounded the desk.

"That's been your opinion right down the line," Parker said sharply, giving way to his temper. "I had no right to marry Julie, no right to a part of Duchess, no right to a decent salary of my own. Did you know that, Sarah: Your precious brother gave me an allowance, damn him, paid to me by my wife—until a few years ago. And then he gave me a lower salary than he pays his secretary."

Sarah shook her head. "Leave me out of this." Her expression remained deliberately neutral.

Parker got out of the chair, his hands bunched into fists. "I didn't do anything so terrible! You could have gone ahead with the product once the story leaked—it's perfectly safe. All I did was pave the way for it and make some money when the stock went up."

"Money!" Arnold shouted. "There are some things a man doesn't do, not even for money."

"Coming from you," Parker shot back, "that sounds ridiculous. Was there ever anything you didn't do for money?"

"Yes," Arnold said, leaning forward across his desk. "I could have made millions exporting to Argentina during the war— millions! But I wouldn't do it, because I knew whatever I shipped to South America would end up in Germany. It was a risk I couldn't stomach, no matter how much profit was involved.''

The others waited. The revelation was as much of a surprise to them as it seemed to be to Parker. Naomi felt a thrill of pride for Arnold; and Sarah a thrill of shame that she had openly doubted her brother at that meeting so long ago.

"Well, there was no risk involved in what I did," Parker said doggedly, looking for a way out. "Not for you or Duchess."

"Jesus!" Arnold said. "What you did was a breach of confidence. And he doesn't even recognize that." He looked at the three women, then back at Parker. "And where did you get the money to buy that stock in the first place?"

Parker had his back to all of them, looking at the city through the picture window. "From Julie," he said.

"But how?" Julie gasped. "You didn't say anything to me about it."

"I signed a few . . . things of yours," he said in a low voice.

"You forged her signature?" Arnold said, unbelieving. "That's theft, that's larceny, for God's sake. I could sue you for it."

"I replaced every penny of Julie's money the day I sold the stock," Parker said, turning back to look at Julie. "And you can't sue. It was Julie's money. If anybody sued, it would have to be Julie."

"And you're sure she won't," Naomi said shortly, getting out of her chair.

Sarah leaned forward slightly as if something she'd been waiting for was about to happen.

"Of course, I'm sure," Parker said. "Why would she?"

"Because what you've done is reprehensible. But of course she'll accept anything you do, God knows why."

"Mother!" Julie said in her I-don't-know-what-you-mean voice. "It isn't that simple."

"Oh, Julie, stop it!" Naomi said impatiently. "It's *very* simple. Your father treats Parker like a dim-witted child, and Parker behaves like one, sleeping around to get even with him. They're using you—both of them—and you're helping them do it." She took a deep breath. "I just don't want to watch it anymore."

"Naomi!" Arnold began, his anger turned to shock.

"Arnold, it's true," she said. "It's low and mean and rotten, but it's all true. I don't like either of you for doing it, and I don't like Julie for letting you.'' She looked at her daughter, and her voice softened. ''Honey, nobody is worth that kind of black-mail, not my husband and not yours.''

''Damn it!'' Arnold said. ''How can you blame me for what he does?''

''You don't trust him, Daddy,'' Julie said. ''You never did.''

''Did I ever have any reason to?''

''You had no reason not to,'' Naomi insisted, ''when they were first married. But you expected him to be what he . . . became, so he did what was expected of him. People usually do.'' She sat down again on the sofa, and her head dropped while she rubbed her forehead wearily. Then she looked up again.

''I'm tired of all of you. I've had enough of smoothing things over, changing the subject, watching you destroy each other while I sit there with my heart in my mouth, pretending we're a happy family. You're not honest with each other, and we're not happy with each other. I am sorry for you, but I'm tired of you.'' She leaned back, exhausted. ''That's all I have to say.''

The room was very quiet. Arnold sat down in the chair behind his desk, his face more confused than angry. Julie and Parker avoided each other's eyes. Finly Sarah moved away from the display case.

''Well, are we going to sit here all night?'' She lit a cigarette.

''Sarah,'' Arnold said heavily, ''what do you expect us to do?''

''Fire him the way you did Ellis—or pick up the pieces and go on. It's not the end of the world just because Naomi finally told you the truth instead of what you wanted to hear. What the hell, it's high time someone did.''

Arnold's shoulders dropped. Some of it was true, even though he would never admit it. He had never given Parker an even break. But Naomi said she was tired of all of them; that worried him more than Parker's scheming. He could understand Parker—grudgingly he could even admire how clever he'd been. But he was afraid to ask Naomi what she meant. He had always been afraid, and he was too old to change now.

''We'll pick up the pieces, I suppose,'' he said, shrugging. ''But that'll take time.'' He looked at Parker, his expression impossible to read.

"I don't want a royal pardon," the younger man said, still belligerent. "I belong here because I've earned it."

"Well, I don't," Sarah said. "Belong here, I mean. Before we had this happy little scene, I'd decided I don't belong here at all. I'm going back to Israel."

"Oh, for Christ's sake, Sarah," Arnold exploded. "There's room for you at Duchess, whether he's here or not."

"I told you—Parker has nothing to do with this. And neither, dear brother, do you. I just don't feel at home here anymore. It's too closed in. I miss Yad Mordechai and all those crazy Jews arguing with each other from morning to night. You people are too polite."

"Shai, don't go now," Naomi said. "It's too dangerous."

Sarah smiled. "I'd feel a lot safer looking at the Gaza Strip than I did a few minutes ago in this office. At least I know what they're going to do. But honestly, I'm homesick. Twenty years is a long time to spend in a place. Whatever its shortcomings, you get attached to it. I have children there and grandchildren. Anyway, they need me. They've mobilized."

"Oh, no," Julie breathed. "When?"

"I heard it today. I don't think there's much chance of stopping a war now. Once it starts, they'll close down the airport, and I want to get home before they do."

"They haven't got a prayer, Sarah," Parker said, looking genuinely worried. "The odds are too great against them. You'll be flattened."

"Wanna bet?" Sarah said. "I'm really not that heroic, Parker. I really think we have a chance."

"Elea," Naomi said. "He'll want to go." The thought of that boy in danger was unbearable to her.

"I can't stop him," Sarah said. She took a yellow cablegram from her handbag. "Joshua asked me to try."

"He won't go if his father doesn't want him," Arnold said.

Sarah and Naomi looked at each other. Elea was used to his father not wanting him. He would go if he could.

"How long before you leave?" Naomi said, resigned to it. Once Sarah made her mind up, it was pointless to argue.

"About two weeks." Sarah's dark eyes moved around the room over each of their faces. "Would you mind delaying your war until we see what happens with that one?"

She bent her head to put the cable back in her bag, hiding her face from them.

"As far as I'm concerned," Naomi said, "ours is over. I'm not going to pretend things haven't changed after tonight, but I really don't care what any of you do. I have other things to worry about." She got up and put an arm around Sarah. "Come on, Shai, if we don't get started, we'll miss the curtain. You need a little real entertainment tonight."

The two women walked toward the office door. After a second Julie followed. Parker and Arnold glanced at each other briefly before they left. Their little war wasn't exactly over, but Naomi was right—things would be different from now on. For years they had all played their roles in a carefully scripted family scenario, with no danger of a disaster while Naomi was willing to keep the semblance of a truce. She had just abdicated that position. They would have to deal directly with each other now. None of them knew exactly how to begin.

54

GIORA
JUNE 5, 1967

Rachel came out of their small cottage at dawn and stretched, still sleepy, not noticing the man who dropped to the ground in the reeds near the lake as soon as he saw her. The table inside was set for two, but she thought she could persuade Benjamin to go down to the lakeshore and have breakfast there, just the way they used to. He would be leaving right after that. Something was going to happen—it usually did whenever Benjamin was on the move—but she mustn't ask him. It was a treat that he was here at all. Joshua was still at Dimona.

Benjamin came out of the house, his hair still wet from a shower, and stood behind her, his hands on her shoulders, looking out over the lake.

"Listen, Mom, I think you'd better stay under cover for the next few days, okay?"

He couldn't see her face change. "Okay," she said. "And you?"

"I have things to do, but I'll be back and forth. Dad should come back in a day or two."

"I'll never get used to your calling him 'Dad'—it sounds so foreign. If you can't say 'Abba,' try 'Papa.' " Her hands held his. She was only talking to keep him near her, to keep him safe. "How is he?"

"You know him—he's always the same."

"Not always," she said. "How about taking breakfast down to the lake?"

He nodded approval and helped her gather the things for a simple breakfast. They went down to the lakeshore, where a breeze rustled the reeds over their secret visitor. When the sun was well up, the breeze would calm. It was going to be a warm day.

Benjamin poured tea from the Thermos and handed her a sweet roll. "When isn't he the same?" he said, picking up the conversation they'd left unfinished at the house.

"When he's too tired to fight what he's really like."

"And what's that?"

"The way he was before the war, remember? He never saw only one side of things, he saw everyone's side. He wanted to make things fair, the way they were supposed to be. I think that was what charmed people so, his belief that the world was meant to be fair . . . that, and how beautiful he is, like you."

Benjamin frowned. "He hasn't been very fair to you."

"That's not for you to judge, Benjamin." Then her voice softened. "There was a moment, a few years ago—he's still there somewhere. Anyway"—she smiled again—"I've had exactly the life I wanted—most people do—and the man."

"You're a hopeless romantic, Mom. Why not say you love him because you love him?"

"Why not? It's true." She took a deep breath. "What a beautiful morning this is—warm for June."

"It's going to get warmer," he said, warning her again.

Rachel looked at him carefully. "When?"

"Today."

"Where?"

He shook his head. He couldn't tell her, but it didn't matter. In such a tiny country anywhere was everywhere.

They sat together in the fresh breeze from the lake. The reeds were tall this spring. A few yards away there was a movement in the reeds that the wind could not explain. The man was lying there, watching this mother and son in the peaceful glory of a June dawn. His feet were muddy and his clothes damp. He had dropped to the ground when the woman came out of her cottage and had been watching them ever since through the sights of his rifle. The barrel moved imperceptibly, pointing first at the woman, then at the man.

"It's time to go in." Benjamin looked at his watch.

The man's finger tightened on the trigger.

"A second more," Rachel said, taking her son's hand. "You always were my buddy, weren't you?"

All of them heard it at the same time: Rachel, Benjamin, the invader, the people at Giora—a rumble, a roar, and a whine. Benjamin only had time to shield his mother's body with his own before the shell, fired from across the lake, hit, just another shell among the many that had showered on the Jordan Valley for years.

Voices shouted from Giora, people ran, shutters slammed, but near the lake, when the dust drifted down to settle on the bank, there was only silence, then the hesitant call of a frightened bird and the rustle of the reeds.

When Isaac came to search for them, it was a shock to see how much they resembled each other in death, the two who were Abraham's and the one who was Ishmael's.

At 7:10 A.M. Israeli planes took off on schedule to destroy the Egyptian Air Force on the ground and the MiG armadas of Iraq and Syria as well. By order of the defense minister all communications out of Israel were shut down. The world held its breath. The Six Day War had begun.

In three hours the Egyptian Air Force was demolished, and Israeli ground forces swept into the Sinai from Khan Unis and Rafah to Al-'Arish. The "impregnable" fortress at Um Catef was taken from the rear—at night. By the end of the second day Gaza was occupied and the Sinai open to Israeli armor. In the once barren desert Russian tanks, deserted by fleeing Egyptian troops, bloomed in profusion.

Still, the only news coming out of the Middle East was Egyptian claims of great victories. In the northern Galilee the men listened, staggered by Egyptian boasts they knew were not true and waiting for their order to attack.

"Joshua's boy."

Elea kept hearing it. Even when it was unspoken, he could see the officers were thinking it from the look they exchanged. It infuriated him. He had a name of his own, he was a person, not just his father's son! And he was twenty—a man, not anyone's boy, above all not Joshua's!

Around him the men fanned out in the Chula Valley, where they had been waiting ever since Elea got there a week before the war began. He knew he was coming as soon as Israel mobilized, despite the efforts of the family to keep him in America. His aunts, Sarah and Naomi, knew he was going too, no matter what his father wanted.

This time there was a choice, but he didn't think of that until he was on the plane. Once the plane touched down in Israel, there was no time to think. He had joined his brigade in the northern Galilee immediately, unable in the chaos of the war to let anyone at Giora know he was here.

And then he waited, along with the rest of the Golani Brigade, for the order from Moshe Dayan to clean out the Syrian gun emplacements on the heights.

Rumors filtered to them. The United States and England were sending a flotilla. De Gaulle had cut off arms and uranium shipments to Israel the day before the war broke out. The Russians accused Israel of "criminal aggression." The Egyptians claimed great victories, then fell silent.

Finally volunteers joined them fron battles already fought and won in the Sinai, in Jerusalem, on the west bank of the Jordan. The men waited, then demanded the attack order that still had not come.

Elea knew how they felt. For them the world was this little corner of the Galilee under constant bombardment for years— and, across the pillaged Chula Valley, the heights they were impatient to climb.

Elea shivered when he looked at the Golan Heights. As a boy he had looked at them from Giora and known that someday Israel would have to do something about them. They were higher, more menacing here than at home.

He wondered if he was going to die on the heights. Something terrible lurked upon those cliffs, something bad for him; he had always felt that. Spending winters at school in the States almost made him forget, but part of every summer was spent here on military training, and the Golani Brigade was named for its ultimate purpose: a battle to end the casual, sporadic rain of death from up there.

An impossible battle, it seemed. Cliffs that were almost unscalable. Defenses ten miles deep in places, on several subterranean levels, protected tanks, artillery, and rocket launchers. Three Syrian brigades defended it; six more backed them up. The most heavily fortified emplacements were at Tel Azaziat, called the Dragon of the Heights by the Israelis, and at Tel Fakr. These were the cliffs General Elazar had chosen to assault when the order came. His men had grown up under Syrian guns, and they intended to silence them once and for all.

The order finally came.

By noon on June 9 they had crossed the Syrian border and started up the cliffs, bulldozers first to clear away the rocks, Sherman tanks for what cover they could offer, and the infantry in the rear.

"Why did he pick the strongest point to assault?" a boy near Elea said, his hand moving on his rifle.

"It's the shallowest point too," Elea said, remembering Ari's description last summer. "If we break through, we can outflank them—"

He heard his name shouted and knew before he turned that it was Ari, with Natan's bellow close behind. Elea turned and held up his rifle. Then he walked on until they caught up with him.

"I knew you'd come," Natan said, pounding Elea on the back. *"Totseret ha'arets,"* he said to Ari. "Our own product. I told you he'd be here."

"Of course he's here," Ari said. "He's Joshua's boy, isn't he?"

The smell of war—bombs and Napalm from Israeli planes

drenching the heights, twisted hot metal, and sizzling human flesh—closed in over them.

I can't do this, Elea thought. *It's too steep, the sun's too hot. Why am I doing this? What do I care who sits on these cliffs, the Syrians or us? Why couldn't they stop shelling us, leave us alone, let us live in peace?*

His eyes filled with tears of frustration. Nothing could have kept him away, but it was so stupid that he had to be here in the first place. He was glad Ari and Natan were somewhere near him. He always felt safe around Ari—and Natan was indestructible. Natan was Giora and Rachel and Benjamin. Joshua was probably at Dimona.

He stopped thinking about his father and went on walking. "Mad dogs and Englishmen," the kids used to sing, "mad dogs and Englishmen go out in the midday sun."

It was a cruel climb to the top under blazing sun and Syrian artillery. It was a crueler fight when Elea reached the Syrian entrenchment. For three hours they fought to take it, knocking out the dug-in Syrian tanks with hand grenades, fighting with rifles first, then rifle butts, then knives, finally fists.

A corner of Elea's mind closed down, and he managed not to watch himself stabbing with a knife, battering other men to death with the piece of wood and metal in his hands. He caught a glimpse of Natan in the thick of it, his huge hands powerful, his enormous torso seeming immune to blows and flying bullets. They had lost sight of Ari.

On June 9 the Syrian representative to the United Nations in New York announced that his government would comply with the cease-fire resolution, along with Egypt and Jordan. By the time it was dark again on the Golan Heights, two Israeli footholds were secure and Damascus not too far away.

Natan and Elea, slipping on pools of blood and pieces of dead men, searched for Ari. They were too exhausted to be sickened by the carnage, too anxious to be amazed that they were alive and unhurt—except for a corner of him, Elea knew, that would never be the same again, that would swing open when he least expected it and poison every sweet thing in life if he let it. The way his father had let it. He went on looking for Ari, but he was looking

for his father too. He didn't mind being Joshua's boy anymore.
He didn't know why; he just didn't mind.

They found Ari propped against the treads of a Syrian tank,
almost gone.

"God Almighty, Ari," Natan whispered, sitting down beside
his friend and taking him in his arms. "Don't go and die now."

Ari's eyes opened for a moment, and he smiled faintly, ac-
knowledging their presence. He looked at Elea. "A good soldier," he whispered. "I always said."

"Ari!" Natan shook him gently. "Ari, don't die! For God's
sake, Ari!" Tears poured down Natan's face. He turned to Elea.
"Get a doctor, get help."

"It's too late," Elea said. He sat down and took Ari's hand in
his. It was cold. Couldn't Natan see that most of Ari wasn't there
anymore?

"Your father," Ari said faintly. "Tell him . . . Lazar's
dead. It's time already." Ari's eyes fluttered closed for the last
time, and Elea stretched out beside what was left of him, listening to Natan's sobs and holding on to both of them, the dead man
and the living, as if they were his life.

55

NEW YORK
JUNE 1967

There was a commotion as the huge limousine stopped on the
tarmac, and Parker glanced at a man in one of the cars on his
left. The private detective answered him with a reassuring nod.

Arnold Fursten was always news—any tycoon was, but particularly a publicity-shy one. And his destination was hotter news
than he was. The world was still unable to believe that Israel had
won an impossible victory in only six short days. The press had
been like leeches, trying to suck all the information they could
out of this family and still hanging on to them as they went to
board a private plane for Tel Aviv.

"How did he get permission to fly into Israel?" said one of the watching newsmen crowded behind the security fence. "That's what I can't figure out."

"Some of his family's there," hie companion said. "A rabbi, I heard. But rabbis aren't news."

"They are now. Hey, there they go."

In seconds the family boarded the plane: Sarah with Paige, Naomi and Julie, Parker and Arnold. The door closed, the motors turned, and the plane taxied to take off. Soon they were airborne, locked together in the narrow space of the plane and the shock of all that had happened in less than a week.

Their incredulous relief when the war ended was cut off by a cable from Joshua that said only, "Rachel and Benjamin killed. Please come."

It only struck Sarah now, as she sat with Paige, that the cable had been addressed to Arnold, not to her. At first she thought Joshua had done that to spare her; then she thought it was because he needed his brother desperately and had chosen this way to let him know it.

Her throat ached, thinking of Rachel and Benjamin. They were part of her life. How had she let Arnold persuade her not to go right back to Israel as soon as they mobilized, the way Elea had done? Arnold was always trying to protect her; he had minimized the danger during the war to protect her from the threat of Lazar's death. But she had known then the magnitude of the threat to Lazar. And she should have known now that the Israelis had to use surprise to tip scales so enormously weighted against them.

Her eyes blurred with tears of grief and regret. If she had been in Israel, Rachel and Benjamin might have come to Yad Mordechai that fatal morning; they might still be alive.

Then she shook her head. No matter how great love was, it was never strong enough to protect anyone from death. Or from life.

She felt a small, comforting arm around her and turned to the thirteen-year-old girl beside her, determined to ease the panic Paige must feel at her first encounter with death. Although she had never met her aunt Rachel or Benjamin, people you only hear about assume legendary proportions, even to a bright, so-phisticated child like Paige.

Paige was her grandfather's pride. Her idea of fun was a trip to one of Arnold's plants, where she watched the manufacture of cosmetics and perfumes with intelligent eyes. She had carried a set of her own tester sticks when she was just a little girl, and she knew more about the business than even Arnold expected from a child her age.

"It's going to be mine some day," was her explanation. "I'm going to be just like my aunt Sarah."

She had been following Sarah like a devoted handmaiden for months, and until now the biggest disappointment of her protected young life was Sarah's decision to return to Israel permanently. But it was something Paige could understand, even as a rival to Duchess. Israel was Elea, and Elea was everything.

Paige took her aunt's hand. "I wish I knew what to say to him. What do you say when somebody dies?"

"You won't have to say anything, honey. He'll know you're there, and that's what he needs."

Paige looked at Naomi, sitting by herself just in front of them. Maybe Sarah was right; Grandma was the most comforting person in the world, and sometimes she didn't say a word.

"What's Uncle Josh really like?"

"It's hard to say. You can't describe a man like my brother just like that."

Paige persisted. "You could if you wanted to."

Sarah leaned back and thought a minute. "Well, I always said I've only known two beautiful men in my life," she began.

"And Lazar was one of them," Paige anticipated her.

"The most," Sarah agreed. "He looked like a walking mop with his thatch of blond hair, but an extraordinary mop—with charisma. He knew what he wanted, he did as he liked, and he was free. I mean his only obligations were the ones he chose, to me, to his children, and to his country."

"And Uncle Josh?"

"He had charisma too, but a different kind. When I was little, there was always something small hanging on to him—a kid or a puppy or a little old lady. He had such dreams, you see. He believed in them, and he made everybody else believe in them too." Her voice faded.

"And then?" Paige asked.

"Something happened to him, I don't know what. I always

thought it had something to do with Lazar. He still talks about Lazar as if he only died yesterday. He's doing what he and Lazar set out to do—but he doesn't believe in it anymore, and for a man like Josh that isn't easy. He hides his feelings away so he can keep on working, when he really wants to run. That takes great courage.''

Paige sighed. ''What will happen to him now?''

Sarah's eyes watched Naomi's head. ''I don't know, honey,'' she said. ''I just don't know.''

Naomi let herself drift in a direction she had deliberately avoided for days. What would happen to Joshua now? Benjamin and Rachel dead—it was frightening to think of that. Benjamin was as dear to her as Elea. For years he had lived in her house. He and Julie had grown up together. And Rachel—a woman who had come to mean so much to Naomi in the last few years.

She wondered if Elea and his father had found each other at last—and fear chilled her when she thought that either of them might have been hurt . . . or killed. No, she would not think of that. Surely the boy and the man would reach out to each other now.

But Joshua hid himself away from people. Even before the war he had asked neither support nor approval from anyone at home for whatever he wanted to do. He had only begged her once to live her life with him, and she had been unable to do it.

No, she had chosen not to. She could never have lived like that. She could never have shared a man with anything or anyone, as Rachel had. It was in Naomi's nature, no matter how it got there, to have to be at the center of a man's life, not somewhere on the fringe of it. The girl she'd been thought he couldn't love her at all if he didn't love only her. Pride had done the rest; all her life she had loved him and been loved by his brother.

She looked across the cabin at Arnold, sitting by himself. If Joshua needed her, was there any reason not to stay with him? It was late for both of them, but he had done enough for Israel now. He deserved a few years for himself. And she had done all she could for Arnold. The pity was that ''all she could'' was not enough for her husband, just as all he could was not enough for her.

What was missing in his utter devotion to her, when it was the very thing she wanted most from a man? Why hadn't she taken it gladly, with open arms, instead of grudgingly, at arm's length. *Oh, Arnold*, she thought, *what was missing that could have made us happy?*

Julie and Parker had said nothing since the plane took off. They had been unusually silent with each other ever since the night Naomi shocked them all out of their complacency. Then the war in Israel turned all of them in another direction—and now these terrible deaths put off any discussion of their private relationship.

Julie barely knew her aunt, but she dearly loved Benjamin. And there had been something about her moody Uncle Josh that touched her, as anyone who was lonely touched her, as Parker had touched her.

He had been so quiet since that night. Except for his good looks, there was nothing rakish about him anymore. His too-ready smile, his too-smooth compliments had vanished. He hadn't apologized to her for all the years of infidelity, as if they could be canceled out if they were not spoken of. Unsaid, but very clear, was that she would tolerate no more of it.

He had organized everything for this heartbreaking journey. Half a family wiped out in seconds, like his own. What must he have felt? What was he thinking? But Parker had said nothing, and her father had left it all to him, too immersed in sorrow to act himself. It was the first time Julie had seen her energetic father stilled, as if he were waiting for something worse to happen. What could possibly be worse than this?

She looked across the aisle at her father, then turned back to the window. Whatever happened, she wouldn't let Parker use her love to hurt her anymore; nor would she let her father do it, ever again.

Impossible, Arnold thought. He couldn't face the fact that Benjamin was gone out of the world with the woman who had brought him into it, Benjamin, the one boy he would have chosen for his Julie, the son he never had.

And he had always wanted to speak to Rachel again, renew that quick companionship they discovered at Julie's wedding party. But he had persistently refused to travel to Israel over the years. It was hard enough to live in his brother's shadow when Joshua came to America—even when he didn't. He could never have been anything but a little merchant in Naomi's eyes if they had seen the man in Israel.

Now they would see him—and now Joshua was alone, as he had always been. Unless Naomi . . . he had been thinking about that for days. "I'm tired of you," she had said. It was true, he'd been hard on Parker, but he never knew how bitterly Naomi resented that. He never realized what he was doing to Julie by involving her in it. He had punished both of them because he was convinced that he, himself, had been punished by life.

And by Naomi. "People do what is expected of them," she had said. All his life he had expected her to say she loved his brother and . . . what? Leave him for Joshua? That had been impossible up to now. But Naomi cherished the people she cared for. It was one of the things he loved about her. She might stay with Joshua. What was there about him, her own husband, that she could not cherish? She was still the only woman in the world he wanted, but that was not enough to make her look at him the way he had seen her look at his brother.

The moments of truth in the years of their marriage had been too few, too brief, to do more than still the rocking boat and let them go on together peacefully. But God Almighty, he didn't want peace. He wanted her to love him!

What can you do, he asked himself, *to make somebody love you the way you want to be loved?*

What am I to do, face to face with this brother of mine who turns to me for comfort, the way I went to him as a child—and who has been a threat to me since I was old enough to know that he was something I could never be?

The motors hummed on, and stillness settled over the cabin while the plane headed toward a rendezvous with sadness in the midst of joy, loss in the midst of incredible conquest, defeat in the heart of victory.

The plane was trundling toward him slowly, once more earth-bound, clumsy, and ponderous. The sky was its place, and there it was beautiful to see. Was it the same for people too—that they flourished only where they belonged?

Where did he belong? Without Benjamin he wondered if he could stay in Israel. Without Rachel he wondered why he had ever come here.

She wandered in his consciousness the way she was when he married her, a dark-eyed dryad with golden skin and long black braids, beckoning and tentative, waiting for him, always waiting for him with a part of herself, while the rest of her was busy with her sons, her work, her life. Rachel, virginal and passionate, accepting but never submissive, demanding very little but taking what she must absolutely have.

Joshua watched the plane turn its side toward the terminal door. His brother took what he must have—but Arnold needed too much. Arnold wanted an impossibly heroic dimension added to his success. He had built a rivalry with Joshua for a quality that existed only in Arnold's imagination. And still he was always there for people, solid as a rock, reliable. Heroes were not reliable.

But once the brothers had known a real rivalry—over Naomi. Thank heaven she was on this plane too. Sweet woman, living her romantic dreams in bed with Joshua, letting him into her fantasies for a few hours of loving that was a kind of love—all he had to give but not the kind she wanted. He had been so grateful to her while it lasted. Naomi, walking away from him because of Arnold. A loving woman. She had sheltered them all: first him, then Benjamin, then Elea. But not even Naomi had been able to keep the boy away from this war.

Elea was safe, he knew that. Tacked on to a radio message to the operations room at Dimona had been a note for him: Ari was dead, but Elea had come through that incredible battle unhurt. In a few days he would get leave and come home; time enough then for him to find out his mother and Benjamin were asleep forever at Giora. Isaac was already there with Natan in case Elea got back before he was expected, before Joshua was there to . . . what? How could Elea want him after all the years of estrangement that a boy would never understand?

Suddenly he wanted to see Elea, just to touch him, to be sure Elea was warm and whole and well.

I want to see him, Joshua thought, *to be sure that life goes on, and it is only the lives that die.*

Gone. So many of my lives are gone. Rachel and my son.

Lazar, my conscience. Ari—you always said what everyone was thinking, and you knew more than you said. And Ben. Oh, God, Ben, it could have been you for my Rachel. She would have been happier with you, but I'm glad it wasn't. I loved her, Ben. I loved her more.

But Elea was left. How would it be now between Joshua and Rachel's son?

He pressed the tears from his eyes while the steps were wheeled over to the plane and the door opened. Surely Sarah's would be the first face he saw, or Naomi's. But it was Arnold in the doorway. His expression changed when he saw Joshua's lonely, longing face, and he went quickly down the stairs to put his arms around his brother for the first time in more than twenty-five years.

56

They had driven north from Tel Aviv, and now they traveled eastward to the Galilee. From there they would turn south to Giora. Joshua and Arnold were in one car, the rest of the family in two others. They had never exchanged trivialities, but Arnold was more uncomfortable than ever alone with his brother.

Joshua suggested they drive together to Giora, much to Arnold's surprise. Joshua was surprising in many ways. The austere personality they had all come to accept for so many years was changed. In his place was not merely the old Joshua wearing a gaunt and haggard face; they could have understood that. In his place was a man tentative and indefinite, turning to all of them—and Arnold most of all—for direction when he had always gone his way alone. The women, even little Paige, knew how to deal with the change; Arnold could not.

It was all the more difficult for its mute appeal. Naomi had obviously been moved by it; that made Arnold hostile, while pity for his brother stirred that old love they once shared before life and jealousy warped it.

How could he love someone who threatened him, not by what he did but because of what he was that Arnold was not?

Arnold turned from his brother's gaunt profile to the passing countryside. "I never expected it to be like this," he said. "This is a wilderness."

"This isn't wild," Joshua said. "The desert is wild, unbelievably savage, but beautiful. I've spent most of the last ten years in the desert."

Arnold listened, watching the scrubby terrain burst into neat quadrangles of yellow sunflowers or green vegetables now and then, only to revert to rock and bracken again. He wondered how Giora would look. There would only be the graves to see, but it was for that they had come, to see where Rachel and Benjamin were, and because Joshua and Elea needed them.

"And now?" Arnold managed finally, trying. "Will you go back to the desert?"

"Yesterday I was thinking of coming back to the States." Joshua glanced at his brother. Even in slacks and an open shirt Arnold looked too well tailored for Israel, too well ordered for grief. When the silence lengthened uncomfortably, he added, "That doesn't seem to strike you as a very good idea."

Naomi would never live in this impossible country—but what if Joshua came back to America? "Why ask for my opinion? It didn't stop you from coming here in the first place. Now that I look at this—nothing—I still don't know why you did."

Joshua considered before he answered. He had never bothered much about his brother's feelings; too often Arnold seemed to have none. But if the first disaster of Joshua's life had made him reject his own dangerous capacity to love, this latest catastrophe had opened doors he believed forever closed. Arnold was visibly worried. Joshua wondered why.

He temporized. "We never did see things the same way. This 'nothing' is wonderful to me. But I want to do what's best for Elea, and I'd like your opinion on that—you know him better than I do."

Arnold's anger blasted through his good intentions. "That's not surprising, is it? You didn't want him in the first place, a wonderful boy like that. There were so many people you didn't want, even if they wanted you.''

Joshua moved uncomfortably, at a loss. It had been easier when he didn't care what he said, easier when he cared about nothing. But the doors, once opened, were impossible to close again.

"I suppose I deserve that," he said, trying to leave everything out of this but the boy. "But Elea was born a long time ago.''

"Do you think that makes any difference?'' Arnold shook his head fiercely, answering his own question. "Some things last a lifetime.''

"I see,'' Joshua said, giving in. "We're not talking about Elea at all, are we?''

"We're talking about Naomi—my wife!'' Arnold's eyes moved rapidly. "I know, only a bastard like me would talk about his wife when yours is dead. But I can't help that. I have to know.'' He clasped his hands tightly.

Joshua pulled the car off the road and stopped it. "Go on, Arnold, say it.'' He waited, looking at the dusty dashboard of the car.

"All right, I will. I love her. You never loved anyone like that, you're incapable of it, you don't know how. But while Rachel was here, at least you had her. I never had Naomi because she always wanted you.'' He had thought the words would choke him. They almost did. His palms were moist.

They sat there on the shoulder of the road, both of them looking straight ahead. It was the first moment of truth for them, but all the truth would make any other moments impossible.

"Maybe she did,'' Joshua began, "but only for a little while.''

"It wasn't all one-sided,'' Arnold said, refusing him an easy escape. "Don't blame her for it.''

It was painfully touching to hear Arnold defend Naomi, even while he accused her. It struck Joshua that for all his many-faceted devotions, he had never loved a woman as single-mindedly and as wholeheartedly as Arnold loved his wife. His neat, precise brother had a depth of passion he had seen in only one other man—Lazar. There was no iota of resemblance between them but this: Each of them could love one woman from the day he found her till the day he died.

"No, I don't blame her for it. We were in love with each other for a few weeks before I left for Palestine. I should never have told her—she was engaged to you—but all I wanted was to take her away from you, to take her with me. It was over almost before it began."

"It wasn't." Again Arnold refused him an escape. "It wasn't over for her. There are—things that say more than words. Every time I touched her, I knew it, I saw it. For a long time I was afraid she'd divorce me. Then you married Rachel. Even then I never knew whether the two of you . . ." He covered his face with his hands. "For the love of God, tell me! Did you? Did you ever . . .?" It was beyond him to say it.

Joshua almost told him the truth. A love affair ended because she loved Arnold more—as Rachel had loved *him* more—because she already had what she wanted. That was the greatest love of all. But truth, he had learned, was not an absolute. It came in different forms for different people. And he loved his brother, after all, too much to tell him the truth.

"No, Arnold, by everything I hold dear." His hand rested on Arnold's shoulder. "She loves you, she always has. Maybe there were times she didn't know it, but she always has."

They sat in silence for a whole until Arnold raised his head and dried his face with a hand-monogrammed handkerchief. Then Joshua started the raspy motor, and the little Renault chugged back onto the dusty road.

All of it was a shock to Naomi. First there was Joshua, his face like an exhausted child's, still the most impressive face she had ever seen. But she had never seen him here, in the place where he lived, where he wanted to be. It made him seem different to her, not in any way diminished but much more himself. And that self was completely strange to her: not merely strange—unattainable. Then there was the way he was waiting to see Elea. Joshua had always been a strong man, a man who dominated without effort. Yet now it seemed that the father needed strength from the son. It was neither weakness nor age nor grief; it was Joshua's consuming need for Rachel's son, so strong that it removed Joshua from Naomi's universe. He might have been on the moon. It was obvious that Joshua would stay where Elea was, and Elea would certainly stay here.

And now, after a night when all of them said very little to one another, Giora was a shock too. Its little buildings, the proud accomplishment of Rachel and her parents, were so simple, even ramshackle by contrast with the steel and cement world Naomi lived in. The beauty was there, not to be denied. The colors and scents of earth and orchard, the blues and whites of the sky and lake. It had Rachel's serenity, unspoiled by any planning. Just looking at this place Naomi felt Joshua sliding away from her—and when he got out of the car with Arnold, she knew he was gone for good.

There was a link between the brothers she had never seen before—or perhaps it was the absence of a barrier. Something had passed between them on the road that made a difference. They not only stood together near the graves, they were together.

Naomi stayed with Sarah, the only one of them free enough to cry, and with Julie and Parker. They were still avoiding each other's eyes, but they stayed close together, with Paige nestled between them. They were alien to this place. Only Joshua and Sarah belonged—and perhaps Paige, because children belong anywhere they are loved.

Naomi felt the focus of everything change, shift to a new reality when she looked at Joshua again. It was not that she had lost him—she had never had him, but only her idea of him. This was the only place on earth for him, but it was the last place in the world for her, as it had always been—and Joshua the last man. He had been the passion of her life, it was true; but Arnold was its love.

She took Sarah's hand to ease the sense of loss. And then she let go of her dream. She would miss it—there was a corner in every life for dreaming, but that was the place for it, a corner. If only that had been so clear to her at nineteen. She might have loved Arnold differently. It was too late for that now.

But it wasn't too late for something else. Whatever happened, she knew she would never lie again. For once she had refused to pretend with her family, had told them the truth. Amazing, the tonic effect of truth.

"Look!" Paige's voice called. "That's Elea!" She started to run toward the road, but Julie held her back. He was too still, standing there smiling by the edge of the road. He needed the time to understand what he was seeing.

The sequence of his perceptions was as clear to Joshua as if he had been inside Elea's mind. The smile on his face had frozen once he saw who was absent from this family circle. His aunts and his cousins would not have come so far right after a vicious war for anything less than . . . His eyes dropped to the two new graves at their feet, and then he knew, and the smile broke into pieces and reassembled itself as cruel, accepting, inconsolable grief. He stood there, looking at them, unable to move.

Joshua walked down to the road, his hands reaching out. Elea, with Rachel's eyes, Ben's smile, Lazar's lazy walk. *Oh my God*, Joshua marveled. *He's all of them and me too. It doesn't matter who his father was—he's my son.*

The others watched the man and the boy together, then saw them turn and walk toward the lake.

"Come into the house," Sarah said. "We'll have some tea."

"I'm glad he has his son," Naomi said, her hand in Sarah's. "He'll be all right as long as he has Elea."

"So you finally woke up. I'm glad of that. I wonder what Arnold will do about it."

"So do I," Naomi said. "So do I."

"Is this where?" Elea said when Joshua told him about the shelling. He seemed to half-expect that death had come from the cliffs across the lake.

"Yes. Do you want to sit here with me for a while?"

They sat together on the bank. Someone had smoothed the earth where Benjamin and Rachel died, and a huge swathe of reeds had been cut down along the lakeside.

"Dad," Elea said after a while, "I'm going to stay in Israel. If you don't want me here at Giora, I'll stay with Aunt Shai."

Joshua took a deep breath. He had so much to make up to this boy. "Of course I want you here. It's your home."

"Okay then," Elea said.

"No, it's not okay. I didn't want you here before—but it wasn't only you, Elea. I didn't want anyone, not even your wonderful mother, and she was the only one who understood."

Sorrow stirred around the young man, there where his mother and Benjamin spent their last morning. But he mustn't cry with his father, much as he wanted to. It was harder to be with his

father now than it had ever been. It seemed they were trying to
draw a new map of their relationship. There were no arrows, no
signs, to tell them how far they should go in any direction, how
long it would take to get home to each other.

"What did Mother understand?"

"That I was afraid to get too close to anyone. If you love,
Elea, that makes you vulnerable. But if you let someone love
you, that's an awesome responsibility. It gives you influence
over those who love you, and that can be more dangerous than
you know."

Elea clasped his arms around his knees, remembering Ari's
voice on the heights and Natan crying. "Does it have anything to
do with Lazar?"

Joshua looked his surprise. "Why do you ask that?"

"It was something Ari said before he died." Elea's voice was
unsteady. "He said to tell you Lazar's dead. It sounded crazy,
but Ari wasn't crazy, not even then."

"So he knew that too, the old fox," Joshua said in a low
voice. "I didn't want anyone to know—especially not Sarah. I
didn't want her to lose Lazar twice."

Elea shivered at that but kept silent. His father's anguish was
almost palpable, too private and too terrible to touch. Whatever
his father meant by that strange remark, he must share it with
Elea of his own volition.

Joshua's hands moved in the earth of the lakeshore. Here they
had sat, his Rachel and his Benjamin, and here they had died.
What was it worth to be born, to learn to walk, talk, read, laugh,
above all love—and have it all go to waste in death?

Live on in his son? *No*, something in him shouted. *That is not
enough, that is not the same. It is my life that will be canceled,
my love that disappears and is not there to lavish on my people.
It is I, myself, who have to give it up, let it go from me; I, this
special, unique parcel of matter that has never before been so
combined and never will be again. Who has felt my pain in
exactly the same way? Who has felt my joy, my ecstasy, my
wanting, exactly as I have? No one. Never. In all the history of
life, past and future, no one else but me. Not my wife—oh,
Rachel, I did love you. Not my son—Benjamin, where are you?
Not my dearest friend, my father, my brother, my lover. How*

*dare I be taken from myself for whatever cause? How dare life be
given to me on such grotesque terms as these, that I must live as
best I may and die whether I will or not in whatever circumstances fate decides, like Lazar—like everyone?*

*How can I find comfort in this beautiful boy who tries to earn
my love, this namesake of one hero and God alone knows how
many unremembered more, who will also be canceled out, with
all his beauty, his knowledge, and his strength? How can I dare
to love him? The joke is so cruel—to have anything is to lose it.
To live is to die. To love is to suffer.*

His hands moved in the earth and felt Rachel. His eyes looked
at the lake and saw Benjamin. His arms felt the whisper weight
he had carried in them since that day near Weimar.

But he loved this boy. He wanted him near. He had to tell
him why he had always been afraid of that, why he was still
afraid.

And then he told his son about Lazar.

Elea moved closer to him as he talked. He put an arm around
his father when he finished.

There was no way to persuade Joshua that he was not to
blame for Lazar's death, that wherever he died, it was his
own choice. People did what they wanted to do and Lazar most
of all.

But if he couldn't wipe out Joshua's guilt, he could listen to
it. That's all anyone really needed, someone to put arms around
and say "I'll listen and I'll hear."

He had never loved a man so much. He would never understand a man so well.

57

Arnold was impatient to leave the place. The hotel in Tel Aviv was tacky and uncomfortable. There were no suites; they had taken adjoining rooms, like Julie and Parker. He could hear Paige talking to her parents across the hall as he went into Naomi's room through the communicating door.

It didn't suit her at all, this place. She was at the window, looking down at the crowded streets of Tel Aviv. The curtains were cretonne, in a violent floral print. They made her look more delicate than ever.

The bags were packed and ready. In a few hours they would be on the way home. But Arnold was still uneasy about Joshua; he wanted to call him once more before they left. They were still worlds apart. They always would be. But they had moved closer to each other in these few days. It might be a long time before they met again, and his brother looked so mortally weary it was hard to leave him.

What was Naomi thinking, there at the window? The same thing? That it would be impossible to leave Joshua and come home with them? She had said she was tired of them—he couldn't forget that. His feelings churned. Whatever he did was always colored by suspicion of his brother and his wife, no matter what Joshua said. It was how Naomi felt that mattered to him.

"Why don't you lie down and rest before the trip?" he asked, suddenly nervous. "You never sleep on a plane."

"I'm not tired," she said over her shoulder. "I'm worried."

"About what?"

"Julie and Parker. If things don't change, she might divorce him—or she might persuade him to have nothing to do with us." She turned to look at him.

"And you think I'd like that? Well, I wouldn't, not anymore. I don't want to lose Julie."

She waited.

"Damn it, Naomi, I'm willing to try again," he said finally, knowing it was what she wanted to hear. "But that was a rotten thing he did."

Her hands made a little gesture of irrelevance.

It was unfair of her. "And naturally it was all my fault!"

"No, Arnold." She came to take his hands in hers. "I just don't think it matters whose fault it was. Things—happen; people make mistakes." Her blue eyes searched his, and he wondered what she was trying to tell him. He was afraid to ask.

"You don't," he said, meaning it.

"I most of all."

There it was, at last. He turned his head away, his hands still in hers. "You mean by marrying me." She would have to tell him now. "It's always been him, and it still is. You're going to stay here with him, aren't you?"

"No!" She was startled. "He doesn't need me."

"And if he did?" Their lives had been governed by what Joshua needed, no matter that he had never asked for anything until now.

She dropped his hands and sat down on the faded armchair. "Arnold, that's ancient history. We're too old for jealousy."

"When you love, you're never too old." He sounded desperately tired. "I've been jealous of him all my life. I wanted to be like him, but I'm not. I couldn't make myself over, not even for you. I was always sure you were lovers." Even now he couldn't believe his brother; he had to hear it from her, whatever it was.

She sat looking at her hands, as if she were debating a very complicated question. Finally she raised her head.

"It's what you expected me to do, isn't it?"

He walked toward her. "You said that about Parker. It's not true. I don't know what you mean."

"I mean that all my life I've done what was expected of me. My father expected me to be pure and pretty. My mother expected me to marry the right man and never have to work. Julie expected me to smooth out all the wrinkles and make everything seem fine. And you expected me to have an affair with your brother. That's what I mean.'' She sounded as she had that night with Julie, as if she were going to say what she had to say, no matter what the consequences.

He was stunned. "Was it so terrible, your life with me? What did *you* want—that I didn't give you?"

She put her head back and opened her arms, half sad, half ironic over what she wanted.

"Everything! I wanted to be marvelous. I wanted to be something more than decorative. But most of all I wanted someone to say to me 'I love you, not for the way you love me or the way I think you should be, but just for how you are.' '' Her arms dropped. "Nobody ever said that to me. They just 'expected.' ''

"My God, Naomi, it was how I felt, you must know that. But I couldn't say it."

"How could I know if you didn't tell me? Why didn't you say it?"

"Because of him." He clasped his hands. "It isn't easy for me to say what I feel, the way it is for him. And knowing about him, about you—you don't know what it's like to say that to someone who doesn't love you. You never said it either."

"What did *you* want, Arnold? Will you tell me that?"

"You," he said. "Just you."

"That isn't true. You wanted enormous success and the kind of wife who went with it and houses to match; you wanted a certain kind of daughter and a certain kind of husband for her. And you wanted me to love you wildly even though you knew I loved Joshua on the day we were married. You wanted everything too."

"All right, then, everything." He was as angry as she. "Well, we couldn't give it to each other." Suddenly he wasn't angry, he was sad. "Nobody can."

Her face changed, watching him. "You're right, darling. Nobody can." She had never called him "darling" like that before. She had never let him love her in his way. She had wanted him to love her in her way.

"We could have been happy—except for him." His hand rested on her head. Her hair was gray, but to him she hadn't changed. Desolation overwhelmed him. "Were you lovers? Tell me, Naomi, I have to know."

She hesitated. Only a few days ago she had sworn she would never lie again. But the man who had come back from the war was not the man she fell in love with all those years ago. She had refused to accept the change, but he was not the man Arnold was talking about.

It didn't matter so much what Joshua had wanted of her. In the weighing and balancing of this moment what mattered most was what she had wanted of him. Most of it was sex, the kind she'd never known, never thought she wanted, didn't really need as much as women like Sarah. Some of it was love—but not for the army captain in his uniform or the rabbi with his guns and his bitter, unsmiling eyes. It was for the man he'd been, so wonderful to see, so marvelous to hear. He had made her believe in everything he said—except that she should marry him and come to Palestine. She had never been that man's lover, and she would not break this man's heart over him.

"No," Naomi said with utter conviction.

"But you were in love with him."

"Yes."

"From the beginning?" They were looking at each other now.

"Yes, all right, yes, from the beginning." She said it with relief and regret. Her face was wet.

"And never with me." His voice was steadier now. He was stating a fact he had spent a lifetime trying to accept.

"That isn't true," she said, tears shining on her face. "I chose you. I could have come here with him, but I chose you. I must have loved you. Of course I loved you—even without the kind of passion Sarah and Lazar had."

"I did," he pleaded, even now.

"I know, and I'm sorry. I don't have that kind of nature." Not for him, and for Joshua only the way he used to be. She hadn't known that for a long time. "I never meant to cheat you, Arnold. I do love you. I tried to make you happy."

He looked down at her. The pity was that she thought she had to try. He had grown up loving her; he wouldn't have known how to love anyone else.

"Arnold." She stood, putting her arms around him. "I want to go home where I belong. But you have to forget it now, all that old story. You have to leave it alone."

He dried her face with a handkerchief that smelled faintly of perfume. For him the old story would never be forgotten, but at least it was over.

"All right, I'll leave it alone. But rest now, you're tired." He walked with her to the bed and folded the spread over her. Then he started going toward the door.

"Where are you going?"

"Just to my room to call Giora."

She stirred slightly. "Leave the door open, Arnold. I don't want to be alone."

He left the door open and went into the adjoining room to say good-bye to his brother.